CW01207219

THE SPECIMEN

- A Novel of Horror -

by Pete Kahle

Copyright © 2014 by Pete Kahle

All Rights Reserved. No part of this book may be reproduced, distributed or transmitted in any form or by any means without the author's explicit written consent, except for the purposes of review

Cover Design © 2014 by Elderlemon Design
http://www.elderlemondesign.com/

ISBN-13: 978-1495230004
ISBN-10: 1495230007

This book is a work of fiction.
Names, characters, places and incidents are either a product of the author's fertile imagination or are used fictitiously. Any resemblance to actual events, places or persons, living or dead, is entirely coincidental.

For Noemi, Zoe and Eli

This novel is the reason for my late nights and grumpy mornings. Thanks for putting up with me.

I love you

Dedicated to my grandfather,

James Campbell Ditty.

He shared his love of the written word with me. I hope it is evident in this novel.

Thanks to all who have supported, encouraged or inspired me over the last 17 months. I'm certain this long process would have been much more difficult to do if you hadn't had my back. It's very likely that I will forget some people, but these folks are at the top of the list:

*Mom & Walter,
Dad & Kathy,
Gabi & Sandor,
Viktor & Leah,
Rudi Anna, Jaime Bell, Sherri Bellinger,
Barak Blackburn, Jack Broderick,
Kealan Patrick Burke, Donna Connelly,
Ian Eller, Anthony Gallotti, Doug Giles,
Deb Gorsky, Steve Harnden, Jim Hawkins,
Catherine V. Holmes, Laurie Huber,
Carol Johnson, Tom & Jenny Kelly,
Yvette Keitel Sulema, Avi Kreitenberg,
Jen Eastman-Lawrence & Jeff Lawrence
Jessica Levenson, Mark Madden,
Tom Martin, Maura Mitchelson,
James Newman, Amanda Scopteuolo,
and Sue Walsh Lopez*

Cast of Characters

Bronze Age Estonia – Kaali Crater (23rd century BCE)
Brunni – A young hunter on a rite of manhood; Steed
Kalev – A young hunter on a rite of manhood; Brunni's brother; Steed
Brom – Brunni and Kalev's father
Tor – Brom's older brother

East Anglia (869 CE)
Thorbjorn Valdersson – An aging Viking warrior
Aksel – A young Viking warrior, Thorbjorn's nephew
Arne Skoog – A Viking warrior
Olf Skoog – A Viking warrior; Arne's brother
King Edmund – The deposed king of Anglia
Ivar Ragnarsson – Leader of the Great Army; The Boneless; Steed
Ubbe Ragnarsson – Ivar's brother and lieutenant
Halfdan Ragnarsson - Ivar's brother and lieutenant

Mexico (1370 CE)
Tlatlaukitezkatl – The living avatar of Xipe Totec; Steed
Cipac – A young Aztec peasant

Cartagena, Spain (1602 CE)
Bishop Juan de Zúñiga Flores – The Grand Inquisitor
Inez Jimena de Lima y Contreras – Prisoner of the Spanish Inquisition.

Springfield, MA (1964-65 CE)
Lucien Roumain – A New Orleans transplant; Steed
Jarvis Harold Varney, Jr. * - See Harry; Steed
Nana Varney – Harry's grandmother
Violetta Rooks – Customer of *Bayou Lou's*; interested in Lucien

Greylock Institute (1965 CE)

Dr. Saul Eckenrode – Director of the Greylock Institute
Dr. Genevieve Coe – Head Scientist – Greylock Project, Acme Group
Ron Fenton – Field Agent, Acme Group
Ed Jameson – Field Agent, Acme Group
Harry* - A young African-American boy; afflicted with vitiligo; Steed
Mr. George Willard – The Greylock Institute's custodian
Angelo Scarpa - A Greylock Institute resident; Steed
Stanley Wick- A Greylock Institute resident
Richard Hutchens- A Greylock Institute resident; Steed

Newark, NJ (1985 CE)

Archie – See Murtaugh (Acme Group)
Vasily – A gun dealer
Wayne Duffy – A serial killer; Steed
Monica – Archie's girlfriend; one of Duffy's victims
Noodle – A dachshund; Thrall

Worcester, MA (1992 CE)

Al – See Grimaldi (Acme Group)
Martin Shawcross – Al's foster father
Gina Shawcross – Al's foster mother
Osman "Ozzie" Hamzaoğlu– Al's foster brother
Kevin – Al's foster brother
Lewis– Al's foster brother
Sneakers – A cat
T-Bird – A delinquent thug in his early 20's

Springfield, MA (2004-05 CE)

Nina - See Valentine (Acme Group)
Wally Vanderhook - Nina's boyfriend
Dr. Colfax - See Colfax (Acme Group)
Shane Corker - Nina's classmate
Bobby Desjardins - Nina's classmate
Teddy Meeks - Nina's classmate

Massachusetts (Modern Day)
Willie Brady – A widower walking in the forest
Chuck Monahan – Former college football player in his 50's
Kate Monahan – Chuck's wife
Hank Monahan – Chuck's son
Sydney Monahan – Chuck's daughter
Dahlia Grossman – Sydney's best friend
Scott Ritchie – Hank's best friend
Milton "Bud" Ritchie – Scott's grandfather
Rosemary Ritchie – Scott's grandmother
Wyatt Ferris – Employee of *Schrödinger's Curiosities*
Sioux Martinez - Employee of *Schrödinger's Curiosities*
Chet Boyd - Owner of *Schrödinger's Curiosities*
Elvira Dombrowsky – Frank's 75 year-old aunt; loves cats
Frank Popecky – Elvira's nephew
Old Harry* - See Harry; Steed
Solomon – Elvira's favorite cat, an Abyssinian; Thrall
Ookla The Mok/Boots – The Monahan's cat; Thrall
Dr. Anita Chacon - Trauma Doctor at St. Frank's
Cindy Orton - ER Nurse at St. Frank's
Mike Murphy/Randy Geist – Field Agent, Acme Group
LaDonna O'Malley/Jennifer Bohannon – Field Agent, Acme Group
The Cluster – Mutant Rider
Sheriff Joe Smucker – Bristol County Sheriff
Deputy Nate Sloan - Bristol County Deputy
Deputy Simone Booker- Bristol County Deputy
C.C. Kenealy – Emergency Medical Tech
Billy Oestreicher - Emergency Medical Tech
Officer Marisa Vega – Cambridge Police Officer
Officer Barry Strickland - – Cambridge Police Officer
Larry Hazewood – A Hazmat tanker truck driver

The Acme Group (1960's-Modern Day)
Al Grimaldi - Field Agent, Acme Group
Archie Murtaugh – Field Agent, Acme Group
Patrick Quillian – Team Leader, Acme Group
Nina Valentine – Field Agent, Acme Group
Delano Stoopes – Field Agent, Acme Group
Dr. Arnold Colfax – Geneticist, Acme Group

James P. "Jimbo" Kilcannon – Field Agent/Team Leader, Acme Group
Tom Jeffords – Field Agent, Acme Group
Gary Koonce – Field Agent, Acme Group
Mike Pfeiffer – Field Agent/Team Leader, Acme Group
Hector Mangual – Field Agent, Acme Group
Jerry Smolensky – Security, Acme Group
Burt LeDuke – Security, Acme Group
Alberto Huerta – Security, Acme Group
Rob Fowles - Security, Acme Group
John Swanson - Security, Acme Group
Todd Brawley - Security, Acme Group
Willie Titus - Security, Acme Group

THE SPECIMEN

PETE KAHLE

Contents

Part 1 - Convergence

Prologue - Forever and a Day	1
Chapter 1 – Welcome to the Monahans	7
Chapter 2 – Run For the Hills	16
Chapter 3 - Monster Meatloaf	20
Chapter 4 - Time to Make the Donuts	27
Chapter 5 – Wyatt Goes Surfing	29
Official Report on the Greylock Incident	34
Chapter 6 - Don't Kill the Messenger	38
From the Personal Journal of Dr. Saul Eckenrode	41
Chapter 7 - The Bottom of the Hill	48
Chapter 8 – All Rivers Flow to the Sea	55
<<ACME EYES ONLY>>	61
Chapter 9 - Old Deuteronomy Takes a Cat Nap	63
Chapter 10 - A Little White Lie	75
Official Report on the Greylock Incident	79
Interlude: The Riders - Where the Sun Fell	83
Chapter 11 - Dream Girl	90
From the Personal Journal of Dr. Saul Eckenrode	98
Chapter 12 - My Bloody Valentine	100
<<ACME EYES ONLY>>	111
Chapter 13 - Extra Crispy	116
Chapter 14 – The Man with One Nipple	120
From the Personal Journal of Dr. Saul Eckenrode	123
Chapter 15 - Code Brown	126
Official Report on the Greylock Incident	135
Chapter 16 – Clusterfucked	140
Chapter 17 – The Stench of Charred Flesh…	148
Official Report on the Greylock Incident	156
Interlude: The Rider - Ivar the Boneless	161

Part 2 - Origins

Chapter 18 – Bayou Lou	175
Chapter 19 – A Cold Wind Howling	181
Chapter 20 – Trichotillomania	192
Video Transcript – Dr. Colfax/Nina V.	197

The Springfield Republican – 11/14/2005	209
The Springfield Republican – 11/17/2005	211
Springfield Morning Union – 11/23/2005	214
<<ACME EYES ONLY>>	216
Chapter 21 – Sneakers	220
From the Personal Journal of Dr. Saul Eckenrode	232
Chapter 22 – Government Men	235
Chapter 23 – Dirt Mall	241
Official Report on the Greylock Incident	259
Chapter 24 – 'Round Back	263
Chapter 25 – Blue Light Special	270
Official Report on the Greylock Incident	276
Chapter 26 – Unleashed	282
Chapter 27 – The Burden of the Beast	288
Chapter 28 – Good Samaritan	291
Interlude: The Rider - The Festival of Red Smoking Mirror	296

Part 3 – Turmoil

Chapter 29 – A Glaring of Cats	305
Official Report on the Greylock Incident	317
The Poughkeepsie Journal – 4/26/1958	322
The Daily Hampshire Gazette – 8/22/1958	323
4The Daily Hampshire Gazette – 8/2/1959	324
Chapter 30 – Body Bags	326
Chapter 31 – Rats in a Cage	333
Chapter 32 – Ookla the Mok	340
From the Personal Journal of Dr. Saul Eckenrode	342
Chapter 33 – Elevator Music	344
<<ACME EYES ONLY>>	347
Chapter 34 – What is Left of Me	354
Chapter 35 – The Dudes Abide	358
Interlude: The Riders - Lucifer's Concubine	364

Part 4 – Entropy

Chapter 36 – A Piece of Me	373
Chapter 37 – Stalking the Bandersnatch	381
Chapter 38 – Ghosts and Shadows	385
Official Report on the Greylock Incident	389
Chapter 39 – A Meeting of Minds	392

Chapter 40 – No Pleasure without Pain   398
Chapter 41 – That Special Feeling   402
Chapter 42 – Opie and Little Miss Psycho   405
Interlude: The Rider - The Night the Lights Went Out in Greylock   410

Part 5 – Maelstrom

Chapter 43 – Exodus   427
Chapter 44 – Demons   435
Chapter 45 – Howl   440
Chapter 46 – Road Trip   451
Chapter 47 – Haulin' Ass   455
Chapter 48 – Comes a Reckonin'   460

Epilogue – Brunni   487

PART 1
CONVERGENCE

Prologue
Forever and a Day

Chesterfield, MA – Last Winter

After the night's rain and a quick freeze, the entire forest was sheathed from trunk to tip in glass. Frost rimed the needles of the pines and all was silent except for the steady crunch of someone climbing in the early dawn. *This is as good a place as any*, thought the bearded man as he reached the top of the hill. He sighed, fogging the early morning air with a plume of exhaled breath, and dropped his equipment to the frozen ground. He walked in a broad circle, looking down all sides of the hill. As far as he could see, bare skeletal branches clawed at the sky in supplication as if pleading their gods for forgiveness for their sins. He grunted softly. *Don't hold your breath.*

No houses were visible in any direction, but he circled one more time to be certain. He needed solitude for this. The chance that someone might happen upon him here at this time of day was extremely low. If he was interrupted, he would be forced to leave and ultimately might lose his nerve to do what had to be done.

Opening his gray canvas knapsack, he pulled out a silver flask with initials WWB inscribed on one side. He had filled it with Maker's Mark as he left his house that morning. Now it was close to empty. Only a swig or two remained. He turned the flask over and silently moved his lips as he read the inscription on the other side:

> ***To William,***
> ***All my love***
> ***Forever and a day,***
> ***Sylvia***

Willie Brady held back his tears and emptied the flask in a toast to his late wife, gone three years from uterine cancer.

The Specimen

"Love ya, Syl," he whispered before returning the flask to the bag and reaching for the shotgun lying next to it. "I'll be there right away."

He had already loaded the shells before he left, but just to be certain, he engaged the breach lever and checked the barrel again. The metal caps of the two shells gleamed in their respective chambers. Brady brought the barrel back up and closed it until he heard the click. He lowered the gun again, holding it with one hand as he pressed against his abdomen with other.

The lump was irregular, the size of a large apple and buried beneath layers of fat and muscle. He knew it was cancer. No need to go through a litany of tests to confirm it. After years of dealing with doctors and the bloodsucking insurance companies during Sylvia's illness, Brady never wanted to visit a hospital again. In a weird way, he considered this turn of events poetic. Coming down with a disease like the one that had sucked the life out of his soulmate was cathartic. Unlike Sylvia, however, he had no reason to fight. The sooner he passed on, the sooner he would see her again.

And then there were the voices …

In the past month, Brady had begun to hear a chorus of chattering and whispering at the edge of his thoughts. Nothing was distinct. No individual words stood out, nor did he recognize any voices, but more and more he had felt as if the whispering discord was telling him something. And he knew that he didn't want to hear it.

This, ultimately, was why he had come to the decision last week to take his own life. This wasn't suicide, in his opinion. Not with death idly waiting for him as life and sanity dripped out of him in a slow leak. Rather, he considered that he was upgrading his ticket on the ferry over the river Styx from Economy to 1st Class. *Might as well go out on my own terms*, he thought.

He reversed the shotgun and raised the barrel to his mouth, resting it on his lower teeth. The barrel tasted metallic and oily, like old blood. He knew that taste well from having coughed up chunks of bloody sputum nearly every morning for the past two months. It was familiar and ferrous, reminding him of what he had to do despite his doubts and fears. He wasn't a religious man at all, but what if this was a sin? *No, I can't turn back now.*

Brady angled the barrel toward the back of his palate. He wanted to safeguard against the chance of the shotgun only paralyzing him, or even worse, just blowing off his face and leaving his brain intact. That would be Hell. This method was the most efficient way he had found on the internet. While conducting his research, he had seen numerous horrific images of teens who had utterly demolished their features with a misplaced blast and he wanted to be certain that couldn't happen to him.

He took his finger off the trigger, pulled the barrel out of his mouth and furiously cursed himself. A dog barked in the distance as if admonishing his cowardice. Legions of birds launched from a nearby grove of barren bushes, circling the summit of the hill before banking off to the south in a hurricane of feathers.

"You know you want to do this. It can't wait," Brady growled under his breath. "Remember Syl!"

Suddenly he felt a dagger-like spasm in his lower abdomen, directly beneath the veiny mass that had inspired this action. A swell of vertigo slammed into him, nearly enough to drop him to the forest floor. The drink he had recently downed threatened to spill out of his throat, but he swallowed it back down with a grimace. *What the hell was that? Nerves?* He needed to push past it. Sylvia was waiting for him on the other side.

Again, he raised the shotgun to his mouth and bit down on the metal. He placed his right thumb on the trigger and braced the cold barrel with his left hand. He counted down … *1 … 2 … 3 …* Nothing. His finger refused to pull it. Brady had the uncanny sensation that someone was resisting his muscles as he tried to push down on the trigger.

He tried once more, but again it was as if there was a mental tug of war. The chattering voices rose up in his ears. Fierce, howling whispers and silent shrieks of insanity. An inner babel that exhorted him to turn away from this path to oblivion. Even so, as the voices rose in volume and

The Specimen

the pressure on his hand increased, he finally broke through and squeezed the trigger just as his left hand pulled on the barrel against his will.

The explosion silenced the world.

Brady collapsed in slow motion to the ground, realizing a number of cold, hard facts in a fraction of a millisecond. Immediately, he knew that he had not died instantaneously, unless there was some truth to the idea that the soul stays with the body for some time after death. Assuming that his first instinct was true – that he was still alive somehow – his next thought was that his shot had missed his head. Considering that he had specifically purchased the most powerful shotgun he could find (he had told the salesman at the gun show that he wanted to be able to take down a bull moose), the back half of his skull should have been a large cloud of red mist just now settling to the earth and staining the frost-rimed dirt crimson, if he had scored a direct hit. Obviously, he had not. He was bleeding quite a bit, but he should have been killed immediately. Some force had interfered with his aim.

He hit the dirt and bounced slightly on the right side of his head. Though his point of view had not changed, Brady felt removed from what was happening, as if he were a spectator. The only part of his body that he seemed to be able to move was his left hand, which kept reaching for his face and somehow just missing it. The shotgun had landed directly in his line of sight, a wisp of smoke curling from the barrel. He could still taste the metal in his mouth.

The keening, high-pitched squeal of the ringing in his ears gave way to an intermittent whistling hiss that ebbed and flowed with each wheezing breath Brady took. His left hand finally made contact with his face and his worst fears were confirmed. All that remained below his left eye was a grisly wet pit littered with shards of bone embedded in the fluttering remnants of his sinuses. His fingers slid down in the meaty mess. His lower jaw had been pulverized, but somehow his entire tongue remained intact, flopping in the bloody dirt like a dying fish.

Gradually drifting away from consciousness, Brady was more than ready to leave this mortal coil. There was no bright light that he could see.

No stairway to Heaven. No elevator to Hell. Just a blurring of the lines. A fading of colors. Everything seemed washed out, as if the color was slowly leeching from the sky ... the trees ... the blood on the ground.

Yet something prevented his final exit. Like a rubber band stretched to its limits, he was hauled back into his body against his will. The voices were still there and they were screaming in terror as the agony of his wounds slammed into him. His left hand and arm were doused with each arcing spurt of blood from his torn carotid artery. His right hand – in fact, the entire right side of his body – was paralyzed. He couldn't have moved even if he had wanted to.

The voices changed in tone. Rather than giving off the unmistakable aura of fear, he now sensed anger and desperation as if they understood he was leaving them soon. Whoever *they* were. Brady knew now that, even though he had completely messed up the shot, he was still bleeding to death. This way was more painful and took longer than he had wanted to go, but perhaps it was better. Perhaps he needed the pain as penance for his mortal sins.

Soon, Sylvia. Soon I'll have you back in my arms.

If he still had anything resembling a mouth, he would have smiled.

Slightly more than three minutes later, as the tide of blood from his gutted throat slowed from a gush to a seeping trickle, William Brady, aged 57, died alone on the frozen forest floor. His last breath exited his body and all was still. For a moment, it seemed as if the woodlands, as one creature, let out a pent-up sigh.

Suddenly, a muscular, undulating ripple flowed up Brady's lifeless torso from the lump in his gut. The flesh of his corpse bulged as the object inched toward the bloody cavity in his neck. It breached the gash, tearing open skin and muscle, while it pushed itself out in a disturbing semblance of childbirth.

Glistening with gore, a small wormlike head with a set of translucent yellow feelers emerged. It tested the edges of the hole before the bulk of the organism climbed out onto Brady's torso. Pseudo-eyes

The Specimen

formed on the ends of the feelers and swiveled to both sides. *Danger*, it thought. It looked back at its bloody cave. *Safety... Food,* it realized. Without hesitation, the alien creature slid back inside its haven and waited.

Eventually another Steed would arrive. They always did.

Pete Kahle

Chapter 1 – Welcome to the Monahans

"No one thinks of how much blood it costs."
- Dante Alighieri

Modern Day – Chesterfield, MA

Chuck Monahan was not a man of many words. "Keep it short and sweet" was his motto. As a former defensive tackle at Clemson University, standing 6'6" and tipping the scales at 335 pounds, he never needed to raise his voice above a normal conversational level. His size was all he needed to get his point across. In all facets of his life, Chuck was calm, cool and in control, projecting a sense of rigid self-discipline. Nothing ever appeared to bother him, which was why his family was shocked to see him hogtied and bloody, sobbing quietly like a petulant child on the kitchen floor of their home in Chesterfield, Massachusetts.

Four more individuals were seated on the floor, lined up against the kitchen wall and restrained with plastic zip-ties on their wrists and ankles. Chuck's wife, Kate, a blonde matronly woman in her mid-forties, was silently weeping with her head bowed, blood from her broken nose intermittently dripping onto an old jersey of Chuck's that she used as a nightshirt.

Next to her was their son, Hank, 15 years old and on target to match or even surpass his father's size one day. Unlike Chuck, however, the younger Monahan showed no interest in football whatsoever, preferring instead to spend the day playing videogames like *Assassin's Creed* or *Call of Duty* on his Xbox, listen to *System of a Down* on his iPod, and letting his blonde hair grow past his ass. Clad only in a pair of flannel pajama bottoms, he had the angry mark of a taser burn on the left side of his neck. He was silent, clenching his fists and staring fixedly at his father bleeding in front of him.

On the end were two hysterical teenaged girls huddled together with tear-stained faces. The one on the left was the Monahans' 17 year-old daughter, Sydney, strawberry blonde and usually cute as a button if not for the streams of tears and snot flowing down her face. Huddled next to her

7

The Specimen

was her best friend Dahlia, a petite girl with short spiky brown hair and, in Chuck's opinion, altogether too many piercings in her ears, lip and nose. Dahlia had made the unfortunate choice to sleep over in Sydney's room last night in order to get away from her mom's lecherous boyfriend-du-jour. One of her earlobes was bloody where an earring had been torn loose in the night's struggle.

Flanking Chuck in the middle of the kitchen were two armed men in identical gray suits with tasers trained respectively on the nape of his neck and the group against the wall. Each also had sidearms in holsters under their jackets. Both could have been pulled out of central casting for a generic corporate goon… thick neck, prominent jaw, sloping forehead and beady eyes with a thousand yard stare. The only apparent difference was the slicked-back hair on one goon and the severely broken nose, scarred cheeks and stereotypical cowboy's salt-and-pepper handlebar mustache on the other.

Twenty minutes earlier, at approximately four in the morning, Chuck woke to the sound of his bedroom door crashing open. As he and Kate were roughly dragged from their bed, his face was slammed into the wall by Slick while Kate was pinned to the floor by Cowboy, bound hand and foot with zip ties, and gagged with a pair of Chuck's boxers (thankfully clean) to shut her up while the rest of the occupants were corralled into the kitchen.

A few strategically placed applications of the tasers combined with kicks to the abdomen were enough to reinforce the notion that screaming and escape attempts would only result in pain. Excruciating and creative torture the likes of which Chuck had never conceived. He now knelt in the center of the kitchen wheezing over a smeared puddle of blood, mucus and saliva dripping from his shattered nose and mouth.

"Now that introductions are complete," echoed a quiet but cheery male voice with a slight Irish brogue from the doorway to the family room. "We can get down to business."

In through the arch walked a man in his early forties, wearing a tailored black suit, pressed white shirt and a power tie the color of oxblood. A few inches shy of six feet, he seemed larger, with close-cropped hair the color of pewter and features that appeared to have been carved from a block of ash. Pale, but not sallow. His face was long, craggy and raw-boned with large fleshy lips, a strong Roman nose and a sculpted chin that seemed a bit too large for a man his size. His most striking feature was his bushy black eyebrows over deep-set dark-brown eyes. He carried a large leather satchel, which he placed on a chair by the kitchen table as he continued to address the Monahans in his oddly merry tone.

"Let's see. Who do we have here?" He continued to smile as he pulled his smart phone from his pocket, consulting it cursorily as he spoke. "Charles Edward Monahan. Fifty-one years old. Prefers Chuck to Charlie. Former football player. Assistant dean. Mm-hmm… packed on a bit of weight there since college. Eh, Chuck?"

He nudged Chuck in the side with his foot, eliciting a moan, and laughed, "Just joshing with you, buddy. I know how tough it is to keep the weight off after you hit a certain age, especially when the little lady isn't exactly keeping up her end of the bargain either, huh?"

He turned his attention to Mrs. Monahan and grinned, "I mean Kate here certainly isn't the limber little pixie you nailed in college. Look at this, Grimaldi."

He pulled up an image on his smart phone and directed Slick's attention to it. The burly tough eyed it momentarily as directed and nodded in approval as Quillian continued, "I would have tapped that ass ten ways to Tuesday."

"Seriously, Kate," he said as he turned in her direction. "Why did you let yourself go so much? Chuckles here might be carrying a few extra pounds, but you, my dear, you have gotten sloppy fat."

Kate looked up from her shirt, sodden with blood, and screamed, "Just tell us what you want! Who are you? Why are you doing this to us?" She broke down again and buried her face on Sydney's shoulders.

"Now, now, Kate. All in due time," he continued, still smiling but now lacking the humor previously shown. His brogue thickened. "We've been monitoring Chuck here for months. Ever since he was identified as a candidate. Thankfully, Chuck here is a charitable citizen who helps his common man by donating blood on a regular basis. Without our screening program, you may have had a big surprise join you in a couple months" He paused and smiled at Kate. "Bear with me, dear. Some events are meant to

The Specimen

be savored. I'll wager that you will understand the importance of our visit within the hour."

He walked on down the line toward the teens and, squatting down to their eye level, addressed them directly, "I'm assuming that you're the children, Hank and Sydney …plus a surprise guest. You three have my most sincere apologies. Our original schedule had planned for this visit to occur later in the day after you had left for school, but you know what they say about the plans of mice and men."

Obviously confused, Hank shook his head negatively while next to him, the girls pressed against each other and moaned. Sydney had her eyes closed in denial of what she had seen, while Dahlia repetitively whimpered, "I wanna go home. I wanna go home."

The man stood up from his crouch and nodded his head sympathetically, "Understandable, lass, but I'm afraid that option has long since passed."

He turned and indicated the two men behind him, "You've already met my brothers in arms, Mr. Grimaldi and Mr. Murtaugh, but I'm sure you are wondering who I am and what reasons I have for being here." He grinned and scanned his captive audience before continuing. "My name is Patrick Quillian. I represent a group of like-minded scientists, organizations and branches of various governments who are dedicated to the sanctity and purity of humanity. We have no official name, though some call us the Acme Group. Acme, as in a pinnacle of achievement.

We strive for anonymity. Working behind the scenes allows us a certain leeway with our projects that individual public corporations and national governments do not possess. As for what we do…let's just say that our guiding purpose is to constantly improve and perfect the human race so we may reach our true potential. Occasionally, we discover threats to our mission, and this requires that we stage an intervention." He smirked at the choice of words, and then turned to one of his men. "Murtaugh, the table, if you will…" The man with the handlebar mustache immediately stepped forward and began clearing the top of the sturdy oak kitchen table of all objects.

While speaking, Quillian walked to the chair on which his leather satchel sat and removed his suit jacket. He placed the jacket on the back of the chair, rolled up his shirt sleeves and opened the satchel to remove a few objects which he placed on the kitchen counter behind him. The last thing he removed from the satchel was what appeared to be a folded square of plastic sheeting. When opened up, it became a full plastic body suit into which he stepped and zipped up to his neck.

Murtaugh finished clearing off the table, then picked up a small glass bottle and a syringe from the pile of items Quillian had placed on the counter. Grimaldi held Chuck still while Murtaugh injected him in the neck with the syringe and the other captives looked on in shock. Seconds later, Chuck slumped bonelessly to the linoleum as his muscles ceased to function. A puddle of drool began to form next to his mouth, diluting the blood from his previous injuries. His eyes rolled back into his skull showing only the sclera as Murtaugh and Grimaldi lifted him off the floor and onto the newly bare kitchen table. They sliced through the zip-ties with a knife, and cut off his pajamas and boxers with the efficiency of ER doctors in response to a victim of a car accident. Soon, Monahan was splayed naked and comatose on his back, arms and legs dangling over the sides of the table, newly zip-tied once again to the table legs.

"Nooooooo!" screamed Hank as he lurched to his feet and dove forward in an attempt to tackle Grimaldi despite the plastic ties still encircling his wrists and ankles. Sidestepping the boy's awkward assault, Grimaldi smashed an elbow into Hank's face, audibly crushing the cartilage in his nose, and sent him to the floor on his back. A torrent of blood and shattered teeth gushed from his nose and mouth while Grimaldi ruthlessly jammed the taser under his chin and jolted him with an extended shock. The teen's body convulsed spasmodically as his bladder and bowels released and his mother and the girls shrieked in horror. The stench of burnt hair, urine, and fecal matter lingered in the air long after the boy had slumped to the floor and his body had been dragged into the corner away from the others.

"Stupid ass kid," Grimaldi muttered, kicking Hank's foot in annoyance. Murtaugh rolled his eyes, but remained mute.

"Not the best idea in the world," commented Quillian. "Though, I have to give him credit. Kid had a set of brass balls on him. He had potential." He paused in contemplation, and then continued, "Let's get

The Specimen

back to business. Time is money....right, ladies?" He waggled his eyebrows in their direction.

Quillian reopened the leather satchel and removed a black nylon bundle which he unrolled on Monahan's hairy abdomen, revealing a small set of surgical tools and a slim electronic device with a screen about the size and shape of a paperback book. Attached to the device by a slim cord was an apparent scanner.

"Okay, class," Quillian continued as if lecturing a room full of students instead of three bloodied women and a teenage boy lingering on the edge of death. "This little object is basically an ultrasound on steroids with a few extra gizmos. Much more powerful than the one used in your obstetrician's office, Kate."

Kate stared at Quillian listlessly, a bubble of mucus forming below one nostril. Her right eye was swelling shut and turning dark purple. She gave no sign of having understood his words.

"Looks like Mommy has gone to her safe place, ladies. I guess you'll have to fill her in later," Quillian said as he turned back to Chuck's supine body. He held the device in his left hand pointed so the girls could see the screen while pressing the scanner into Chuck's midsection. "Bear with me now as I show you the reason for why we're all gathered here today. Keep your eyes on the screen, girls."

The teens whimpered and leaned into each other, but they heeded his directions, watching the display for any anomaly. Something. Anything that would explain why they had suddenly been thrown into this hellish mirror of their lives. Chuck lay comatose and oblivious to the procedure about to be performed upon him.

Quillian applied pressure to every inch of Chuck's belly in a sweeping side-to-side motion, gradually working his way from just above his groin to the faded Tasmanian Devil tattoo on his left pectoral muscle. Indistinct shadowy images came in and out of focus on the screen as the scanner was pressed into Chuck's abdomen and chest while Quillian muttered sotto voce, "No....no....that's not it. Where are ya, you bastard?"

He continued scanning down Chuck's flanks and up into his left armpit where he discovered a large protruding nodule buried under Chuck's flab.

"Bingo!" crowed Quillian. "It's a whopper, gentlemen! At least a ten pounder." Palpating the lump under the layers of skin and fat, it was soon obvious that it was slightly larger than a softball. The skin over the swelling was discolored and bruised. Quillian pressed harder with the scanner and an image of the spherical mass came sharply into focus on the screen.

"Just look at that, ladies," whispered Quillian. "You may not know much about human anatomy, but I'm sure you realize that this is not normal." He circled the man while trying to find a better angle. "Your father is host to an alien parasite that will eventually suck the life from him. We need to remove it to determine its source. When we find the ultimate origin of the creature, we will hunt it down and we will obliterate it."

The girls gasped in fear as they saw the picture. It was completely unnatural. Rather than the fatty tissue or fluid-filled sac that one might expect to see, this had teeth (fangs), bones and other anomalous features. A myriad of tendrils of multiple sizes wrapped around a spine-like structure in the center of the object. Nerve clusters and tangles of blood vessels permeated the mass. Amid the snarl could be seen organ-like masses that pulsated slightly, in time with Chuck's heart.

"Sydney," asked Dahlia in a whisper. "What is that thing inside your dad?" Sydney shook her head in denial and squeezed her eyes shut, refusing to answer. *None of this could be real. It's impossible.* She willed herself to wake up from this horrendous nightmare, but when she reopened her eyes, Quillian had removed a scalpel from his medical kit and was slowly slicing away the skin surrounding the mass on her father's side. Blood began to seep onto the kitchen table, causing her to look quickly away out the kitchen window. Looking for anything to blot out the sight of her father getting filleted by this maniac.

Storm clouds obscured the moon, making the night black and unforgiving. At least an hour remained until the sun would rise and dawn would encroach upon the impenetrable shadows. Sydney was not sure she would even be alive to see the next day. Normally she loved the fact that her house was private and set back from the road on their wooded ten acre

The Specimen

lot, but now she would have traded it all for a set of nosy neighbors who would call the police for the slightest disturbance.

The window above the sink was narrow and cluttered with some of her mother's collection of ceramic gnomes. Lined up according to their size and the color of their pants, they appeared to be a final phalanx against any window-based intruders. The reflection of the kitchen in the glass obscured her view at first, but she continued to stare out the window, sending her thoughts through the darkness so she would no longer be here.

"Oops," muttered Quillian, cursing under his breath.

She heard a couple of wet slaps as something heavy hit the linoleum but she refused to look and see what it was. *Pieces of my father's bloody flesh sliding off the table.* Dahlia sobbed in horror and buried her face in Sydney's nightshirt.

"Pass me that garbage can, Murtaugh," said Quillian as he cut away the layers of fat and folded back the bloody flaps of blubber on Chuck's abdomen. "This is getting a bit messy."

The bald thug walked across the room to do as Quillian asked, looking directly at Sydney as he passed.

Sydney clenched her lips together, holding back her gorge. She stared directly out the window and refused to look back at the operation on her kitchen table. *Wait*, she thought to herself as she looked more closely. *Is that a handprint?* Sydney froze and looked even closer without appearing to stare. *No... I think it's a hand!*

Suddenly the shadows just beyond the glass of the kitchen coalesced into a set of familiar features that she never thought she would ever be happy to see.

SCOTT!!

She let out a short gasp as she recognized the face of a terrified boy. Scott Ritchie. Her brother Hank's pathetic best friend. He stared in at them, frozen in fear, through the window, then bolted away into the darkness.

Behind her, Sydney heard Murtaugh grunt in surprise. She turned and saw that he was holding the garbage can, and staring out the window as well.

Milliseconds later, Murtaugh drew his gun from his holster, yelled, "Fuck! Some kid's outside!" and rushed out of the kitchen, rocketing for the living room and the back door. Sydney shrieked after him in pure panic, "RUN, SCOTT, RUN!!"

She turned back to the others just as Grimaldi swung his fist and backhanded her across the jaw, sending her deep into unconsciousness.

The Specimen

Chapter 2 – Run For the Hills

"I am not afraid of death. I just don't want to be there when it happens" - Woody Allen

Modern Day – Chesterfield, MA

Scott Ritchie already felt like he was going to puke. It was a bad idea to break into his grandfather's liquor cabinet and finish that bottle of Johnny Walker that he found. It was an equally stupid idea to ride his bike over to his best friend Hank's house at four in the morning to see if his sister Sydney had left her blinds up again. The most idiotic idea of all, though, was sneaking right up to their house to look in the window after he heard screams coming from their kitchen. *What the hell had he been thinking?* He and Hank had watched hundreds of horror movies together and the worst thing to do was to explore anything that wasn't normal. That was an express ticket to a gory and painful death. *Should've just called 9-1-1*, he thought. *Even if you had gotten in trouble for peeping, you could've saved them.*

He was probably going to die anyway. Shot in the back of the head by some goon with a shaved head and a porn star mustache. Brains exploding through his forehead all over the forest floor. *Frickin' vivid imagination. Cut the crap. You're just scaring yourself,* Scott thought as he stumbled through the trees.

Knowing his grandparents, he doubted that he would even be missed until tomorrow evening. Hank hadn't even known he was planning to come over, so his body wouldn't be discovered until a week or so went by. *Isn't this the place where that old guy shot himself last year? They didn't find his body until over a month later and it was a total mess.*

Like that body, his corpse would rot and bloat, turning a rainbow of colors while maggots feasted on the smorgasbord of his flesh. It was entirely possible that he would never be found. Perhaps a burrowing creature like a mole or a badger would lay claim to his hollowed-out chest cavity and make it into a dwelling for generations of its descendants. *Damn it. Did it again.*

He could hear the man crashing through the trees behind him, getting closer every minute. The ground was muddy and covered with wet leaves, making full speed nearly impossible. He leaped over a small creek, landing in the far shallows and thoroughly soaking his sneakers before clambering up the muddy slope. The burly man followed, loudly cursing as he fell to one knee in the mud before lurching to his feet and continuing the chase.

Scott's breathing became labored as the urge to vomit increased. He dodged around rocks and weaved through saplings, getting smacked in the face and neck more than once by low-hanging branches. Sweat burned his eyes and he bled from multiple scratches on his arms and legs. If only he hadn't worn his bright white Patriots jersey, he wouldn't present such a glaring target to the man behind him. With the moon almost always behind the clouds, he should have been almost impossible to see, but his unfortunate wardrobe choice made him stand out like a red flag.

He heard a soft cough, then a branch inches above his head exploded, showering him with splinters and chunks of bark and moss. *He's shooting at me*, thought Scott. *Holy shit! This can't be real! I just wanted to hang out with Hank, smoke a bowl and ditch school. Now I'm getting shot at!*

Scott was a year younger and a grade behind Hank in school, but they had quickly bonded five years earlier when he moved here to Chesterfield from Wisconsin to live with his grandparents after losing both of his parents within a month. His mother had lost an agonizing two year battle with breast cancer and his father took a one way trip down the carbon monoxide highway in their garage three weeks later. Scott was the one who found him when he came home from school and heard the car running in the garage.

If not for Hank, Scott may not have recovered from his depression so quickly after moving in with his grandparents. A mutual interest in horror films, video games (especially ones with zombies) and comic books cemented his and Hank's friendship within days of meeting him on the school bus to middle school. Unlike Hank, who was blonde and towered over most of his classmates by a few inches, Scott was short and a bit chubby with dark brown hair and grey eyes the shade of storm clouds.

The Specimen

When Scott met Hank's older sister Sydney a few weeks later, he knew he was in love and he made a point to catch a glimpse of her every chance he got. Now, his obsession would be his downfall.

Scott barely ducked under an arm-thick branch that came close to beheading him. Swinging around the next sapling, he snatched a glance back behind him and saw that his pursuer was about twenty to thirty yards back, but steadily gaining as each minute passed.

"Shit!" cursed the stocky teen as he redoubled his efforts and flung himself forward through the maze of trees. Up ahead, a hundred yards or so away, lay a steep incline that seemed completely insurmountable in the daylight, much less while being chased by a killer in the pre-dawn hours. At the top of the hill, if Scott remembered correctly, was Route 138. If he made it to the crest, a chance still existed that he could run onto the road to flag down a passing car and escape. He wheezed with every step. *I'll never smoke pot again if I can make it up that hill*, he promised to whatever god watched out for derelict teens.

Phwwt! Phwwt! Two more muffled shots echoed simultaneously with blasts of tree splinters peppering his face and body from more near misses. The shots were getting closer. Scott whimpered in fear as his gorge rose in his throat. He tasted blood trickling into his mouth from a cut above his brow. Lightheaded, he staggered forward and began the climb up the muddy rise, grabbing at any roots, branches or stones that would help stabilize him.

The sounds of his pursuer slowed and he risked a glance back when he reached a point midway up the slope where the incline leveled off for a couple of feet. The bald man stood at the bottom, panting heavily with his gun at his side, and yelled up at Scott in a raspy growl, "Kid! Come back down here. I don't wanna shoot, but I will if you don't stop climbing!"

"Fuck you!" shrieked Scott as he turned again and attempted to claw his way to the top of the ridge. "You already shot at me!" His pace quickened. It was his last chance to save himself and the edge was within reach. He only needed to make it over the edge and the gunman would lose sight of him. There was no way that he could climb it as fast as Scott had. Safety was close at hand.

Below, Murtaugh shook his head slowly in disgust and aimed his gun carefully at the boy's back. "They never make it easy," he muttered to himself. "Damn, I hate shooting kids." He pulled the trigger three times in succession.

Scott reached the top and pulled himself to a standing position a few feet from the road, just as an angry wasp buzzed past his ear. An invisible sledgehammer bludgeoned him twice, just above his right hip and in the meat of his left forearm. Three deadened retorts echoed in his ears as he spun forward, took two stumbling steps and fell toward the pavement when his vision went blinding white. He heard the angry wailing blare of a horn ending in a crash and white-hot agony, and then all sound stopped, and he was soaring, flying, and tumbling end over end until he hit the road and the night swallowed him whole.

The Specimen

Chapter 3 - Monster Meatloaf

"Life is a hideous thing." – H. P. Lovecraft

Modern Day – Cambridge, MA

Wyatt Ferris looked up as the first visitor of the day came barreling through the door, shattering the morning peace with the jangling of the entrance bell. The woman maneuvered quickly around the displays and made a beeline in his direction. With both hands and an audible grunt, she hefted a bulky green canvas bag onto the counter.

"I've got something very special to show you today, Wyatt," she said to the gangly red-headed man in black t-shirt, hoodie and jeans perched on the stool reading a magazine and sipping a cup of coffee at the cash register. A sturdy woman who looked to be in her late sixties, shaped like a toad and smelling faintly of Vick's Vapo-Rub, Mrs. Elvira Dombrowsky was a frequent visitor to *Schrödinger's Curiosities*, the shop where Wyatt had worked for the past three-odd years. She was a local spinster with numerous cats, an obsession with plundering estate sales, and arguably too much time on her hands. Mrs. Dombrowsky was also the self-appointed supplier of discovered objects… items that she deemed worthy of enshrinement in *Schrödinger's* eclectic window display. Regrettably, her opinion of the value of her discoveries was often in opposition to their actual merit.

"You've said that before, Mrs. D.," Wyatt stated, peering reluctantly over the latest issue of *Fangoria* at the object she withdrew from the bag. It was large and unwieldy, nearly a foot high and bundled in a garish red and yellow afghan that had been secured with a couple of bungee cords. A distinct sound of liquid could be heard sloshing within the container under the knitted blanket.

Normally, if they were busy, her finds would only receive a cursory glance before Wyatt deemed them worthy of the store or not, but that Wednesday was the slowest day the store had seen all week. He couldn't just brush her off this time.

Quite honestly, there had been a few occasions when she did bring in items that fit the requirements of *Schrödinger's*. Old photos and animal skeletons were her usual donations. One time, she had managed to locate a well-preserved hydrocephalic pig fetus with a gigantic cyclopean eye in the center of its forehead, but a good portion of her discoveries were either verifiable as fakes or were in such poor condition that the potential resale value was not worth the shelf space. Today, something about her excitement piqued his interest and he sat forward to examine her contribution.

In her haste to unveil her latest discovery, she lurched forward and deposited it heavily on the counter where it wobbled precariously on the edge. Wyatt dropped his magazine and reached out instinctively, steadying it with his hands to avoid any potential disaster.

"Good catch, Wyatt," she tittered nervously. "That would certainly have been messy... and unpleasant for both of us."

"Should I be nervous?" he asked, recalling the purportedly mummified cat she had brought to the store last summer which had begun to rot weeks later during a particularly humid stretch. The store had smelled like road kill for weeks afterwards and *Schrödinger's* owner, Chet, had considered barring her permanently from the premises.

"Of course not," she said. "It's just a large sealed jar that hasn't been opened in over 50 years. I imagine it would stink if opened, though... and how many times have I reminded you to call me Elvira? Even if I am old enough to be your grandmother, I prefer not to be reminded of it."

"Please forgive me," Wyatt replied, holding back a smile.

"Apology accepted. Now help me with these cords so I can show it to you. It's a real humdinger."

The bungee cords were wrapped around the container multiple times and the afghan was secured in place with an excessive amount of red duct tape. After multiple muttered profanities on his part and the judicious use of a box cutter, the tape was separated and the cover was removed, revealing an enormous, antique specimen jar with something floating inside it.

He was staggered.

At *Schrödinger's*, they were renowned for the various oddities they put up for sale to collectors across the country. From the aforementioned fetal pig to jars filled with gallstones to tribal jewelry made

The Specimen

from animal teeth, its inventory was quite different from that of your average antique shop. *Schrödinger's* had found its niche selling objects weird, taboo, and often grotesque, to a select yet extremely loyal clientele. Wyatt liked to think that he'd seen it all, but, on rare occasions, a client surprised him with something utterly unique. Generally, he was still able to identify the object, or at least hazard an educated guess that was in the ballpark. This time, however, he was wholly confounded. The object was obviously organic, but other than that, he could not determine its source.

Drifting in the jar in an indeterminate yellow-amber liquid (most likely formaldehyde) was a vaguely ovoid object of apparent organic origin. It was about the size and shape of a lopsided football, mottled in color and texture. Wyatt immediately felt a wave of revulsion tinged with fascination wash over him when he placed his right palm on the side of the jar to turn it for a better view. An earthy musk emanated from near the lid, despite the seal. *Is there an opening?* thought Wyatt. A small, peeling, yellowed label written in a cramped hand was glued to the bottom half of the glass, but Wyatt ignored it as he turned the jar for a closer look.

The glass surface felt warm as he rotated it on the counter and an oily residue remained on his fingers after he removed them. The brass-colored lid was sealed tight with what appeared to be a solder, blackish-silver in heavy threads lining the mouth of the jar. Soon, Wyatt's nausea subsided and he absently wiped his hand on his tattered jeans while sliding the table lamp closer for more illumination.

The light pierced the liquid and emanated throughout, giving the jar an unnatural glow that wept onto the scarred wooden counter. Rotating the specimen jar had caused the object to bob slightly giving off an impression of respiration and internal motion. Dark reddish sediment stirred, clouding the bottom of the jar for a few seconds before settling again in a thin layer.

Blood, Wyatt thought, yearning to tear his eyes from the thing, but unable to pull away. He was entranced. Blotchy pink and grey with cordlike vessels erupting through the skin, it was an abomination. *Yet it's mesmerizing*, he thought. *Horribly beautiful in its design.* Wisps of multicolored hair sprouted in random patches along skin with multiple textures. Striated, smooth, scarred and scaled. Its hide was marred with blisters, boils, bony protrusions and calcifications in haphazard patterns.

One center nodule about the size and texture of a golf ball protruded from the right side, brownish-purple like a week-old bruise. Along the left flank, in a patch of skin that resembled a charred hamburger, over a dozen pseudo-teeth sprouted in a facsimile of a demented lopsided grin. An array of slits resembling gills ran along the bottom edge and flakes of peeling tissue swayed, disturbed by the motion of the liquid medium in the jar. *Breathe*, Wyatt thought. *Show some signs of life!* It remained inert, but he was unconvinced.

"I knew you would appreciate it," Elvira stated matter-of-factly. "Care to hazard a guess on it?"

Wyatt looked up, as if dazed, and then shook the cobwebs from his head. "Huh? Oh... maybe a mutated animal of some sort? I can't see anything that would be a clue. Looks like parts of many animals here, yet nothing that stands out."

She grinned and said, "Why don't you check out the label?" pointing to the small parchment affixed to the bottom third of the jar. He turned the jar again, to bring the label closer. The glass was still warm and slick, but this time he sensed a vibration, so low it bordered on subsonic, thrumming under the tips of his fingers like the heartbeat of a mouse.

The label was made of a waxy yellow parchment, glued in place and stained in a couple places by a variety of liquids over the years. Beneath the stains, in a barely legible scrawl, it stated:

Specimen #73
[JHV – M/Negro/13]
10/11/1965
Greylock Institute
Dr. G. Coe

"Specimen of what?" Wyatt muttered to himself. "Some sort of deformed fetus?"

The Specimen

It certainly bore some resemblance to one, but a fetus of what species? Wyatt could see skin of various colors, hair, and even scales, both piscine and reptilian. He even could make out tiny knoblike forms that bore vague resemblances to fingers, toes, and tentacles (suckers and all) outlined under the diaphanous membrane covering the mass, but there wasn't rhyme or reason to any of it. *It's like a monster meatloaf,* he thought. *Looks like someone tossed a bunch of random creatures into a mixer which then spit them out in one large lump.*

"What the hell is it?" he repeated again in a more audible tone. "I need to be certain that it's something we can sell. Chet wouldn't appreciate any more legal violations."

That was an understatement by any measure. Months earlier, *Schrödinger's* had been cited and fined for selling the skull of a polar bear, which was illegal to sell under the regulations of the Endangered Species Act. Though it had been mislabeled as a grizzly bear skull, Chet was culpable, because according to the citation, it was his responsibility to verify the source of his purchases. Since that blow to his bottom line, Chet had been hyper-vigilant with regards to the purchases made for the store. Anything that was questionable had to be cleared through him. No exceptions to the rule.

"I did a bit of research and I think it's an extremely large teratoma… or maybe a fetus in fetu."

"English, please."

"Basically it's a rare type of tumor that often resembles a fetus," said Elvira. "Usually they're much smaller, found in infants, and immediately removed. Some doctors think that they are twins that never formed in the womb. This particular one, as you can see on the label, was removed from the body of a teenaged boy over fifty years ago."

"That's a tumor? It's huge!" Wyatt sputtered. "Are you certain? It looks like it weighs twenty to thirty pounds. At least."

"As sure as I can be… unless you want someone to unseal the jar and run some tests. I doubt anyone has opened it since 1965. That's what it says on the label, right?"

"What about the hair? And the teeth? Tumors can't grow hair and teeth."

"Believe it or not, these can," she stated. "They can even grow organs and spinal columns. I've found thousands of photos of teratoma on the internet, but none of them were half as large as this one."

"Freaky," he said with an excited grin. "You know I can't make a decision until Chet approves, but you were right. This is special. I love it and I know Sioux will, too. Where'd you find it? And how much are you asking?"

"My nephew Frank – I think you met him a while ago - went to one of those auctions where you can bid on abandoned storage units and get whatever you find inside them. Old Lumpy here… he was locked in a trunk with some other specimens and antique medical equipment. As for money, tell Chet same deal as the pig. Fifty percent consignment."

"Lumpy?" Wyatt snorted. "And how did you decide it's a he? I didn't know tumors had genders." His attention continued to be pulled back to the jar where the supposed teratoma was drifting slowly to a stop in the urine-hued soup.

"It's my pet name for him. He reminds me of an ex-boyfriend. Just seemed to fit," she said as she gathered her afghan and packed it into the green bag. "So, have Chet call me… okay? No hurry. If he likes this, he might be interested in the rest of the stuff I found. Nothing else was as interesting as Lumpy, though."

"Will do, Mrs. Dom… Elvira," Wyatt corrected himself with a grin and waved as she headed out the door. He turned his attention to the jar once again, touching the side lightly with his fingers. It was still slick and warmer than the ambient temperature of the store, but the subliminal thrum had disappeared and he felt a bit let down. He moved the jar awkwardly from the counter to the broad shelf directly behind him to keep Lumpy out of harm's way. *Damn, it was heavy. How did Mrs. D carry it?*

It had to be at least thirty pounds. Later, after Sioux arrived to man the register in the afternoon, he would move it back to the storeroom to await Chuck's verdict. *Take a nap, Lumpy*, he thought. *You look like you might need one.*

The bell rang again and Wyatt turned to greet the new customer with a practiced air of boredom. Soon after, while he was attempting to

The Specimen

satisfy the young man's request for "something weird and kinky" for his girlfriend, the sediment in the jar had resettled from its most recent jostling and the teratoma no longer rotated on its axis.

If anyone had been watching the specimen jar closely while Wyatt was busy with the customer, they would have seen the slightest fluttering of the gill-like flaps as a small flurry of bubbles escaped and rose lazily to the surface of the liquid. And if they had walked around to look at the jar from the opposite side, they might have seen the large nodule on its side peeling open for a second or two, revealing a pustular sulfur-colored ball with a narrow slit for an iris. By the time Wyatt rang the man up, though, the eyelids had closed again and any measure of disturbance in the jar had long since gone still.

Chapter 4 - Time to Make the Donuts

"Some mornings, it's just not worth chewing through the leather straps" – Emo Philips

Modern Day –Dorchester, MA

Bells were ringing and there was no way to stop them. The girl on the rumpled bed flailed blindly at the clock radio on the table next to her and knocked it onto the floor. The bells did not stop their clarion call as she rolled over, screamed into the pillow, and then looked up blearily when she realized the ringing was coming from her cell phone in the pocket of her jeans… the jeans she had left in a pile on the floor when she crawled into bed after closing the bar at 4:00 am that morning.

"Ugh, I'm getting too old for this shit," she muttered into her drool-covered pillow. Sitting up, she rubbed her eyes and staggered to the mound of clothes to retrieve her phone.

She looked at the screen, noted the caller ID and audibly groaned, "Please, don't be Chet. Don't be Chet. Don't be Chet," before pressing the answer button, holding the phone to her ear and grumbling, "This is Sioux."

"Wakey, wakey, sunshine. Time to make the donuts!" chirped an intentionally overly cheerful voice in her ear.

"Oh…Wyatt. Thank the Goddess it's you. How late am I?" she sighed in relief at the sound of her co-worker's voice. The recent altercation with her alarm clock had reset the time, so she had no reference and her body clock was completely unreliable lately. She stood up with groan and stretched, wearing only a 4XL neon pink Hello Kitty t-shirt that hung to her knees, which she had used as a nightgown since high school, and padded over to her closet to choose her outfit for the day.

"You're not late yet, Suzi-Q… but you will be if you're not here in half an hour. I had a feeling you would need to be roused from your coffin," said Wyatt. "Chet's coming in and he's been on your case about your lack of punctuality, so get a move on."

"Pffffft," Sioux snorted. "I'll just wear something to distract him and he won't say a thing about it… and don't call me that. You know I

The Specimen

hate it." She reached into the closet and took out her patented Japanese schoolgirl outfit, knowing that Chet would be helpless and incapable of forming complete sentences in her presence if she wore it. Whenever she was bored, she regularly dressed in outrageous outfits designed solely to make Chet a babbling fool. Come to think of it, they helped with sales as well.

"Okay," he agreed. "Just get in here soon, Miss Martinez. I've got something to show you. Mrs. D. brought in something truly amazing."

"Like that dead cat? I can still smell it in my dreams," she wrinkled her nose in disgust at the memory. "I had to throw out my favorite blouse because I couldn't get the stench out no matter how often I washed it."

"No, it's sealed up in a jar. No stink on this one. This is some Discovery Channel shit. Freaky as hell."

"Now I'm intrigued. You know I like the freaky stuff."

"So you've told me in detail… multiple times. I don't need that mental image now, though. Just get your ass in here before Chet arrives."

"I said I would, Wyatt. This better be worth the hype."

"You'll love it. I promise. Definitely your style. Chet will bitch about it at first, but I think it could easily pull a few thousand if we find the right buyer, so he'll keep it no matter."

"Mysterious," Sioux smirked, then yawned as she said, "Okay, I'll rush out the door and be there ASAP. Thanks for the call, babe." She hung up after saying good bye and ran to the bathroom for a lightning speed shower that barely moistened her hair. After some perfunctory makeup (heavy on the eyeliner), she tied her hair up in pigtails, put on her clothes, chugged some almond milk straight from the carton, scarfed down a banana and raced out the door to catch the 3:35 bus and hopefully sneak in the back door of the store before Chet arrived.

Chapter 5 – Wyatt Goes Surfing

"It's Not a Tumor!"
- Arnold Schwarzenegger in Kindergarten Cop.

Modern Day – Cambridge, MA

Wyatt ended the call with a chuckle and slid his phone into the pocket of his hoodie. He tapped the specimen jar with his fingernail and peered again into the murky yellow soup. The specimen drifted and collided gently with the opposite side of the jar. Flakes of skin came loose and drifted to the bottom to join the sedimentary layer of prior shedding. Wyatt grimaced slightly, then turned the jar so he could read the label again and copy it down. Time to hit the internet to get some info on this Greylock Institute that was listed on the label.

He was not the type of person to slack off when there was work to be done, but on the other hand, if no work was on his immediate radar, he felt no guilt at all in taking a little leisure time for himself. With free Wi-Fi (provided generously by Chet) and a perpetual assignment to scour national auction websites and Craigslist for upcoming events and rare items that fit the eclectic needs of *Schrödinger's* clientele, Wyatt spent much of his free time on his laptop.

Opening his browser, Wyatt tried searching for "Greylock" and "Greylock Institute" on the usual search engines with no luck. The majority of the results referred to the highest mountain in Massachusetts, Mount Greylock, and the Mount Greylock State Reservation, an animal preserve that covered the mountain and surrounding peaks. No entries for the Institute, though. They were slowly improving, but these search engines were problematic in Wyatt's experience, tending to search for the exact phrase instead of finding related pages. The more words that were typed in the search box, the more the results were narrowed down and eliminated, often to the point where nothing usable was found.

After a few dead ends, Wyatt had a hunch and typed in "Mount Greylock Institute". One second later and he struck gold. The 3rd link on the page was the Wikipedia entry for The Greylock Lunatic Asylum. He clicked on it and began reading.

The Specimen

The Greylock Lunatic Asylum
From Wikipedia, the free encyclopedia

The Greylock Lunatic Asylum, also known as the State Lunatic Hospital at Mount Greylock, the Mount Greylock Institute, and the Greylock State Insane Asylum, was a high security psychiatric hospital located in Adams, Massachusetts on the border of the Mount Greylock State Reservation in the Berkshire Mountains of Northwest Massachusetts.

History

Built in 1888 to meet the increased need for residential psychiatric hospitals in New England, the Greylock Lunatic Asylum was designed by the celebrated architect Tobias Duncannon, only months before he took his own life at his home in Holyoke. Mount Greylock would be his final design. It opened in 1890 and was at full capacity by the next year with the majority of its population coming from the overflow of its more renowned sister facilities, The Northampton State Lunatic Hospital and The Danvers State Insane Asylum.

The Institute was a self-contained psychiatric hospital originally consisting of a central administration building with six radiating wings organized according to security level, with the outermost ones reserved for patients with a history of extreme violence. Beneath each of the residential wards was a maze of tunnels that connected to the multi-leveled basements and each other, branching off like spokes from a central hub beneath the main administration building. Originally designed with patients of both genders in mind, the Institute changed to male-only in 1912 when the Sunderland State Women's Asylum opened its doors and all female residents were relocated to the newer facility.

After 1912, the former women's unit was converted to a pathological research laboratory, and a medical facility with multiple operating theaters. Greylock Institute was originally designed to accommodate 750 patients. Once the women's unit was relocated south, the official capacity of the Institute was downgraded to 500 patients. Even so, by the late 1930s and 1940s, overcrowding was quite severe with over 1,000 patients being housed in cramped and unsanitary conditions.

Eugenics Controversy

In the early 1920s and 1930s, multiple reports surfaced that the Institute was involved in the controversial Eugenics Movement. Dr. Herschel Toomey, director of the Mount Greylock Institute from 1907 until his retirement due to poor health in 1937, was known to be an associate of eugenicist Charles B.

Davenport of the Eugenics Records Office, as well as a close colleague of psychologist Henry H. Goddard around the time he wrote the controversial book *The Kallikak Family: A Study in the Heredity of Feeble-Mindedness*. Less than a year after retiring to his home in Hartford, Connecticut, Toomey passed away due to complications from a gastric ulcer.

Responding to complaints filed by the families of both former and current Greylock patients, the Massachusetts Board of Health, Lunacy and Charity inspected the Greylock Institute soon after Dr. Toomey's departure. After an extensive audit, it was determined that there had been numerous violations involving the care and treatment of the patients. Among the procedures in regular use that drew the loudest criticism were electroshock therapy, drugs, immobilization by straitjackets, and surgical intervention such as lobotomies, but the policy that caused the greatest outcry was the compulsory sterilization of any patient deemed socially or intellectually "deficient." It was estimated that approximately 1200 patients had been forcibly sterilized since the 1910s. These revelations led to the dismissal of a large number of employees and the Institute being placed under state supervision for the next two decades.

The Blackout Murders

On the evening of November 9, 1965, the Greylock Institute was affected by the Northeast Blackout of 1965. Parts of Ontario in Canada and the states of Connecticut, Massachusetts, New Hampshire, Rhode Island, Vermont, New York, and New Jersey lost power for over thirteen hours. During the outage, two unnamed patients overpowered and killed a staff member, then used his keys to gain access to the entire facility. According to a compilation of eyewitness reports on the incident, the patients did not make any attempt to escape the Institute. Instead, they used the blackout as an opportunity to satisfy their most primal, homicidal urges. When the power finally returned the next morning, eleven patients, five staff members and one doctor had been killed, and the two patients were captured and charged with multiple counts of homicide.

Closing its Doors

Declining patient population in the aftermath of the murders, large state budget cuts, and a national trend towards alternative methods of treatment, deinstitutionalization, and community-based mental health care led to most of the wards being closed and sealed off over the next few months. Eventually, the Greylock Institute shut its doors for good on September 30, 1966. Since closing, mainly due to its isolated location, the Institute campus has been left to decay and rot for decades. It has reportedly been listed on urban explorer message boards as a prime candidate for exploration. To date, no images of any successful foray have been published.

The Specimen

Wyatt scrolled to the bottom of the Wikipedia entry, but nothing else struck him as interesting. He clicked back to the search results page, but none of the other links seemed even remotely related to the Greylock Institute. A brief scan of the image results also led nowhere. He was ready to give up until later when he remembered Mrs. D.'s words about teratomas.

Typing the term "teratoma" into the Google image search, Wyatt was surprised at the amount of results he found. He scrolled down past pictures of distorted tissue with hair, teeth and miniature limbs embedded in masses of chaotic flesh. Some were whole. Others had been dissected. The photos were posted in both color and black and white. After a couple of minutes of looking at these monstrosities, Wyatt felt nauseated.

Most of the images showed excised flesh that was only a couple of centimeters in diameter, but there were a few specimens that were much larger, usually attached to the back or the face of an infant before removal. None of the results, however, showed anything comparable to the size of Lumpy. Wyatt examined it again, turning the jar. It bobbed slowly in the liquid, rotating on its axis like a bloated meat cantaloupe. He had to disagree with Mrs. D. about its origin. This was no chaotic amalgam of random cancerous tissues and pseudo-organs. No. He was certain that it had a purpose to its design.

The bell over the door jangled, and Wyatt looked up to see Sioux sauntering in nearly ten minutes late for her shift in her usual soiled kitten motif. He knew he should have been pissed at her, but he couldn't muster any anger at all. She may be completely irresponsible when it came to being anywhere on time, but without her presence at *Schrödinger's*, the clientele would have had more of an escaped mental patient vibe rather than the sorority girls looking for a naughty Halloween costume that they always saw around this time of the year. Wyatt thoroughly appreciated the diversion from the usual nut jobs and everyday tourists.

"Awesome! I made it in time," said Sioux as she reached the counter and looked around for Chet. "Please tell me I'm right ... and what sweet hell is this thing? You'd better not tell me this is your booger collection, Wyatt."

Wyatt laughed and beckoned for her to come behind the counter and take a closer look. Within minutes, she too was mesmerized.

The Specimen

Official Report on the Greylock Incident

January 23, 1966
To: Members of the Governing Council, ACME Group
From: James P. Kilcannon, Agent-in-Charge
RE: Greylock Incident

Esteemed Council Members:

Enclosed please find a collection of relevant entries from Dr. Coe's laboratory notes. Although most of her data were destroyed in the fire, we were able to salvage enough to provide you with an overview of their discoveries. Unfortunately, her primary specimen is missing. The search is ongoing. As we restore pages to legibility, they will be passed on and, of course, any progress will be reported to you immediately.

- JPK

* * *

Day 1

I am en route to Greylock per orders of the Council. Two handlers, named Jameson and Fenton, have been assigned to work with me, but I will reserve my opinion of them when I meet them at the site tomorrow. They have been guarding the subject for nearly a week since they took him into their custody.

The subject is reportedly a young colored boy from Springfield, Massachusetts, who was discovered to be hosting a symbiont by a relative at a family outing. Unfortunately for him, this relative has a history of psychiatric problems, and she receives therapy on a weekly basis. The therapist is an associate of mine who regularly reports issues that seem beyond the usual everyday occurrence. I immediately recognized the description of what the patient had claimed to have seen for what it was. If reality matches his perception, we could be in for a long stint at the Institute.

There is a strong possibility that this symbiont has only become recently attached to the child. This would be the chance of a lifetime for me, if it is true. In the centuries since our organization has been collecting data on the symbionts, none have been attached to the host for less than a few years. Examining how consciousness transfers will be most enlightening.

GC

Day 2

We have arrived at Greylock. The subject has been in residence here for six days, but he has had minimal contact with the other patients of the Institute per our instructions. Jameson and Fenton have performed quite better than I had expected. I believe I will keep them on the project.

The Director of the Institute, a Dr. Saul Eckenrode, is a wart-covered little toady that serves as a figurehead for the public. He is a truly unpleasant little man with clammy hands and hair that is slicked back with sort of foul-smelling pomade. I swear he uses some type of animal fat.

I thoroughly dislike him, but if he is the individual that ACME has placed in charge, he is surely under their thumb to the point where he will be afraid to contradict any of my instructions. ACME is quick and brutal with its punishment.

In my initial examination of the boy, it was soon apparent that he continues to lack any memories from before the symbiont joined him. Judging from our conversations and the age of the scar tissue at the borders of their flesh, I estimate that the encounter occurred 12 to 18 months ago, though it could be less, considering the increased healing effects of their union.

The symbiont still appears to be deep in a stage of torpidity. The last time it was subjected to electrical shock, it took nearly a week for it to become active once again, but we must remain vigilant.

The Specimen

       In order to fully determine the effects of symbiosis, the subject and symbiont will not be separated in the near future until all tests have been exhausted. Instead, samples will be frequently excised from both and put through a number of strictly designed tests. On occasion, if additional subjects are needed, Greylock residents will be encouraged to volunteer as often as is deemed necessary.

GC

Day 3

       The facilities are dreadful, barely adequate for our needs. Eckenrode revolts me. Our rooms are stiflingly hot. The food is industrial waste. Our subject is refusing to participate today, so I've given him one day to acclimate to the new setting, but tomorrow we will begin, regardless of his opinion. Other than that, everything is wonderful.

GC

Day 6

       Ten cell samples were removed from the symbiont today while subject was placed under sedation. Five were cut from the neural core of the symbiont; five taken from the boundary between subject and symbiont. Additionally, a large sample was excised from the subject's left flank to use as the control.

GC

Notes:

       Neural Core – The cells excised from the neural core resemble some types of human neurons, mainly Purkinje, Pyramidal and Renshaw cells with one great difference: exponentially more dendrites and synapses.

       Boundary cells – All five samples confirmed conclusions from prior experiments. The structures found in each sample closely resemble those reported in Gurdon's stem cells from his work in the UK in 1962 as well as our colleagues McCulloch and Till in Toronto. All the stem cells have structures resembling tangled golden fibers present in their cytoplasm. The functions of these strands have yet to be discovered. As the location of the specimens move closer to the neural core, the ratio of neurons to stem cells increases until the stem cells are nearly nonexistent...

The Specimen

Chapter 6 - Don't Kill the Messenger

"He who laughs has not yet heard the bad news" - Bertolt Brect

Modern Day – Chesterfield, MA

The flashing red and blue lights cut through the rain like neon lights at a club. Murtaugh was honestly impressed at the number of vehicles and the speed of the response. Considering the location of the accident and the spotty cell phone service in the area, he hadn't expected anyone to arrive for at least 10–20 more minutes. Hidden in a thicket at the edge of the road, Murtaugh counted at least five police cars, two fire engines, and three ambulances lined up in the early dawn light.

It was pointless, though. The kid was a goner. No one could be shot multiple times, then get hit by a mini-van that was travelling at least fifty miles per hour. *That kid went flying like a rag doll,* thought Murtaugh. *No chance he's surviving that without a miracle. This would cause problems, though. It's not every morning that a teenager is shot a couple times before getting hit by a car.*

The local police would be on high alert and the kid's trail would very likely lead back to the Monahan household. Once he was loaded into the ambulance, the officers would investigate the surrounding area and Murtaugh wanted to be long gone when that happened.

Needless to say, Quillian had to be alerted…and soon. Murtaugh was not looking forward to that conversation. Better to call as soon as he was able to get reception than tell him in person. Even with the advanced resources at the disposal of the Acme Group, they were still bound by the limits of their crappy cell phones. *Typical,* thought Murtaugh.

 The road where the kid had been hit wasn't a main thoroughfare, but there was still a reasonably high amount of traffic for this early in the morning. One lane had been closed off and a policeman in an orange raincoat directed traffic past the site of the impact. A line of rubberneckers was already forming because nothing stops traffic like a little morning drive carnage.

Murtaugh climbed back down the muddy incline, miraculously without falling on his ass, and headed back through the woods toward the

Monahan house. The rain had subsided to a meager drizzle, just enough to make his clothes damp and uncomfortable. On the walk back, he checked his phone, hoping for a couple bars of reception so he could report the situation to Quillian before arriving. The return trip was taking much longer than he had expected and he wasn't certain that he was taking a direct route. Even though there were very few houses out this way, he didn't want to walk into the wrong yard and create another situation. There was already enough of a mess to clean up and that greasy mook Grimaldi would only get in the way. He was good at killing, which is why he was one of Quillian's favorites, but other than that, Grimaldi was pretty worthless for anything that involved more than a third grade education.

Murtaugh checked his phone again and noted that reception had increased to two bars. Pressing "1" on speed dial, he connected with Quillian after only one ring and braced himself for a tongue-lashing and a threat of bodily harm. Surprisingly, though, the team leader was calm and reasonable upon hearing the turn of events. Unsure whether he should be relieved or concerned at Quillian's even temper, Murtaugh asked if he should head to the local hospital and check on the situation.

"No, I'll send someone else out for that," answered Quillian. "I want you back at the house ASAP. You need to take the two girls and the van to the Center to be processed. Grimaldi and I will clean things up here and meet you later."

"What about the other three?"

"The dad's dead…mom's on her way out…and we need the boy to wrap things up nice and neat."

"You need any supplies?"

"No, we've got it covered. Both of their cars had full tanks. Grimaldi siphoned them clean."

"Roger that," confirmed Murtaugh, ending the call. Immediately, he dialed another number. This one was longer – twenty-one digits. No record of this call would ever exist, either on his phone or in any federal database.

A woman with a French accent answered, "Yes. Identify."

Murtaugh cleared his throat and responded, "The process of delving into the black abyss is to me the keenest form of fascination."

The Specimen

"Identity confirmed. Report, Agent Murtaugh."

Murtaugh related the entire incident to the woman on the line, detailing casualties and complications, and requesting instructions. Once finished, he waited for a response.

"Determination – Actions within mission parameters. Continue monitoring Colfax and contact us with each new development"

He ended the call, pocketed the phone, then leaned back to look up at the dreary, gray cloud cover. The rain spattered his face intermittently as if God himself were spitting from Heaven… as if he actually cared about the individual fates of the mindless swarming insects below Him. He stood that way for a minute or so, enjoying the white noise of the drops hitting the leaves, then held up his right fist and saluted the sky, middle finger held high in defiance.

Pete Kahle

*From the Personal Journal
of Dr. Saul Eckenrode
Clinical Director
Mount Greylock Institute*

August 24, 1965

      This damnable heat wave has all the residents agitated, and I will admit that it has me on edge as well. I must remember to have Mr. Willard purchase another couple fans. One for the common room, and one which I will appropriate for my own comfort. As director, I have only a few privileges and I intend to take full advantage of them whenever possible...

      The boy arrived today. If I had a choice in the matter, he would not be here, but since I have no say, I will bite my tongue and restrain myself. I must remember that, if not for my benefactors, my life could very well have gone down a different, much shorter path and I most certainly would have been unable to pursue my own medical studies. I am afraid this will lead to a permanent arrangement where I must share my space with... others. Others who may question my methods.

      He arrived accompanied by two Acme watchdogs, both of whom looked like ex-military and were probably armed to the teeth. Overkill, in my opinion. How would a thirteen year old colored boy present a threat to any adult with military training?

      They escorted him directly to my office, which unfortunately took him right past the common room. Who knows how many residents saw him? It is safe to say that the house cats we keep on the property for therapy saw him, because they began yowling as soon as the three of them crossed through the room.

      Luckily, despite the caterwauling, very few of the residents looked over during the brief transit, but enough saw him that I will have to integrate him into population earlier than expected, even though he is the youngest by at least six years. He'll probably be targeted because of his race and age, but some things are just unavoidable. According to my employers, the boy's interaction with the other residents is necessary, despite my warnings. I have never thought that it was a good idea to combine the state residents with those brought from the private sector. But I digress...

The Specimen

  I gave him a room on the South Wing, near the medical facilities as requested. When I escorted him there, I attempted to engage the boy in conversation, but he was either shy or in a monosyllabic mood. The only information that I could get out of him was that he preferred to be called Harry rather than Jarvis. Both of the men accompanying us were equally mute. One carried Harry's suitcase, a large battered leather satchel with brass latches, large enough to contain his entire life. Now that I think about it, it probably did.

- S.

August 30, 1965

  This morning I was met at my office by the two new Acme goons, Jameson and Fenton, both of whom I will struggle to distinguish from the other. Each is well over six feet tall, with buzz cut brown hair. Jameson has a large reddish mole at the corner of his left eye and the hairiest hands I have ever seen on an individual. Perfectly designed for strangling a troublesome doctor who doesn't know when to keep his mouth shut. The other one, Fenton, must have stock in Old Spice considering the amount with which he douses himself. I find myself breathing through my mouth every time I have to speak with him.

  Accompanying them was a diminutive, elfin blonde woman who introduced herself as Dr. Genevieve Coe, pronouncing it "John-vee-ev". I don't think we'll be friends. She seemed condescending and dismissive. I would normally consider her attractive if not for the clinical "I'd like to castrate you and examine your balls under a microscope" glare she gave me when first introduced. Some men might find that attractive. I do not.

  Obviously she is unaware of my extensive qualifications. That will change in time. I may be in debt to our mutual employers, but I will not kowtow to anyone. She introduced herself, and without missing a beat, informed me that they would be commandeering a surgical room for the indefinite future, and that they would be bringing in a few pieces of large medical equipment to store there.

  I didn't protest, knowing it would be futile, but you can be sure that they will keep no secrets from me. What is the importance of the young boy to warrant such an expense? And why cloak the entire project in such mystery at an asylum off the beaten path like this one? Unless it requires a suspension of ethics that would invite questions from the authorities. Intriguing, indeed. I will have to investigate more.

- S.

August 31, 1965

Dr. Coe is earning my wrath in numerous ways, not the least of which is how she has ensorcelled Mr. Willard under her spell. He is neglecting his duty as groundskeeper of the campus and has become her personal chauffeur, furniture mover, electrician and all around bootlicker. She has him moving all of her equipment into her surgical rooms and office, as well as making certain that she has the necessary wiring to support the amount of power she will need.

A parade of large crates and boxes have been hauled in by another squad of interchangeable muscle-bound goons over the past two days. In addition, she has replaced all the doors to her rooms with ones constructed of solid metal, and all the original locks have been removed.

It seems like overkill to me because the doors are at least 6 inches thick and they do not appear to use standard keys. One of the men installing the doors informed me that they utilize a new form of locking mechanism that involves electromagnetism. These new doors are supposedly impenetrable, requiring a special type of key that disengages the magnetic field.

Of course, I have not been given a key.

This is yet another example of Dr. Coe excluding me from decisions made about my own facility. Since this discovery, I have avoided the South end of the building. I find it easier to restrain my fury if I am not a witness. You can be certain that I will file an official complaint with her superiors, but I rather doubt that it will make any difference.

Logically, I always pretend to approve of everything. I need to be trusted by Acme if I hope to advance up the ladder and get my due, so I will play well with others and bide my time until opportunity presents itself.

As for the boy...

He was introduced into population on the 15th and was immediately targeted by the usual suspects. Angelo Scarpa and his mumbling sidekick Stanley Wick approached him, planting themselves on either side of him on the institutional grey canvas couch at the far end of the community room. I observed this happen from the other side of the

The Specimen

room while doing morning rounds checking on specific residents. Mainly, however, I wanted to see how Harry's incorporation into the community was handled by everyone involved.

Jameson and Fenton were in the room as well. Rather than their usual Jehovah's Witness ensemble of white shirt, black tie and slacks, they wore the official uniform of the institution and blended in with the rest of the staff. It was unlikely that most of the residents would even notice the new blood. Most of them were on extremely high doses of medication and were unable to distinguish new staff from old. Even then, as I scanned the room, I saw at least five residents already slumped in their chairs in torpor from their morning pills.

Most of our patients are male, from their late teens to well into their fifties. Younger patients are housed in a children's facility near Springfield and our geriatric clients are often shuttled off to nursing homes when they are incapable of caring for their own basic needs. There were some exceptions to the age rule in special circumstances. Harry fit those criteria, apparently.

Jameson and Fenton looked in my direction to see whether they should intervene, and against my better judgment, I shook them off. I thought he should feel things out on his own at first. He wouldn't learn anything if he was coddled and protected constantly. Besides, the sole purpose of integrating him into the community was to foster peer interactions - be they positive or negative.

The two looked at me steadily, obviously suspecting something, and then nodded their heads nearly in unison. They have creepy dead eyes - like lizards. I'm sure they both wet their beds and tortured small animals when they were younger. I have also realized why Fenton uses so much Old Spice. He has a shockingly powerful body odor that can make your eyes water if you get too close. With the summer heat at its peak, his aroma is especially pungent.

Angelo Scarpa has been a resident here for nearly seven years. Hard to believe it's been that long. He came here in the fall of '59 after being deemed unable to stand trial due to insanity. I have never had any doubt that he is insane, but he does know that actions have consequences, and I have yet to discover any proof that he did not understand that his crimes would definitely harm people.

Scarpa is an unrepentant pedophile and a confessed murderer. He has scarred dozens of young boys and girls over the past two decades by satisfying his vile needs, and although Harry is a few years older than most of those boys were… well, let's just say that, in this place, beggars can't be choosers.

I slowly angled my path closer to the couch to get a better view, clipboard in my hands so I could feign the distraction of daily paperwork. The young Negro boy was almost swallowed by his oversized bathrobe and pajamas, causing him to appear even smaller than his actual twelve years. I expected to have to send Jameson and Fenton over to the couch within two to three minutes. Scarpa sat on Harry's left, hunched, sunken-chested and scrawny, with tufts of greasy black hair at his temples. Wick slouched into the right side of the couch, sandwiching the boy between their bulks.

Wick is built like a fire hydrant and has about as many brains. He has been a resident here for most of his adult life after suffering repeated brain damage as a child from multiple beatings at the hands of his parents. At age fifteen, Wick repaid them both when he bludgeoned them to death with a sledgehammer. He was picked up by the police sitting on his front steps, covered in gore to his elbows and cradling the bloody weapon like a toddler clutching his teddy bear.

One week later, he was brought to Mt. Greylock and he has been here ever since… nearly twenty years. If he somehow gained a few more points of IQ, he would quickly realize that he was just being used by Scarpa as a loyal lapdog, but that wasn't likely. Barring a miraculous regeneration of brain tissue, he will remain stupid and loyal to Scarpa, our very own Lenny to Scarpa's psychopathic George.

I watched them intently. As soon as Scarpa made any attempt to intimidate or manipulate Harry, we would be all over him and, if Wick jumped in, they would both be cuffed and sent off to solitary confinement for a little "attitude adjustment".

Scarpa leaned toward the boy with a smile, snaking his right arm behind Harry and resting it on the back of the couch like a tentacle poised to tangle a victim in its clutches. The boy ignored him. Scarpa spoke again and held out his left hand in greeting, but Harry continued to sit silently, refusing to respond. I circled around the room and noted that Harry's eyes were clenched shut. He was shaking his head vigorously, saying, "No!" over and over again while pressing his hands to his ears.

The Specimen

At first, I assumed that he was responding to Scarpa's overture, but the skinny little man seemed equally confused. He glanced at Wick and nodded. The burly man nudged the boy roughly, grabbed his shoulder and growled at him in warning. Jameson and Fenton started heading in their direction with me right behind them, but by the time we arrived seconds later, the shit had already hit the fan.

Wick yanked back his hand as if he had been shocked, yelling in pain and backing away from the boy. Scarpa looked on in confusion as the boy turned to Wick and whispered to his sidekick. I couldn't hear what he said, but as soon as he said it, Wick had what appeared to be a sudden muscle spasm before going slack, staring over Harry's shoulders at Scarpa.

It became a bit confusing at that point, because I and seemingly everyone else in the common room were suddenly overcome with stomach pains and hunger pangs when a musky scent filled the room. I was staring directly at the couch or else I might have missed what happened next.

Harry deftly jumped off the couch, leaving Wick and Scarpa facing each other. Scarpa shouted at Wick to go after him, but the squat muscular man did not respond. His eyes rolled back to his head and he began to shake violently. Foamy spittle began seeping from the corners of his mouth.

I yelled out, "Seizure!" to alert the staff and followed the Buzzcut Twins in a hurry. Scarpa had finally realized that something was seriously wrong with Wick. He scrabbled backward over the arm of the couch, but Wick lashed out with his right hand, grabbed his buddy's ankle and yanked.

Scarpa lost his balance and flung his arms back to catch himself. He fell backwards and smacked his head on the floor, biting his tongue in the process. Blood sprayed from his mouth all over his robe. He held up his hands to hold off Wick, but it was futile.

Wick launched himself over the side of the couch and landed with his knees on Scarpa's chest. I heard his ribs crack like kindling. Scarpa howled shrilly in agony, spraying Wick's face in a mist of scarlet. Jameson and Fenton were only a couple strides away when Wick reared backward, mouth open and dripping gouts of saliva, then slammed his head down and clamped his teeth on Scarpa's beak-like nose.

One time when I was a child in Brooklyn, I saw a stray mutt catch a rat the size of a puppy and break its back with a vicious shake of its jaws. The sound of Wick chewing through the cartilage of Scarpa's nose was eerily reminiscent of the sound of the rat's spine snapping.

Jameson and Fenton pulled Wick off of Scarpa and I saw that his eyes were still completely rolled back in his skull. I dragged Scarpa to the side and pressed a cloth someone had handed me to the bloody mess of his face. Where his nose had been, there were only two gaping holes leading to his open sinuses. Wick was pinned to the floor by multiple orderlies, but I could see he was calm and content, working on the pieces of Scarpa's nose like it was a piece of beef jerky. Standing off in the corner was Harry, face filled with fear, completely shocked at what had happened and apparently unaware of his part in the carnage. I must find out more...

- S.

The Specimen

Chapter 7 - The Bottom of the Hill

"I guess I just prefer to see the dark side of things. The glass is always half-empty. And cracked. And I just cut my lip on it. And chipped a tooth."
- Janeane Garofalo

Modern Day – Cambridge, MA

"Shit flows downhill," muttered Chet Boyd to himself as he pulled onto Massachusetts Avenue in his 1963 Dodge Dart. "Boy, were you ever right, Dad. The rich get richer. Screw the little guy!" He smacked his hand on the steering wheel and gritted his teeth. If he couldn't find a way to increase sales soon, he'd have to consider selling *Schrödinger's*, the only real piece of his father he had left. The proverbial wall of shit was rolling down the slope towards him at a breakneck pace and, barring a miracle, all he could do was freeze in place and wait for the deluge.

His father had been fond of that adage in times of stress, when money was tight and the Boyd family had to cut back on "non-essential items" like new clothes, cable television, and utilities. Marvin Boyd's entire philosophy could be boiled down to those three words. In his mind, society was rigged. Life was inherently unfair. The corporations controlled everything, especially the government, and if you weren't one of their minions, you would be smart to just bend over, stick your head between your legs, and kiss your hairy ass goodbye.

When people first met him, with his greying dreadlocks and trademark Che Guevara t-shirt, they often came away with the impression that Marvin was a rabble-rousing radical, but once you got to know him, you realized that he was just a grumpy old bastard who liked to complain about the faults of the system, but lacked any serious motivation to act upon his values.

Marvin's cynicism proved prophetic twelve years earlier when he had a fatal heart attack in a hospital waiting room after sitting for over seven hours to be seen. He had complained of severe chest pain and tingling in his extremities, but he was ignored. Any competent doctor would immediately have recognized the symptoms of cardiac distress and bumped him to the front of the line, but since he was a poor African-American with minimal health insurance, he was continuously passed over for other patients with less serious conditions.

It wasn't until he keeled over after midnight, prompting a fellow triaged patient to call for help, that he was finally brought to a doctor's attention. Regrettably, he had already slipped into unconsciousness and was unable to be revived. It was too late. Within minutes, he had expired. The system which had continuously been his nemesis had buried him in an avalanche of shit.

Chet hadn't even been aware that his father was at the hospital. His mother had lost a battle with pancreatic cancer over a decade earlier, and Chet had drifted away from his father since college. They spoke on the phone weekly, but Chet's disinterest in "fighting the cause" proved to be the main reason for their distance from each other. Chet was aimless after college, drifting from jobs as a bartender, a waiter, and subsequently, manager at a video rental store, where he became an expert on all topics related to science fiction and horror films. In retrospect, his lack of direction was inherited directly from his father. Marvin was simply more vocal about who pissed him off and freely shared his opinion on what needed to be done to set things straight.

Additionally, Marvin was notoriously private, so he hadn't even called to let Chet know he was in the emergency room. Chet was informed of Marvin's passing by a faceless representative of the hospital who called at noon the following day and gave him the news in a practiced monotone before asking about arrangements for his father's body.

And that was how he inherited the shop. Marvin had run it for decades as a generic thrift store with the occasional revolutionary apparel, but Chet took it in a different direction when business was lagging a couple years after his father's death. Originally called Boyd's Thrift Shop, Chet renamed the shop *Schrödinger's Curiosities* in homage to the infamous cat and box scenario posed by the great physicist. He began featuring items marketed to a more eclectic crowd, specifically individuals whose taste tended toward the morbid and bizarre. Later on, after he was called Mr. Schrodinger a few hundred times, he realized that his average patron did

The Specimen

not make the connection nor did they consider it witty. Curiosity. Cat. Seemed obvious to Chet.

Initially the format change was a huge success. Rarely did a day go by in the first year or two that the shop was empty of customers at any time of the day. Profits were sky high. Chet had stumbled into a niche market and *Schrödinger's* was the only place in the Boston/Providence metro area that catered to his clientele. Slowly, though, sales had decreased steadily for the past five to six years until this past one when he began losing money on a regular basis. If it continued this way for much longer, Chet was seriously considering closing shop and putting the store on the market.

Even so, as long as he budgeted his savings well, he would have enough to retire within a couple years at age 50… enough for a small bungalow in the Florida Keys where he could while away his midlife crisis in sunny isolation. Chet despised modern society as much as his father had, but instead of constantly vocalizing his displeasure, his main motivation was to find a way to escape it. Until that moment, all he could do was bide his time and hope for a sudden resurgence in the bizarre antiques market.

Traffic finally let up and Chet was able to untangle himself from the snarl of the late afternoon Boston rush hour, taking the side streets of Cambridge to the small parking lot in an alley just off of Harvard Square. There were only twenty-four parking spaces in the lot, but each was completely paid for by a cadre of shop owners who, along with his father, had pooled their money together decades earlier to purchase the miniscule property. As long as they paid the annual property taxes, they all had free parking forever. Next to the store, this was the most valuable inheritance he had received from his father. Eventually, he might have to consider putting his space up for sale. Over the years, Chet had received multiple offers in the tens of thousands of dollars to purchase it, but he had resisted temptation so far.

Chet pulled up to the chain link gate, unlocked it and maneuvered into his parking space. Back row. 2nd from the left. He shut off the engine and sat there in the silence with his eyes closed briefly, then sighed deeply, grabbed his beat-up leather satchel, and exited the car, locking the gate on his way out. From there, it was only a three block saunter to the shop, located in a lower level space between a Russian grocery store and a tattoo shop that Chet suspected had an alternative source of income, considering the fact that it was rarely open and he had never seen anyone actually get a tattoo there.

Seconds after leaving the lot, a weak drizzle spattered from the sky, sending pedestrians scurrying to find shelter under awnings and concrete overhangs. Chet ignored the rain and continued stolidly toward his shop, satchel swinging in time with his strides, ignoring everyone he passed, with the exception of a quick nod to Old Harry, one of the career panhandlers found on nearly every corner in Harvard Square.

Old Harry had been manning the corner near *Schrödinger's* for as long as he could remember. An African-American man who looked as if he could be anywhere between the ages of 50 and 70, Old Harry seemed barely to have aged at all over the years. His main distinctive feature was a mild case of vitiligo on his hands with smaller patches of the loss of pigmentation at his right eyebrow and hairline and on his left ear. The condition also affected his hair with a large shock of white on his left temple.

Every so often Old Harry would wander in to the store and study the items on sale, but he never purchased anything. Chet didn't mind. Old Harry wasn't aggressive like some of the other men and women working the passing crowds for change, nor had he ever bothered any of the customers and he was always cleanly dressed in a Harvard University hooded sweatshirt and jeans. He wasn't much of a conversationalist, though. Chet had tried to talk to him many times over the years, but he always responded in one or two words at most. When words were unnecessary, he would crack a smile or make a subtle gesture.

The most that Old Harry had ever said to him was nearly a year after his father had passed away. On that day, Old Harry had come into *Schrödinger's* quietly, almost tentatively, walked around the store once, and then stood alone for a while as if contemplating something unknowable. Chet had walked over to see if he could be of any service, somewhat apprehensive because it had been the first time he had seen Old Harry anywhere other than the streets.

The Specimen

"I knew your daddy," he had mumbled to Chet when he approached. "He was a good man. A very good man." Old Harry looked up at Chet, swiped at a tear trickling from the corner of his eye, then turned abruptly and walked out. In the eleven years since, Chet had always made it a point to keep an eye out for him on the streets, especially when the weather was bad. He occasionally felt a twinge of guilt that he didn't know whether Old Harry had any shelter, but in Cambridge, it was likely that he had a place to stay provided by some charitable organization. The community was quite liberal and Harvard Square was its epicenter. Old Harry never appeared malnourished or neglected. His clothes, though worn, were clean and honestly, he fit right in with the style of the college crowd that always frequented the area.

Normally Chet would have had some change for Old Harry, or occasionally a cup of coffee or a sandwich, but today he had been too preoccupied to pick up food and hadn't even eaten anything since breakfast. His stomach gurgled at the reminder and he picked up the pace, remembering a box of *Cheez-Its* that were in his desk drawer. That should hold him over until he had something delivered for dinner.

Rounding the corner, he sidestepped a massively pregnant woman pushing a tandem stroller with twin boys shrieking in unison that they wanted some ice cream now. He stopped to briefly apologize for nearly bowling her over, skirted around an inordinate amount of stray cats at the entrance to the alley next to the store, and then continued on until the black cast iron storefront of *Schrödinger's* loomed in front of him.

One of the first things Chet had done after inheriting the store was to rebrand it in order to attract a different clientele. Instead of the backwoods radical/deer hunter/survivalist/aging hippy vibe that Marvin had cultivated for so many years, Chet wanted to attract a higher income yet equally eclectic type of patron… namely the suburban upper middle class gothic teen.

In his video store days, Chet had worked in a rundown strip mall next door to a *Hot Topic* franchise where many of his friends worked. One thing he had learned from them was this fact: Goth kids were almost always spoiled little rich brats whose parents were in such shock that their children had embraced the androgynous black eye-liner pseudo-suicide cult style that they would do anything to lure them back from the brink of eternal freakishness. The most common method they tried was bribery. Throngs of ghostlike teens in various garments of black, white, red and purple would descend upon Hot Topic on the weekends to spend their cash. When they finished, more often than not, they would venture to Chet's video store to browse the latest horror and anime films.

Years of trying to convince Marvin to change the format of the shop were unsuccessful, but once Chet took over, he put his plan into action. The front of the store was now covered with repurposed cast iron fences welded to the original brick storefront. Above the entrance was the name *Schrödinger's*, also shaped from cast iron, fashioned by a friend who worked as a blacksmith in a traveling Renaissance Faire.

Chet realized that he had probably spent more than was necessary for the extra ornamentation, but he thought the investment had been worth it. The entrance to *Schrödinger's* had become an iconic sight of Harvard Square. It guaranteed that the shop would always have a regular flow of visitors, but sadly it did not always translate to a steady, predictable stream of income.

Chet sighed deeply. *Relax, boy. Something good will come along*, he thought as he pulled open the shop door to a blast of cold air and the sounds of Volbeat over the speakers. *Damn it, Wyatt. I can't hear myself think.* He saw Sioux and Wyatt toward the back, huddled around a large glass bottle behind the counter. *Looks like Sioux made it on time for once. What the hell are they so interested in?* Whatever it was, they were thoroughly mesmerized by its contents. Wyatt held a flashlight, which he shone into the interior of the jar illuminating a shadowy silhouette. Sioux was in her usual soiled schoolgirl outfit, obviously calculated to distract him from anything she might happen to do wrong. Currently, she was running her hands over the jar slowly, almost erotically, up and down the glass sides and over the sealed metal lid.

The store seemed unnaturally warm with a musky undertone to the usual shop smell. Chet sniffed, looking around for the source of the scent, when the air was split with a high shriek of pain. Sioux whirled away from the jar, clutching her right palm, rivulets of blood trickling down her arm while she hissed in pain.

The Specimen

"It bit me!" she yelled uncomprehendingly. "It fucking bit me!" Chet and Wyatt both rushed to her aid, hustling her off to the washroom for some towels to staunch the flow. Left behind on the counter, a dim golden glow emitted from the jar. A few drops of blood had leaked into the interior by way of the lid and were now dissipating into the liquid solution. The dim spark of life gleamed from a latticework of miniscule filaments on the surface of the teratoma. Its skin swelled slightly and retracted when a line of bubbles escaped from the base of the organism. Gradually the light dissipated as motion slowed to a standstill in the viscid soup.

Soon, except for the smear of blood on the lid, no evidence of anything out of the ordinary remained.

Chapter 8 – All Rivers Flow to the Sea

"Death is the only god who comes when you call"
– Roger Zelazny

Modern Day – Scott Visits Comaland

It won't matter if he plans to go down a different path this time. If Scott takes a new fork, eventually that side path will bend back and rejoin the original trail. The dream always begins the same way.

All rivers flow to the sea…

All rivers flow to the sea…

At first, Scott remembers nothing of the waking world. The seal between dream world and reality is pristine. He is watching cartoons, lying on the ancient couch in the living room of the two bedroom ranch he shares with his father in Rhinelander, what he considers to be the most boring rural town in northern Wisconsin. Definitely not the center of high society, Rhinelander's main claim to fame is the reputed existence of a legendary creature known as the Hodag.

Much of the town's economy revolves around reinforcing the myth of this animal. There is a statue of the legendary creature in town, and an annual festival where locals hawk t-shirts, coffee mugs and stuffed Hodags for little nieces and nephews around the country. And the food? All things fried were always available at numerous booths around the festival, probably the only redeeming aspect of this town. Otherwise, Scott thought it was total bullshit (but he would never say that out loud because his dad would whoop his ass). It wasn't like they had any proof like they did with Bigfoot or the Loch Ness Monster.

The couch is lumpy and smells faintly of sour milk, residue of a bowl of Cheerios he spilled last week but he is too lazy at the moment to get up and get the air freshener. He almost calls out for his mother, before remembering she is not there. Gone. It has been almost three weeks since the cancer finally took her and he still feels her presence throughout the house. Always in the other room, puttering around and wiping down imaginary spots on the counters. Arranging the dishes in almost military formations in the cabinets. Checking all the expiration dates of the food in

The Specimen

the refrigerator. Melanie Ritchie would have been the first to admit she had a slight case of Obsessive Compulsive Disorder, but she would rationalize her many quirks by stating, rightly so, that she was a perfect foil for her husband Vic's perpetual hyperactivity and apparent aimlessness. She focused him while he enabled her to occasionally let loose. Even with Vic around to buff her sharp edges, her compulsion for cleanliness became less of a quirk and more of a psychological necessity once she learned of her breast cancer. Each germ eliminated by Mr. Clean represented a cluster of cancer cells down for the count.

Scott misses her terribly, but he is accepting her loss incrementally more each day. His father, however, is taking things much harder. Vic seems irretrievably lost without his life partner, drifting through each day like debris on a gust of wind. The once spotless house has quickly become the embodiment of the disarray they now felt in their lives. Plates and cups litter the room, some with food from last week still caked on them. The couch isn't the only source of foul odors in the room. A few items of discarded clothing lay on the floor and an abandoned pile of laundry sits in a basket atop the dining room table, unfolded, wrinkled and utterly disorganized. Scott occasionally attempts to pick up some of the mess, but let's face it; he's nine years old and his idea of clean most likely doesn't meet the standards of the average person.

A few drops of the present sweat through into his dream, rendering the walls of his house diaphanous. Through the walls, he sees familiar shadows. A butchered man on a table, innards steaming and wet. Another man chasing someone through the rain-soaked forest. A series of explosions and a blinding light and the walls rematerialize. Scott remembers much more and he begins to separate dream from reality.

He realizes he should have gone to school today, a Wednesday, but his father didn't wake him on time for the bus. Vic was already in the garage working on his Toyota when Scott finally crawled out of bed just after 10 am. Now it is nearly 1pm and his stomach is beginning to growl like a feral dog gnawing on a bone. Two stale Pop Tarts and a glass of chocolate milk doesn't seem to be cutting it today. Since there is nothing else remotely edible left in the house, maybe his dad would let him order pizza. They could eat it for lunch and dinner.

He forces himself to stand up and stretch. Grandpa Bud would say he was sitting there growing mushrooms and to get up before his ass grows into the couch. Mom always said that Grandpa Bud had "a way with words," yet she seemed to be the only one who truly understood him. Dad just says Grandpa Bud's an uptight asshole conformist. Scott doesn't know what a conformist is, but he's pretty sure that Dad doesn't mean it to be a compliment.

After taking an epic piss worthy of a young man twice his size, Scott knocks on the door to the garage and calls out for his dad. No answer. He raps on the door a bit louder because the car engine is running and his father is probably in his own little world, mourning in his own way. Scott yells a couple more times, and then gives up. It looks like he'll have to venture outside and enter the garage through the main door.

The car engine is even more audible when Scott goes out the front door and heads to the one-car garage. The door is down in a locked position and, strangely, it appears that the lights inside are turned off. Scott touches the door and finds it a bit warm. Noxious fumes from the car leak out through the dog door in the center, causing tears to leak from the corners of his eyes and trickle down his cheeks. He holds his nose and bangs on the door, yelling for his father to open up and let him inside. No answer. He didn't expect one.

He begins to get concerned. Maybe there was an accident inside. His father could be bleeding to death on the concrete. On the other hand, he could also be passed out on a chair after drowning his sorrows in a bottle of Jack. It wouldn't be the first time. Scott is too short to look through the window in the garage door, so he can't verify if any of his morbid thoughts prove true.

There is a small wooden door to the garage around the back that they rarely use, but Scott has been through this many times before and he knows the only lock is a flimsy hook and latch screwed into the door frame. Unless the dream takes a previously unknown path, he can probably knock the door open with a couple of swift kicks. A couple times he punched out the window, but he usually ends up cutting himself pretty severely. Not that it matters, but the pain feels real and he would like to avoid it if possible.

The Specimen

Scott hurries around the side of the house and peers through the window. He knows what he won't find and he can't change a thing, regardless of how much he prays, but still he looks with a glimmer of hope in his heart that this time would be different. His father is not fiddling with the engine under the Toyota's hood, nor is he lying on the floor in a pool of blood. No, he's sitting inside the car and it looks like he's sleeping or perhaps listening to the radio. Scott can't see much through the window because the lights are off and he only has the sunlight streaming through the windows to provide illumination.

He kicks the door and it flies open on first impact. A cloud of exhaust fumes rolls out and envelops him in its foul embrace until he is hacking and spitting up his Pop Tart breakfast on the grass. At this point, while he is on his knees, it becomes apparent something is very wrong. Something long, thin and bright green is attached to the Toyota's exhaust pipe. He crawls closer and realizes that the object is his mother's garden hose. The dream and reality are now bleeding into one another.

The hose has been attached with what appears to be a few dozen yards of duct tape sealing it to the pipe. The other end of the hose is threaded through a narrow gap at the top of the driver's side window. Right where his father is sitting...

Scott pushes himself off the grass and rushes into the garage, yanking the hose from the car window and pulling his father's door open. His father lays there with the seat reclined and his hands folded in his lap. His face is a mottled bright lobster red and his lips are cracked and bloody with dried saliva ringing around the mouth.

Right off the bat, Scott realizes his father is dead. He shakes him, screams at him and presses the horn. Anything to pull him back from the other side. Spinning around, Scott rushes to the door leading into the house and pulls up short. The door has vanished. Where the stairs and doorway once were, there is only a smooth blank wall with no sign of there ever having been any sort of entryway. Scott looks back to the car and sees that the door through which he had entered is now dissolving into the walls of the garage. The main garage door is also affected. A curtain of skin gradually grows from the floor to the ceiling, sealing off any access to the outside. Scott is frozen. Nothing like this has ever happened in this dream before. All bets are off now.

After the initial shock subsides, Scott returns to the car to look at his father's corpse, only to find that Vic's body is not alone. Another figure sits behind his father in the back seat. Someone very familiar. Someone he thought he had lost. Someone he never believed he would see again.

Melanie Ritchie looks up at her son from the rear passenger seat. She is dressed in blue scrubs, her outfit of choice back when she had been a nurse – before the cancer.

"Hey there, little bruiser," she greets him smiling widely. "Just in time to help your mom clean up this mess."

Scott stands there frozen before whispering the words, "Mom? Is it really you?"

"Of course not, honey. I'm dead," she teases him. "You're dreaming, remember? I'm still watching you, though. I'll be with you when you need me."

Tears slowly trickle down Scott's face. "I miss you so much, Mom." He hesitates. "Dad didn't take it well."

"My death? No, he didn't," she says as she leans forward and strokes Vic's cheek. "That's pretty obvious ... considering his condition. Don't you think? Now where are the keys? I need to turn off the car so we can open the doors and windows and clear the air."

After searching for a few seconds, though, it becomes obvious. No keys can be found and yet the car is running without them.

"They must be hidden," she mutters, ignoring the impossibility of the running car.

She grimaces as she looks around the interior, and covers her nose and mouth. His dad has let it go as much as the house has been ignored. Coffee stains the gearshift. The windows are streaked with grime and receipts, wrappers and napkins litter the floor. Spotting something metallic sticking out from beneath a floor mat, she leans down and retrieves it.

"Just what I need. Now I know where they are." she grins, raising a rusty scalpel to the light. Scott stares at it incomprehensibly.

The Specimen

"Why do you need that?" he mumbles, though he is afraid he already knows. He looks from his mother to his father's body and back, "No, you can't. Please, Mom. Don't!"

Melanie shakes her head in a manner with which he was extremely familiar, sympathetic yet determined to act. She clambers into the front seat, jostling Vic's corpse and momentarily causing the horn to blare in the sealed garage. Scott catches his father and pushes the body back into the car. He then turns away in revulsion as Melanie cuts open Vic's shirt and begins to slice into the dead man's flesh.

There is no way he wants to watch his dead mother carve up his newly dead father, but there is no place else to look in this sealed chamber. The walls ripple and pulsate, reminiscent of the interior of a beating heart. He shuts his eyes at the sight and plugs his ears. Must think of something else to keep his mind off the horrific act being performed behind him.

All rivers flow to the sea...

All rivers flow to the sea...

At first, Scott remembers nothing of the waking world. The seal between dream world and reality is pristine. He is watching cartoons again, lying on the ancient couch in the living room of the two bedroom ranch he shares with his father...

<<ACME EYES ONLY>>
What We Know: An ACME Group Primer on the Riders
J.P. Kilcannon/G. Suares/K. Morimoto, 11th Edition

Section A. – Overview

Disclaimer – This document is designed to provide an introduction to the alien creatures to whom we refer as Riders. As always, this edition is only a catalogue of the most recently compiled information. It is solely meant to serve as a set of flexible guidelines. Agents must always remember that there are exceptions to every rule regarding these creatures. How a specific Rider's abilities may manifest with one individual may not align with which abilities manifest when bridled to another. Always be prepared for something never before seen.

*Note – instead of the word "Steed", we have chosen to use the term "Host" throughout this booklet. "Steed" is what the Riders call their enslaved humans. "Host", on the other hand, is a much more accurate term, representing the parasitic relationship between the two creatures.

Section B. – History of ACME

Introduction – The first recorded meeting of Le Conseil de l'Atlantique sur Médicaux Enigmes (The Atlantic Council on Medical Enigmas) convened at Montpellier in Provence, France at the end of the 17th century. Among the original members were some of the greatest medical minds of that era, most notably Martin Lister, Daniel Whistler and Clopton Havers from England, François Bernier and Raymond Vieussens of France, and Dutch physician Frederik Ruysch.

They had been corresponding for years regarding numerous medical topics, but more and more frequently the discussion had turned to the preponderance of cases involving the creatures that we now know as Riders. We now are aware that the sudden increase in Rider population in the 17th to 19th centuries was a result of many global societal factors causing a die-off of the Riders in the 12th to 16th centuries (see Section G – Rider History)

The Specimen

For the next century, Riders were believed to be mindless parasites of terrestrial origin that caused delusions and breaks with reality. It was not until the mid-19th century that the idea of their extraterrestrial origin began to take root in our circles.

As the Council grew, it was decided that the best course of action was to become more proactive by seeking out these creatures and their unfortunate minions, rather than constantly reacting to events after the fact. More resources were committed towards the capture, study and, in many cases, elimination of the Riders. We have succeeded in more ways than we had ever expected, and yet the threat has also proved more resilient than we first imagined.

In the years since our modest academic beginnings, ACME has evolved from a gathering of some the top medical minds of their generation into one of the most powerful yet anonymous multi-national intelligence organizations in the world.

In the 20th century, our influence has expanded beyond the Atlantic, from Europe and its North American colonies to virtually every corner of the globe. What began as a quest to understand one of the planet's greatest mysteries has become a centuries-long mission to preserve the purity of the human race. If you are reading this, you are now part of this mission.

Chapter 9 - Old Deuteronomy Takes a Cat Nap

"Old Deuteronomy's lived a long time; He's a Cat who has lived many lives in succession…"
<u>Old Possum's Book of Practical Cats</u>, by T.S. Eliot

Modern Day – Cambridge, MA

Once the sky clouded over and it began to rain, the morning's pickings grew slim and Harvard Square cleared out. It was midweek, so there weren't many tourists and the Harvard students didn't venture out much until the late afternoon. Harry didn't mind the break. It was nearly time for his nap and he was looking forward to the sound of the raindrops on the pavement lulling him into slumber. He sat down on a bench to count the money in the venti Starbuck's cup he had liberated from a trashcan. $26.85 - A bit slow for three hours of work, but more than enough to cover the day's expenses.

He rolled the bills up and wrapped them with one of the many rubber bands he kept on his wrist for just such a purpose. The coins stayed in the cup for the afternoon, but now Harry was off to take his daily siesta in one of the numerous secret places he frequented throughout the year.

He pulled his Kansas City Monarchs cap, a gift from a store owner in the neighborhood, down to his eyebrows and his hoodie over the cap to keep from getting too wet. The rain was more of a mist, though, so although his hat was protected, his face received the full brunt.

Harry turned down a side alley behind *Au Bon Pain*, wriggled past a dumpster filled with day-old bread, and turned again to squeeze into another narrow alley that had been hidden behind the dumpster for as long as he could remember. Then again, his memory hadn't been that reliable for quite some time now. He rarely remembered people's names and any event beyond the past few years were lost in the tangled weeds of his mind.

At the end of the alley were a few sheets of plywood leaning vertically against the wall, hiding the entrance to the abandoned storeroom of a shop that went out of business years earlier. When the space was finally bought by another business four summers ago, major remodeling in

The Specimen

the interior had blocked off the doorway and a six foot by ten foot alcove behind a new wall. Harry had capitalized on this architectural anomaly and laid claim to the space immediately. It even had a working outlet in the wall that he occasionally used.

Over the span of a month, he populated the small room with a variety of furniture he cobbled from the street. An old bookshelf. Some milk crates. A dresser missing one drawer. Best of all, though was the used La-Z-Boy that he found on the sidewalk one morning near dawn and rescued from an ignominious fate at the local landfill. Sure, it had a few undefinable stains on the mustard-colored fabric, and someone had repaired a couple of large tears with copious amounts of duct tape, but it was extremely comfortable. So comfortable that this tiny space was Harry's preferred hideaway.

Someone had repurposed the door to the room long ago, so Harry had tacked up a heavy wool blanket over the open doorway to keep out the weather. He pushed aside the blanket and entered the dark interior. Sometimes he turned on a lamp that he used late at night to read, but today he was only here for one purpose… to take a long nap. Setting his coffee cup on a milk crate and his bag on the floor, he crawled into the recliner and drew a stained orange afghan up to his waist. He leaned back, extending his feet, then dozed off to the lulling sound of the rain rhythmically falling on the pavement.

* * *

In his dreams, Harry remembered everything. He had no lapses or fugues. He could speak in full sentences without his throat seizing up. He made logical connections between unrelated topics with simple rational explanation. He remembered…whether he wanted to or not.

The first thing he always remembered was the fact that Harry was not his birth name. He was born Jarvis Harold Varney, Jr., the fifth of eight children, to Jarvis, Sr. and Virginia in Toms River, New Jersey on March 4th, 1952. That was not all he remembered, though. "Don't call me Jarvis. Don't call me Junior. Call me Harry."

For the first twelve years of his life, his memories were nearly eidetic. He could recall exact conversations he had with his brother and sisters and be able to recite them back verbatim. He could recite the title *of every book he had ever read in the order in which he had read them. He remembered the smell of his grandmother's rhubarb pie cooling on the stove on Christmas Day 1959, and he could hear the sound of his big brother Eddie's right elbow popping out of joint and tearing through the skin when he suffered a compound fracture sliding into 3rd base during a game of sandlot baseball the next summer. He could still feel his eldest sister Loretta's kinky hair as she woke him from his nap by dangling it in his face and tickling his nose. That always made him giggle. He felt the pain as he was strapped by his father for giving his mother backtalk when she told him to dress for Sunday Worship. He heard the soothing tones of his grandmother's voice as she read him tales of Rum Tum Tugger (his favorite cat and Nana's pet name for him), Mr. Mistoffelees, Bustopher Jones and Old Deuteronomy from his favorite book, <u>Old Possum's Book of Practical Cats</u> by T.S. Eliot. He didn't like Macavity, though. He was a bad ol' cat.*

Around the age of twelve, though, his memories became somewhat convoluted. Both of his grandparents became ill in 1962, when he was ten, so Harold and his family uprooted themselves from New Jersey and resettled in Springfield, Massachusetts, down the street from them in a much smaller apartment than the previous one. Some of his sisters helped clean their house, while others cooked the food every day. Since he was the youngest, his job had been to care for all of his grandparents' cats, and that was not an easy job. They owned between 15 and 20 of the animals, depending on who you asked, and they were always running away for days and coming back with injuries or smelling like they had been crawling through a refinery.

Not all of his memories were pleasant. He also remembered an older skinny white boy with bloody knees and elbows lying on his back under a thorn bush... and he saw the faces of the men in the Dodge Lancer. The one with the grossly hairy knuckles and the mole on his face, and the other one who stank of dirty socks all the time. He felt a gaping hole getting carved out of his wrist, but when he looked at it, a weeping yellow eyeball looked back at him from the depths of the wound.

The images ran together like rain on a windshield. He recalled events that could not have been pulled from his memories. Bloody, horrid

The Specimen

images that sparked dreadful thoughts and hungers in him. Eyes that crawled with motes of gold. Scarlet-fanged beasts danced with abandon. Savage eagles soared with bits of torn flesh in their talons. A bearded man riddled with arrows, tied to a gigantic oak tree. Severed heads rolled down the gore-stained stairs of stone ziggurats. An elderly man in fine silk robes engulfed in flames, writhing in agony on a stone floor. Mottled strips of bloody torn flesh dangled from a teen's back in the shape of wings. A skeletal child scaled the walls of a vast pit filled with a towering mountain of bloated cadavers.

All of these visions were simply a prelude to what was lurking under the subconscious cobblestones of his mind. Occasionally a dream would pry one up and reveal buried knowledge of what had been done to him in his teens. The violations he had experienced at the hands of his captors. These hidden Easter eggs would crop up every few weeks or so, but they would always fade before he awoke.

This time was different. This time his specters peeled away the skin and meat of his armor to lay his guts open. Old Harry found himself lying face-down on a metal table, strapped down with leather belts across his neck, back and knees. It felt familiar. A rush of icy dread crawled over his skin.

He tried to pull at his bonds and realized immediately that he could not move his limbs at all. He was completely paralyzed below the neck, but he retained all feeling of pain, pressure and temperature. The ability to react to stimuli was gone. His arms were extended to his sides, pierced with tubes and needles attached to a large rack of ancient beeping machines that were sucking his life out drop by drop. As his blood and other fluids pumped out through the tubes, he could see his skin growing paler, blanching by the second. His vitiligo crept up his hands and forearms like maggots eating a rotting carcass leaving bones in their wake.

A heavy mass lay diagonally across his spine, encircling his torso and left shoulder. It felt as if it were a part of him, melded with muscle and sinew, but it moved independently. Harry craned his neck to its limits, trying to see what was riding him, but he could only see a bit out of the corner of his eye. Muscular, ropy flesh with bristles of hair along its length. Turning his head in the only remaining direction, he was unable to catch a better glimpse of the creature beyond his initial impression. He did hear a voice, though …

Soft and smoky, his grandmother's voice was like a balm on his wounds. Hers was the first voice he heard in the morning, and the voice that read him bedtime stories as he drifted off to sleep.

<BLINK! - One of the light bulbs on the ceiling flared, then returned to normal levels.>

He lay his head on the cool metal slab and saw her seated next to him in the flower-patterned love seat that had been her preferred place to collect her thoughts and watch nature through the window in her reading nook. Harry knew that her presence was not possible and these were the hallucinations of a dying or insane man, but he felt comforted by the sight and sound of her anyway. She began reading one of his favorite passages from the book that was their nightly ritual.

"To understand its character.
you now have learned enough to see
that Cats are much like you and me...
And other people whom we find
possessed by various types of minds.
For some are insane and some are just sad
and some are good and some are bad
and some are better, some are worse--
and some, my dear Old Deuteronomy,
can't decide what they want to be.
No matter how much they scream or shriek or shout,
So many pieces of them need to be cut out"

Harry was confused by the narrative. He croaked in a phlegm-filled voice to his grandmother, "Nana, you changed some of the words and added a whole new verse."

She smiled at him and looked directly into his eyes, "Just because you haven't seen or heard this version doesn't mean it doesn't exist, my little Deuteronomy."

The Specimen

"Ain't I your Rum Tum Tugger anymore?" he asked.

"No, little man, I wish you were, but you grew out of that nickname a long time ago. Now you're like Old Deuteronomy with your many lives inside of you."

"And you can call me Macavity," purred a sibilant whisper in his ear.

Harry flinched at the sound of that voice, just centimeters from his ear. He turned quickly toward the source and found that his passenger had become an adult cat, somehow intertwined in the muscles around his spine. Scrawny, ginger with matted fur and long spider-like limbs. He licked the old man's earlobe with his rough sandpaper-like tongue and muttered, "We've been together a long time, but now I think I have convinced the good doctors will help release me from your too, too solid flesh."

A third voice joined the conversation.

"The patient has been given a paralytic, but he will not be sedated during the procedure in order to monitor cognitive function during the excision..."

Harry turned his head back to his grandmother and found that another woman had joined her. Dr. Genevieve Coe. Clad in a white lab coat, she was petite and blonde in her late thirties to mid-forties, though she could easily have been older. He knew not to let his guard down with her, not that his situation would improve much now through his vigilance, but it was better to be safe than sorry, as the old saying goes. Her elfin stature was deceptive and disarming, hiding a ruthless, clinical disposition. She stood with one hand on his grandmother's shoulder and spoke into a handheld tape recorder with the other, "After the procedure, the patient will resume residence at Greylock, to be monitored on a regular basis but he will no longer be required as a focus of the study."

Harry wanted to scream, but he couldn't. Something was preventing him from opening his mouth. He angled his face toward the reflective metal of the table and realized then that his mouth had been sealed shut somehow. The flesh had melted together like candle wax, leaving shiny purple-blue keloid scars in place of his lips. He shrieked behind the tight skin barrier, but no words could escape. Only muffled whimpers.

Coe placed the recorder next to a metal tray, upon which sat various types of medical tools and implements. She pulled a mask over her face and picked up a scalpel that appeared not to have been cleaned in decades. Stains covered the scalpel, either from rust or dried blood from the last patient.

<BLINK! - The lights flickered again>

The jellicle cat on his back sank its claws into his flanks and whispered in a voice that somehow carried, reverberated throughout the cavern:

> "Macavity, Macavity,
> there's no one like Macavity.
> For he's a fiend of many shapes,
> a monster of depravity."

"I guess we changed the words again, buddy boy," said his grandmother with a gummy, toothless smile. Only, no, it was not his grandmother anymore when he glanced her way. Oh no. She had leaned back in her chair and pulled the old switcheroo. Seated there now was a tall cadaverous young man who appeared barely out of his teens if not for his hairline. Ghostly pale with spiky ginger hair prematurely receding in a widow's peak. He was wearing a lab coat to match Coe's, but rather than seeming comfortable in it as Coe had, his uniform hung from his bony shoulders like a threadbare shirt on a scarecrow. He smiled at Harry, but no emotion reached his deep-set eyes.

"Finally tracked you down, Harry boy," he stated in a barely audible baritone with a faint Southern accent. "It took some time, true, but I am a patient man. When an individual has something I want, time does not matter to me. I know that it will eventually come my way."

He stood and approached the table, bending low to meet Harry's gaze.

"Come on, boy! Don't you remember your old friend Dr. Colfax and our little visits? You have no idea just how much I've looked forward

The Specimen

to resuming our little friendship and hopefully connecting up with our other amigo. It's been quite some time since we last saw each other, but I'm certain we'll pick things up exactly where we left off. Huh, buddy?"

If he had not been rendered paralyzed by the drugs, Harry would now have been frozen in terror. Dr. Colfax placed a hand on his arm in a gesture meant to comfort him, but Harry felt as if his heart would explode in his chest. The doctor's hand was the worst part. Half of the last two fingers on his hand had been twisted and scarred from a brutal amputation.

Of all the individuals he had met over the past five decades, from doctors to mental patients to fellow abductees, not one had inspired an overwhelming sense of dread as this young doctor had. Dr. Coe was horrible with her complete detachment and apparent lack of a soul, but Colfax was an entirely different species of monster.

In Harry's extensive experience, there were four types of monsters that populated this cursed little planet. First of all, there were the ones who were utterly unaware of the fact that they were monsters. They often thought that they were acting in a manner that was genuinely benevolent, and if they ever discovered their true nature, the sheer horror would torment them the rest of their lives. Quite often these individuals were driven to end their own existence upon the revelation of the true consequences of their business.

The second type of monsters were aware that their actions were completely against the morals of society, but they rationalized their evil by deluding themselves that it was far outweighed by the greater evil that they prevented with their deeds. Many of these individuals entered politics or joined the military and moved their way up the ranks with ease. Dr. Coe would fit rather nicely into this subgroup of psychological profiles.

The third subgroup consisted of people whose malignant sides were unleashed at random with no apparent cause. These sufferers were well aware of the obscenities that they had perpetrated, but they were helpless to do anything to prevent anything similar from happening again, unless they decided to take themselves out of the equation by prematurely ending their own lives.

The last breed of monster was not quite as common as the previous three. Members of this strain were completely conscious of their evil and, simply put, they didn't care about the cost. It was enjoyable. Life-affirming, even. In many cases, their actions inspired greater and greater evils in such a person. Most such people eventually burned out or were put out of their misery by fellow monsters. A scattered few, however, aspired to a new level of monstrosity. Dr. Arnold Colfax was one of them. This was a fact that Harry unfortunately knew quite intimately. He had not seen Colfax in nearly five decades, but it would take much more than time to erase the stains this man had left upon his soul.

Coe inserted the scalpel between the layers of skin and scar tissue defining the border between the symbiont and Harry. Much of the connective tissue was tough and unyielding, only separating from host and parasite after multiple passes of the razor blade. With each cut, the weight on Harry's shoulders grew lighter, yet his heart grew heavier. Colfax watched the procedure in rapt attention.

Though he knew this was a dream sequence, he also felt that this event had happened in a manner close to what was being depicted. He had been bonded with a symbiont for a few months as a child, and it had been forcibly excised as well. The benefits given him by the symbiont had slowly faded to nothing in a few months, but the yearning for its contact would always remain.

<BLINK! BLINK! – The lights flashed incandescently, leaving a white afterimage on his retinas. Coe disappeared and Colfax now stood next to him in her place.>

Harry was no longer paralyzed, but he was still strapped down tightly to the metal table. The weight on his back was gone, replaced by a searing sensation as if his skin had been severely sunburned over his entire body. He reared back in an attempt to pull free of his leather restraints, but he was only able to gain a few more inches in his range of motion than he had before. The pain flared white-hot and he collapsed to the metal wheezing in agony.

"Within minutes of the excision, the patient immediately shows signs similar to narcotics withdrawal," narrated Colfax into a small microphone attached to a reel-to-reel recorder. "Symptoms in the hours following the procedure include high fever, heavy perspiration, severe shivering, and overwhelming anxiety."

The Specimen

The long-limbed doctor circled the table as if performing for an invisible audience. As he passed into view, Harry saw that Colfax was dragging another object behind him. Some sort of wet cloth or sheet. A trail of moisture marked his path around the room, like the path of a mop - a scarlet mop.

The doctor drew closer, continuing to speak, "Surprisingly, the specimen has reacted quite well to its removal from the patient. Its new host will be ready to bond with it within a few days or so. Dr. Coe was quite concerned that the transfer would encounter numerous obstacles, but for once her dire predictions have not been fulfilled."

Dr. Colfax paused right next to the head of Harry's table and peered down at his captive patient, a man who he had called "an old friend". He looked directly into Harry's eyes and smiled so widely that it seemed as if his face would split into two bloody halves, continuing into his microphone, "I guess it's true what they say. There's more than one way to skin a cat. Behold the glory of Xipe Totec, The Flayed Lord!"

He held up his other hand, revealing the object he had been trailing behind him like Linus from Peanuts with his security blanket. It was both dreadful and familiar at the same time. Held in the air near Harry's nose was the complete skin of someone who had been flayed from chin to ankles. It dripped gore and gobbets of flesh onto the grey-painted floor while Harry pulled away as far as he could retreat.

Harry recognized this dreadful, gory trophy. This wasn't just any flayed skin. It was his own flesh, peeled from his body with meticulous care, vitiligo and all. A Harry suit ready to wear. Colfax continued to grin, teeth like pebbles gleaming in the fluorescent light of the operating room. He laid the skin suit over Harry's back and began to disrobe, baring his pale sunken chest, prominent ribs and surprisingly thick reddish chest hair.

"Hmmm… it's not my size," the doctor said with a wink. "But I'm sure I'll grow into it. After all, you won't be using it much longer. Will you, boy-o?"

The long-limbed man spread the bloody skin in front of him on the floor and stepped into it one leg at a time, like a pair of painter's coveralls. The skin seemed to stretch past its limits as Colfax pulled it up over his shoulders and zipped it to his throat. A zipper? Where did that come from? He reached back and yanked the rest of the dangling skin over his face like a hood before sealing the slit shut.

"I forgot to mention somethin', Harry," he said, muffled through the saggy folds of flesh. "An old friend of yours want to say hello."

A hissing sound, like a monstrous snake in a bad mood, sounded from beneath the metal table where Harry was strapped. Panicked, he craned his head over the edge and saw a rubber tube connected to the skin suit now worn by Colfax. As Harry's gaze travelled up, the hissing coincided with the skin expanding, inflated by the air blown from the connected hose. The skin-suit grew wider and taller. The timbre of Colfax's voice deepened, gaining a Louisiana accent as the new figure before Harry became recognizable.

A goliath of a man, dark as mahogany, laughed heartily as he loomed over Harry. His borrowed skin, formerly blotched white here and there with Harry's vitiligo, had become an even ebony. Slick with blood, as if he had just entered the world from a cavernous womb, the naked fat man smiled wide and said, "You didn't think I'd miss this chance to see ya, son. Did ya?"

"Lou?" Harry asked. "What's happening to me?"

"Oh, I just came around to give you a message, boy. A warning. I wish we could do more, but it's hard doing anything except sending messages from where I am."

"Warning?"

"It's back, Harry. Someone found it, and this time it's not fucking around. It will find a Steed that it is certain it can control, and it will raise some Hell. After five lost decades, you can be sure it's gonna make up for lost time."

"What? What am I supposed to do? Why me?"

"It's not like you have an option to ignore it, Harry Boy. Eventually, it's gonna search you out and get reacquainted. You can either give in, or try to stop it. Make your choice before you no longer have one."

* * *

Harry woke in the middle of a soul-wrenching scream, wailing so loudly that he was heard three streets away. Even though he couldn't remember why he was screaming, he knew that the nightmares were just

The Specimen

beginning. He curled up into a fetal position on his chair, stuck his thumb in his mouth and shuddered violently for the next few hours.

Chapter 10 - A Little White Lie

"All the truth in the world adds up to one big lie"
- Bob Dylan

Modern Day – Cambridge, MA

Elvira Dombrowsky sipped her green tea and stroked the reddish brown Abyssinian lounging in her lap. Nine other cats of various shapes and sizes sprawled in random spots around her cluttered living room, but only Solomon merited the place of honor in her lap. Solomon purred in contentment, but that did not alleviate the fact that she was feeling somewhat guilty for her earlier deception. When she had brought in the jar to *Schrödinger's*, she had lied to Wyatt about its origin. Just a tiny fib. A white lie, but a lie nonetheless, and Elvira did not enjoy hiding the truth from her friends and colleagues. Her only exceptions to this rule was when doing so would protect them or keep them out of harm's way… or in this case, give them plausible deniability.

As she had revealed to Wyatt, the specimen had been found by her nephew Frank. However, he had not won it in auction of abandoned storage units (which, in retrospect, was an excellent idea for future endeavors) as she had stated. Instead, he had acquired it in a slightly less legal method.

Frank was an urban explorer.

In his spare time, Frank was a member of a select cadre of individuals who enjoyed going into abandoned buildings and examining every last cellar, storage room, and hallway for abandoned treasures of the past. Over the years, he had explored factories, subway tunnels, sewers, prisons and most recently, an abandoned private hospital in the Berkshires in northwest Massachusetts three weeks earlier. *What was its name? Greyskull?* It was in this building that he discovered the jar with the large teratoma.

According to her nephew, the unspoken credo of urban explorers is to "take nothing but photographs, leave nothing but footprints," and until now he had always followed that rule. This time, though, he felt

The Specimen

inexplicably compelled to remove the jar from its hiding place and take it with him.

He had discovered many interesting sights over the years, from fully furnished libraries in abandoned tunnels of the Boston subway system to boxes of 19th century medical tools with stains that looked suspiciously like old blood. He had also encountered other people in his forays: fellow urban explorers, teens looking for a private place to party, and indigent souls who had retreated from modern society. One time, Frank had related to her, he had found a fully-articulated human skeleton sitting in the front row of an abandoned theater in Binghamton, New York. Upon examining the bones, he saw what appeared to be marks of heavy gnawing… much too large to be the teeth marks of rats or other small animals. Spooked by the grisly implication, he immediately exited and never returned to Binghamton.

Last week, Frank had called her about the specimen jar, asking if she knew any place that would be interested in purchasing it. As strong as his compulsion to remove it from the hospital had been, his need to find a person to take possession of it was even more powerful. Elvira had agreed to take a look, but privately she had thought it would be unlikely to find a home.

Her opinion completely changed upon seeing it. The object in the jar seemed to speak with her, regardless of how ridiculous this idea seemed to her now. The second Frank unveiled the jar, Elvira was mesmerized. Thinking back, she had reacted similarly to the way Wyatt had when she revealed it in the store earlier. The first sight of Lumpy was all that was needed to convince people that this object was special. Once she had left the store, however, the nearly hypnotic sensation she had experienced subsided gradually.

Elvira dialed her nephew's cell phone for the 4th time in less than an hour. Voicemail again. The theme music to Raiders of the Lost Ark followed by an interminable beep.

"Frankie, it's Aunt Elvira again. Call me as soon as you can. I have good news, but you're worrying me by not answering your damned phone. Check in….please."

She hung up and placed her phone on the table. Turning to the window, she sipped her tea and vacantly stared at the motley group of pedestrians rushing by in the rain on the street below, skirting around a strange gathering on the far side of the street. A lone man in a trench coat and hat sat on a bench surrounded by a mewling pride of alley cats. He fed them sardines from a tin. On the pavement, some of the felines were jostling each other to get at the half dozen empty tins lined up in a row beneath the bench. Occasionally the man glanced at one of the pedestrians as they stepped behind the bench or into the gutter to avoid the cats, but not one of them met his gaze. They were compelled to avert their eyes as if they had seen something horrific and unnatural about him and they didn't want to get caught staring. Elvira squinted but she was too far away to see his features.

"Where is that boy?" she muttered under her breath as she suddenly turned away from the window in exasperation. She considered Frank more of a son than a nephew. His mother had succumbed to pancreatic cancer when he was only eleven, and his deadbeat father, Elvira's younger brother Stanley, had been drowning himself in whiskey ever since. Frank came to live with her when he was thirteen after his father had left on one of his frequent benders for over a week, and he never went back. Stanley had protested slightly, but eventually realized that his life would be much easier this way, and if Elvira didn't mind, who was he to argue?

Even though he had left for college and lived on his own nearly a decade ago, Frank still visited during the holidays and every other chance he got. This was his home. He always called Elvira back immediately upon receiving her messages. Today was especially strange since he had been expecting her to call after she visited *Schrödinger's*.

She finished her tea with one gulp and stood, ejecting Solomon from his throne and waddled heavily to her kitchen. You never know, she thought hopefully. Perhaps Frank met a girl. Sensing an opportunity to finagle a snack, the nine other felines immediately scampered after her, but Solomon lingered behind. The cat leapt to the window sill and began to pace back and forth all the while eying the figure in the trench coat below.

The Specimen

Mere seconds later, after the last sardine was distributed, the dozens of cats and their hulking benefactor lifted their heads and stared directly at the window in which Solomon paced. Both sides froze as their gazes met. Solomon's green eyes rolled back into his skull as he stretched his mouth open in a silent wordless scream. Translucent golden feelers were visible at the back of his throat, wriggling and tasting the air. After nearly a minute holding this pose, Solomon closed his eyes and sunk gently to lounge on his side in Elvira's rocking chair. When she returned a couple of minutes later, the Abyssinian was already asleep in her spot. She shook her head in amusement and glanced out the window. The bench was clear, and the crowd was off in search of more sardines.

Official Report on the Greylock Incident

January 25, 1966
To: Members of the Governing Council, ACME Group
From: James P. Kilcannon, Agent-in-Charge
RE: Greylock Incident, cont.

Dear Council Members:
    The subsequent notes from Dr. Coe detail the events at Greylock from the arrival of Dr. Arnold Colfax onward. The content of these notes should illustrate the upcoming problems without any comment from me or my fellow agents. It is our opinion that you will all come to the same conclusion about the cause of the failure of the project without any biased synopsis of the events interfering with the facts.
                      - JPK

*   *   *

Day 9
    The Council is testing me. They sent that sycophantic child prodigy Colfax to join the project. Anyone else would have been acceptable, but of course they sent my least favorite colleague to "observe and learn". Regardless of their attempts to insinuate themselves into the experiments, I will not let this bother me. If I follow the science correctly, there is nothing that he can do, short of sabotage, to derail the results. The Council obviously does not want the experiment to fail. They simply want complete control over any of the results.
    I will need to monitor Colfax's contact with the subject, however. If the rumors are true, individuals with his proclivity often have difficulty in restraining their most primal urges when unsupervised. Any interaction with the subject outside of the project is to be avoided at all costs.

The Specimen

Fenton and Jameson will need to be informed of the potential problems. Colfax will not taint anything in this project with his personal issues. Not if I have anything to say about it.

- GC

Day 14

Data from the first rounds of exposure have been collected. The cell samples which were excised have been subjected to extremes of temperature and various other tests to ascertain their vulnerabilities and defenses.

<u>Exposure Test Results</u>

Fire – Prolonged exposure results in the destruction of both the neural core and boundary cells. Regeneration will happen unless the entire sample is incinerated.

Cold – Freezing induces neurological torpor with some destruction to boundary cells from a condition similar to frostbite.

Acid – Exposure to acids with a pH of 0.3 or less causes burns. Prolonged exposure to acids of 0.1 or less result in complete tissue destruction.

Electricity – Exposure to charges greater than 500 kilovolts incapacitate the symbiont temporarily. In comparison, charges of 100 kilovolts can incapacitate the average human male. Charges greater than 5 megavolts have damaged the neural core of a symbiont permanently.

Sonic – No visible effect on symbiont. It can be assumed that the host could still be disoriented or even injured by sonic weapons.

Magnetism – No visible effect

Radioactivity – Exposure to high levels of radioactivity has been shown to distort or reduce the regenerative abilities of the symbiont and host. Long term effects have yet to be determined.

Next steps:
- Attempt communication with symbiont on patient JHV
- Surgical removal of symbiont from patient JHV
- Recruit potential hosts, preferably residents
- Monitor growth of exposed tissue samples compared to control group.

- Transfer symbiont to new host
- Document abilities of host and symbiont both solitary and fused

- GC

Day 19

Success! In Lab B today, on our fifth attempt to separate the consciousness of JHV from the symbiont, we were able to determine the correct dosage of anesthesia. JHV's primary personality was put under while the subconscious personality of the symbiont was induced to rise to the surface. Once it was fully in control of JHV's motor functions, we attempted to hold a conversation with the creature through JHV.

The contrast between JHV and the other entity is astounding. JHV is a young boy, but the mind within the symbiont is obviously powerful and ancient. How old is the symbiont after all?

Communication results were mixed. Due to its ability to follow simple instructions in English, we are certain that it can understand us. However, the ability to understand English does not seem to grant the ability to communicate with us in English. It speaks in a language that seems similar to Nahuatl or one of the other Uto-Aztecan languages... at least to our uneducated ears.

Despite our inability to understand the words, we were able to understand its tone. Where JHV begged for us to release him, the other one spoke as a master to a slave. Its disdain was palpable in every word. We disgust it. This was extremely apparent to me and Colfax. For once we agreed completely. We must always remember to use every caution with this creature.

- GC

Day 20

First I am placed under the watchful eye of my young colleague Colfax, who reports my every decision back to the council. Now I have to worry about this meddler Eckenrode snooping around the labs.

Last night after dinner, Fenton discovered the good doctor attempting to gain entry into Lab C, which just happens to be where we

The Specimen

have housed the cell samples, along with the majority of our imaging and sterilization tools.

It looks like changing the doors and adding the electromagnetic locks was a good idea after all. He put up a fuss and stated that any changes to the physical environment here at Greylock need to be run past him. He can believe that all he wants, but it won't make it true. I have carte blanche here, but for now his delusion of importance serves a purpose.

Of course, now that Eckenrode knows about the lock changes, his curiosity will certainly lead him back for another attempt. Fenton and Jameson will have to take turns monitoring him. Perhaps I shouldn't express my displeasure that he and JHV are meeting on a regular basis. If Eckenrode believes that he is involved with the project by playing a few games of chess with the boy, then he may rethink his attempts to enter the labs again.

- GC

Day 22

JHV was placed under anesthesia again this morning, and communication with the symbiont was much more successful. Gradually it seems to be learning English at an exponential rate. I suspected that it would soon be able to develop a form of conversation with us, but this rate of learning is beyond my greatest hope.

Apparently, direct contact with the brain of the host accelerates the learning process.

Questions to answer:
- Does the learning process work the same way in reverse?
- Do memories transfer with the symbiont from the old host to the new host?
- Are skills transferred as well?
- What else results from bonding with a symbiont?

Once we reach the next stage – transferring the symbiont from HV to another host, we will attempt to answer these puzzles.

- GC

Interlude: The Riders
Where the Sun Fell
Kaali Crater, Estonia – 23rd Century BCE

The legends said that the sun fell *from the sky into the islands of the northern sea. Brunni and Kalev had heard them all. Their father, Brom, had been telling them every night as long as they could remember. He in turn had heard the legends from his father, who had heard them from his father who heard them from fathers upon fathers before. The young men could recite them back word for word, and often corrected Brom when he skipped a key part. He would laugh and blame the lapse on his age or too much mead, then continue as if he had never stopped.*

There were many tales of the exploits of gods and demons, but the one of which Brom most often spoke was the time when the old Sun was stolen and the new Sun fell to the earth on an island far to the north. As he told the tale, the blind whore-witch Louhiatar, Mother of the Nine Plagues, was so jealous of Man that she plucked the Sun from the sky and erased the knowledge of fire from their minds, sending the entire world into darkness.

Seeing her theft, Ukko, the Sky Father, became angry. He declared that a new Sun would be crafted from a spark so that light would be returned to the world. On his command, Ilmatar, an air spirit, took the spark and began the long journey to place it in the sky, but in her haste she lost her grip and the spark fell to the earth below. The spark skipped along the earth, leaving many scars and a path of fire, finally crashing on one of the islands in the sea to the north.

For generations, the tribes had brought their young men to visit this island as a rite of manhood. Some were called by the gods to stay and some returned home. As a youth, Brom had travelled there with his four brothers. His eldest brother, Tor, had remained to tend the crater with others who took the oath. Now Brom brought his two sons along for their turn, knowing all too well that he may make the return trip alone.

When the weather was warmer, the only way to travel to the island was by sea. Due to the rough waters, though, it was considered quite

The Specimen

dangerous by mainlanders and islanders alike, especially since access to boats was rare. Only the Saarlased, local pirates, dared the open seas on a regular basis. Most pilgrims to the crater chose to travel by foot over the ice bridge that formed every winter. Brom and his sons had crossed it two days ago, arriving on the southern coast the morning before last just as the herds of coastal seals woke with a chorus of raucous barks.

Once they scaled the cliffs, they headed inland through the dense thicket until nightfall, resuming the hike through the forest this morning after a restless night of intermittent sleep. Just after midday, the gleam of the water in the craters was visible from a high ridge. Eight small round pools were scattered along the path leading to the main lake. According to the tales, each hole had been created by pieces of the New Sun as it scorched the skin of the earth. In the centuries since, the craters had filled with water, creating the series of small ponds. The largest pond was soon considered a holy place and a wall was built to allow in only those who truly believed.

The three men crested the ridge and began the descent. The afternoon sunlight cast an amber glow over the frozen earth, patches of ice scattered among the black skeletons of the trees. As they came closer to the crater, they realized that a wall of earth had been built to the height of a man, surrounding the entire area. The wall had been reinforced by water that had been poured on the top multiple times and frozen in order to strengthen it against incursion, not that anyone would dare.

Brom led the way, followed by his sons, heading to one of only two entrances in the fortifications, a gap only wide enough for two men to pass. The entrance was unguarded, so they passed through without a problem. On the other side of the wall, a path led down a steep slope to the water's edge where a number of figures in robes circled the crater. Kalev was disappointed. The oval basin was barely a pond, not the immense hole in the earth he had envisioned. The crater was slightly more than a stone's throw across at its most narrow point and only a few paces longer than that at its widest. A light layer of mist hovered near their feet as they clambered down the slope. Reaching the shore, they saw that only a thin skin of ice covered the water, even though the ice bridge they had recently crossed had been much thicker. The air within the enclosure was noticeably warmer. Not enough to melt the ice, but enough that plumes of fog would not accompany every exhale.

"Remain here," Brom instructed his sons before heading toward the closest robed figure. Kalev and Brunni were silent as they watched him genuflect and kneel before the man. Too far to hear their words, they were able to examine the man and his attire. He pulled back the hood of his robe and, to their surprise, revealed a man only a few summers older than themselves.

Once the ritual greeting was completed, Brom leapt to his feet and embraced the man roughly, laughing with joy. He turned and walked with the man toward his sons, renewed energy in his step.

"Boys, meet your Uncle Tor," he grinned as he reached them. Tor smiled at the two young men and held out his hands in welcome. At first, they were too stunned to take his hands. Something strange had happened here. Tor, despite being nearly ten summers older than Brom, looked as if he had only aged one summer for every four summers that his younger sibling had advanced. His black hair was tied back with a leather strap, and he was beardless in the manner of the coastal villages. He wore a thick robe made from a patchwork of small multicolored furs sewn together in a random pattern. Kalev noted this design with interest. The camouflage of the pattern would be quite useful on a hunt.

Tor embraced the two young tribesmen, then stepped back to inspect them.

"Both are excellent candidates, Brom. They will bring glory to your name whatever the outcome. Come, let us eat before the ceremony."

With that, Tor turned and led the three men down the shore to a slow-burning fire encircled by stone. Several other robed men sat around the coals cooking a variety of game from the surrounding forest. Rabbits, boar and even the haunch of an aurochs were roasting on spits over the fire. The four men sat on the ground nearby and eagerly accepted the roasted meat. For Brom and his sons, this was the first meal in days that didn't consist of salted fish, dried nuts and berries. Kalev and Brunni were amazed at the feast, but they followed their father's lead and did not question the source of the plenty, simply enjoying the flavor of greasy fat dripping down their chins.

The Specimen

While sucking the marrow from a boar's leg bone, Brunni looked around and noticed a couple of the robed men leave the circle with scraps of meat wrapped in fur. He nudged Kalev and both watched the men walk down the shore to a point where they tossed small bits of the charred flesh into a small opening in the ice… as if feeding something. Ripples in the pool of water and flashes of pale flesh near the surface seemed to confirm this theory. Another serving of boar followed by a skin of mead was enough to distract the two young men, and by the time they finished, sleepy and bloated, the activity at the shore had ended and all had been forgotten. They settled down to rest their weary bodies and sank into unconsciousness.

* * *

After a long nap on the embankment of the crater, Kalev and Brunni were shaken awake by their father and told to strip naked in order to bathe in the pool. Normally, swimming in a partially frozen body of water would not be an activity they would relish, but Brom had prepared them for this part of the ceremony. Once their clothes were removed, they realized that the cold barely bothered them. They were hypernaturally alert. Colors were more vivid. Sounds were sharper. Odors more pungent. Every shard of stone beneath their feet was individually felt. The air, though still chilly, seemed much warmer than before. The thin layer of ice on the crater had melted and the water appeared to churn under a shallow layer of white mist. A subsonic hum permeated the area, causing the hairs on their arms and legs to stand on end.

Gathered on the shore were dozens of robed individuals at regular intervals, circling the crater. Kalev realized that the hum was coming from them, eyes focused on the roiling water. After disrobing, he and Brunni were led to the shore by their father and Tor, both of whom remained silent in their reverie. No words were exchanged. No signals were given. Once the two young men reached the water's edge, Tor and Brom retreated to stand humming quietly with the other men in robes.

They stood frozen for a moment before realizing that the men were waiting for their next move. The water continued to bubble. Shadows *flitted and darted beneath the surface, but whether they were living creatures or a trick of the light was not clear. The brothers looked at each other warily then, as one, stepped into the water.*

The pool was surprisingly warm, considering that ice had covered the surface only hours before. Prepared for a painfully frigid shock, the brothers looked at each other and grinned in relief.

"This is good, Kalev. I can feel it," Brunni spoke softly. "Look below. The spark is still there. It summons us."

Kalev followed his brother's gaze and saw a dim phosphorescence emanating from the center of the crater floor beneath the water. He heard no call, though. Turning to Brunni once more, he was unable to voice his concerns for his brother had already descended beneath the surface.

"Join him, Kalev," called Brom from the shore. "Make the journey together."

Kalev nodded despite his fears, took a full breath and plunged under the water, kicking to catch up with Brunni. His brother was closer than he had expected, only two body lengths ahead of him and swimming at a slow, steady pace toward the glow on the floor of the crater. Kalev kicked vigorously and was soon even with Brunni. He reached out and grasped his brother's hand, receiving a reassuring squeeze in return.

They swam deeper and their vision sharpened… as well as they would have been able to see above the surface. Though they had already been under for nearly a minute, their lungs seemed to be easily withstanding the lack of air. All their senses had become more acute as the thrum from below intensified, reverberating through their teeth, their bones… the very meat of their bodies.

The seemingly endless motes of dust and silt in the water came into focus, revealing themselves as a swarm of miniscule creatures darting around the two of them in an intricate dance. Kalev looked at his brother and was stupefied at what he saw… millions upon millions of the organisms teeming over Brunni's skin. Under his robes. Through his hair. In and out of every orifice. Brunni even had some of them crawling on the whites of his eyes. He smiled and his teeth glittered with the waving cilia of hundreds more creatures. Kalev peered at his arms and hands and found a similar amount covering his skin. He swiped a hand through his hair and

The Specimen

was astonished at the sparkling cloud of glittering specks that filled the water surrounding him. Shimmering, swirling, writhing, they glided back toward him. His brother was now barely recognizable beneath the sparkling carpet that covered him. Brunni waved and pulled him deeper towards the glow which had begun to throb with the same tempo as the hum that permeated the water. They sank together and the light overwhelmed and consumed them.

* * *

Above, hours passed as the lake continued its incandescent maelstrom. The sun sank below the horizon and the glow from the water illuminated the basin with its ghostly sheen. Shadows danced on the faces of the men gathered at the shore. Brom and Tor stood at the front of the group, waiting for the two teens to reappear.

"This is lasting much longer than I remember, Tor," whispered Brom. "Should we be concerned? Could something have gone wrong?"

"Do not worry, brother," replied Tor. "The rituals have been taking longer and longer in the years since you were last here. We must trust the gods whether or not we understand them. It is pointless to question what we cannot comprehend."

Brom sighed, nodded tiredly and resumed the wait for his sons to emerge or the sun to rise… whichever came first.

Their vigil continued until the first light of dawn crested the eastern horizon. As the mist dissipated at the top of the crater and the rays of the sunlight pierced the canopy of trees to brush the roiling water, the surging waves subsided and the glow receded into the depths.

Seconds later, first Kalev, then Brunni emerged from the crater. They were alive and unscathed, despite having spent over ten hours beneath the water. They walked slowly to shore and collapsed to the ground as their father and uncle reached them. Concerned, they herded the two young men to sit next to the fire and wrapped them in fur blankets.

"Sons," asked Brom. "Are you well? Can you speak? What did the gods say to you?"

"Calm yourself, Brom," interrupted Tor. "They may need some time to recover. Remember, we were unable to speak for days after we emerged. Give them space---"

Brom grudgingly agreed, stepping back from them and attempting to rein in his emotions. A few seconds passed. Kalev opened his eyes and stood.

"Come, brother. We must begin our journey," he said to Brunni. Brunni nodded wordlessly and rose to his feet, joining him as they walked up the incline toward the exit in the mud wall.

Brom was confused, as was Tor.

"Journey? What journey?" sputtered their father.

Tor gaped in dismay and called, "Won't you stay and tend to the lake?"

Kalev grinned, "The lake's purpose is nearly complete, father. We must now go out and sow the seeds." He turned to Brunni and they smiled together.

Their eyes crawled with golden filaments that glittered in the morning light.

The Specimen

Chapter 11 - Dream Girl

"Some women pick men to marry - and others pick them to pieces"– Mae West

Modern Day – Mt. Greylock, MA

Where the hell have I ended up now? Frank Popecky thought blearily as he woke in darkness with a blinding headache. Groaning, he soon realized that his hands and feet were bound behind his back with what felt like a zip tie. His ears rang and a massive lump on his left crown throbbed in time with his heartbeat. The reek of gasoline and antifreeze surrounded him and he heard the muffled rumbling of an engine down shift as it careened around a turn, causing him to slide from one side to the other.

I'm in the trunk of a car? What the…? The car turned again sharply, banging his head against the interior and sending a wave of burning agony and nausea through him. His forehead became wet with blood. A cut at his hairline had reopened and a slow stream trickled through his right eyebrow to pool near his ear. As his eyes adjusted to the darkness, he realized that he was facing the front of the car. A reddish glow entered the trunk from behind him, illuminating the interior enough that he could see shapes, but not details.

After futilely struggling with his bindings, then rocking back and forth, Frank was able to roll over, shifting his position so he faced the rear of the vehicle. A tsunami of nausea washed over him, nearly knocking him unconscious once again. The red light was a bit brighter from this angle, entering through an inch-wide rusted-out patch near the taillights, allowing him to crane his neck and check out his surroundings. There wasn't much to see in the trunk, just a half-empty bottle of windshield wiper fluid, a stray plastic bag and an ice scraper with the UMass logo on the handle.

He groaned, suspicions confirmed. *In the trunk of my own damn car. Are you kidding me? What did I do now?* This wasn't the first time he had been thrown in the trunk of a car, but previously he hadn't been tied up. During his junior year at UMass-Amherst, he passed out at a fraternity party and some of his housemates thought it would be hilarious to strip him down to his boxers and toss him in the trunk. The plan had been to deposit him unconscious on the steps of the Student Union in all his glory. Luckily he woke up and prevented that from happening by lunging out in a drunken fury and breaking Ryan Murphy's nose with a boot to the face when they opened the trunk. That ended the night on a sour note, but it guaranteed that they never tried anything like that again with him.

  This situation seemed unlikely to be the result of a prank. The zip ties somewhat gave that away. This wasn't the action of anyone he knew. No, he had definitely been abducted and his life was in serious jeopardy. *But why? Who would want to kidnap me?* That one fact escaped him.

  He heard a recognizable sound through the back seat of the car. The ringtone from his phone. Someone was trying to call him and the driver of the car was ignoring it, letting it go to voicemail. Most likely his Aunt Elvira. *Was I supposed to call her?*

  If so, she would be frantic by now. *Damn, I can't remember anything.* Every time Frank tried, he faded in and out of consciousness for the next few minutes. The wound on his head crusted over and the ringing in his ears began to subside. He felt the car slow down, then make a left turn up an incline. The ride became rougher as if the road was now unpaved, filled with potholes and debris that made the car bottom out and slide sideways. Frank bounced around the trunk like a sack of potatoes, cursing in pain with each bump. His car's shocks were taking a beating. He hadn't driven on a road this bad since he went exploring in that abandoned hospital way up in the Berkshires. *What was its name? The Mt. Greylock Asylum?* Suddenly it all came back in a sickening wave. The hospital. The jar. The freaky specimen floating inside it and his uncontrollable urge to take it with him. Aunt Elvira was going to try and sell it in her favorite shop tomorrow. There was always someone out there who would pay top dollar for that weird shit. *Or was that today? Could he have been unconscious that long?* Where had he gone after visiting his aunt? *Shenanigans. Oh shit. Crystal. That's where I was last night.*

* * *

The Specimen

Shenanigans. Whoever came up with that name for a bar should be taken out back and bludgeoned with a two by four. Despite that, it still was Frank's favorite watering hole in the area. Cheap beer. A large dance floor. A couple of pool tables, dartboards and some scoreboard sized televisions. Throngs of young men and women in their twenties ready to let loose most days of the week. All you can eat Buffalo wings on Thursday nights and $10 domestic pitchers during Sunday football. A perfect bar for someone like Frank. Who cared if it had a permanent early nineties vibe?

Frank dropped by at least once a week, and more recently he had been increasing the frequency of his visits. His favorite stool at the bar was all the way at the end and the entire staff knew him by name. Even the guys in back knew his favorite dishes.

Regardless of his comfort at Shenanigans, Frank rarely gathered up enough courage to talk to any of the girls there, much less flirt with them. Inherently, he was your average shy guy.

So when his ideal woman sat in the stool next to him last night, and ordered herself a green apple martini, he was rendered speechless. Petite, just over 5', fit but not overly muscular, short-cropped strawberry blonde hair, green eyes, with a raspy voice that was sexy as hell and a crooked smile that foreshadowed her sharp wit. It was as if he had drawn her according to his specific wishes and ordered a prototype. Her name was Crystal. When she turned to Frank and started up a conversation about the fact that Star Trek was infinitely superior to Star Wars and anyone who thought otherwise could kiss her skinny white ass, he was instantly infatuated.

They spent the next couple hours at the bar chatting about a vast array of topics: movies, politics (she was a devout liberal in all facets of her life; he was socially liberal, but tended toward the conservative side when it came to finances), sports (they both were diehard Red Sox and Celtics fans, but despised the Patriots), and books (science fiction with a smattering of horror). Frank was astonished at how easy the conversation flowed. He was never this smooth, but Crystal (plus a half dozen or so Newcastle Brown Ales) seemed to have unlocked the floodgates of his perpetual social anxiety and he was never at a loss for words. Even the intermittent pauses in conversation were natural and organic. Nothing awkward at all. He was entranced.

Just before one in the morning, as he was pondering how to ask for her number, she leaned over as if to whisper in his ear, entwined her fingers in his hair and pulled him to her for a long, lingering, tangy green apple kiss.

She pulled back, smiled wickedly at him, and kissed him again... this time giving his lower lip a quick bite at the end.

"Let's go somewhere more private, so we can... talk more," she whispered in his ear. Afraid he would ruin the moment with an attempt at speech, Frank smiled, nodded and tossed a twenty on the bar as he shrugged into his leather jacket. Buck, the bartender, winked lasciviously at him and flashed the thumbs up in approval. Crystal clasped his hand in hers and led him up the stairs and out the door into the parking lot behind the bar.

The chill was bracing. Crystal giggled and pulled her jacket tight as they walked through the intermittent spotlights down the row of cars to his maroon 1994 Honda Civic. Not exactly a chick magnet, but at least he had cleaned the floor of fast food wrappers and soda cans the day before yesterday. It wouldn't be too embarrassing to show it to her.

They weaved their way through the shadows. The night was crisp and silent, a stark, serene contrast to the constant noise in the bar. The only sound breaking their reverie was their footsteps on the gravel.

"Oh, fer Christ's sake," Frank groaned as they reached his car. Next to his Civic was parked a large blue van with an airbrushed panther on the side panels. The driver had squeezed in a bit too tight next to his driver side, making it nearly impossible to open the door. "No way can I squeeze in there," he grumbled.

"Babe, let me try. Gimme your keys," offered Crystal. "I'm pretty flexible, you know." She gave him a naughty wink as he handed over the keys and started to wriggle between the two vehicles.

Frank admired the view and mentally thanked whichever angel was looking over him tonight when he heard steps in the gravel behind him and a deep voice said quietly, "Did I block you in? Let me take care of that."

The Specimen

Frank turned at the sound of the voice just in time to see a large aluminum baseball bat on a path to slam into his skull. It hit him with a flash of blinding white pain and everything went black.

* * *

Frank had been in deep shit before, but nothing compared to this situation. Bound and beaten in the trunk of his car, which was being driven by some unknown attacker on a back road somewhere in the rain. He could hear a voice, but the noise of the downpour on the trunk drowned it out. *What about Crystal? Was their assailant an ex-boyfriend? A husband? A psychopathic stalker?* Frank's mind whirled with images of her being raped in the parking lot by some Neanderthal with a baseball bat while he lay bleeding and unconscious on the gravel next to her. She could be dead already, buried in an unmarked grave or tossed down an abandoned well.

No, she's alive. She had to be alive. No matter how desperate things might seem, Frank needed to hold on to that one strand of hope. She wouldn't have been raped in the middle of the parking lot where anyone could have left *Shenanigan's* and seen them. Odds were that she was in a similar situation, bound and helpless in another car, or maybe even in the back seat of his Civic, just inches away from Frank in the trunk. Even if escape from this ordeal seemed infinitely impossible, he had to watch out for any opportunity whatsoever and try something. To do otherwise would be equivalent to suicide, and despite Frank's complete inexperience in actual fights, he would not go down as easily as if he were a dog being led to receive a euthanasia injection.

The car slowed down, turned left and started up an even steeper incline. Frank hit his head and bruised other vulnerable body parts numerous times as he ricocheted around the trunk. His swollen right temple slammed on the wheel well so sharply that he began retching, eventually vomiting last night's beer all over himself and the interior of the trunk. He continued to gag and groan for the next few minutes as he felt the car crest a hill and coast to a stop. The driver left the engine running and exited the car. A squeal of grinding metal and a rattle of heavy chains were audible over the rumbling of the Civic's engine and the rain on the trunk, before the driver got back in and drove around a sharp bend onto a smoother paved road.

Frank's head stopped spinning somewhat and he was able to concentrate on the motion of the car. He didn't know why, but the sensation of the road and the pattern of turns felt very familiar to him. The car could not have been traveling at more than 20 miles per hour. For the next few minutes, Frank sensed that they were moving in a wide counter-clockwise loop, steadily climbing, as if they were circling a mountain on the way to the summit. Occasionally, it was apparent that the vehicle slowed down and avoided an obstacle in the road. Frank imagined a downed tree or some hillside debris that had slid in a torrent of mud down onto this unused roadway.

His clothes were soaked in his vomit and the trunk smelled like mop water from a dive bar after a night of drunken revelry. Even so, he felt better. More alert. His nausea had subsided and he could focus his thoughts, even if all he could think was his approaching death. It wasn't likely that the person who had tied him up and tossed him in the trunk had good intentions. The way Frank saw it, there were only two possibilities.

Option #1, the guy had raped and killed Crystal and he was going to do the same to him and dump both of their bodies in a ditch somewhere. *God, if I'm about to get killed, please skip the raping part.* Option #2, the thug had kidnapped Crystal and he was going to kill Frank to prove his undying love. Probably in a creative manner just to prove how batshit crazy in love with her he was. Either way, Frank was monumentally screwed. There was no way he was going to magically find a sharp object secreted in the trunk with which he would astonishingly free himself seconds before the trunk opened. That crap never happened in reality. Only in Hollywood. He knew that meeting a girl like Crystal had been much too good to have actually worked out. There always was a catch.

To be honest, it was doubtful that Frank would even be in this situation if it were scripted for the movies. Frank was not leading man material. Someone had once told him that he looked like "a taller, younger

The Specimen

Paul Giamatti". Great actor, but not known for his looks, nor someone who you would expect to attract a girl in Crystal's league.

Finally, the road flattened out and the car slowed to a stop. The engine was shut off and two doors slammed consecutively as the passengers came around to the trunk of the Civic and popped it open. A large flashlight shone directly in his eyes. Frank squinted in the glare and attempted to avert his gaze.

Shielding his eyes, he was able to make out two separate figures. The one closest to him was obviously male, bulky and swollen in a rumpled suit that stank of stale cigarettes. Frank could smell them over the reek of his recent puke and nearly felt his gorge rise again. The other individual was short and wiry, stepping out of sight nearly immediately.

"Damn! Looks like your boy here upchucked all over himself. I am not touching that," the man said as he leaned in covering his nose and mouth. He was a large African-American man in his mid-fifties with a hangdog face, bloodshot eyes and a thick bushy mustache that appeared to be the only thing he ever groomed. His teeth were long and stained brownish-yellow from a perpetual diet of coffee and cigarettes. Reaching into the trunk, he gave the zip ties around Frank's limbs a pull to test their strength. "I'll lift him out and put him in the chair, but after that he's yours. He stinks to high heaven. Maybe we should let him sit his ass in the rain a bit so it washes some of that sick offa him."

"Who are you? What do you want?" yelled Frank from the trunk. His eyes were slowly adjusting, but he didn't see the man wind up and backhand him across the face. Blood and spit flew from his mouth and his vision went grey for a few seconds.

"How about you shut the fuck up now unless you want more of that," growled the big man.

"Calm down, Stoopes," called a familiar voice. "You don't want to have another episode like last time. Last thing I want to do tonight is drive your fat ass to the emergency room."

That voice. It couldn't be. As the other individual stepped back into view pushing an old wooden wheelchair, it immediately became apparent that there was a third possibility that Frank had never considered.

"Hi there, Frankie," smiled the woman he had met last night. "I guess you probably figured out by now that my name isn't Crystal. You can call me Valentine." Behind her, illuminated by the Civic's taillights was a building that he quickly recognized: **The Mt. Greylock Institute for the Mentally Insane.**

The Specimen

*From the Personal Journal
of Dr. Saul Eckenrode
Clinical Director
Mount Greylock Institute*

September 15, 1965

    I have befriended the boy. After the incident with Scarpa and Wick a couple of weeks ago, few of the residents or staff will even hold a conversation with him. They avoid Harry whenever he enters the room and whisper that he is insane. Rotten. Possessed by legions of hungry demons. The former is likely true, but what do they expect? If he was sane, he would not be here at Greylock.

    I believe that I overreacted in the common room two weeks ago, seeing things that didn't exist, assigning impossible abilities to a young boy. Wick obviously had a psychotic break with reality. He has been in isolation since the attack, and Scarpa is still in the hospital undergoing multiple surgeries in an attempt to reconstruct his damaged face.

    At times it feels like Dr. Coe sees Harry only as a specimen, only good for use in experimentation. She initially thought that the games were a bad idea, but she now agrees that our interactions could be beneficial. Of course, I am required to file reports with her on a regular basis, but that shouldn't be too difficult. Dr. Coe doesn't seem to be the type who would actually read the reports. Rather, she is more likely to make certain that they are completed or otherwise, she would get a bug up her ass if they were not submitted.

    We play chess nearly every day during lunch in my office. Either Fenton or Jameson were initially to be present all the time, but they have recently grown lax and often leave for a cigarette or an extended lavatory break. Harry seems to like me, and I am not ashamed to admit that I have grown fond of our games and conversations. He has a creative mind and he has become quite effective with his unorthodox style. He also has an uncanny ability to distract me from his actual game strategy. If I wasn't looking directly at the board, I would swear that he was somehow moving my pieces without my knowledge. Initially I won all the games, but he has learned quickly and he now wins more often than not. It is somewhat disconcerting to lose to boy of his age, but it proves he has an extraordinary intellect and I haven't had such a challenge playing chess since my university years.

I must admit, though, that I do have an ulterior motive. To date, I have been unable to deduce the actual reason for Harry's presence here at Greylock. He is the subject of Coe's study, but much of the day he spends in his room or watching television in the common room. He has a preference for westerns and mysteries, mainly *Gunsmoke*, *Bonanza*, *The Twilight Zone* and *Alfred Hitchcock Presents*. I could do without the first two, but on evenings when the latter two shows are broadcast, I often find myself staying late to watch them as well.

I can only assume that he has a medical condition that affects his neurological functions and that he is undergoing some sort of medical treatment. Dr. Coe remains inscrutable. Perhaps I can dig some information out of Fenton or Jameson, both of whom have been a smidgen less hostile to me in recent days...

- S.

The Specimen

Chapter 12 - My Bloody Valentine

"The only way to find true happiness is to risk being completely cut open." - Chuck Palahniuk

Modern Day – Mt. Greylock, MA

When it came to torturing people, Delano Stoopes didn't fuck around. Why waste time? It wasn't a complicated job. No need to be creative. In his experience, efficiency was the answer when the collection of information was the goal. Unlike some people - little Miss Valentine for one - torture was not something he enjoyed. He didn't get his jollies when he broke someone's nose. His nipples did not become erect when he was pulverizing someone's kneecap with a sledgehammer. He didn't get sweaty thinking of new methods to try. That kinda shit was for them Jeffrey Dahmer and John Wayne Bundy types. Guys who had mommy issues. Guys who would have fit in here at Greylock.

Not Del Stoopes. Del's method was boiled down and simple. If you don't answer my questions, I will inflict pain. For him, it was a job, and as his daddy always told him before he got killed, "If you're gonna do a job, do it right the first time. Otherwise you just have to go back and fix all your mistakes." Not bad advice from a guy who barely graduated high school. His daddy may have been a mean bastard, quick with his fists and angry at the world, but he never lied to Del. If he said something to say to you, positive or negative, he meant it with all of his cold cruel heart.

Even though his father had been dead for over forty years, Del could still hear his voice and see him sitting at the kitchen table in his SFPD blues cleaning his piece. That was his father's routine every night, whether or not it had been fired. His memory of it was so clear that he swore he could still feel every chip on the green Formica table, including the place where he had carved his initials on the underside when he was nine. He could smell the gun oil and the beer on his father's breath. His old dog, Rufus, a mutt of unsubstantiated origin, sat at his feet snoring and farting. He could still hear the *telenovelas* his grandmother had always watched on the Spanish channel in the living room, even though she couldn't speak a lick of Spanish outside of the swear words. This was Del's last truly positive family memory. Within the next month, his father would be killed in the line of duty because his gun misfired when confronting a would-be stick-up. *Irony is a bitch.* He grunted under his breath and ended his reverie. That was a long time ago and he had a job to do now. *Back to work*, he thought as he stared at the bound figure before him. This kid was tougher than he looked.

Once removed from the trunk, Stoopes and Valentine had lashed Frank to the wooden wheelchair and transported him back inside the abandoned hospital into the main lobby where they had set up shop. Stoopes had stripped off his jacket, rolled up his sleeves and begun questioning him vigorously and methodically for the past half hour, alternating punches to the face and chest with kicks to Frank's unprotected groin. By now his *cojones* should be buried deep inside his torso or swollen to the size of ripe avocados. Either way, if he somehow managed to survive the night, his chance for children in the next few years had decreased greatly.

Stoopes put a little extra into the next punch, breaking Frank's nose for the second time. Blood and mucus spattered on the floor and a long string of reddish drool hung down the young man's chin onto his shirt.

He moaned incoherently from the bloody remnants of his mouth, "Uhdun noway knee thin… uhswe-ah," Frank coughed up a gob and spit it to the side of the chair. His swollen mashed lips and broken teeth garbled his speech, but Stoopes had a lot of experience interpreting this type of dialect. "I was juss lookin' for a place to explore."

Delano smirked, "That may be true, Popecky. But sometimes people are reluctant to share the entire story because it incriminates them in other ways. I don't give a shit if you were stealing shit to sell or running around in here naked as a jaybird. All I care about is what you found and where it is now. So, you get to make the decision. Tell me now or tell me later. All the same to me."

"Frankie, I actually believe most of what you told us," called Valentine from her spot sprawled on a moth-eaten couch a few feet away. "Yet we're pretty sure you left some things out. Why you chose this place.

The Specimen

How you found the jar when a team of our people scoured the building thoroughly years ago. And most of all, who sent you here?"

Stoopes chuckled under his breath, "He'll give it up soon, sister. I don't believe he's working alone. What kind of dumbass goes into abandoned building by himself just for fun?" Quickly he backhanded Frank again, causing a fresh line of blood to trickle from his right nostril.

"Let's give him a breather, Stoopes," commented Valentine. "We can't get any answers if he's unconscious."

"Whatever you want, cherry pie," Stoopes muttered as he backed away and pulled a battered pack of American Spirits from his shirt pocket. He lit one with his Zippo and gestured with the pack in her direction, offering her one. Valentine brushed off the cherry pie comment and waved off the smokes. She stood up from the couch while her burly partner slouched over and took her place. Frank looked up at her approach, flinching as she straddled his lap in what would normally be a provocative position and raised her hand to his face.

"I said we'd give you a little break, honey bunny," purred Valentine as she cupped his bloodstained chin in her hand and wiggled closer to whisper in his ear. "Give you some time to regain your memory." She looked down at his lap in surprise. "Well, lookie here! I guess Stoopes didn't permanently damage you after all. Little Mister Popecky is wide awake and ready to play. Maybe I can convince you another way. Huh, big boy?"

She leaned in and kissed him roughly on the mouth, savaging his lip in a sadistic parallel to her playful bite from the previous night. Frank screamed in agony as she pulled away, teeth clenched on his lower lip, stretching it out to its tearing point. Just as it seemed she would rip off a significant chunk of meat, she released him and licked the blood from her mouth like a cat that has drank her fill of milk. Her teeth marks formed a jagged semicircle on Frank's lower lip and blood dripped from the wound to join the older stains on his shirt.

"So," she continued quietly. "Let's try this again. How and where did you find the specimen in this building and where is it located now?"

* * *

One month earlier...

Frank was ecstatic. He had found it - the Mt. Greylock Institute. Just like he had hoped, even though he had harbored some doubt that it still stood after having been abandoned so long ago. Closed for nearly five decades, the immense building was nestled on a wooded plot of land in the Berkshire Mountains in northwest Massachusetts right next to the Mt. Greylock State Reservation. It was overgrown with vegetation and one boarded-up wing in the back had some severe fire damage on the exterior, but other than that it seemed to have weathered well.

The grounds were littered with deadfall from the trees ringing what had been the front lawn and parking area, but there was no evidence that anyone had been here since 1966, the year it was closed. Frank could possibly be the first person to enter the building since then. In urban exploration, a find like this was legendary. In fact, it was entirely unheard of for an edifice this large to completely "drop off the map."

Despite this, that was exactly what happened. The asylum was shut down a few months after two inmates committed numerous murders and set fire to the medical wing of the Institute. In the aftermath, the remaining patients were gradually transferred to other psychiatric facilities or released to their families, and that was that. The gate was locked and all signs directing visitors were removed. Soon after, any detailed reference to the institution disappeared. It was no longer listed on state or county maps. Only Wikipedia had a minor entry on the building and the murders. There were no references listed at the bottom of the article.

If he had been one to believe conspiracy theories, Frank would have thought that there had been a concerted effort to erase the memory of its existence in local records. Some of his "more colorful" friends might have believed such an idea, but Frank tended to ignore the black helicopter whacko theories.

Frank had left his car a mile away to avoid drawing attention to his trespass. He easily circumvented the chain link fence at the entrance by hiking in from a side road. The way up the mountain bristled with overgrown shrubbery and decades of fallen limbs from the surrounding trees. The pavement was pockmarked with cracks, potholes and a few

The Specimen

young saplings that had sprouted in the small crevices formed by the yearly freeze and thaw. In order to drive a car up the slope, these and other obstacles would need to be cleared out. Otherwise, anyone else who felt like visiting would be hiking their way in as well.

The hike had taken just over half an hour. Frank had expected it to be rough going, but the eight foot gully he crossed halfway up the mountain was unexpected. The rainstorm the night before had softened the earth and a small brook rushed down the gully in brownish muddy torrents. Frank was drenched to his waist and lathered with mud above that from a face-first tumble he suffered when crossing.

Even so, it had been all worth it. Aches and bruises were forgotten. Here he was about to enter a building that had most likely not heard the footsteps of man since the late 1960's. He pulled out his digital camera and verified that it was fully charged. The urban explorer credo was "Take nothing but pictures. Leave nothing but footprints."

Frank lived by this code whenever he took off on one of his adventures. Though he often discovered objects both rare and sometimes disturbing, he was religious about maintaining the sanctity of the buildings. On the other hand, Frank also took his time with a new place, exploring every corner. No matter how mundane the site, Frank often took hundreds of pictures to upload to his personal blog where fellow urban explorers and the occasional online lurker could peruse them at leisure. This batch of images was bound to be a huge hit with his followers. Finding a new pristine location was always a virtual badge of honor in the urban explorer community.

The door was chained shut, of course, years of rust and filth coating the metal. Frank probably could have broken it open with a few blows to the hasp, but that was an option only to be used in an absolute emergency. A couple years back, a fellow urban explorer who went by the handle Pillager44 posted dozens of images online of items he had "retrieved" from various sites across New York and Pennsylvania. Within days, numerous anonymous reports had been filed with the authorities and Pillager44 was taken into custody and charged with multiple counts of felony burglary, vandalism and other assorted crimes.

You don't mess with the code.

Acting on a sudden hunch, Frank walked around to the rear of the building. This was where the patient dormitory had been according to the minimal information he had been able to glean from his research. Halfway around to the east, Frank found the fire escape – exactly what he had hoped to see. It was rusty as well, but once he pulled it down and tested it, the ladder appeared to have been constructed from cast iron and remained quite sturdy.

Swinging his backpack over his shoulders, Frank clambered up to the 4th floor, bypassing the 2nd and 3rd floors on another hunch. The window was unbarred and most of the glass had already been broken away, giving him access to the inside latch. He reached around the remaining shards, unlatched the window and climbed into what appeared to have been an office. He had done it. It seemed almost too easy. Normally he might have to search for hours to gain access to a structure, especially if it had not yet been catalogued by past explorers, but this time it had been abnormally easy. He had felt a yearning, an unconscious need to follow his instincts, and he did just that. It had almost felt like a voice, but without words, leading him exactly where he needed to go.

The elements had thoroughly annihilated the room over the decades. Rotting remnants of books littered the floor. A dingy gray couch was half covered with a wispy yellowish mold that looked like rancid cotton candy. The carpet had curled up from water damage and portions of the industrial linoleum beneath it bubbled up like necrotic tissue.

Frank scanned the room and took a few pictures for his blog. The door was closed shut. If he was fortunate, the damage had not extended much into the hallway and the rest of the building. He opened the door and looked left and right into the hallway. Extending approximately twenty feet in either direction, the corridor had a stairwell at each end leading up to the top floor and down to the residential areas. The right end of the corridor ended at the stairwell. On the left side, the corridor turned right and continued toward the front of the institute where Frank had entered through the gate. There were five other doors in the hall, all but one of them open. Debris was strewn across the floor and there was obvious water damage coming from two of the rooms across the hall. Most likely, those windows were broken as well, allowing snow and rain to

The Specimen

accumulate and melt in the rooms many times over the years. On the third floor and below, all the windows were barred. Perhaps there would be less damage there.

Frank turned right and opened the door to the stairwell at the end. Though he had much more to explore on this floor, he felt uncharacteristically compelled to see what was below. As to be expected, the stairwell was pitch black. This was pretty common in these abandoned sites. Obviously, there was no electricity, and windows were a luxury in many buildings that he explored.

He was prepared for such a situation, though. Reaching into his bag, Frank pulled out a key tool of the modern urban explorer, an elastic cloth headband into which a small halogen flashlight was sewn. He slid it over his head and clicked it on, immediately illuminating the depths below with a white light that seemed more powerful than was possible by such a small bulb.

Except for an instant of motion at the edge of the light's range, the stairwell was empty. Perhaps a rat? Frank didn't mind them, but cockroaches gave him the heebie-jeebies. He muttered a short prayer that they would stay out of sight. Cockroaches were everywhere, so it was fruitless to hope that they were absent here. A couple months ago, he had slipped on a wet patch in an old textile mill in Waltham and fallen face first into a pile of rotting fabric. To his abject horror, a nest of roaches had been living there and he immediately found himself covered with hundreds of the foul insects. That incident had led to weeks of nightmares and extra-long showers.

Frank started down the stairs, right hand firmly on the railing to steady himself. There was a musty stale smell that reminded him of his Aunt Elvira's attic. Dry, yet with a subtle hint of rot like an animal had died here decades earlier. He paused at the 3rd floor stairwell for a few seconds, took a couple pictures, then passed on by, once again compelled to look in another area of the building. In the back of his mind, Frank knew that this urge came from an outside source, but as soon as he wondered why he wasn't fighting it, he immediately forgot his concern and his thoughts meandered. He was looking for something and he would know what it was when he found it.

He passed the 2nd and 1st floor doors without pause, continuing to the bottom of the stairs where the walls changed from brick to concrete as he went below ground. A metal double door labeled "FACILITIES" in large red letters stood in a shallow alcove in the wall.

The door was cracked open. It should have been locked, but Frank thought nothing of it. He noticed numerous sets of footprints in the dust when the door swung open, but he looked right past them into the vast basement. Nothing registered except for the compulsion… the urgent need to find whatever had been hidden from sight for nearly fifty years overrode the realization that he was not the first to search the asylum since it closed. He ignored the thoughts bubbling inside him. Paid them no heed. The sole focus was to search and find what called him here.

When he was much younger, before his mother had died of the Big C and his dad subsequently found new love in a bottle, his childhood had been full of joy and laughter. His memories of that time weren't always clear because he was so young, but certain images were vivid as if they had happened yesterday.

One of his fondest recollections from the years before his mother became ill involved a game his parents called "Hot and Cold". It was a modified version of Hide and Seek where his parents would take turns hiding from him in their back yard. The one who did not hide would follow Frank around the yard as he sought his target, calling out hints. "You're getting hotter" or "Oh no, that's too cold". Obviously it wasn't the most complicated game, but for a young boy playing with the two most important people in his life, it was the greatest game ever invented.

Now, in the dark, cavernous basement strewn with debris, boxes and machine parts, he remembered that game again and he had a sensation that someone – something – was guiding him in the same manner. He swung his head left and right, aiming the narrow beam of light in a sweeping motion across the floor. Patterns of multiple footprints were visible throughout the room, but they were much more concentrated on the left side and closer to the door. Frank noticed this anomaly, but his concentration was solely focused on his need to find what had pulled him to this space. As he stood in the doorway, he sensed the ghosts of its former residents in the objects strewn on the floor. He walked a few feet into the

The Specimen

room and was immediately overcome with a sense that he had lost his equilibrium. Chills raced up his left flank and a burning feeling tingled the right side of his face, as if he had lain too long in the sun. This bilateral confusion intensified as he continued to walk down the barely defined center aisle. Hot…Cold….Hot…Cold.

He moved to left and felt colder. Aiming to right rear section of the room caused his face to flush with droplets of sweat forming on his brow. He spun around slowly counterclockwise. As he rotated, the side facing the left of the room rapidly covered in goose bumps, while the other side felt as if he were in a tanning booth. The dichotomy was not pleasant.

Hot…and Cold. Hot and Cold! Frank shook himself out of his mental fog. This was like that game he had played with his parents so long ago. Something was communicating with him. Frank felt a chill run up his spine that had nothing to do with previous feelings. He normally wasn't the superstitious type, but now he was beginning to doubt his convictions.

Frank angled his path toward the warm side and took a couple steps in that direction. The warmth increased, but now it was pleasant, as if he were walking toward a comforting fire after having been standing outside in the elements, cold and damp and grey. The compulsion, which had receded somewhat when he entered the room, now overwhelmed him. He had to escape the Cold region and enter the Hot sanctuary where he would find what called him.

Frank pushed aside boxes and climbed over old furniture, bedsprings and outdated medical equipment that appeared to have been tossed in a pile. Hotter. The light from his headlamp illuminated what seemed to be the only undisturbed corner of the cellar. A pile of neatly stacked bedframes and ancient mattresses stood before a section of the wall that, unlike the rest of the room, was made of brick. The rest was industrial gray concrete.

One by one, Frank moved the moldy mattresses and wooden frames to the side, revealing a gigantic fireplace. The hearth was empty, clean of ashes and any debris, but this was definitely the source of the Heat. He could feel the radiating waves of an invisible fire coming from inside the chimney. Without a second thought, he ducked into the fireplace and looked up the long vertical brick tunnel. A musky perfume *filled the shaft. Metal rungs were set in the side wall, leading to an apparent alcove approximately ten feet above him.*

Frank began climbing, the urge to complete his quest throbbing in his brain. Sweat poured off his brow and decades of soot painted his hands and face as he clambered up the metal ladder. He whimpered in anticipation as he reached the hollow opening in the bricks. Leaning his head in, he saw a cylindrical object at the back of the shelf. He shifted his angle and aimed the lamp toward the back, revealing the jar glowing in the light.

It was glorious.

* * *

Nina Valentine paused in her interrogation at the sound of footsteps from the corridor. After Frank had revealed how he had been led to the hiding place, Stoopes had left to check the basement and verify the story while Valentine continued to question him. When the topic turned to the current location of the jar, though, Frank clammed up, giving her a chance to demonstrate her other talents. Stoopes emerged from the shadows in the hall, returning from the basement, cursing to high heaven and covered in soot.

"You're almost as dirty as me, Stoopes," giggled Valentine as she stood up from Frank's bloody form. Bites, cuts and cigarette burns covered his naked torso. He had finally slipped into unconsciousness a minute ago when she chewed off his left nipple along with a couple square inches of surrounding flesh with an overly zealous love bite, then spat the chunk of flesh into her palm and held it up to his eyes. Now, she was tossing the nipple in the air offhandedly, as if she were flipping a lucky coin.

Stoopes stared at Frank, then looked away, nose wrinkled in disgust. *That little girl is one twisted fuck*, he thought to himself. *She gets the job done, though. Can't deny that.*

"Looks like he was telling the truth," he responded. "The chimney was there and there was an alcove inside with a large circular impression in the soot. I can understand missing the alcove, but how did they ever

The Specimen

overlook that chimney? Quillian is going to be pissed. I'm glad we aren't the ones who did the initial search last year"

"Oh?" she answered, raising her eyebrows.

Stoopes nodded, "They did a half-assed job. The evidence is right there in the dust. Only one set of footprints goes anywhere near the chimney, and I'll bet they belong to Mr. Nipples here. It looks as if they were actively repelled from searching that area."

Valentine froze in surprise at the last statement. "Wait…repelled?" She shook her head. "Oh, no. This is not good, Stoopes. Do you have your phone? Never mind. I have mine. We need to alert Quillian immediately."

"Quillian? Why? Isn't he on a hunt today?"

"He is," she said as she pulled out her cell phone. "But he's the only one who has personally tangled with them within the past couple years. He'll want to know."

"Your call, l'il buddy," he sighed. "As long I'm not the messenger, I could give a crap."

"You may crap your pants just yet, Stoopes. I hope to hell I'm wrong, but I think you just described something that is only within the power of an Elder, and if that's the case, we're in for a shit tsunami."

<<ACME EYES ONLY>>
What We Know: An ACME Group Primer on the Riders
J.P. Kilcannon/G. Suares/K. Morimoto, 11th Edition

Section C. – Our Adversaries, the Riders

Origin – Convincing evidence of Rider influence on humanity has been discovered as far back as 8th Century BCE in the Assyrian Empire, and there is reason to believe that the Riders have lived among us for much longer – possibly since the 14th or 15th Century BCE.

The earliest recorded indications of Rider existence center on the Baltic Sea, Scandinavia and Eastern Europe. Later records expand outward in all directions across all continents. Specific instances of Rider intervention will be highlighted later in this primer.

Only within the past two to three decades has it been confirmed that the Riders are not of terrestrial origin. Rather than the double helix, four nucleobase model of terrestrial DNA, all Rider cells have a triple helix and eight nucleobases in their analogue of DNA. Even within this design, much is in flux. Just as all Riders are able to change appearance and transform between types of tissue in its body as needed, some of the oldest ones have developed the ability to change their forms on a molecular level.

Life Expectancy/Other Benefits – For all intents and purposes, a Rider is immortal. They can be killed and they can be injured or maimed; they can be scarred, but they do not visibly show the effects of age. As a Rider gains years, it also develops more control and power. A Rider's ability to influence people and creatures around them increases as its pheromones become more potent and concentrated.

Most Riders encountered in the field are between seventy to four hundred years old. This spike in numbers is the result of a natural phenomenon that will be explained later in the section on Reproduction. To be considered an Elder by the measures we use, Riders should have close to one thousand years of experience. Years spent in hibernation do not count toward that total.

The Specimen

The Rider/Host relationship is not always one-sided. In fact, many benefits are extended to the Host as well. It can survive up to double the life expectancy of a normal human (between 150 and 200 years), depending on a number of factors:

1) The age of the host when originally bridled
2) The host's original health
3) The age of the Rider. Older Riders can extend a host's life longer than one with little experience.
4) The level of empathy between Host and Rider
5) Whether the relationship is Rider-dominant or Host-dominant

Along with an extended lifespan, Hosts also develop a combination of abilities which manifest differently depending on the individual. Some of the most commonly reported abilities are detailed below in Section D.

Section D. – Rider Abilities

Rider/Host Relationship – The level of control divided between the Rider and the Host can be illustrated as a spectrum ranging from Rider-Dominant to Host-Dominant. There appears to be no obvious determining factor with regards to whether the Host or Rider is the dominant of the pair. Even in the case of Elder Riders, individuals with an extremely strong willpower can resist their influence.

One theory illustrates the relationship as a battle of the minds. Some humans are simply more able to handle stress. Others collapse in the face of any pressure. This ability to compartmentalize situations translates into a mental barrier that locks the Rider personality inside the Host mind.

1) Rider-Dominant – The overwhelming majority of Rider/Host pairings are dominated by the Rider. This can exhibit in multiple ways. The most common examples are when the Host personality is completely submerged and the surface personality is that of the Rider.

2) Host-Dominant – This type of relationship is much less frequently seen than the more commonly encountered Rider-Dominant pairs. In a Host-Dominant pair, the host is able to suppress much, if not all, of the Rider's control.

Most often, these relationships occur in instances when the Rider is very young and the Host is mature, though there has been at least one recorded case where an immature Host has been able to resist the influence of an Elder Rider the vast majority of the time.

In cases where the Host personality is dominant, but the Rider can sometimes break through, the Host personality can fracture and lose its ability to submerge the Rider's personality. This can result in a nervous breakdown and, eventually, a reversal of dominance.

Personality Assimilation – A key fact to remember regarding interaction with Riders is that they are *aliens*. No matter how human one may seem, the personality that you see is inherited from the multitude of Hosts ridden by that specific Rider during its entire existence. It is not the Rider's personality at all, but rather an extremely realistic mask they use to emulate us.

In Host-Dominant pairs, the Host personality remains on the surface and the Rider's personality only surfaces during times of extreme stress, or, much less frequently when the Host is sleeping. When the Host dies or in the rare case when the Rider involuntarily moves on to a new Host, only a ghost of the Host personality continues on with the Rider.

In Rider-Dominant pairs, the surface personality is an amalgam of the previous hosts. The longer an individual stays with a specific host, the greater a portion of the Rider's personality reflects that particular Host. Each subsequent Host alters the personality with its own quirks, passions and insanities.

Theoretically, a newly born Rider is a completely blank slate before it finds a Host. Once it has bridled a human Host, it takes on its core personality traits. If the Host is a violent individual, the Rider adopts its violent tendencies and magnifies them. On the flip side, if the hypothetical Host is gentle and benevolent, these traits will also be transferred and magnified. The fact that we have never encountered a Rider that is even remotely benign is a sad testament on the true characteristics of the human race.

Telepathy – In all recorded cases, Riders have exhibited some level of telepathy. As Riders age, the range and strength of the telepathy increases. Initially, only the Rider and Host can communicate with each other. The next few levels of telepathy are as follows:
    1) Skin-to-skin contact/Larvae ingestion
    2) All individuals within sight
    3) Any individual who has had previous contact with a Rider within a specific radius. As the Rider ages, the range of effective telepathy increases.

Empathic Projection – The ability to influence the emotions or urges of humans and animals is common in Riders, but the strength of such influence varies greatly. Often it depends on the Host/Rider interaction. The Rider may exhibit minimal empathic projection with one Host then suddenly become a master of manipulation with a subsequent Host. Those with strong pheromones are usually empathically strong as well.

Telekinesis – **(Unconfirmed)** The power to move objects with the mind is so rare that it has not been reported since the beginning of the 19th century. Even when documented, evidence has been shaky.

Pyrokinesis – **(Unconfirmed)** The power to create fire has been rumored, but no evidence other than anecdotal has been discovered.

Accelerated Healing Rate – This ability is a universal benefit given from all Riders to their Hosts, regardless of whether the Host or Rider is dominant. As with most of the abilities, the older the Rider is, the stronger the effect will be. The healing ability can also be transferred to other individuals who have ingested a Rider Larva (See Section E: Reproduction).

Injuries that would normally heal in months take weeks. Organs grow. Bones regenerate. Spinal cords, once severed, have been repaired. Amputated limbs can even grow back over time. Other than a bullet to the brain, decapitation, or complete exsanguination, there are very few ways to kill a Host with a completely healthy Rider on her back.

The Specimen

Chapter 13 - Extra Crispy

"White smoke of burning flesh hangs in the motionless air."
- William Burroughs, <u>Naked Lunch</u>

Modern Day – Chesterfield, MA

The mouthwatering aroma of bacon and eggs greeted Milton "Bud" Ritchie when he entered the kitchen with Sherman and Patton loping in after him. As he hung up the dogs' leashes and his windbreaker on the coat rack, the two young Weimaraners scooted past him to pester his wife Rosemary at the stove.

"Don't even think about it!" she reprimanded them as they crouched at her feet displaying the most pitiful faces they could muster. She swatted at them distractedly with her spatula as she looked with amusement at her husband of thirty-eight years, "You were gone a while. I had to take it off the burner for a bit, so I wouldn't ruin your breakfast. The bacon's a bit crispy, but you like it that way."

"Puts hair on your chest," he replied.

"Exactly why I don't eat it," she smiled, then squinted at him, immediately sensing his distraction. "Anything happening that I should know?"

"Looks like there was a big fire a few blocks over on the other side of the woods. Maybe Belcher Road or Mason Place," he remarked as he kicked off his boots. "Must be the reason for all those sirens around dawn." He nodded at the two dogs snuffling around the kitchen for stray scraps. "The boys were whining at me to head over in that direction, but it's best to stay out of the way. Maybe Scotty and I will drive over to check things out later. He still in bed?"

"I believe so. I knocked about half an hour ago, but all I could hear was that fan of his," she replied. Frowning in contemplation, she gestured toward the stairwell leading to the second floor, "I think he might've snuck out again last night. We should talk to him about it soon before it becomes a problem."

"He's beginning to remind me of Vic more and more," grumbled Bud.

"I would think so. He's the spitting image of our son at this age, but it doesn't mean he'll make the same bad decisions. Don't convict him before he commits the crime, Milton Ritchie."

Bud winced. He knew by her tone and the use of his full Christian name that he was treading on thin ice and he had best rein himself in before he got himself into more trouble. Despite what Scott may believe, his grandmother was fiercely protective of him and anyone who didn't give him a fair shake would get a piece of her mind. *A piece? They'd get the whole damn pie,* he thought.

"I'm gonna give Chuck and Kate Monahan a ring later and compare notes," he continued carefully. "Maybe they have some strategies that have worked with Hank that we haven't tried."

"I wouldn't hold your breath, honey," sighed Rosemary as she scooped half of the eggs and nearly the entire pile of bacon onto his plate. "Hank isn't exactly a Boy Scout either. Sit down and have your breakfast first. Coffee's ready to go. I'll go wake up Scott."

Bud poured himself a mug of coffee, muddy black just as he liked it, and sat down at the sturdy wooden table to eat. Rosemary may not have been the fanciest cook, but he would take her eggs over a diner breakfast any day of the week. She fried the bacon first, then cooked the eggs in the leftover fat. No namby-pamby egg white omelets in this house. The Ritchies ate hearty meals filled with cholesterol and flavor. The groan of pleasure he released as he took his first bite attested to this fact.

Minutes later, as Bud was shoveling the last of the eggs in his mouth and the dogs were wolfing down a couple of bacon strips that had been conveniently dropped on the floor, Rosemary hurried down the stairs and called out, "Bud, he's not there."

"What do you mean?" he frowned. "Did he sleep in his bed or not?"

"I don't think so. The sheets are rumpled, but not as much as if he had slept there. There was an empty alcohol bottle under his bed and his phone is still charging next to the alarm clock," she said with a haunted look of déjà vu. "You don't think…"

The Specimen

Bud cut her off before she could voice her fears, "I know what you're thinking. Don't go there. He's all right. I'll call up Chuck and Kate and see if he's over there."

Reaching into his right pant pocket, Bud pulled out his cell phone and dialed the Monahans' home phone number. A minute later, he ended the call in frustration after well over twenty rings with no answer. No voice mail. Not even an answering machine.

"No answer?" asked Rosemary from the open sliding glass doors which led to their back yard and the forest beyond. Bleak clouds of black smoke still stained the sky above the trees and a breeze redolent of pungent smoke and soot carried through the air.

Bud grunted, "Nope." He turned and retrieved his car keys from the hook by the garage door and continued, "I'm going out looking for him. I'll try the Monahans' house first."

"I'm coming with you, too," said Rosemary.

Bud walked up to her and held her hand, "I don't think that's the best idea, sweetie. Someone needs to stay here in case he comes home."

"That's a load of crap, Bud, and you know it," she snapped. "I saw where the smoke was coming from. You even mentioned it…"

"Even so, hon. I need you to stay. I'll leave the boys with you, too. I've gotta follow my gut and check a few things out," he responded in a serious tone. "I'll call you immediately when I hear anything. Cross my heart, sweet pea."

His wife let out an exasperated sigh at his use of her pet name and he knew that he had convinced her. She would reluctantly follow his wishes, but he had used up quite a bit of his stored brownie points.

Less than fifteen minutes later, he rolled out of the driveway in his 2007 Dodge Ram pickup and headed up the gravel-covered side road to the main road leading to Monahans' house. He had tried to reach them by phone again, but, just as before, no one picked up. This was getting worrisome.

Bud felt a gnawing in his gut, tightness in his throat, and his temples were pounding with each drum of his heart, a sensation he had experienced only three times before in his life. He considered them his omens. Each had portended a catastrophic event that forever changed the direction of his life. Each time he had been helpless to do anything but witness the chaos.

Most recently, he had experienced a foreboding sense of disaster hours before learning of the suicide of his son, Vic. As a result, Bud had collapsed from what doctors called "a cardiac incident of unknown origin" and was rushed to the emergency room. Scott's father took his life that afternoon, only weeks after his wife Melanie's passing. Cowardly as always, in Bud's opinion. His son had never faced up to his responsibilities in life, and his death was a permanent reminder of his failures. While Bud was lying on a bed at St. Frank's, Vic was duct-taping a garden hose to the exhaust pipe of his Toyota Corolla and threading it past the driver's side window. In Bud's opinion, the only thing Vic had ever gotten right in his life was choosing Melanie as his wife and contributing half of Scott's chromosomes. Apparently Vic agreed with this sentiment, deciding to cut his losses and end it all.

Prior to his son's suicide, he had not been subjected to a premonition since the spring of '69 in Vietnam. Bud was stationed in country with the 1st Battalion, 7th Marines outside of Đà Nẵng when he came down with what had seemed to be the worst case of dysentery in the history of infectious intestinal disorders. Judging by the way he was avoided, many of the medical staff believed it as well. For over two weeks, Bud recovered in a military hospital in Đà Nẵng while the rest of the 1/7 were clearing out Quang Nam Province to the south. Combat was relentless, heavy and bloody. By the time he was well enough to rejoin his battalion, the majority of the fighting was over and thirteen of his friends had been killed. He was distraught. If not for his lack of intestinal fortitude, Bud had no doubt that he would have been among the casualties

Yet, despite the loss and trauma he had experienced on those two occasions, the first time he felt the now-familiar symptoms of oncoming catastrophe would always been the most memorable… and the one that pulled him out of his nightmares screaming a couple times per year.

The Specimen

Chapter 14 – The Man with One Nipple

"Fear is pain arising from the anticipation of evil."
– Aristotle

Modern Day – En route to Hartford, CT

My nipple! Holy shit*, I think she ate my fucking nipple*, thought Frank as he regained consciousness. He realized immediately that he was no longer at Greylock. Every part of his body hurt, from his face down to his feet, but the burning hole where his left nipple had once been was pure agony. He was once again hogtied with plastic zip-ties on his wrists and ankles, wearing only his blood spattered jeans. The rest of his clothes - shirt, socks and shoes - must have been left behind at the asylum. His face was pressed flat on a cold metal floor, highway thrumming the tires beneath him. Blood from his broken nose and lacerated lips had congealed on the cold metal surface in a small pool around his right cheek, but he did not move a muscle. Not that he could move much tied up as he was, but he wanted to be able to evaluate his current situation before his two captors figured out that he had woken up from his involuntary slumber.

Looking carefully around him, he realized that he was now riding in the back of the van that had been parked next to his car in the back lot of Shenanigans. He could hear muffled voices from the front seats, most likely the sadistic nipplevore, Miss Valentine, and her goon partner Stoopes.

Frank closed his eyes again and listened to the tires hum their vibrating dirge. By the dips and hills on the road, he sensed that they were slowly descending from the mountains, but he couldn't figure out the direction they were heading. From what he knew of the region, the only possible destinations were north to Vermont and Canada, west to Albany, or south towards Connecticut. Whichever way they were going, he hoped they would feed him soon or at least give him something to drink. He was parched and extremely lightheaded. The series of bare knuckle roundhouses from Stoopes had certainly rung his bell.

Despite the pain, Frank shifted his position and angled his head to try and hear what was being said in the front of the van. Each inch he moved pulled at a different bite or cut, sending slashes of agony through his brain as he tore his flesh again. Valentine seemed to be speaking with someone on a cell phone while Stoopes slouched in the driver's seat and stared at the winding road ahead of them.

He looked around the back of the van searching for anything that might help him escape… but it was bare except for some crumpled up take-out bags under the seat. Looking forward again, he caught the tail end of Valentine's conversation as she said, "Yes, Ma'am. We'll see you then," before ending the call. Glancing back behind her quickly, she caught Frank watching them before he could shut his eyes and feign unconsciousness.

"Well, lookie here, Stoopsie," sang Valentine gaily, craning for a look at Frank. "Somebody woke up from his nap." She swiveled her seat around and faced him, all the while grinning like The Cheshire Cat. "Feeling better, sleepyhead? You were out for a few hours there."

"And you snore like a motherfucker," interjected Stoopes. "Couldn't listen to my Kenny Rogers, 'cause you were so loud."

"I didn't snore before you broke my nose," Frank croaked.

Valentine cackled and swatted Stoopes on the shoulder, "He's got you there, partner. You did a number on it. His nose looks like a mini eggplant."

Stoopes just grunted, rolled his eyes and muttered, "Your boy better shut his mouth, less'n he wants me to smack him round once again and make him look like Porky Fucking Pig."

"Simmer down now," she responded. "No need to poison the air with hostility. Sheesh! You can certainly give it, man, but you can't take it. We still have a couple hours until we hit Hartford… and then we have that side trip as well to do some more research."

Frank watched as his two captors bickered, still searching for anything to use to his advantage, when something he saw stopped him cold. As the two up front discussed what Valentine perceived as Stoopes' utter lack of a sense of humor, she accentuated her point with something she held in her hand. Something metallic and rectangular, with a logo and an image on the other side.

The Specimen

Nausea bloomed in the pit of his abdomen. The image may not have been obvious to your everyday man of the street, but to a dedicated fan of science fiction like Frank was, the image was iconic – Han Solo frozen in carbonite after he was betrayed by the scoundrel Lando Calrissian at the end of The Empire Strikes Back. But what made the image even more memorable to Frank was the fact that he had the same exact one on the back of his iPhone. In other words, the phone which Valentine held in her hands right now.

Eventually Valentine noticed that everyone else had gone completely silent… Stoopes due to the fact that he was accustomed to tuning her out when she was on one of her tirades, and Frank because he was filled with dread, staring at his phone in her hand and imagining a myriad of horrendous outcomes.

"What's so interesting, Frank?" Valentine asked with a knowing smile on her lips. She continued as if he had responded. "Oh, wait … you think this looks just like your iPhone? No, it's just a coincidence. A lot of people have this picture on the back of their phone, right? Wear your geekiness like a badge of honor. Am I right?"

Frank did his best not to scream and beg for his life as Valentine stared him down.

Stoopes chuckled, "Give the man a break, girl. You already gave him some permanent reminders of your date. Just cut to the chase."

She glanced in her partner's direction with an annoyed look, then turned back to Frank and continued with a rock-steady gaze to impress upon him the importance of her next statement, "Your Aunt Elvira sounds like a sweet old lady, Frankie. I can't wait to meet her when we stop off in Cambridge after we drop you off with the rest of our guests. Dr. Colfax is especially looking forward to meeting you."

Frank could only cry out in horror as Nina stabbed him in the thigh with a hypodermic needle and he was sent back into the dark abyss of his subconscious.

*From the Personal Journal
of Dr. Saul Eckenrode
Clinical Director
Mount Greylock Institute*

September 28, 1965

Harry had quite a disturbing episode today…

I am being vague for a reason. What happened today at lunch does not seem to have any specific triggers or symptoms (somatic or psychological) that would lead me to diagnose him with any commonly known malady.

We were playing our daily game of chess. He had only picked at his food (a delicious beef stew, I might add) and seemed under the weather. I was winning the game by a significant margin and probably could have placed him in check within two to three moves. This was quite unusual, to say the least, considering that he now wins 3 out of every 4 games. Harry was obviously too tired and distracted to play.

When I asked about his general health one time (when Fenton was outside on a smoking break), he shrugged his shoulders and stated that he wasn't sleeping much lately. I asked if Dr. Coe met with him at night, he mumbled something noncommittal and clammed up, unwilling to add anything else. Obviously that is a taboo subject.

A few seconds later was when it happened. I had just placed his king into check after an abnormally careless move on his part when I noticed that Harry was drooling. A long, swinging strand of saliva hung from his chin as he stared fixedly at a spot on the floor between his feet.

"Harry?" I asked him tentatively. "Young man, are you okay?"

He didn't answer and I stood from my chair, calling for Fenton. No response there either. I opened my office door and peered down the long, dark corridor. No one. He must be smoking outside, or on one of the open balconies in the South Wing. I returned to Harry's side and gently shook his shoulder. Again, no response.

I reached down and grasped his left wrist to take his pulse. It was rapid, but quite strong, so it was unlikely that his sudden catatonia was result of any circulatory problems. I released his arm only to have my right wrist suddenly and brutally clutched by Harry with a strength that belied his scrawny frame. His nails cut into me, leaving white half-moon

The Specimen

indentations in my flesh. I yelled in surprise and agony as he drew me closer to bring his mouth to my ear.

For one panic-stricken second, I was certain that he would clamp down upon my ear and gnaw it down to a ragged nub, crunching the cartilage between his teeth. Just like Wick had done as he had ground Scarpa's bony beak like a piece of gristle and then swallowed it down with a shit-eating (nose-eating) bloody grin.

And then he spoke.

"Nehuatlahtec... Nehcuecuetzotoc... Tlayohua... Tlatlaukitezkatl"

His voice was... how can I explain? It was his voice, yet it was not. It was as if some other individual was speaking through him with his voice, but it was forced, as if this person did not know how to use his throat to speak, nor did he know English. It wasn't gibberish. The words sounded like they were from an actual language, but not one with which I was familiar. Something ancient and primal.

Then his eyes welled with tears and he said one more word. This one I understood.

"Help," he whispered in anguish as he turned around and pulled down the collar of his shirt, baring his shoulders and upper back.

At first I didn't know what I was looking at. It was too alien. I initially interpreted it as a horrific keloid scar to the right of his spine that wrapped around his torso under the shoulder blade to finish on his abdomen. He must have had an unbelievably monstrous injury for a scar that size, I thought. But then my perception shifted and I saw it for what it truly was... a horrid, living creature embedded in his flesh.

I must have flinched and cried out in shock, because Harry was suddenly himself again. He found me pulling his collar low, staring at his passenger, and he looked ashamed. Claiming that he felt ill, he pulled away from me and fled out my office door to return to his room. I was still extremely shaken from what I had just seen, so I did not follow him out of my office.

One thing is certain, though. Now I know why Dr. Coe was interested in him, and I want to learn more. It's time to find out what she plans on doing to him. I think it is time to investigate...

- S.

October 2, 1965

    Coe's little sidekick, Dr. Colfax, always seems to be working in his lab whenever I attempt to investigate. I have not been able to learn anything yet. That kid – inexperienced child, if you ask me – creeps me the hell out. He looks like Lucille Ball and Don Knotts had a son. All long arms and legs. Bright red frizzy hair slicked back with an overload of Vitalis. And his personality is even worse.

    In my rounds, I often see him stationed in the corner of the general recreation room observing a variety of patients. He is obviously quite interested in Harry, but there are others who have caught his eye as well – namely Angelo Scarpa and, for some unknown reason, one of our permanent residents, Richard Hutchens. The three of them couldn't be any different.

    Scarpa returned from the hospital a few days ago. He was given a prosthetic nose, but he refused to wear it. Can't blame him. It looks like it was removed from a pair of Groucho Marx glasses. Instead he leaves the rough gash of his sinus cavity open to the air. We allow him to carry a handkerchief around with him so he can blot the mucus that continuously leaks from the ragged hole.

    He is subdued now because we have increased his dosage of Thorazine, but the staff is always watching him for the eventual violent outburst. It's anyone's guess why Colfax would be interested in him.

    His interest in Hutchens is another thing entirely. The man is one step away from catatonia. I can only surmise that he is being considered for one of their behavioral experiments. Truly disturbing. He looks at the patients so clinically, as if they were rats in a maze. I often wonder if he has any emotions. Coe might be a cold fish, but this one has the charm of a corpse.

    -S.

The Specimen

Chapter 15 - Code Brown

*"Boys, set the terror level at code brown,
'cause I need to change my pants."*
– The President of the United States in *Monsters vs. Aliens*

Modern Day – St. Francis Children's Hospital

Dr. Anita Chacon was not in the best of moods. Close to sixteen hours into a double shift in the Emergency Room at St. Francis Children's Hospital in Waltham, Massachusetts, she was already counting the minutes until she could rush home, strip out of her toxic scrubs, shower off the layers of filth that had accumulated overnight, and dive into bed for a well-deserved slumber. It had been an extremely rough night. For the first time since she clocked in just before four yesterday afternoon, she was able to sit down, drink some coffee (even if it was hours old, concentrated and oily) and catch her breath. The only food she had eaten since her double shift began was a barely edible Hot Pocket and a handful of communal E. Coli-flavored gummi bears she had swiped from a bowl at the nurses' station.

This was absolutely the last time she covered for a colleague at the last minute, even if it was her best (and only) friend, Colleen Breslin, also an ER resident. They had attended the same school since they were roommates in undergrad and they had both been hired at St. Frank's within days of each other. Now, in their second year of residency, they shared an apartment, but they rarely saw each other more than a few minutes per day because they worked different shifts. It was almost like they were married, without the sex. Not that she had seen any activity in that department since graduation from medical school, either. For the past few years, her social life was a vast barren landscape strewn with the corpses of blind dates and drunken encounters.

Each industry has its own internal language or slang - acronyms or euphemisms for situations that crop up frequently. Some terms are unique to a specific location, while others are universal throughout the field. Medicine is no exception. One of the most commonly used terms is a Code Brown, meaning that a patient has lost control of his bowels, usually on the floor or bed, and someone is needed to clean it up. Chacon had her own personal definition for the commonly used term, meaning that the proverbial shit was in the process of hitting the fan. Today was definitely one of those days.

She had realized almost immediately that it was going to be a Code Brown shift with the first case she saw. Milo, a young man with a shaved head and numerous tattoos, had hobbled in with a 103 degree fever and severely infected wounds in both hands and feet. His extremities were swollen to nearly twice their size and green, foul-smelling pus was leaking from all four wounds. His hands were the worst. Fingers swollen like hot dogs, purplish and tender. The injuries were in the center of the palms of his hands and the soles of his feet, approximately the diameter of a dime, penetrating through and through. Homemade stigmata, apparently.

Milo was self-proclaimed "guerrilla street artist." Three days earlier, he and a few fellow artists had put on an impromptu exhibit in Faneuil Hall in Boston. As the central component, Milo had been crucified on a home-made cross constructed from used railroad ties and wheeled around the marketplace by a half dozen flagellants whipping themselves with ropes made of braided Twizzlers. Milo had been painted from head to toe in dog feces, wearing a sign around his neck with the statement "GOD BLESS OUR CORPORATE OVERLORDS."

Regardless of the artists' message, what was obvious was the fact that they hadn't consider the potential negative effects of fecal matter smeared over open wounds. After they had been chased off by the Boston police, Milo and his friends had washed off by tripping on shrooms and bathing in the fountain in a local park, not exactly the most sanitary of swimming holes. Anita was amazed that he had not required immediate amputation of at least one body part. As it was, he could still end up with permanent nerve damage and some loss of movement in his hands.

The next couple hours were a parade of the four standard Friday night casualties: bar fights, domestic violence, car accidents, alcohol poisoning or any combination of the above. There was even a Goth girl drama queen who claimed that "something in a fucking jar" bit her on the hand. The hand was cut pretty deeply, but it was a smooth laceration requiring seventeen stitches in the meat of her palm - nothing resembling

The Specimen

teeth marks at all. It was definitely the result of a very sharp blade of some sort. Anita was sure the girl was probably stoned on something anyway, considering the way she carried on. Once she had been stitched and bandaged, they sent her on her way, bitching and moaning all the way out the door.

A few minutes after midnight, at the start of Anita's 2nd shift, the ER welcomed a rare occurrence, a case that involved all four of the categories, known among the hospital staff as a Grand Slam.

The patient, Dennis Boyle, had gotten into an argument with his on-again, off-again girlfriend Maggie while out at a local *TGIFriday's* with a group of friends. Catching Dennis ogling another woman, Maggie had coldcocked him, smashing the glass pitcher of beer over his head.

Large glass objects tend to be sharp when shattered and this instance was no exception. Dennis fell immediately to the floor gushing blood from a jagged three-inch gash across his forehead and left temple. Fortunately for them, their friend Marcus was an EMT with a large first aid kit in his car. They bandaged Dennis' wound immediately and drove off to the hospital. Their luck had apparently run out though, because Marcus' car was T-boned by a fellow bar-hopper in Ford pickup as they pulled out of the parking lot. None of them were wearing seatbelts. In the ambulance ride from the accident site, all three victims were discovered to have blood alcohol levels well above the legal limit, but Dennis topped them all with a mark of 0.29. As a reward, he earned himself a stomach pump. *Grand Slam.*

With those three cases, tonight would have easily earned a spot on her personal list of All-Time Crappy Days at Work, but her most recent case may have bumped today's shifts directly to number one… with a bullet. Despite the fact that the ER was crowded, rather normal for a Friday overnight shift, Dr. Chacon desperately needed to take a moment by herself and decompress after this latest case.

About four and a half hours ago, a boy in his early teens was flown in from Chesterfield by helicopter to the ER, victim of a motor vehicle accident. No identification and in critical condition. Near dawn, he had run out of the woods onto a road right into the path of a minivan. The minivan won hands down. The boy had broken his collarbone, both

128

femurs, his right ankle, his left ulna, eight ribs (one which punctured his left lung), multiple fingers, and his pelvis was shattered in five places. As far as internal injuries, the aforementioned lung had collapsed, plus he had burst his spleen and shards of his pelvis had perforated his colon. To top it all off, he had a tremendous road rash on both forearms and the right half of his face.

Any one of these injuries were serious enough that he could soon die of complications, but they weren't what made his case extraordinary. Dr. Chacon had treated many instances where individuals had been struck by a vehicle and the results were never pretty. Simple physics. The object with the most mass will deliver the most force in a collision of two objects traveling at the same velocity. If that object is traveling at a much faster velocity than the smaller object (in this case, the boy), then the damage caused is exponentially higher. Even without extenuating circumstances, survival from such an impact would be miraculous. In this case, it was even more unlikely.

Before his clothes had been sliced off, it had been assumed by everyone that the young man was simply an unfortunate casualty of a night of drinking and debauchery in the woods away from the prying eyes of parents and the police. The stench of whiskey emanated from the boy's blood-and-vomit-soaked shirts and jeans. Once the source of much of the external blood was revealed, the reason for his early morning flight became apparent. He had been shot twice: once in his right hip, barely missing his femoral artery, and once in the meat of his left forearm, splintering the ulna. Someone had obviously been chasing him and trying to kill him. There was much more to this story than had initially been apparent. *What could such a young boy have done to become the target of a killer?* she wondered.

Chacon was amazed he had survived so far. Once it was known that he had been shot, the hospital had immediately alerted the police. This had gone from a tragic accident to an attempted murder. Until more was known about the patient, it was quite likely that he would be placed under protective custody with round-the-clock officers sitting outside his room. In her time at St. Frank's, she had seen situations like this only a few times. Usually it involved medical procedures for inmates from one of the

The Specimen

nearby Massachusetts Correctional Institutions, either Cedar Junction in Walpole or Bay State over in Norfolk. A few months back, an officer was posted outside the room of a gangbanger who had been shot thirteen times in a drive-by, allegedly by a rival gang. Protection was deemed necessary in case of retaliation for a prior beef or an attempt to make a name for oneself. Similar precautions were likely to take place in this boy's case. At least until his family was found.

She gulped down the last of her coffee, grimacing at the gritty grounds that always seemed to collect in the bottom of her cup. Just one more pass through the ER to see if there were any new cases to treat, then she would check in on the boy and leave instructions for the incoming shift before she could go home and crawl into bed. She was off until Monday evening and she intended to live in her pajamas until it was absolutely necessary to return from her self-imposed isolation. Colleen was off tomorrow, too. Perhaps they could split a couple bottles of wine and watch a couple old Molly Ringwald movies. Colleen might want to go out to a club, but that just wasn't Anita's style anymore. In the immortal words of Danny Glover in the *Lethal Weapon* series, "I'm getting too old for this shit."

She returned to the ER at 7:30, surveying the waiting room and the patients currently being examined. The waiting room was surprisingly empty except for a towering man in a trench coat watching soap operas on the television in the corner. Something was wrong with his face - burns, scars - whatever they were, it wouldn't look good if she was caught staring, so she surreptitiously averted her gaze and checked the list of patients who were already getting treated.

There were two motor vehicle accident victims, an 18 month-old with a nasty-sounding case of croup, a young woman with alcohol poisoning who was on her way to getting her stomach pumped, and a 73 year-old man who had fallen off his roof after getting the urge to clean the gutters on his house just after dawn. After checking the gutter cleaner's back to make certain he hadn't injured his spine, she spent a little time with the toddler, comforting the family more than the child who was currently gobbling up a free popsicle.

As she was about to call it a night, a timid voice behind her said, "Dr. Chacon?"

She turned with a raised eyebrow and found Cindy Orton, one of the 3rd shift nurses, standing there. Cindy was in her first year and, unlike most of the ER nurses who could probably match up with any patient they encountered, Dr. Chacon rarely had any patience for her, considering her too skittish to succeed in the ER. She would be much better off handling cases in the Prenatal Intensive Care Unit (PICU).

In her first year at St. Frank's, a gunshot victim had been brought in coked up to the gills and screaming obscenities in two different languages: English and her native Russian. Add the fact that Olga the Cossack (the name Chacon gave her when retelling this tale to her friends and colleagues) was pregnant and weighed well over 300 pounds, and one could imagine the scene she made. It took Chacon and three nurses to pin her down on the gurney while restraints were put in place by a fourth nurse. In the process of Olga bucking like a rodeo bull, one nurse was scratched across the face and Dr. Chacon had her left eye blackened when she was blindsided with a kick from a mud-covered Timberland boot. When they finally had Olga restrained, Chacon turned around to see Cindy shaking in a nearby corner, eyes boggling at what she had just seen. Since then, Chacon had no use for her except to deliver messages between floors.

"Yes, Cindy," she answered as she held back a sigh. "I hope this is important. I'm working a double shift and I'm due to go home in less than ten minutes."

"I'm sorry, Dr. Chacon," she stammered. "It's just that the police are here about the boy who was hit by a car. You had us call them?"

"Crap," she cursed. "Fine. Where are they?"

"They're out in the lobby. Should I bring them in? They want to visit the boy".

"That's not going to happen right now. He's in an induced coma and it's unlikely to stop until he heals for a few days. Bring them into the conference room. I'll talk with them there."

Cindy nodded and hurried out to the hospital lobby. She returned two minutes later, towing two individuals behind her, just as Chacon was

The Specimen

opening the conference room door. Plainclothes detectives apparently, since neither wore a uniform. One was a short, smiling, stocky man in his late 30's with flaming red hair buzzed short and more freckles than Chacon had ever seen on a single person in her life. The other individual was a tall angular woman, at least six feet tall, with mousy brown hair in a tight bun, minimal makeup and a grim, humorless gaze. Hopefully this would be quick and painless. She did not need to stay long after her shift ended to kowtow to a couple of detectives.

"Please, sit down," she said, gesturing to a leather chair as she took a seat across from them. "There's no need to stand and I'd like to get off my feet for a bit after the night we've had."

"I completely agree," responded the redheaded man with a shit-eating grin. "Detective Mike Murphy at your service and this is my partner, Detective LaDonna O'Malley. We're here to follow up on the young boy who was struck by a vehicle earlier this morning."

"I'm Dr. Anita Chacon, head resident here," she responded, forcing a grin. She hoped it didn't appear as plastic as it felt. Murphy reached out, clasped her hand and shook it in greeting. His palm was rough and calloused, bringing to mind industrial sandpaper. O'Malley kept her hands clasped tightly in her lap and nodded in greeting.

What a cold fish, thought Chacon. *Even her eyes look dead. Girlfriend needs to get laid more often.*

"I worked on the young man when he arrived. Obviously he's lucky to be alive. Even more so, considering the bullet wounds we discovered in addition to the broken bones and head trauma he suffered from the impact."

"Bullet wounds?" Murphy asked. He cast a sidelong glance at his partner.

"Yes, weren't you told? We reported it as soon as they were discovered. Initially, all the blood was believed to have resulted from his other injuries. Honestly, it's a miracle he didn't die immediately."

"That's definitely true," he agreed. "Luckily for him, the speed limit on that road is only thirty-five miles per hour. That may be what saved him. Otherwise, we would have needed the medical examiner rather than an ambulance. I once saw someone who jumped off an overpass into the path of a semi…"

O'Malley coughed, interrupting Murphy, "Let's not get sidetracked now. I'm sure the doctor has things to attend to." She locked eyes with her partner and continued, "We'd like to post an officer outside his room until he regains consciousness."

"I sincerely doubt that will happen any time soon," replied Chacon. "He has a long road ahead of him, if he even makes it through the next day or so."

"Be that as it may," Murphy jumped in. "We still have no idea who this young man is. Even if he only wakes for a moment, we'd like to contact his family before they learn of his condition."

"That's certainly our wish as well, Detectives," Chacon agreed. "However, I'm not the person with the authority to approve something like this. I'm pretty sure that needs to be cleared with the hospital's administration."

O'Malley sighed, obviously growing impatient, "Dr… Chavez, was it?"

"Chacon," Murphy corrected her. *Bitch.*

"Yes, excuse me. Dr. Chacon." she repeated, glaring daggers at her partner. "How can we expedite this? With whom should we speak? I'm sure you agree this is an important matter."

"You'd most likely want to speak with our Chief of Staff, Dr. Charles Jarvis. He makes all the decisions regarding the day-to-day functioning of St. Frank's." She paused, "If I had to guess where he was right now on a Saturday morning, he's probably teeing up at the Norfolk County Country Club. He never schedules surgery on the weekends," she said sheepishly. "We can page him, but he's not likely to answer unless it's a 911."

"And this wouldn't qualify?" asked Murphy.

"Unfortunately, no. Not in his mind. The boy is in critical condition, but he's stable."

Murphy sighed and pushed out his chair in exasperation, stating, "Damn bureaucracy, huh? Whole damned world is run by the fuckin' bean counters."

The Specimen

He stood as if to leave, but O'Malley stayed seated, silently scowling and brooding while fixating at a spot on the wall above Chacon's head.

"I'll be sure to have someone call you when we know, or when he wakes up. Either one," Chacon stated as she got ready to leave as well. *God, do I need to sleep. This day can't end any sooner.*

O'Malley remained silent for a few more awkward seconds, the stood up slowly and turned to Murphy, "Change of plans, Spooky."

Murphy glared up at his partner and growled, "Don't. Call. Me. Spooky." He looked over at Chacon, then back at O'Malley, "You sure you want it to go down this way? You know he won't be happy."

"I don't care anymore. Time to clean up this mess."

Chacon looked at the two detectives in confusion. The vibe in the room had thoroughly changed. What had been a polite, congenial meeting suddenly took on an air of menace. She realized belatedly that neither detective had presented her with any ID. She had simply assumed they were who they said they were. They probably weren't even with the police.

Fucking Cindy, she thought acidly. *She is so fired after this. So goddamn fired. This is the last time she fucks up. I'll make sure of it.*

O'Malley smiled for the first time since she had entered the room. The smile was broad, cold and predatory with a full span of gleaming white teeth. Her eyes remained dull black and dead, like a shark's.

A fucking shark. That's what she is. I should have seen it before.

"What's going on here?" she asked, pushing back from the conference table and rising to her feet, hands in her pockets. "Are you detectives or not? Can I see some identification? Why are you really here?"

The woman who had been introduced as Detective LaDonna O'Malley chuckled abruptly, "Don't worry, Doctor. You'll find out soon enough." She reached down to her holster and pulled out her gun, pointing it directly between Chacon's eyes. "Right now, though, take us to the boy. Immediately. Unless you'd prefer to have your brains blown out the back of your skull."

Code Brown Alert.
Shit just got real.

Pete Kahle

Official Report on the Greylock Incident

February 1, 1966
To: Members of the Governing Council, ACME Group
From: James P. Kilcannon, Agent-in-Charge
RE: Greylock Incident (Thralls)

Dear Council,

    The following entries in the diary should illuminate Dr. Coe's activities in the days leading up to the blackout and the chaos that followed. We believe these notes may reveal the decisions that were made to alter the focus of the study, and would eventually lead to the catastrophic events on which we are compiling evidence now.

                            - JPK

                *   *   *

Day 31

    It is time. Tomorrow we will finally be ready to remove the specimen from the boy's back. When I informed him of the imminent procedure, the boy actually became quite excited. Unlike previous operations, he seems eager for the day to arrive. He wants the creature removed. Understandable.

    Even so, I chose not to tell him of the risk - that we have no idea how deeply connected the Rider's tissue is intertwined with his spinal cord and brain. There is no need for him to know about the emergency procedures that may need to be performed. We are prepared for the worst case scenario. Regardless... all great discoveries come with casualties.

The Specimen

On a side note, Colfax had an idea for another experiment and, truthfully, it intrigues me. Is the Rider able to infect animals? Once the Rider has been safely removed and both the boy and creature are stabilized, I gave him permission to move ahead with his experiment. You would have thought I had given him the keys to Dr. Frankenstein's laboratory. He was so happy. Maybe this will keep him busy for the time being.

- GC

Day 32

We are ready for the procedure. The boy is about to be sedated and prepped. Colfax will be at my side assisting with the removal. In addition to the electromagnetic locks, Fenton and Jameson are keeping watch in the hallway to prevent a certain Dr. Eckenrode from snooping again.

This morning, I attempted to speak with the creature one final time before it and the boy are separated. It barely spoke with me... as if it were sulking. I shouldn't anthropomorphize it, though. Though it originally spoke in a tongue that originated in Mesoamerica and it appeared to learn English in less than a week, I do not believe that it is inherently intelligent. If my theory holds, I believe we will learn that the creature only gains intelligence if its hosts are intelligent and that the effect is cumulative. Its personality is a combination of all the personalities of its hosts, both past and present.

The more Hosts one of its kind Rides over the decades – even centuries - the more "human" it may come to appear, but in the end, I believe that it is still an animal mimicking a person. If it had a series of hosts that are animals, my belief is that it would present itself as an amalgam of the beasts that it had ridden. The length of each Host's Ride would determine how much of the creature's personality would consist of each one's contribution. Most interesting would be a case where the creature has been hosted by both animals and humans. Would the result be a human intelligence with animal instincts? Or a savage animal with the intellect of man? Just one of the many interesting queries we should file away for later.

- GC

Day 33

I have successfully separated the creature from the boy, and the operation appears to have been relatively smooth. The Rider has retreated into a state that resembles the torpor we have seen when it is exposed to electric shock, while the boy is still under heavy sedation. We will take our time bringing him out of the induced sleep in order to ascertain if he has suffered any neurological damage from the procedure. The risk was significant, but no complications were noticed at the time.

- GC

Day 34

Both the Rider and the boy remain catatonic, but I have our other experiments to occupy me while we wait for them to revive.

There have been some astonishing results with samples 45-64, the ones which were exposed to increased levels of radiation. Of these, samples 61-64 have exhibited cellular breakdown and samples 45-51 showed no change at all, but the remaining nine samples have all shown extraordinary growth rates. Unbelievable, in fact. Though their initial sizes were less than a cubic centimeter on average, they have increased their mass approximately one thousand-fold.

The Specimen

As of today, the nine of them are each about the size of a small tangerine. Their combined mass is greater than the original specimen. Despite their size increase, none of their cells appear to have undergone any specialization. All the cells resemble human stem cells in structure, but it is difficult to determine whether they stay that way when the organism is conscious. Due to their abilities, it has always been deemed necessary to keep them sedated when examining them. If their growth doesn't slow down, we could be in for quite a surprise. I will need to develop a protocol for these specimens ASAP.

Is it possible that, through exposure to a certain spectrum of radiation, we have induced a mutation that has induced some form of spontaneous reproduction? Prior to this, we have always assumed that Riders need a host to reproduce, and that reproduction happens only in extremely rare cases. If this is indeed the case, I need to determine whether this development is unique, or if it is reproducible in nature, and if that turns out to be the case, countermeasures must be developed. Immediately.

- GC

Day 38

The boy finally woke up today, but he is barely responsive, so far. His eyes show response to stimuli and he vocalizes random sounds when addressed, but in truth, I believe this only to be an involuntary reaction. For all intents and purposes, he is in a vegetative state. How long he remains in this condition remains to be seen. His memories, or what remain of them, are likely buried in his deep subconscious.

At this point, I estimate his chances of recovery as 50/50, but regretfully there will always be some deficits in his cognition and memory retention. This is a truly unfortunate result, but I believe it is all for the greater good.

Eckenrode has been a nuisance since he learned of the boy's condition. He has even gone to the paranoid lengths of claiming that we intended to leave him in this condition... not that he knows anything whatsoever about what we were doing. He is under the laughable impression that the procedure we performed was a prefrontal lobotomy. An unsuccessful one at that. Ridiculous. If I were to perform such a barbaric operation, the boy would never have been left in this state. No, this is the direct result of how deep the parasite was intertwined with the boy's central nervous system.

Unlike my dear Dr. Eckenrode, I am simply not an emotional buffoon who despairs at unfavorable results. I examine them, learn from the compiled data, implement new precautions and move on. Now is time to focus on the future. Dwelling on the past is completely counterproductive.

Next on the agenda is the transfer of the Rider to another host. We have a number of candidates already here. Why not use such an opportune resource? Fenton and Jameson could easily abduct an indigent from Springfield, but that would be unnecessarily time-consuming. Here we can choose the candidate with the characteristics most appropriate for the program. Additionally, despite their deep pockets, the Council does appreciate thriftiness.

- GC

The Specimen

Chapter 16 – Clusterfucked

"Everyone carries around his own monsters."
- Richard Pryor

Modern Day – St. Francis Children's Hospital

"**LaDonna? Are you serious?** I should kick your ass for that, Geist," scowled Jennifer Bohannon as she pulled a zip-tie out of her pocket and secured the unconscious doctor to the wall bar in the handicapped stall. "Next time I'm picking the names."

Guarding the door to the hall, her partner, Randy Geist whispered, "Fine. Just speed it up, Jen. I don't like it in here."

"Are you seriously afraid of getting caught in the ladies' room?"

"Old habits die hard. We should have stuffed her in a maintenance closet like I suggested." He shook his head in frustration, "Besides, I don't want to draw any more attention. Let's just do this, head back to the kid's room and remove the threat"

"Listen, Spooky. Shut the fuck up and quit bitching. I'm almost done," she said as she crossed over to the sinks and grabbed a long swath of paper towels. She crumpled the towels up in a ball and shoved them in the mouth of the doctor, so she couldn't scream.

"How long will she be out?"

"Not certain. She'll be paralyzed at least a couple hours from the injection, but I did hit her pretty hard, so that could make it last longer," Bohannon guessed. "This should prevent anyone from finding her for a while."

She taped a paper sign on which was written OUT OF ORDER in large red, block letters on the stall door, and then placed a yellow folding WET FLOOR sign on the floor outside the stall. For good measure, she poured some water outside the stall door.

She continued and chuckled, "Few things are avoided like an overflowing toilet, especially in a hospital. Now let's get back to the kid."

* * *

Under duress, Dr. Chacon had led them to the boy's room: 5th floor, Room 515 in the Critical Care Unit. Once they looked in the door and confirmed that it was in fact his room, they moved to the closest ladies' room and, resisting the temptation to kill her, instead knocked her unconscious and tied her up. Quillian had specified that he wanted as few complications as possible and they were not about to intentionally defy him and incur his wrath. Both had experience with it, and it was not pretty.

They entered Room 515 and closed the door behind them, leaving the lights dim to avoid attention. The room was double occupancy, but only the bed on the far left was filled. The other bed had been stripped because its most recent tenant had passed away in the night. Bohannon approached the boy's bed while Geist stood watch at the door.

The boy was wrapped in plaster and bandages from head to toe. Tubes, electrodes, pulleys, ropes, metal stabilizers and a myriad of other medical contraptions were strewn around his bed. His face was swollen to a grotesque size and remnants of dried blood were still evident in his ears and nose. A tube snaked down his throat to help him breathe, while monitors on a cart next to the bed tracked his brainwaves and heart rate.

"He's not going to wake up, Jen," stated Geist. "Just take care of it like Quillian said and let's get out of here. No need to drag it out. It's a simple contract."

"It's never a simple contract, Randy. That's why you'll still be doing this shit in a decade and I'll be running my own division in the Group. You follow orders without thinking. You lack ambition." She turned and looked at the medical chart before continuing, "Whoa... Johnny here is fucked up. Probably would have been better if Murtaugh had put him out of his misery. Quick and easy. I guess it doesn't matter now that we're here. Am I right?"

Geist ignored her question and continued his line of thinking aloud, "You ever think that I may be happy doing exactly what I'm doing? It's a straightforward job. The hours are terrific. I get to travel all over the globe. I'm making more money than I'll ever need," he protested. "I don't lack ambition. My goals are simply different than yours. Hell, in a decade,

The Specimen

I'll be retired in the Florida Keys, tanned and sipping on a cocktail in a lounge chair in my Speedo thong."

"Thanks for that horrific mental image. Not sure you'll tan much with your pigmentation, though, ginger man," she said while pulling a large syringe filled with a transparent golden liquid from her pocket.

"Bite me... but you get what I'm saying, right? You can have your promotions and increased responsibility. I just want to do my time and live out my life in paradise," he said. "What the...?"

Bohannon immediately tensed and asked, "What's wrong?" She stepped back from the bed and unsnapped her holster.

"Shhh... I thought I saw something move," he whispered as he crouched near the door. "Oh Shi--!!"

Crashing open, the door slammed into Geist mid-sentence, knocking him across the room with such force that he made a massive dent in the opposite wall before collapsing to the floor. Bohannon cursed loudly and dropped to her knees, pulling her pistol from its holster.

A bald, hulking silhouette stood framed in the doorway. As it strode into the light, she could see that the intruder was well over six feet, wearing hospital scrubs and a face mask covering everything below the eyes. Or to be more accurate, where the eyes should have been. Above the mask was a smooth expanse of skin, reminiscent of a birth caul, translucent and glistening with fluids. A small nodule migrated from its left temple, rippling beneath the skin to where the eye socket would be. A slit formed on the surface of the nodule, splitting open to reveal an eye. Yellowish sclera and a large green iris filled the newly born organ, pointed directly at Bohannon.

"Oh, Christ! Geist, you gotta get up now! It's a Cluster! It's a fucking Cluster!" Bohannon screamed at her partner. She pulled the trigger several times in succession, hitting the interloper twice, once in the abdomen and once in the right shoulder. Three other shots went wide. Two hit the wall and door frame. One became embedded in a metal water fountain ten yards down the hall. A chorus of screams filled the corridor as nurses, visitors and patients ducked into rooms or behind counters to get out of the line of fire.

The figure staggered when hit, but there was surprisingly minimal blood. A second later, two masses of flesh – one from each wound site – sloughed off its body and landed on the floor with a muffled splat. The flesh liquefied quickly, leaving puddles of slime and the two bullets in the center of them. Two more eyes sprouted on its face, one focused on Bohannon and one on Geist. The first eye slid up the behemoth's forehead over its scalp and reformed on the back of its skull to watch the hall behind it.

Obviously deciding that Geist was the less immediate threat, it moved toward Bohannon, lashing at her gun. Its right arm had reformed into a long whip-like appendage that wrapped around the gun and her hand. With a sudden wrench, her wrist was brutally snapped and the gun went flying across the room. It hurled Bohannon to the floor and turned to face her partner.

Against the wall, Geist came out of his daze and fumbled for his gun. He pulled himself up, grabbed the window sill and sent two shots in the creature's direction, winging it with one bullet and imploding the television on the wall with the second. A blaring alarm sounded in the hall and a voice repeated over the loudspeaker, "Code Silver. 5th floor. Security, please respond. Code Silver, 5th floor." Another lump of flesh fell off the creature to the floor and quickly dissolved into a pool of pinkish sludge.

Bohannon cried out from the floor, "Geist, aim for the primary node. The primary! Use the taser!" Her right wrist hung limp and twisted as she pulled herself under the bed and fumbled for her taser. She had lost the syringe in the struggle with the Cluster, but an extended jolt from the electrical device should serve the same purpose. In his current condition, the boy's heart would easily be stopped. It wouldn't be subtle, but she would deal with Quillian later. They had already screwed the pooch on this mission. Time to salvage what they could, if they even survived the attack. Clusters rarely left survivors.

A chorus of muttering resonated from the Cluster. A random cacophony at first, the varied syllables merged to form a single communal voice that sounded as if a swarm of insects had discovered speech. "Leeeave... The... Booooy... A... Looone," it buzzed as it lumbered

The Specimen

towards Geist. He aimed his Glock at its "head" and center mass and fired the remaining seven rounds from less than ten feet away. He hit his target six times, with only one shot going astray, blowing a hole in the ceiling. The first hit carved a 2 inch-deep divot out of its left temple, while the other 5 shots all hit directly above where its sternum would normally be if its anatomy was an actual analogue of the human body.

It listed to the right with the temple shot, but the other wounds appeared to have almost no effect. Geist scrambled to clutch his taser with his right hand, while reaching out with his left to hold it off for enough time to give it a jolt. He grasped its scrubs to fend it off, but was unable to dodge the pile-driver roundhouse that slammed into his jaw and sent blood and teeth flying. The back of his head connected with the windowsill sending a blinding pain throughout his body as he was hoisted up off the floor, and hurled at the glass window. His pistol and taser tumbled to the floor and rolled under the bed as he reached for any handhold to prevent his fall. In a last ditch effort, Geist held onto the front of the cluster's scrubs, but they easily tore away and he flew out in an explosion of shattered glass. A few branches slightly broke his fall as he plummeted through the tree next to the room's window. Even with their occasional interruption, he hit the pavement with a sickening thud, and lay there in a pile of broken limbs. A pool of blood soon stained the sidewalk next to his head.

Five stories above, the battle continued unabated. Three hospital security guards barreled into the room in response to the alarm and stopped short in shock at the scene of destruction. The oldest of the three took one look at the towering intruder and instantly turned tail, yelling, "OH, HELL NO!" as he fled down the corridor. The Cluster's scrub shirt was hanging in rags. Any doubt that it wasn't human was gone. Its torso rippled with muscles intertwined with irregular bony plates that served as organic armor. Geist's five bullets were embedded in this carapace, and as the seconds passed, they were slowly extruded, grotesquely reminiscent of boils being lanced, and the bullets covered in oozing discharge dribbled out of the wounds to land in a metallic clatter on the floor.

From beneath the bed, Bohannon shouted, "Shoot it! Shoot it! Move your fat asses and shoot the bastard!" She pulled herself out from under the boy's bed on the side opposite the cluster, clutching her right hand to her chest and Geist's gun in her left. The closest guard fumbled with his gun, raising it to aim at the Cluster just as it threw an end table that hit him directly in the face. His nose and mouth burst in a shower of teeth and blood and he was knocked out before he hit the floor.

The last remaining guard dove to the left and rolled behind the unoccupied bed. Crying and screaming, "Oh my God, Oh my God, Oh my God!" she popped up and unloaded her pistol into the creature that had laid low her colleague. All eight bullets miraculously hit it dead center in the head, bursting it like an overripe melon. The chattering voices stopped immediately and its massive body slumped to the floor, leaking blackish-green ichor from the many holes in its pulverized flesh.

Meanwhile, Bohannon climbed out from under the boy's bed and placed the gun next to him. She reached into her jacket pocket and pulled the taser out, then leaned over him to properly apply it to his temple. At full power, it would thoroughly broil his brain and eliminate any chances that he could give pertinent information on what he had witnessed. Inches away from pressing the tips into the boy's skull, she heard the security guard yell out, "Step away from the boy, officer. I'm warning you. I will shoot."

Bohannon turned calmly and smiled at her as she put the taser on the bed and cradled her right arm, "Pretty convincing, except you're out of bullets and that means you're shit out of luck. Thanks for taking care of Big Boy there, though." In one fluid motion, she lifted Geist's gun and shot the guard point blank in her face. The guard's corpse toppled to the linoleum in a spray of bone shards, blood and gray matter. Shaking her head in regret, Bohannon gingerly placed the gun on the bed and picked up the taser once again.

"Kid, you are a serious pain in my ass," Bohannon whispered, turning to the frail bandaged figure once again. "You're not having the best day either, are you? Just a few more seconds, baby, and I'll put you out of your misery." She pressed the taser to his temple again, heard a noise and hesitated. Someone was sliding across the floor on the other side of the bed. She leaned over the bed to see what was causing the noise and suddenly something latched onto her legs, yanking her off her feet. The

The Specimen

back of her head smashed against the floor and her broken wrist took most of her weight as she instinctively tried to brace against the impact. The pain was blinding. Once again, she lost hold of the taser as she instinctively clutched her shattered limb in agony.

Peering down at what was holding her legs, her worst fears were confirmed. The Cluster was not dead. Despite taking an entire clip directly to the head, its primary node had not been damaged enough to make it go dormant. Its two upper limbs no longer resembled arms. Entwined around her legs, they looked like flesh-colored snakes and were slowly, inexorably, pulling her under the bed closer to the bloody remnants of its former head. Bohannon began to wail in sheer terror.

In hindsight, Bohannon should have known better. Though this was the first Cluster she had faced in combat, what was known about the general anatomy of these monstrosities had been drilled into her memory during her training with Acme Group. The main point that was constantly repeated was that the primary node was nearly always located in the center mass of the body which was highly protected. If there was a head, it was simply where the sensory organs were located. Even with this knowledge, it was difficult to override one's instinct to shoot for the head.

Now, though, any rational thought had long fled her mind. All that was left was gibbering fear as she was dragged closer to the Cluster. Any resemblance to a human figure could no longer be seen in the pulsating form on the floor. The two fleshy tentacles clinched tighter on her legs, constricting them like a pair of boa constrictors. A loud pop sounded as one of her knees was disarticulated, followed soon by a series of cartilaginous crunches. Her lower body was being pulverized as the cluster slowly crawled up her thighs and pelvis, compressing each bone into multiple pieces.

Bohannon was dead by the time the cluster reached her mid-torso. Blood and other body fluids were squeezed out of her flesh through all orifices and even her pores. Still, the cluster continued sliding upwards until it had engulfed her whole and proceeded to grind and macerate her entire corpse into a meat pudding.

Out in the hallway, the alarms continued their clarion wail and a mass exodus of staff and patients locked themselves in rooms or fled to other parts of the hospital. Less than five minutes had passed since the start of the combat. The only movement in the room was the wet, meaty flow of the Cluster slithering its way up the side of the bed. The only sounds were the beeping monitors tracking the boy's vital signs. The probing appendage snaked its way to rest upon his chest. After a few seconds, the tip of the tendril, about the size and shape of a caterpillar, detached itself from the main mass of the cluster and settled on Scott's chest.

Once separated, the fleshy finger retreated off the bed and was reabsorbed into the main body of the cluster. The gaping hole that was once its head had healed over seamlessly and its body was now barely half the size it had been when it entered and started the attack. It headed for the broken window and slid out, climbing up the outer wall towards the roof. Left behind were two corpses, one without a face and one which looked like a Hefty bag of tenderized hamburger. Lying in the doorway, a grievously injured security guard with months of plastic surgery ahead of him breathed laboriously through a destroyed mouth and nose.

On the boy's chest, the remaining piece of the Cluster shivered slightly and sprouted cilia-like legs, skittering into his mouth, past the breathing tube and down his throat. Seconds later, he began convulsing, choking and writhing on the bed. Hands grasping and clutching blindly, he reached up to his mouth and pulled the breathing tube from his throat, gagging and retching as the entire length was removed. Finally the last bit came out and he was able to sit up, open his eyes and look around the room.

"Holy… What the hell happened here?" Scott Ritchie rasped as he looked down at the casts and bandages covering most of his body and at the three bodies on the floor of his room. After a few seconds looking around in shock and horror, he fumbled for and frantically pressed the call button to the nurse's station.

The Specimen

Chapter 17 – The Stench of Charred Flesh Leaves a Bad Taste that Lingers in Your Mouth

"MMmmmm ... barbecue!" – Homer Simpson

Modern Day – Chesterfield, MA

Bud could smell it long before he arrived. Sweet and smoky, simultaneously appetizing and revolting at once. He had smelled it many times before and he would never forget it. Roasted human flesh. Reminiscent of the Class of '95 pig roast he had regrettably attended when Vic graduated from high school, but even more so, it brought back memories he had buried for nearly four decades. Images of charred corpses strewn across the remnants of villages. A young girl with keloid scars over half her face and body and the reminder of the beautiful woman she would never be on the unscarred half. Parents wailing next to the scorched remains of their children. The numbing horror when one realizes that the blackened figure smoldering on a pyre is that of a toddler and not the child's doll you initially thought it was. The tremendous guilt you feel when you realize that all this time you have been salivating at the smell of cooked human and thinking about barbeque back home in America.

Bud slowed his truck to a crawl, stricken mute by what he saw. His dread grew as he drew nearer to the hanging ashen murk and realized that, more than likely, the Monahans' home was the site of this morning's blaze. A lingering haze of smoke hung in the air near the treetops, like a layer separating heaven and earth.

The street was lined with police cruisers, and a number of fire trucks from Chesterfield and neighboring towns could be seen down at the end of the Monahans' long driveway, leading to the house around the bend. Bud parked immediately behind one of the cruisers and unbuckled his seat belt. He closed his eyes and took a deep breath, preparing to step out and ask the officers what had happened, when one of them beat him to the punch, walking hurriedly up to his truck and tapping on his window.

Bud rolled it down and greeted the young officer, "Good morning, Nate." The young deputy was the son of one of Rosemary's close friends,

Rita Sloan. Bud had shared a few beers with him at summer barbeques at her house a number of times over the years and they often saw each other about town. Nate was a good kid. Someone he would describe as having a solid head on his shoulders. Although, truth be told, he wasn't exactly a kid. He had graduated high school a couple of years after Vic, which would make him close to 40 years old. *Damn, I'm older than dirt*, Bud thought with a grimace.

"Mornin', Bud," responded Deputy Nate Sloan. "Sorry for being a pain in your rear, but I've been instructed to ask you to leave. This is officially a crime scene. I know you were their friends, but we can't have everyone traipsing around in there."

"Oh God… not Chuck and Kate?" Bud groaned. "You said 'were their friends' as in past tense, Nate… how bad is it?"

Nate turned red. Frustrated at his poor choice of words, he replied, "Damn it, Bud. I shouldn't have said anything. We're still waiting to dig through the debris, but it doesn't look good." He paused briefly, looking over his shoulder. "I still need you to leave, though. Sheriff Smucker is in a foul mood. He doesn't want any chance of evidence contamination."

Bud thought to himself, *When is Little Napoleon ever in a good mood?* Joseph J. Smucker had been Sheriff of Bristol County for nearly two decades, ever since his appointment in 1995 when his predecessor, Gordon Wurley, keeled over and died of a myocardial infarction just minutes after ending a speech at the local Kiwanis Club. Since he had finished out the remainder of Wurley's term, Smucker had been reelected three times, despite being universally considered to be a uniquely arrogant asshole. A common graffiti message in the local area was often found in various tunnels, rocky outcroppings, and on the sides of abandoned buildings stating that "SMUCKER IS A MOTHERFUCKER". Personality aside, he was good at his job. The county crime rate had been on a steady decline during his tenure, especially in the last three or four years, due mainly to the fact that Sheriff Smucker never let go of anything into which he had sunk his teeth. The man was a pit bull.

"I understand, Nate, but this is an emergency. I'm looking for my grandson, Scott. He's good friends with Hank Monahan… and he may have snuck out to visit him here last night. Has there been any word?"

The Specimen

Shaking his head, Nate replied, "Wish I had more to tell you, Bud. I can say that as far as we know that we haven't discovered anything that leads us to believe your grandson was here, but it's been a rough shift. We may have simply missed him in the chaos.

"First we had that horrible hit and run out on Belcher Road, then this…" He paused, eyebrows furrowed in thought before continuing, "Um … listen. I'll talk to the Sheriff. I only got here an hour ago, but the Sheriff has been here from the beginning. He might have some news for you, but after that you'll need to head home. Agreed?"

Bud nodded in assent and Nate walked a few yards back toward the house before speaking quietly into the microphone attached to his shoulder. After a number of exchanges back and forth, Sloan said loudly, "Roger that, Sheriff. We're at the bottom of the driveway. See you in a few." He shut off his mike, stood silently for a few seconds, then turned back to Bud with his mouth set in a grim line, "Sheriff'll be down in a jiffy, Bud. He wants to talk to you in person."

"Is something wrong?"

"I'm not certain, Bud. We'll see him in sec"

Bud felt ill. A minute passed in awkward silence as they waited for the Sheriff to arrive. Finally, a white police cruiser with a thick green stripe down its side rolled around the bend of the driveway and parked parallel to Bud's truck. Disregarding the grey, dreary sky, Joe Smucker stepped out wearing his trademark mirrored sunglasses, alligator skin cowboy boots (with rumored two inch lifts) and chewing on a toothpick. It was common knowledge around Chesterfield that Little Napoleon, as he known by his opponents, was perpetually attempting to quit smoking. Once the election took place in November, he would most likely pick up the habit again. Voters in Massachusetts didn't like tobacco.

As the sheriff approached him, Bud made a conscious effort to rein in his customary sarcasm. He needed this strutting mustached rooster to help him out, and whether or not he would vote for him in the fall had nothing to do with the sheriff's ability to find Scott.

"I wish I could say good morning, Sheriff, but it looks like you've seen better ones," he greeted the man, offering his hand.

Smucker hesitated, then shook Bud's hand quickly, "Mr. Ritchie, I'm guessing."

Bud nodded and proceeded to explain why he was searching for Scott over by the Monahan's residence.

Smucker listened quietly, then spoke in a somber voice, "There's no other way to tell you this, Mr. Ritchie. A young boy about Scott's age was hit by a car early this morning when he came running out of the woods over on Mason Place. He was brought by ambulance to St Francis a few hours ago and, last we heard, he was out of surgery and listed in critical but stable condition. Doctors think he could come out of his coma within a few days, but for now they're using regular anesthesia."

Bud felt as if he had been kicked in the gut. He stammered, "Why do you think it might be Scott?"

"We found a bike lying at the edge of the driveway. Black with red trim and stickers all over the frame. One of the deputies thought she recognized it as Scott's because he and the Monahan boy were always loitering at the pizza place on Main St. I was just about to give you a call."

"That sounds like his bike, but I need to see it, Sheriff. I need to verify it with my own eyes," stated Bud. "If the bike is his, I'll have to head to St. Frank's immediately."

Smucker nodded, puffed out his chest and continued, "There's more to tell, Mr. Ritchie. Once the ambulance had taken the victim to the ER, we retraced the boy's trail through the woods." He paused dramatically and began stroking the sides of his mustache, obviously enjoying the captive audience. "It led right here, and that's not all, Mr. Ritchie. When we were only a couple hundred yards from this property, there was a tremendous explosion. By the time we broke through the trees, the whole house was ablaze. It took over four hours and five fire trucks to put it out. And then, I received a message from my officer at St. Frank's…"

Smucker paused again, obviously savoring the story. Completely unaware of the tension in the air. Bud was on the verge of assaulting the man and strangling him until his eyeballs shot out of their sockets. *Stop dragging things out, you little shit! What happened?*

The Specimen

"When they cut the boy's clothes off to examine his injuries, they discovered why he had run out into traffic", the sheriff continued. "Someone shot him. Twice."

"Wait a minute. Shot? In Chesterfield?"

"Exactly my question… so if we put all the pieces together and follow the logical sequence of events, the boy was running away from someone near the Monahan's house. Perhaps he witnessed something, or maybe he was involved in it. No way to know yet. He was chased through the woods and climbed the hill to Mason Place. The pursuer shot him, hitting him twice, which caused the boy to fall directly into the oncoming path of a minivan. The minivan hit him, and now he is lying in a coma at St. Frank's."

Bud nodded after he took it all in and said, "I'd like to see the bike now."

Sheriff Smucker gestured to the passenger door of his cruiser and said "Hop right in. I'll take you back to the house if you can promise not to interfere."

"Last thing I'd want to do is to stop anyone from finding the people who did this, Sheriff."

"The bike is with the rest of the evidence. Just be sure stay out of everyone's way. If it turns out to be Scott's bike, I'll call the hospital and give the okay for you to visit him. They'll do what I say."

Bud grit his teeth, restrained himself from making a snide comment and got into the cruiser. *Not now, Bud,* he thought to himself. *Just ignore him for now. He can't help being a pompous twit.*

As the cruiser came around the bend, Bud gasped at the scope of the destruction. The Monahans' house was nearly completely razed. Blackened timbers still smoked and steamed in puddles of sooty water. Only the far wall of the attached garage remained standing. Both of their cars had been reduced to carbonized metal skeletons in the garage. Here, the stench of molten rubber somewhat overpowered the smell of barbeque that filled the air. Bud's stomach churned with nausea as he covered his nose.

The police cruiser pulled up behind an ambulance and a quint pumper with two firemen still hosing down the edges of the charred frame. Sheriff Smucker and Bud stepped out of the car and surveyed the scene.

"How many did you find?" Bud asked somberly.

Smucker hesitated then replied, "Three. We think it's the parents and their son."

"Hank… Scott's best friend… you know they have a daughter, too?"

"Yeah, Deputy Booker mentioned that. Her son is a classmate of the daughter. Cindy, is it?"

"Sydney"

"Yeah, that's what I said. Anyway, Deputy Booker is the one who recognized the bike. In fact, here she comes now," he said nodding to an attractive uniformed African-American woman approaching with a phone in her hand.

"Joe," called the deputy. "I've got Corona on the line at St. Frank's. Something big just went down. I think we need to get over there."

"All right, let me talk to him, Simone," said Smucker as he held out a hand for the phone. "Can you show Mr. Ritchie the bike that was found? We want to verify that it belongs to his grandson."

Deputy Booker nodded and smiled at Bud, crooking a finger to follow her around the side of the house while the sheriff turned and spoke on the phone to his officer at the hospital.

"I know he seems full of himself most of the time," she said as they turned the corner. "But he hasn't been elected three times based on his personality. He gets things done around here, so everyone has learned to ignore his bluster."

Bud grunted, "It's difficult to ignore, but I'm more concerned with my grandson at the moment."

"Definitely," Deputy Booker grew somber. "I know him and Hank from around town. Not to say that they were troublemakers, sir. They just seem a bit aimless and bored most of the time, riding everywhere on their bikes or playing the old video games at Nando's Pizza." She paused a bit, searching for words, "I truly hope the two of them are okay, Mr. Ritchie. They're good kids."

The Specimen

They turned the corner of the only remaining wall that was standing and Bud's stomach dropped to the earth. The bike was definitely Scott's. His pride and joy was lying on the grass with a small yellow evidence flag next to it. It was a black Jamis Diablo with red trim, a pretty expensive bike, once owned by his father, Vic. Scott had covered it with stickers naming a variety of heavy metal bands: Avenged Sevenfold, Five Finger Death Punch, Turbonegro and Halestorm… none of whom Bud recognized. *What ever happened to simple names like The Beatles, Jefferson Airplane or The Rolling Stones? Music nowadays was so aggressive and angry.* He had said something in that vein to Scott many times, but in reality, he somewhat empathized with his grandson's generation.

When he was Scott's age, he had always felt that there were opportunities around every corner, even with the horrors he had seen in Vietnam and the chaos of the 1960's before that. No matter the problem, it always seemed solvable. Scott's generation was faced with a world that was increasingly faster and more demanding. The deck was becoming progressively stacked in favor of the haves rather than the have-nots. It was no wonder that they would rather immerse themselves in video games where they could control the world rather than spin their wheels in reality.

Noticing the expression on his face, Deputy Booker whispered, "Damn it." She placed a hand on his upper right arm and squeezed it in sympathy. "I had a feeling that it was his bike, but I had nearly convinced myself that I was mistaken."

Bud was silent. He felt somewhat disoriented as if he had been betrayed by someone who he trusted implicitly.

"We have to hold on to the bike for evidence," she stated as she flipped her internal switch to efficiency mode. "Once they examine it, take samples for processing and file reports, Scott can have it back. Right now, we should see about heading over to St. Frank's with your wife to check in with him."

Bud nodded distractedly and followed her as she led the way back to the cruiser. A white van with the Bristol County seal pulled up next to the burnt ruins as they reached the driveway. A man and a woman in navy jumpsuits with the block letters BCME on their backs exited the van, removing a hospital stretcher with piles of black plastic stacked on it. Bud swallowed down some bile that had percolated to the back of his throat. Those must be the body bags, he thought. He followed the two of them with his eyes as they wheeled the stretcher through the remnants of the garage and lifted it over the blackened threshold into the hellish interior of the house.

Sheriff Smucker was waiting for them by the cruiser with a grim cast to his features. He called Deputy Booker over and said, "I need you to follow Mr. Ritchie back to his house so he can gather his wife and meet me at Mass General in Cambridge."

Bud was confused. He asked, "Not St. Frank's?"

The Sheriff shook his head and replied, "Scott's being transferred there for his safety. I've been informed that there was a serious incident at St. Frank's less than an hour ago and we believe your grandson is involved."

"Wait!" Bud called as the sheriff got into his car. "How do you know that it's definitely Scott? Isn't the boy in a coma?"

"He *was* in a coma. He woke up," said Smucker. "Not only did he wake up from what were supposedly life-threatening injuries, but he did so surrounded by three dead bodies in the intensive care unit after someone tried to kill him and a random stranger intervened… and to top it all off, he identified himself as Scott Ritchie."

The sheriff started the ignition and said, "There will be an officer waiting in the main lobby for you. I'll see you in a couple hours." With that, he rolled up his window and took off, leaving the two of them and their many unanswered questions behind.

"Such an asshole," Bud grumbled under his breath. Deputy Booker bit her lip and looked in the other direction to keep from laughing. *No argument there.*

The Specimen

Official Report on the Greylock Incident

February 13, 1966
To: Members of the Governing Council, ACME Group
From: James P. Kilcannon, Agent-in-Charge
RE: Greylock Incident (Cluster)

Respected Members of the Council,

As instructed, with the assistance of Dr. Colfax, we have collected and catalogued all evidence of Dr. Coe's activities that extended beyond the original purview of the mission. We have learned that Dr. Coe pursued side projects when the interactions with the original Rider became limited. As a result of the previous injuries suffered by the symbiont during 1) the forced excision from Mr. Roumain, the escape and the subsequent recapture in Springfield, and the 2) the second surgery to remove the creature from young Master Varney, it was often in a form of hibernation.

Dr. Colfax reports that Dr. Coe began to display increased interest in the growth and development of the irradiated samples, spending what he considered an inordinate amount of time on what he termed an "unnatural aberration". He also adds that he disagreed with many of her decisions from this point on, as can be seen in the bundle of letters he submitted during his stay at Greylock. These letters have been read and filed away due to the absence of anything relevant.

- JPK

*   *   *

Day 43

We have returned the boy to the general population ward since he has surprisingly recovered enough physically to no longer require our care. His mental state is another story entirely, but those are the risks of scientific studies. The main reason I chose this venue was the lack of scrutiny and the ready supply of "volunteers". After all, few of the residents have anyone who cares about them. Most are prisoners or wards of the state who have lived in the institutional system for decades. At least they can have a purpose in life by aiding us in our experiments. I have a number of candidates in mind for the next host of the Rider.

- GC

Day 45

Dr. Eckenrode was especially bothersome today. He still seems to be under the illusion that he has any say over what happens to the patients that I choose for my projects. I may need to discuss this problem with my esteemed colleague. Dr. Colfax will certainly report it back to the Council and they will most likely remind Eckenrode of his place as a public figurehead. Nothing more.

This will keep Colfax busy for some time and solve the problem with Eckenrode without the appearance that I am unable to handle these problems by myself. If the Council insists on monitoring me, can I be blamed for engineering results that benefit me?

- GC

Day 49

Within the hour, with Colfax's assistance, I will attempt to graft the Rider onto a new host. The patient chosen for this operation is a longtime ward of this institution, named Richard Hutchens, a 48 year-old Caucasian male with a diagnosis of early infantile autism. He has been institutionalized for well over four decades, since his biological parents abandoned him to the state.

In that time, he has never received a visitor. No letters. No birthday cards. He only speaks in monosyllabic responses, such as "yes' or "no". This, along with the fact that he is considered to be one of the most passive and compliant patients in Greylock, makes him ideal for the

The Specimen

next phase of the project. Hutchens should be a blank slate, easily subdued by the Rider, and hopefully this will hasten its communication with us.

Day 50

I now know what Jules Verne meant in *A Journey to the Center of the Earth* when he wrote that "science is made up of mistakes... that lead little by little to the truth."

Since the beginning of this project, I have been getting less and less sleep, and I finally realize that it is affecting my work. In my exhaustion yesterday, I made a dreadful error, a lapse of attention, which could have contaminated a number of the samples. Regardless of what could have happened, something wonderful has resulted. Something that I struggle to describe.

Through pure chance, I have created life. A new form of life.

Before we get into that part of the project, everyone should be aware that the graft of the Rider was a complete success. No complications at all. Once the blood vessels and nerve endings were exposed on Hutchens' back, the Rider apparently sensed what was being done and immediately melded with the man's new flesh.

With Mr. Hutchens still recovering for the next day or two, today I turned my attention again to the samples that were harvested last month. Specifically, I was interested in monitoring the growth rate of the irradiated samples.

After their initial growth spurt, each of these samples stabilized at the approximate size of a large grapefruit. Initially they appeared translucent with golden threads peppering the interior like capillaries. Recently, as the size stabilized, the surface of each thickened, becoming opaque.

When I looked at cellular samples under the microscope again, the cells had not yet specialized as I had hoped. It's a complete surprise, but they continue to appear to be solely composed of what resemble stem cells.

The error occurred yesterday as I was taking the daily measurements of each sample. Mass. Volume. Temperature. As was routine, each sample was to be removed individually, measured, and replaced in its container before moving on to the next one. It had gotten to the point where the process was so automatic that I did not think while I moved from sample to sample... a fortunate oversight.

Before returning the first sample to its container, I removed a second one and placed it on the table a few inches away from the first one. I realized my blunder within seconds, but that short moment was all that was needed to initiate what happened next.

A small bubble appeared on the surface of the first sample and that was enough to make me hesitate. The bubble suddenly stretched out, forming a pseudopod that plunged into the mass of the second sample before pulling it close and engulfing it. The similarity to an amoeba in the process of phagocytosis was uncanny... if the amoeba had been the size of a cantaloupe. Now, with the two samples melded into one, it was as nearly as massive as a watermelon.

In hindsight, I have no idea what compelled me to the next action, but I didn't even wait once I saw two samples creating one combined organism. I opened another container and placed two more lumps of irradiated alien tissue on the table. They were enveloped within seconds and the organism was now the size of a very large pumpkin, already about three times the size of the original Rider from which we had excised the samples.

It was then that I realized that I had a new problem. How would I store this new organism? It was as twice as large as any container we had, and I wasn't about to leave it out in the open for Colfax to view. For someone who calls himself a scientist, the man has no sense of wonder whatsoever. Most likely he would have recommended destruction of the newly formed organism and I simply could not allow that to happen.

The Specimen

    I scoured the rooms for anything that might work, but it was soon obvious that no container was large enough to hold the organism. Thankfully, except for a slight pulse rippling along its skin every five to ten seconds, it remained motionless throughout the search. Twenty minutes later, I had emptied the storage closet in the corner of the laboratory and repurposed it to serve as a new home for this creature. After rolling the mass onto a metal wheeled cart, I pushed it into the small space and locked it inside. Soon after, I double-locked the lab and left for my room to take a well-deserved nap.

                              - GC

Interlude: The Rider
Ivar the Boneless
East Anglia – November, 869 AD

Thorbjorn Valdersson shivered in the morning fog as the sun crested the East Anglian coast. The mist slithered around his ankles with diaphanous tendrils. Barely penetrating the grey soup, the meager dawn light offered no heat to combat the chill that had settled into his bones while he stood guard over the prisoner lashed to the tree behind him. Frost rimed his heavy reddish-blonde beard from the plume of his breath, forming crystals of ice in the ruddy tangle of hair hanging down his chest. Even though he had endured much more frigid weather in his homelands to the north, this constant damp brought on a dull ache that made his battered bones throb. He leaned on a massive double-edged battleaxe for support as he valiantly fought off sleep. Thorbjorn shook his head and snorted. Today would not be a good day to be found napping while on duty. Not that any day was, truthfully, but with the leaders of the Great Army soon to arrive, Thorbjorn had to be especially careful, else he be tied to the tree next to this so-called King Edmund.

Ivar Ragnarsson and his brothers, Ubbe and Halfdan, were each, in their own way, brutal taskmasters. If they gained knowledge of dereliction of duty on the part of any of their men, those individuals would serve as an example to the rest of their force. Halfdan and Ubbe were usually inclined to keep the punishment simple by cleaving the offending warrior's skull in two. Ivar, on the other hand, was much more creative. The brother named The Boneless was known to enjoy prolonging the lesson he would teach. In Ivar's opinion, the longer a subject was on display, the longer the example would remain at the forefront of the minds of the rest of the soldiers. If not for Ivar's obvious disfigurement, he might have been known as The Bloodless for his seeming lack of emotion in any situation. Unlike Halfdan's propensity for uncontrollable rages or Ubbe's obvious glee at bloodshed, Ivar approached every situation in the same manner. Coldly and methodically, like the massive glaciers of their homeland.

The Specimen

Thorbjorn sighed and grumbled under his breath, "I should be home playing with my grandchildren." This campaign to Anglia had taken years longer than expected and the end was not in sight for long into the future. Despite being decades older than most of his fellow soldiers, he had joined his countrymen in this invading army to escape the grief caused by the death of his beloved wife Anneke. He soon realized that he had made a rash decision in leaving Denmark. His family needed his presence and he in turn needed them.

The grizzled warrior looked to both sides for the other three sentries. His nephew Aksel hunched against the cold to his left, wrapped in his prized bearskin cloak. Even though the cloak smelled like a pile of fresh bear scat in warm weather, Thorbjorn would have welcomed its warmth without complaint. His own cloak needed to be restitched or replaced soon. The fur was bald in places and the exposed hide was cracking. It stopped the wind, but did little else to stave off the cold.

To his right, the nearest Skoog twin coughed up a large wad of phlegm and spat it into the dirt. Thorbjorn glanced his way and saw Olf engaged in one of his usual activities, one finger buried knuckle-deep in a nostril while staring off into the distance. Both Skoogs were short and squat, resembling toads both in stature and mind. His brother Arne sat slumped against a small boulder on the far side of the clearing. Whether he was asleep or not wasn't apparent, but Thorbjorn would have wagered on the former. They were distant cousins of Ubbe Ragnarsson's wife, though, so any repercussions of their incompetence always fell on others. If Edmund's men ever gained the courage to try and rescue their leader, the Skoogs would probably have been cut down in seconds, but most able-bodied men had fled to the west after the initial slaughter.

Because of this unspoken fact, whoever were assigned to work with the twins were always on high alert. This morning was no exception. Thorbjorn and Aksel covered most of the clearing's edge, leaving little chance for the Skoogs to make a fatal error. Arne and Olf appeared content with the arrangement, though they were always the first to greet visitors of importance with details of their perpetual vigilance. With Ubbe soon to arrive, they were certain to demonstrate new levels of bootlicking, which the middle Ragnarsson brother did nothing to discourage. Ubbe welcomed sycophants and the Skoogs had realized early on that the other brothers had no patience for their tribute, so they focused their sniveling upon the vainglorious Ragnarsson brother.

Thorbjorn yawned again with a loud growl and stomped his feet in the muddy turf to shake himself awake. The sky was growing markedly lighter as the sun rose above the horizon and the mist was slowly dissipating. The leaders were expected to arrive within the hour. He almost felt pity for their captive. Almost.

He looked over his shoulder to check on the prisoner. Still alive, though barely conscious. The bloodied man hung from a massive oak tree near the center of the large meadow, tied spread eagle by the arms and legs around the base of the scarred, gnarly trunk. This was Edmund, purported king of this wretched land of thickets and fens. His elbows, knees and shoulders had all been wrenched from their sockets. The unnatural angles of the joints disturbed even Thorbjorn, who normally could stomach looking at the most graphic injuries on the battlefield.

Torture, however, didn't appeal to him. His belief was that the enemy should be killed expediently and without ceremony. Prolonging agony was sadistic unless it served a purpose. He even disagreed with the use of the traditional Blood Eagle, when a victim's ribs were cut away through the back and his lungs were pulled out through the holes and spread to the sides like the great span of a raptor. Ivar had used this method to kill King Ælla of Northumbria a couple of years earlier. Thorbjorn would never forget the sight of the lungs slowly inflating and deflating on the king's back like a couple of gory pig bladders. Death had taken longer than expected and the rhythmic wheezing of the extracted organs were all that could be heard by the gathered warriors as it slowed and eventually ceased.

Edmund's face was raw and swollen, his lower lip torn and hanging like a discarded piece of meat. Numerous teeth were shattered and his left cheekbone was staved in like a sinkhole in the bloody black bramble of his beard. The rising sun cast its rays across Edmund's eyes and he moaned quietly. He had been stripped down to his breeches. Dark yellowish-purple bruises covered his torso where he had been beaten and kicked with clubs and boots after his capture. Only when Ivar interceded

The Specimen

had the assault ceased. The Boneless had not wanted to waste this opportunity to make an impression on the people of this miserable land.

The king had been strung up on the oak tree three days earlier. Visited numerous times by one Ragnarsson brother or another, he had been beaten into his current bloodied state, and today, with all three soon to arrive, it was assumed by all that his end was near.

"Oy!" yelled Olf Skoog to his dozing brother. He hurled a clump of day-old horse dung through the air to splatter on the boulder above Arne's right shoulder. "Open those eyes and git off your hairy ass! Ubbe and his brothers're comin'. It's gonna be a good show!"

Arne shook himself awake and slowly pulled himself to his feet with a series of loud grunts and farts. He yawned and grinned at Olf across the clearing, "Tell me when you can see them comin' up the hill. I need to take care of my business. Olf cackled out loud and nodded his head as his brother approached the tree to which King Edmund was bound. Aksel and Thorbjorn glanced at each other in disgust. They knew what was going to happen, but neither made a move to intercept Arne. Some fights were simply not worth any effort.

The stout sentry slouched up to the tree and lowered his breeches, saying "Here's some piss for yer pot, my king! Fresh like the sweet morning dew!" A steaming yellow arc cut through the air and splattered the bound man. Arne snorted with glee and wagged his organ in an attempt to wet the monarch's face with his gift. Edmund sputtered as some of the piss splashed off his forehead down into his eyes and swollen mouth. He weakly tried to turn away, but Arne's aim was too accurate.

"Here they come," yelled Aksel, pointing to a line of horses far down the hill. Thorbjorn turned to see a column of more than twenty men on horseback climbing the path from the army's encampment below. Leading the group were the Ragnarsson brothers, in a line three abreast. Halfdan on his fiery roan stallion, Ubbe on his grey gelding giant, and Ivar seated in his bulky saddle on a midnight black destrier.

The two brothers straightened to attention and resumed their posts, preparing to put on their usual theatrics for Ubbe. Thorbjorn and Aksel maintained the positions they had throughout the night. Minutes later, the group arrived and Olf stepped forward to greet them before

Thorbjorn or Aksel could utter a word. Arne soon joined him, abandoning his post.

"Today will be a good day, will it not, Brother Ubbe?" shouted Olf to the hulking warrior as he clambered off his horse. Ubbe shook his blonde locks away from his face and walked forward to meet the squat Skoogs with a grin. Behind him, Halfdan spat on the earth in disgust, as he dismounted, while Ivar was silent and brooding in his saddle.

"One can only hope, my friends," Ubbe said as he smacked each of the twins on the back with a mighty paw. Olf nearly stumbled with the force of the blow, while Arne managed to stand still, only slightly grunting in pain from the exuberant greeting. He turned, beckoning to Thorbjorn and Aksel, and asked, "Quiet night, then?"

Thorbjorn nodded in assent and stated, "We heard nothing but the sounds of the forest and Olf's constant breaking of wind. That was enough to keep the demons at bay."

Ubbe leaned back and roared with laughter as the remaining entourage of soldiers joined them around the perimeter of the field. Olf scowled in Thorbjorn's direction, fingering the hilt of his sword.

"Keep your blade sheathed, Olf," the blond goliath chuckled. "You and I both know that he speaks the truth. Many times have you woken me at night with the braying of your ass. Thank Frigg that my lovely Hulda did not inherit that trait from your kin."

"Have you all finished with your womanly chatter?" Halfdan growled as he squeezed through a mass of soldiers into the circle. "I left our lands to escape the endless bickering of my wife and here it is. Worse than ever!" He looked back at Ivar and barked, "Can we begin, brother?"

Ivar rode forward on his muscled steed until the group of soldiers stepped aside for him. Thorbjorn forced himself not to stare, despite the fact that many of his fellow warriors could not look away. Ivar was not a typical Danish warrior. He wore a long, grey, woolen cloak that wrapped around his shoulders and fell below his knees. Though nearly as large as his brother Ubbe and much larger than Halfdan, his legs were twisted and withered, making it impossible for him to walk. The curvature continued up his spine, ending in a pair of large protuberant humps above his right shoulder. Looking at his deformity, a stranger might think that he could

The Specimen

not possibly draw a bow, yet he carried a large one made from polished yew on his lap. He was easily the most accurate archer in the army, able to shoot an enemy through the throat at over one hundred strides away. No one was foolish enough to challenge him.

Ivar sat in a reinforced saddle which he rarely left. Unlike his lower torso, his arms and upper body were massively muscled, rivaling even Ubbe's in girth. Years of ambulating on his hands as a child had given him forearms the size of large hams. His hands were scarred and calloused, capable of crushing a man's throat effortlessly. Thorbjorn had seen just that happen a few months earlier when a group of locals attempted to ambush them to the south. Ivar had simply grabbed one of them by the throat and lifted him dangling above the ground. It would be a long time before Thorbjorn forgot the sound of the man's windpipe being crushed like a gourd within Ivar's grip.

Normally, a child with a deformity like Ivar's would have been abandoned in the wild to the whims of Hödr, god of winter. The next morning, the child would have disappeared with barely a few spatters of blood left in the snow as evidence it ever existed. As a son of Ragnar Lodbrok, the legendary Viking king, however, Ivar was spared. In the ensuing years, he proved his mettle as a warrior and soon became feared throughout Scandinavia.

The throng of soldiers parted and Ivar approached the prisoner. Circling the tree, he paused before Edmund and stared at him with a dead shark-like gaze. The former king stirred and cracked open his eyes, sticky with the bloody residue of the ragged gashes on his face.

"Why the delay?" croaked Edmund. "Kill me… and be done with it, heathen bastard."

Ivar remained still, only raising his hand to quell the anger of the soldiers at his back. "Worry not, dog. Your time is near," Ivar rasped. "And be certain… your death will be remembered long after the flesh rots off your bones."

"My kin will avenge me," coughed Edmund, blood trickling down his chin…

"Then our axes will drink their blood as well. This will become a land of widows and orphans."

166

The Boneless slowly turned his horse and rode back to the rear of the group where Thorbjorn stood with Aksel. As he approached, the men who had arrived with the brothers all dismounted and spread out in parallel semicircles around the tree. Bows at the ready, they nocked arrows and waited for the command to fire.

Stopping his horse directly next to Thorbjorn and Aksel, Ivar nodded at the two of them in brief acknowledgement and turned toward the prisoner. He scanned up and down the line of bowmen, and called, "As discussed, my brothers. All at once. 1… 2… 3… NOW!"

A wave of arrows streamed to the prisoner as one, pinning his arms and legs to the trunk, leaving all vital organs untouched. Edmund screamed a long wail of agony as more than two dozen shafts pierced his limbs. Five arrows skewered his hands, two in the left palm and three in the right. Arrows jutted up and down his arms and legs. Streams of scarlet blood flowed down the bark of the tree from multiple stigmata as Edmund slumped into unconsciousness.

Ivar raised his hand to the archers, signaling them to hold fire, then nodded to Ubbe and Halfdan. His brothers walked up to Edmund and examined the placement of the arrows. Thorbjorn noted that they were especially focused on the colors of the fletching, and surmised that the two brothers were competing again in one of their well-known wagers. Half the arrows had white fletching and the others were marked with Halfdan's traditional black feathers. Ubbe hooted with joy and Halfdan cursed Odin and all his bastard spawn when it was realized that the white feathers had impaled Edmund much closer to his torso than the black.

Unable to take his fury out on his hulking younger brother, Halfdan turned to the prisoner and backhanded him across the face with his spiked leather gauntlet. One of the spikes carved a deep furrow, further mutilating Edmund's already ravaged cheek. A red spray filled the air and shards of his splintered teeth littered the ground. Thorbjorn looked away in disgust… and that was when he saw it.

Seconds away from impact, a long ash spear sliced through the air toward Thorbjorn, Aksel and Ivar. With a guttural cry, Thorbjorn barreled into Aksel, knocking him to the ground. The spear whistled inches past their heads and plunged into Ivar's horse's left flank. The black stallion

The Specimen

reared, shrieking in agony and hurling the Danish chieftain from his saddle. Its hooves struck the dirt, grazing Thorbjorn's head and causing his vision to go grey for a moment. Aksel rolled away and clambered to his feet, only to be perforated with a flurry of arrows plunging from the sky. One arrow hit the crown of his head and burst through his left eye. He fell to his knees, surprise permanently etched into his features, and collapsed with gouts of blood pouring from his eye sockets.

"Aksel! No!" shouted Thorbjorn. He crawled quickly to his nephew's side, howling with grief. All around him, fellow Danes were turning to face the wave of ragged Anglo rebels pouring from the forest. Emaciated and wild-eyed, the attackers were of all ages. Some were armed with swords and axes, while others wielded only clubs, pitchforks and scythes. The dozen or so individuals with bows stationed themselves at the far edge of the field and released waves of arrows toward them.

Ubbe and Halfdan eagerly rushed at the attackers, bloodlust gleaming in their eyes and battle cries sounding around them. Within seconds, each of them had cut down a pair of rebels with powerful swipes of their weapons. Halfdan cleaved through the ribcage of a young farm boy barely out of his teens while Ubbe decapitated a stout grey-bearded combatant with a backhanded swing of his axe.

Steps away from Thorbjorn, Ivar pushed to a seated position and rapidly unslung his bow, notching an arrow and sending it through the throat of an opposing archer in one smooth motion. He repeated this action twice more, each time with deadly accuracy. Thorbjorn left his cousin's body to protect Ivar's flank, when a lone arrow hit the Danish chieftain in the right shoulder, piercing the large hump on his back and knocking him screaming to the earth.

Maneuvering around the fallen bodies of allies and adversaries alike, Thorbjorn rushed to his leader's side and rolled him over on his side. The arrow protruding from his clavicle prevented him from lying on his back. Ivar was still conscious, but blood leaked from his mouth and he struggled to speak. The battle continued, but the action had shifted away from them to where Ubbe, Halfdan and a dozen other Danes methodically pressed back against the remaining assailants. Thorbjorn made a quick decision and lifted Ivar in a bear hug to carry him closer to the tree. He tried not to jostle the wounded man, but Thorbjorn's pace and the uneven ground made for a bumpy ride, eliciting a long painful cry from the crippled leader.

So much blood, thought Thorbjorn. So much blood.

Ivar's survival seemed unlikely with that much blood loss, but he would be damned if he did not try to save him. His shirt was soaked in gore by the time he leaned Ivar up against the tree mere feet from the riddled body of Edmund, still defiant as he bled out.

"You may still join Death first, heathen," whispered the Anglo king with a pained smile.

Thorbjorn swiped at one of the arrows protruding from Edmund's leg, eliciting an agonized scream and causing him to slump into unconsciousness again...

"Ignore the fool. Take out the arrow," choked Ivar, coughing up some more blood.

"I can't! You'll bleed to death in seconds!" exclaimed Thorbjorn.

"Do it," he said through scarlet-stained teeth. "It needs to be removed now."

Thorbjorn looked around desperately for someone to help him, but all were either engaged in the battle or lying in their own pools of gore around the tree. He had no other option. He must follow the command of his leader. Muttering a prayer to Valhalla, he grasped the end protruding through Ivar's shoulder and snapped off the head so he could pull the shaft through from the other side. Ivar screamed shrilly and passed out.

In the distance behind him, Thorbjorn heard a yell as he rolled the unresponsive man over and began pulling the shaft through the wound. He recoiled in shock as a sharp keening sound pierced the air, much like the yowling of an animal in pain. The screech did not come from Ivar's mouth. He was definitely unconscious. The source of the noise appeared to be located on his back where the arrow had struck, directly beneath the blood-soaked cloth.

Gritting his teeth in determination, Thorbjorn pulled on the broken shaft again and resumed removal. The howling reached a peak as the arrow finally came free. Thorbjorn tossed the fragmented piece to the

The Specimen

earth and started to peel back Ivar's tunic to expose the wound and see what damage had been done.

Ivar moved... or rather the flesh around the humps on his back was moving. Writhing and squirming unnaturally beneath Thorbjorn's grasp. Concerned that the Viking leader was beginning to seize, he reached under the bloody tunic and began to roll him onto his back.

Something bit him.

He yanked his hand out and immediately saw a round, jagged wound on his palm directly beneath his third finger the size of a silver Anglo penny. It wept blood, trickling down his forearm in a steady trail.

"What in Odin's name?" he yelped, for he had felt more than teeth while under the clothing. Ropy, sinuous coils. Scales and hair. Bony spurs. This and many other unrecognizable features were felt along Ivar's back.

"No. Wait!" he dazedly heard Ubbe shout from his right as his hands moved their own volition and pulled back Ivar's collar to see what was hidden.

It was a monstrosity. Approximately the size of a large cat, a lumpy, mottled creature hugged the man's back with three muscular appendages. One tentacle appeared to have entwined through Ivar's flesh around his spine, while the other two gripped his midriff like it was riding him. A sucking mouth, ringed with lamprey-like teeth in the center body mass, shrieked when revealed to the light. Its skin was mottled, scaled, and piebald with scattered patches of hair. Its lone yellow eyeball stared at Thorbjorn with an alien gaze, causing the old battle-hardened veteran to reel back from Ivar with a wave of nausea.

A fresh wound in the creature's upper left quadrant bled freely. The arrow must have been slowed by its flesh before piercing Ivar. It was completely unnatural, and Thorbjorn suddenly realized that this thing had always been there. Ivar had not been living with a twisted spine his entire life. This beast had been attached to him for years... perhaps since birth. What did that mean?

"Demon!" he exclaimed, reaching for his battleaxe. Every hair on his arms was standing on end. He had a visceral need to destroy it. On a subconscious level, he knew that its existence was an abomination.

Rearing back, he readied the killing blow when a muscular arm encircled his neck and applied pressure.

"Stay your hand, Thorbjorn," said a rough voice at his shoulder. "If you kill it or tear it from his back, Ivar will certainly die. It is a part of him." Ubbe pulled Thorbjorn back out of reach of his older brother, then released him. The blonde giant was covered in sweat, mud and gore, his axe blade red to the haft. A long gash on his right forearm dripped blood steadily to the earth. He pulled Ivar's collar to his neck, covering the baleful yellow eye from view.

"What?--" Thorbjorn sputtered. "What is that thing?" He backed away with his axe held out before him, eyes on the mass beneath Ivar's tunic. The revulsion he felt was receding now that he couldn't see it, but the fear remained. It was a constant struggle not to spring forward and cleave the wriggling mass into pieces.

Ubbe shrugged, "Ivar has had it as long as I can remember – since we were children. Since before I was born, at least. Our father had always insisted that we keep it a secret. We think it helps him live. Don't ask me how. He has healed from grievous wounds before… wounds that should have killed him many times over. It is part of him."

"So, brother…" growled a voice behind him. "What are we supposed to do now?"

Thorbjorn recognized Halfdan's gravelly tone just as he felt the other brother's blade at the nape of his neck. He froze in place. The sounds of battle had dissipated, but the smell of blood and death still hung in the cold morning air.

"First we take care of business, then we worry about this one," Ubbe nodded at Thorbjorn and raising his axe. Quick as lightning, Ubbe whirled and buried the blade of his axe in the tree, neatly severing Edmund's head just below the jaw line. The king's skull fell to the ground and rolled to a stop near Ubbe's feet.

Ubbe leaned over and picked up the head with a grin on his face and said, "…and now for our wonderful friend." He signaled his brother with a nod and began walking towards Thorbjorn.

* * *

The Specimen

Two weeks later, the colder weather had passed and Thorbjorn stood on the deck of a knörr finally heading home. Next to him, wrapped in heavy cloth was Aksel's corpse. Ubbe and Halfdan had agreed to wait for Ivar's recovery to make a decision. It soon was apparent that Ivar would be back to normal within days. Normally, an individual with a wound as severe as his risked death from infection or blood loss, but the eldest Ragnarsson brother had recovered at an abnormal rate. He made it clear that Thorbjorn was to be trusted with the knowledge of his secret and rewarded with a voyage home to his family. Now that trip finally neared its end.

Once they landed in Heiðabýr, he would deliver the body to Aksel's wife before continuing on to his children's homes where he hoped to live out his days in peace, playing with grandchildren and drinking the day away. No thoughts of battles or bloodshed. No thoughts of demons riding the backs of warrior-kings. Let other men fight that war.

PART 2
ORIGINS

The Specimen

Chapter 18 – Bayou Lou

"I think that there's a hidden darkness inside all of us." - Matthew Fox

Modern Day – Springfield, MA

Harry hadn't eaten all day. Since the vivid nightmare about his time at the Greylock Asylum half a century earlier, all he could stomach was hot tea and some crackers. Anything else came up within seconds. He was curled up on his battered recliner again in the same position, wearing the same clothes. Even though he had his other outfit in a locker at the Harvard Square T station, he had been too weak to head over there and fetch it, so he remained in the chair smelling of sweat and fear.

Occasionally he drifted into a restless slumber where shadows of his past were eager to emerge from the caves of lost memories and give him more of himself to sift through and reclaim. He was remembering more and more as the hours passed. Each revelation was like a thunderclap inside his head. The lightning flash of the recovered memory, followed by the impact of the resulting implications on his lost life.

Of all the scenes from his past he had recovered, one in particular stood out. The summer before he was brought to Greylock and the choices he made. All eventually led to a chance meeting with a goliath of a man in a porkpie hat… a man who he eventually would come to regard as a surrogate father figure.

* * *

August 1964 – Springfield, MA

"Whatchoo doin' down dissaway, child?" A deep voice full of smoke and gumbo growled at him from a bench as Harry walked down Alden Street in a hurry. "Don'tchoo know this part o' town got some dangerous peoples just lookin' for a l'il boy like you?"

The Specimen

Harry turned around and stared at the gigantic man sitting in the shade of an immense oak tree overhanging the entrance to a small local shop – Bayou Lou's. He clutched the money in his pocket – a sweaty dollar bill wrapped around a few quarters and other coins – as if it would vanish when he let go.

He wanted to buy a couple packs of baseball cards and some black licorice whips, and the only store that sold the kind he liked was at least a half hour walk from his apartment building. Today, since the sun was particularly brutal, even for August, he was trying to cut a few minutes off his trip by taking a new route and cutting through a neighborhood that was known to be a bit rough. He could handle it, though. At least, he thought he could. Now, after getting accosted by this stranger, Harry questioned his bravado.

Despite all the warnings he had heard over and over again from both his parents and his grandparents - especially Big Daddy, his grandfather – that he shouldn't talk to anyone who he didn't know, he felt compelled to correct the fat old fool.

"I ain't no little boy," he spat over his shoulder. "I'm gonna be thirteen soon."

"Okay, son. Excuse me for openin' mah mouth, but you gotta realize dey ain't gonna ask your age when dey cutting your guts open, boy."

Harry bit back a sarcastic retort and looked closer at the man in the shadows. He had been so lost in his thoughts, he would have walked right by without even registering that anyone had been seated there, even someone that looked like this man.

Staring back at him was the fattest man he had ever seen. Damn close to the blackest, too. He had to be at least 400 pounds and a few inches taller than Harry's father, who stood 6'3", and his skin was so dark it bordered on blue. Despite the sweltering heat, he wore a voluminous jacket over a plain white tee. A red porkpie hat with a broad black band perched on his head and he fanned his face with a rolled magazine. A ragged chewed cheroot hung from his lips, trailing a haze of pungent smoke in the muggy afternoon air.

"What's your name, boy?" the man smiled, revealing a row of ivory-stained teeth, except for one gold lower canine. "You being shy? Your Momma and Poppa said not to jaw with strangers, am I right? Okay, can't blame them for thinkin' dat, 'specially wit me. Ain't nobody much stranger than l'il old me."

Harry remained silent, a bit dazed by the onslaught of questions.

The huge man laughed and continued, "How 'bout I tell you first, then you tell me. Sound good?" He continued without waiting for an answer. "My name is Lucien Roumain. I run dis marvelous shop behind me where I sell things that come from my home in Nawlins. I moved here right 'bout seven years ago after Hurricane Audrey hit Louisiana in '57 and I been here evah since." He paused and grinned in Harry's direction, "Okay, I told you who I am. You owes me. Now, pay up. What's your name?"

Surprising even himself, Harry answered him - told him his name and much more. Harry found himself moving closer and revealing details about his life and concerns regarding his family that he had never told any of his friends, much less a strange man on the street. Something about Lucien Roumain made him feel comfortable. He knew that Roumain was the exact type of individual his parents and grandparents had warned him to avoid, but the longer he spoke to the large man, the less he cared about the warning.

Soon he was sitting next to Roumain on the bench and talking about the Red Sox and his beloved Boston Patriots. At one point, the gentle goliath stood slowly and hobbled into the store for a couple of glasses of mint tea. Harry noted that his back appeared to have a bit of a hunch, slightly twisted and off center as he walked away with his cane.

"My mother's recipe," he stated proudly as he handed the frosty glass to Harry a few minutes later. The tea was absolutely delicious.

They spoke for another hour before Harry had to return home, and even though he hadn't been able to purchase his cards and licorice, he

The Specimen

had enjoyed the conversation and the fact that he had made a new friend more than made up for the detour.

* * *

A week later, he returned to Bayou Lou's and visited his new friend once more. Inside the store, Roumain sold an eclectic variety of items. From the spices needed to make anything in a true Creole kitchen to recordings of Zydeco music, books on voodoo, and Havana shirts in every color of the rainbow. For such a small space, Roumain managed to pack the entire Mississippi Delta culture into the store quite easily.

The store was much busier than it had been the last time Harry was here. Roumain manned a gigantic metal register near the entrance while a throng of bustling Creole women examined his wares and bickered with each other. Roumain deflected the invitations and flirtations that Harry would eventually note always seemed to come his way. Even though he was a very large man, he always had three or four widows sniffing around him as if they were alley cats and he had just covered himself with catnip. He always brushed it off, claiming that the women were just interested in his store, but from what Harry would eventually see, the women seemed to be focused entirely on the romantic potential of the Creole bachelor.

Harry stayed for more than two hours that day, spending his time familiarizing himself with the products Roumain had on sale and the aisles in which they were stocked. He looked at bottles, cans and bags of spices, even helping a few customers find items he noticed in his explorations. When the flow of customers slowed a bit, Roumain stepped out from behind the counter and approached him, limping and leaning on a large, carved wooden cane.

"Next you gonna ask me for a job. Am I right, mon frère?" he smiled around another cheroot. Looking closely, though, Harry suspected that the soggy battered cigar might very well be the same one from the last week.

"Ain't I too little?" he mumbled.

"Sometimes, little is better, ya know? You can reach the top shelves with my stepladder and you can bend down for the items on the bottom… That's something I nevah want to do again if I can help it." Roumain paused and wrinkled his brow. "How does 75 cents sound?"

"A day?" asked Harry hopefully. It had taken nearly two months for him to save up the two dollars he had the other day. Lucien's offer was nearly incomprehensible to him. He would be richer than he ever had imagined. It wasn't likely that he could make it to the store every day. Things would slow down during the school year, but he could still count on a couple bucks each week if he worked on the weekends.

Roumain laughed so hard he nearly spit out his cheroot and fell over.

"A day?" he sputtered. "I don' think I could do that and remain in good standing with the Lord. No, son, I meant 75 cents per hour. I figured to need you in the store about nine to ten hours per week… at least until you go back to your learnin' in the fall. How's that sound to you?"

Harry was speechless. He nodded his head, afraid he would say something to jinx his good fortune. Like most boys his age, he had never been able to save more than a dollar or two at most by doing odd jobs for his parents or neighbors when they asked him. With this job, he could easily save ten times as much within a couple of weeks. Unlike most of his peers, he had a plan for the money. He would save the majority of his earnings for years and use it to get the hell out this city when he was old enough to take care of himself. Maybe he would even go to college someday. Well… he would save a lot of it, but he might buy himself a bike before college.

Roumain grinned, pulled the sloppy cigar from his mouth and chuckled, "So, we got us a deal, huh?" Seeing Harry nod again, he continued, "Okay, then let us settle for today and I'll see you at the start of next week."

He lumbered behind the counter and pushed a key on the metal monstrosity of a register. The cash drawer unlatched and slid out on metal

The Specimen

tracks. Roumain counted out 6 quarters and placed them gently into Harry's palm. The boy stared at the coins in glee, thanked his new friend profusely and raced out the door with, despite his promises to save the money, ideas of possible purchases bouncing around his head.

Roumain stood in the store's doorway watching Harry run down the street. His mouth turned up in a smile, but his eyes remained squinted as if holding back a wave of pain. After Harry's silhouette disappeared in the distance, Lucien Roumain winced visibly, grabbed the doorjamb with one big paw and clutched it until his nails bit into the wood.

"Don't get any ideas, mon frère," he growled. "You ain't thinkin' 'bout finding no new Steed, are you? No, you gonna be stuck with me fo' a long while now."

With that, he turned and reentered the shop, leaning heavily on his cane. On his back, the misshapen protrusion under his baggy shirt seethed and rippled beneath the fabric as if he had a coiled snake embedded in his flesh. One thing was true about snakes, though. Every so often, they outgrow their old skin and start growing a new one.

Chapter 19 – A Cold Wind Howling

"Evil is whatever distracts." – Franz Kafka

March 5, 1965 – Springfield, MA

The chill wind was swirling the sodden leaves that had been revealed in the gutter by the spring's early thaw. A misting of rain hung in the early morning air. Piles of grayish-brown slush and pools of oily water were scattered haphazardly along the sidewalk as the heavy black man lumbered on the daily path to his store. Lucien Roumain felt all fifty-two of his years in his bones this morning as he walked the four blocks from his apartment to his store. Especially his knees. He knew very well that he carried much more weight than he should, especially for a man his age. The local widows told him so often enough every time they came by the store, but if they truly were worried about him, they wouldn't constantly bring him dishes of their most recent culinary creations, would they?

Soups. Ribs. Fried Chicken. Casseroles. Pies. Stews. Cakes. Even some of that blessed clam chowder he adored. Next best thing to gumbo in his mind. What was a man to do? Deny the generous offerings they brought? Besides, since he couldn't give them what many of them truly wanted - male companionship – he had to accept their offerings and eat every last bite.

Considering his "condition", Roumain was just glad he could maintain a semblance of a normal life. Glad he had finally learned to control his urges and muffle the voices that often spoke to him. He could never reveal the creature that was melded to the muscles just below his left shoulder. Sadly, he had tried to confide in someone once before, years ago when he first became burdened with this parasite, and it had resulted in a series of horrifying events which culminated in a complete loss of control – a fugue state – where he had apparently killed some men.

Even now, he couldn't remember any specifics of the event that caused him to flee New Orleans. He only recalled the aftermath and a few brief images. The rain and the rage and the blood. Hurricane Audrey had

The Specimen

hit the Gulf Coast less than a month after he left the area and everyone he met had automatically assumed that the monstrous storm had been what caused him to pick up all his belongings and move north.

In the years since the incident, he had learned to exert his will over the Rider. This was a talent that most Steeds never exhibited. Unfortunately, this wall of resistance he had been able to build also blocked many of the physical benefits that supposedly came as part of the symbiosis. He had partial access to many of the Rider's memories, but they were intermittent and foggy, as if read through a piece of cheese cloth.

The rain intensified, coming down in intermittent squalls, thoroughly soaking Roumain as he limped around the corner to Bayou Lou's. It was nearing nine o'clock and the entire sky was a foreboding wall of gunmetal grey. He squinted as he approached his store. As expected, Harry was already there with his new bike. His pride and joy. Bottle green with orange flames on the crossbar. Even though he only worked on the weekends during the school year, he had saved up enough money to buy it in December, but he hadn't been able to ride it much at all due to the usual New England winter.

"You shoulda stayed home, young man," called Roumain. "This storm's looking like a big 'un. My bones ain't feelin' so good today. I don't think that anyone's gonna come to buy anything in this weather."

"I just wanted to get out of the house anyway, Lou. Too many people live with me," grumbled the lanky teen. Harry had sprouted at three or four inches over the winter. He was even cultivating a few stray hairs on his upper lip with the hope that they would eventually bloom into a glorious mustache.

"I hear that, Harry!" laughed Roumain. "A man needs his space."

He turned and opened the shop door, gesturing for Harry to enter. The boy wheeled his bike inside and leaned it against the wall in the back storeroom, before donning a slightly stained apron and meeting Roumain up front to work his four hour shift.

Harry stocked the shelves with new product, but it soon became apparent that the weather was so bad that no one would be venturing out in the storm. Not even Lucien's most fervent admirers Miss Rooks and Miss Aubuchon would brave the elements to visit him with their meals du jour. Harry was disappointed because Miss Aubuchon always brought extra gumbo for him, too.

Due to the dearth of customers, Roumain decided it would be a good day to clean the shop from top to bottom. For the next two hours, Roumain and Harry scrubbed, swept, mopped and polished every inch of the shop. Roumain hated cleaning, but when he did it, he threw himself into the job with a vengeance. Only once did a customer venture from the storm into the store, and she was in and out with her groceries within five minutes, barely giving the two them enough time to catch their breaths and drink some of Mama Roumain's famous mint tea.

The storm wailed, battering the plate glass window and threatening to tear the awning from it moors until Roumain hobbled out and cranked the handle to roll it in. He was thoroughly drenched in the few seconds he was outside in the squall. Huffing like a broken accordion, he came back in and leaned on the counter to catch his breath. Rainwater dripped all over the floor. When Harry asked if he wanted to sit down for a bit, the large man just coughed, shook his head and went back to work.

By the end of the chore, Harry was more tired and sore then he had been in months, but Roumain was looking extremely ill. He was wheezing, with rivers of perspiration running down his face and neck. Stumbling forward, he slumped in his chair and hung his head, sweat dripping from his nose into a small puddle on the floor. He sat that way for a couple of moments, occasionally twitching, long enough that Harry became concerned.

The muscular young boy stood up and approached his friend cautiously, thousands of frightening scenarios swirling in his head. He crouched down and looked in Roumain's eyes. They were rolled back in his skull with only his bloodshot sclera visible. Harry saw his lips move as if the unconscious man was attempting to speak to him.

The Specimen

"Lou? Lucien? Are you okay?" stammered Harry as he touched him lightly on the shoulder. "Say something, please. You're scaring me. Should I call a doctor?"

Roumain lashed out with his left hand, catching Harry's wrist before he could flinch away. Relentless, he squeezed it fiercely, causing the boy to yelp in pain as his wrist bones audibly ground together.

"Aauuggh! Lucien!!" yelled Harry. "Let go of me! You're hurting me!" He tried to pull away from his friend's implacable grip, nearly crying from the agony.

Roumain lifted his head and stared into Harry's eyes, his gaze drilling through to the back of his skull. Harry wanted to look away, but the psychological pull was almost magnetic. Roumain's eyes were normally a deep chocolate brown, barely distinguishable from the pupils. Now, as Harry stood there transfixed, he could see an inner gold-toned ring on the inner portion of the iris. On each eye a few of the golden strands grew past the iris into his sclera, twisting and bending like pale yellow worms behind the orbs.

"Conetl!... Cahuayoh!" hissed Roumain.

The words made no sense to Harry, but he knew they had meaning. Even to his untrained ears, they sounded as if they came from an ancient savage language.

Roumain's eyes crawled up the length of Harry's body as if inspecting a potential purchase of livestock. He licked his lips slowly, a string of spittle dangling from his chin and falling to the floor to land in a puddle of rainwater. He pulled Harry closer to him until the boy was within a foot of his leering face. His breath smelled of sweet tobacco and rum that Harry knew was in a flask in his pocket. Normally the scent would have been pleasant, but now it nauseated Harry and reminded him of the sickly sweet smell of decay.

"Lucien! Please stop it!" shouted Harry at his suddenly incoherent friend as he tried to pull away. "What's wrong with you? STOP!! You're going to break my wrist."

Roumain's grip lessened slightly as he leaned in even closer to Harry. He whispered in English with a bizarre intonation. His speech was completely free of the usual Creole accent, "My chiiiild. Fiiiinally. We meeeet…"

Harry felt as if he had lost his ability to speak, so paralyzed was he with fear. Someone… some Thing was using Roumain as a puppet. The entity speaking could not possibly be his friend, Lucien. He didn't know how he knew this, but he felt it to his core. Some other entity – something ancient, inhuman, and preternatural – was wearing Roumain's body like a stolen coat. The man's mouth moved, but it didn't seem to match the serpentine voice emanating from his throat.

"Aaare you frightened, liiiittle one? There issss no need to be friiiightened. You and I will sssoooon be one together."

Harry clenched his eyes shut. *This is all a dream*, he thought. *I will wake up in my bed and discover that it was all a bad dream. A terrible nightmare. It's still dark out and I haven't even left for work.*

A sharp pain shot through his wrist, forcing him to reopen his eyes to a dreadful sight. Roumain appeared to be having a convulsion. No longer speaking in the strange voice, he had bitten through his lower lip and a stream of scarlet was flowing past his chin and spattering on the floor. His eyes were once again rolled back and his right hand was swinging in random directions.

Harry was still trapped by Roumain's grip, but the pain in his wrist wasn't coming from his friend's hand. If anything, the pressure had let up significantly to the point where he soon might be able to pull away. Snaking out from beneath the left sleeve of Roumain's black shirt was a segmented worm-like tendril at the end of which grew a small dime-sized mouth. Bloody and nightmarish with its serrated barb-like fangs as far down its pink mucus-lined gullet as Harry could see.

Oh. My. God.

The lamprey mouth was chewing something soft and wet. Harry turned his wrist over and realized what was causing his pain. A

The Specimen

centimeter-deep pit the approximate size of a quarter had been scooped out of his inner wrist by the tentacle mouth.

Harry screamed. He yanked his arm away from Roumain and tumbled onto the floor as he was abruptly released. Now that he had actually seen his injury, his arm was throbbing and weak. The wound leaked some blood, but not as much as you would expect from something that deep. The wound edges were red, slightly cauterized by contact with acid or extreme heat. Harry sobbed to himself, sliding backwards until his butt hit a shelf of canned goods. This was NOT happening. His friend was not possessed by some horrible demon. It all had to be some sort of dreadful joke.

Suddenly, Harry's vision doubled and wavered before coalescing again into one clear image. His perception had changed. He felt something archaic and inhuman lurking inside his skull. A voice thundered inside his mind...

<CHILD, YOU WILL BE MY STEED ONE DAY. YOU HAVE NO CHOICE IN THE MATTER, BUT IT WILL HAPPEN. I. WILL. BE. YOUR. MASTER.>

Incorporeal talons carved open his cerebral cortex, peeling back layers of memories from birth to present day... raping his mind and leaving the shattered shell of Harry's psyche laid bare to the elements. The attack continued for what seemed like hours and days of torture, but Harry instinctively knew it was barely seconds since the creature had bitten his wrist.

Abruptly, a new presence entered his mind. It seemed younger. Benign and familiar. It was Lucien! His friend's spirit immediately launched itself into combat with his current foul tenant. Harry vomited from the internal chaos swirling in his head. He slumped bonelessly to the filthy floor and began writhing. Arms and legs flopped uncontrollably. Spit leaked from both corners of his mouth.

He banged his head against the shelves in the aisle, knocking a few cans to the linoleum. An industrial-sized can of stewed tomatoes fell from the top shelf and smacked him right above the right eye. The pain was blinding, but strangely clarifying. After a couple of seconds of gut-wrenching dizziness, he felt the voices fade and he had a sudden epiphany. He wasn't entirely helpless. If he could gather the energy, he could fight back, too! They were in his mind. His home field! His hero, quarterback Babe Parilli, wouldn't have given up. He wouldn't let his Boston Patriots pack it in without a fight and neither would he.

Gathering all his fury and mental energy, he sent out a psychic command full of wrath and screamed, "GET OUT OF MY HEAD!!!" A dazzling burst of cleansing vitality detonated inside his consciousness. A split second later, he knew that both intruders had been hit with the full power of his mental blast because, suddenly, they were gone. No trace of either specter remained. Exhausted, Harry slipped into welcome oblivion.

*   *   *

When he awoke, he was dry, warm and covered with quilts in his own bed in the room he shared with his little brother Marvin. Early morning light was streaming through the window onto the wall above his head. Shadows swayed in the breeze, matching the dance of the trees outside their building. Marvin's bed was empty, but their grandmother was in the room, seated on a rocking chair next to the bed with her yarn and knitting needles. He tried to sit up, but quickly became dizzy and had to lay back down to regain his equilibrium.

"Nana?" he croaked. "How did I get home?"

His grandmother looked up from her afghan-in-progress and smiled, "Look who's back among the living! You had us worried there, Rum Tum Tugger." She stood up and walked gingerly to the side of his bed. She lifted his chin delicately, examining the dark, swollen lump on his forehead. It was the size and texture of a small overripe peach, hanging over the bridge of his nose and his right brow.

She peered into his eyes, searching for a hint of subterfuge as she asked, "How did you get this whopper over your eye?"

Leaving out the part about the monster on Roumain's back, he explained that a shelf full of cans had fallen on him after he slipped on the wet floor. Nana stared into his eyes for a few seconds, then, nodding as if

The Specimen

satisfied by his answer, she stated calmly, "That's pretty much what your friend said when he brought you home yesterday afternoon. Your daddy wanted to call the police and check out his story, but we convinced him not to do it. Mr. Roumain seemed genuine to us and we saw no reason to stir up any trouble."

"Thanks, Nana," he replied, glad that his father wasn't getting involved. He had a temper on him worse than most could handle and who knew what might happen if he got riled up.

"Your bike is on the porch and he gave me your books. I put them on the table next to you, Tugger." she smiled as she gave him a peck on the cheek and headed for the door. "You must be ravenous by now. I'll get you some soup and some of your momma's bread now. Don't you get out of bed yet... you hear me?"

"Yes, Nana," he said, forcing a smile as she went down the stairs to the kitchen. Once she was gone, Harry's thoughts turned immediately to what had happened in the store. Part of him wanted to dismiss what he remembered as a hallucination. He had been hit on the head, after all. The memories were too vivid, though. He could not deny it. He had seen what he had seen. Roumain had a monster growing on his back.

Of course, there was no chance anyone would believe him. He was just a kid. Very few adults even seemed to remember their childhood vividly. If they heard him crying about aliens and monsters, he was more likely to be punished for making stories up than for any information that might cast the Riders in a bad light.

Maybe it was a demon or an alien like the ones in the horror comics his Uncle Sherman had given him last year – Weird Tales or that new one, Creepy. Regardless of what it was, he had proof that it hadn't been a delusion. The perfectly circular wound on the inside of his wrist was enough to convince himself that it had actually happened. It had scabbed over, but it still throbbed in time with his pulse, reminding him of the alien tentacle that had once been attached to his flesh. Strangely, it hadn't seemed like it was trying to eat him, more like he was being sampled. Tested to deem him worthy. Worthy of what? The voice in his head had said he would be its "Steed" and had promised to "Ride" him. Did that mean what it sounded like?

Harry was well aware that Roumain was not a very healthy man. Even though he was extremely strong, he never had any stamina and he needed a cane to walk long distances because his knees constantly pained him. Harry's friend was grossly overweight and could have a heart attack or stroke any day, but until now his poor health had never been fully acknowledged. If he, a 13 year-old boy, could figure that out, then it stood to reason that this creature – this Rider – knew that Roumain's time was limited.

It needed a new Steed and it had set its target on him. Somehow, unless Harry had misinterpreted the events in the store, it seemed that most of the time Roumain was able to repress the Rider's commands, unless weakened or incapacitated. With his failing health, those opportunities to take control would become much more frequent.

Harry rolled over, wincing as his vertigo returned, and reached for the books on the table. He was confused because, despite what Roumain had told his grandmother, these books were not his, nor did he recognize them. There were three paperbacks, all battered and creased. He looked at the titles and realized that they were books that Roumain had promised to lend him one day: <u>The Body Snatchers</u> by Jack Finney, <u>The Puppet Masters</u> by Robert Heinlein, and <u>The Midwich Cuckoos</u> by John Wyndham.

If not for his nightmarish experience yesterday, Harry would have found the thematic similarity of the three novels to be amusing. Now, however, he realized that Roumain had left them with him for a particular reason – to send Harry a message.

A message! Harry instantly began flipping through the pages of the books, searching for a piece of note paper. He found nothing loose inserted between pages. However, when he flipped through the books at a slower pace, he found a message from Roumain on the last page of <u>The Puppet Masters</u>. The note read:

My friend Harry,

The Specimen

It was never my intention to expose you to my unfortunate situation. In my ignorant pride, I believed that I could control the creature as I have for years, but it is now painfully apparent that this is not true anymore. My health is suffering and I grow weaker. Soon I may not be able to control this thing anymore.

I have decided to move on from Springfield and restart somewhere else — somewhere more isolated. I can't change what has happened, but I can make certain you and my other loved ones are no longer in danger.

Please do not attempt to contact me. This is for the best.

— Lucien

Harry read the letter twice to be certain he wasn't misinterpreting anything that Lucien had written. Once he was finished, he sat there staring dumbfounded at the page. This couldn't possibly be true. He recognized Lucien's elaborate signature, but he couldn't believe that their friendship was going to end like this. And it wouldn't. Not if he had anything to say about it.

Swinging his legs over the side of his bed, Harry stood up, intending to put on some clothes from the closet and head over to Bayou Lou's right away. He took one step and immediately tumbled to the floor. The room spun in circles as he stared at the ceiling, and before he could clamber back to his bed, his mother and grandmother found him sprawled on the carpet. They picked him up from the floor, taking turns berating him for his stupidity and clucking like a pair of hens around an injured chick. Soon, he was tucked back in bed and threatened with all sorts of disciplinary action if he tried something that idiotic again.

Obviously, it would take some time for him to heal, but when he was able, he aimed to ride his bike to the store and do whatever he could to change Lucien's mind. They could find a way to fight the monster together.

Chapter 20 - Trichotillomania

"Dogs never bite me… just humans" – Marilyn Monroe

As long as she could remember, Nina Valentine had always suffered from an acute oral fixation. She bit her nails so frequently that her nail beds were permanently scarred and disfigured. When she was a child, she chewed on her fingers so often that she sometimes had no nails at all, just sores at the ends of some of her fingers. A couple times her fingers became infected and the pain from the swelling around the wounds would force her to find another outlet for her habit. Her parents sent her to a therapist to get some help, but nothing worked. Even when they painted her remaining nails with something called denatonium benzoate (supposedly the most vile-tasting substance in existence), she still nibbled and gnawed without stopping. Eventually, she learned that her behavior was called onychophagy, a type of obsessive compulsive disorder, and although it was quite common, the severity of her case was likely to lead to future health problems.

Throughout her adolescence Nina had cycled through a number of obsessive compulsive disorders, but her fallback obsession was always her nail-biting. She went through a period of trichotillomania where she would repetitively pull out her eyebrows and eyelashes. When she developed acne in middle school, she compulsively washed her face dozens of times per day. When a pimple appeared, she lanced it immediately with a needle and scrubbed her face with a cloth soaked in hydrogen peroxide. This resulted in plenty of scabs, and of course she would pick at them, creating numerous pockmarks over her cheeks, forehead, legs and forearms.

Bulimia. Body Dysmorphic Disorder. Olfactory Reference Syndrome. Name the psychological disorder, Nina was likely to have had it at some time in her life.

Counseling. Group Therapy. Numerous medications. Nothing succeeded at completely stopping the compulsions. The only way she was able to end one was to start another, which was why she kept returning to the nail-biting. Out of all of the monkeys riding her back, this was the least harmful and therefore, the most tolerable.

Her first two years at Holyoke High School were utterly dreadful. An outcast due to her physical appearance, she had no true friends and only a few acquaintances, all of whom were as damaged as she was. Nina spent most of her freshman and sophomore years sitting in a corner of the classroom reading novels and occasionally answering questions to maintain her masquerade.

Her junior year was entirely different. That was when Wally Vanderhook moved to town and Nina discovered her true self. Wally's first day of school was in late September, 2004, a couple of weeks after classes had begun. He was assigned the only remaining desk in class, directly in front of her. As he took his seat, he glanced her way and offered up a shy smile. Nina flinched and buried her nose in the latest Laurell K. Hamilton vampire porn novel. In retrospect, the book might be what ultimately compelled him to introduce himself the next day.

"Good series once you get past all the sex," he commented as he slumped into his chair. Nina looked up and answered him with a shrug.

"My name is Wally, by the way," he continued, holding out his hand. She stared at it in confusion for a few seconds before clutching it quickly and responding in a whisper.

"Nina"

He smiled widely, friendlier than any of her classmates had treated her in years, and in doing so, kindled a spark in her that would smolder for weeks. They continued their conversation, comparing favorite authors and films. He preferred H.P. Lovecraft, August Derleth and Brian Lumley, while she gravitated toward Kathe Koja, Charlee Jacob, and Poppy Z. Brite. They both had cut their teeth on the King.

He sat next to her the next day and the next. Soon they were speaking every day in class and Nina actually began to look forward to school just to see Wally. She had never experienced such emotions about anyone before. In hindsight, she realized later that the magnitude of her feelings were probably due to a shift in her obsessive behaviors to an obsession with him, the first person outside her parents who had seen her as anything other than a freak.

The Specimen

On the surface, he was the typical suburban Goth kid, maybe taller than most at 6' 4", but otherwise seemingly interchangeable with all the other disaffected youth of the early 21st century. At any Marilyn Manson concert, he would have faded into the crowd like a shadow in an alley: skinny, shaggy black hair hanging over his oh-so-soulful eyes, black eyeliner, black tee with the Goth band du jour, black skinny jeans with the requisite chains hanging from the pocket, black nail polish, black spiked leather bracelets, etc... The only accessories that weren't black were his bright red Converse All-Stars and an array of red hoops in both his ears.

Within weeks, Wally and Nina had become friends, and Wally had joined her as an outcast within the caste system of the average American high school. It came as a complete surprise to Nina that he chose her over the status quo, but Wally took it in stride. Did it really matter how a few high school students with delusions of their own importance treated them? A throng of anorexic cheerleaders might make snide comments as they passed them in the hall between classes, but it was easy to shut them out with an iPod and a pair of headphones. A couple of gangsta rap wanna-bes might make suggestive catcalls after them as they leave the building after classes, but an anonymous tip to the principal that they were selling drugs in school was a sure way to create an opportunity for the police to conduct an impromptu locker search... K-9 officers and all. Odds were that a few dime bags might be found in the sweep anyway. And of course, there were always a few inbred redneck linemen on the football squad who might intentionally drive through a puddle and splash the two of them as they walked home together, but it was child's play to break into their lockers during football practice and pour a bottle of urine (saved for just such an instance) all over their belongings.

Nina had discovered a talent for devising a variety of methods for getting even with their tormentors, especially in ways that were untraceable to the source, and Wally was eager to be the instrument of her vengeance. For now it was sufficient to wreak some temporary damage upon the classmates who felt they were better than the others in their school, but the best revenge would be in a few years when the former elite will have crested their peak and begun the downward slide into suburban mediocrity. The unspoken social rankings would fade and everyone would be judged according to what type of cog they could be to perpetuate the endless cycle of Holy Capitalism.

As the school year went on, her friendship with Wally was having a visibly positive affect on Nina. The spark inside her eventually became a searing blaze that burned away the protective carapace Nina had built for years. Her nail-biting and scab-picking faded. Her skin cleared up and she adopted the Goth style as well. Though Wally had never given any impression that he was interested in Nina physically, she soon decided that he would be her first... *and there wasn't anything he could do about it.* She made intricate plans for an alcohol-induced seduction and waited for an opportune moment.

The big day arrived during their school's winter vacation, a couple days after Christmas. Nina's parents were visiting an elderly relative for the weekend and they had thankfully allowed her to skip it (her recent style changes would not have gone over well with Aunt Gertie). Nina invited Wally over for a night of horror movies, popcorn and a bottle of Cuervo Especial that she had managed to swipe from their liquor cabinet the morning after her father had hosted a business party at their house the previous weekend. The amount of alcohol consumed by her father's colleagues, spouses and significant others at the party had pretty much guaranteed that her parents were completely unaware of what remained in their liquor stash. She could have taken an entire case of liquor, but hadn't wanted to tempt the Fates. One bottle would suffice tonight.

Nina had planned the entire night to the second. She had rented a couple of science fiction movies that neither of them had seen yet, *Donnie Darko* and the recently released *The Butterfly Effect*, both of which she had read positive reviews on websites which she trusted. She had popcorn and chips ready to go, and she had banished her dog Fenris to the garage for the night. A Mastiff/Rottweiler mix, he was an affectionate brute who loved Wally, but few things will kill the mood more than a hundred twenty pound slobber factory sprawled across your lap.

Wally was to arrive by seven, but the hour struck and he had not yet appeared. Nina called his cellphone twice - at quarter past and half past the hour – but there was no answer and she began to get concerned. He had never even been one minute late before, so this was extremely

The Specimen

unusual. Had he chickened out? Had she scared him away? At nearly ten to eight, Nina was considering calling once more, but she didn't want to act desperate for his attention, when she finally heard the sounds of tires on the gravel in her driveway. Relieved more than annoyed, she yelled at Fenris for barking relentlessly in the garage, rushed to the front door and opened it ...

[Below is an excerpt of the video transcript of a counseling session between Dr. Arnold W. Colfax (DC) and his patient Nina V. (NV). The session occurred at 10:35 am on the morning of October 25, 2005 in the Sunderland State Women's Asylum in Sunderland, Massachusetts]

DC: What did you see? When you opened the door… who was there?

NV: If you had read my file, you should already know, Doc. It's right there. I've told the story dozens of times to so many people.

DC: Yes, Nina… but you haven't told it to me yet. I may notice something that my colleagues may have missed. Or perhaps I may ask a question in a manner that sparks a memory you didn't know you had.

NV: This is fucking pointless. It hasn't worked for the ten months I've been here and it won't work now.

DC: I see that you're angry. Understandable.

NV: Are trying to provoke me with your bargain basement psycho-babble?

DC: Just stating a fact, Nina. *[5 second pause]* I notice that your compulsions have increased dramatically in the past few weeks.

NV: You mean you notice that I'm half bald now from pulling out all my hair? And all my

The Specimen

nails are gnawed down to the quick? How observant. No wonder they sent you here to pick my brain.

DC: I know you feel that this is completely unnecessary, just as you know why we keep going over that night.

NV: I'm not gonna suddenly discover some buried memory, Doc. I've remembered all I can…

DC: Please try, Nina. I can understand how angry you must be at the constant repetition, but it does serve a purpose. If you want to be released into your parents' custody, they need some reassurance that you have recovered enough from your experience so they can be sure that you won't try to harm yourself again.

NV: Who are you again? And why am I even talking to you? I've never seen you here before today. I don't like meeting new people… especially shrinks who look at me like I'm a bacteria culture in their own personal petri dish.

DC: If I introduce myself once again, will you agree to return the favor and answer some questions for me, Nina? I promise my intentions are solely to help you to confront what happened and that is all. We have the same goal, Nina. To help you heal. [A lengthy pause of 20-30 seconds passes as Nina stares defiantly at Dr. Colfax, then shrugs and nods her head. Colfax then continues]. My name, for the record, is Dr. Arnold O. Colfax. I hold doctorates in Psychiatry and Neurology with specializations in Cognitive Neuropsychiatry and Behavioral Neurology.

Drs. Brewer and Weingarten have asked me to consult on a number of cases in this facility, including yours, Nina. Cases which involve severe Post-Traumatic Stress Disorder. I've had a significant amount of success in aiding patients in retrieving repressed memories due to mental trauma… and your doctors believe that my expertise can help here.

[Another 5 second pause.]

Does that answer your question, Nina? May we continue?

NV: Fine. I'll answer the questions.

DC: Good. Now, you opened the door expecting your friend. Is this where we were?

NV: Yes, that's right.

DC: And what did you see?

NV: Wally. On his knees. His face was all battered and bloody. There was so much… so much fucking blood. He fell forward and I tried to catch him, but he hit the ground anyway. *[She bites her fist to hold back a sob].* God damn it…

DC: Take your time with the next part, Nina. Try to recall it with all your senses, Sounds. Smells. Anything could be important.

NV: He was hurt… so bad. He began retching and spitting up blood. It got all over my hands and shirt and it was so sticky. I couldn't get

The Specimen

it off me and I couldn't stop screaming. [5 second pause as she grits her teeth at the painful memory and composes herself]. And then they were suddenly there...

    DC: Who showed up, Nina? Describe them in as much detail as you can remember. The smallest fact could be important.

    NV: There were three of them. They had masks. Rubber Halloween masks of famous monsters. Dracula, Frankenstein. A zombie, I think. I could tell right away those fucks were from our school. Their voices sounded familiar and they immediately started calling me the same names that I was called in school. The same names that made me flip out last week when they used it.

    DC: And what names would that be?

    NV: Witch Bitch and... Little Skank Ho. They pushed me into the house and shoved me so I fell onto the floor next to Wally.

    DC: Did you notice anything else when they came in? Describe them as best as you can.

    NV: I didn't know then that I was right, but they looked like some of the football players from our school. Two white boys and a fat black guy. They reeked of alcohol and they were slurring their words. I'm absolutely sure they were the ones who had beaten Wally. There was blood on their hands and clothes. The black guy had a large splash of it on his shoelaces.

DC: These three individuals… Would they be Shane Corker, Bobby Desjardins, and Teddy Meeks?

NV: I didn't find out their names until later. To me they had always been a bunch of interchangeable dumbass jocks who thought they were better than everyone and treated girls like pieces of meat. They didn't deserve my attention at all. I avoided them in school whenever I could.

DC: They seemed to think you deserved their attention.

NV: They assaulted me! They almost killed Wally! He deserved better!
[She throws her chair against the wall, screams and Dr. Colfax abruptly stops the tape after the sound of a door opening followed by loud voices and a scuffle. After five seconds of silence, the recording resumes.]

DC: Miss Valentine. Now that you have had a few minutes to let out some of your aggression, are you ready to continue? [short pause] I'll assume that your nod signals your agreement, but I must request that you speak out loud in the future.

NV: Fine. Just get on with it.

DC: You left off with three intruders entering your house with their faces covered by Halloween masks. How long was it before you realized they were your classmates?

The Specimen

NV: Almost immediately.

DC: How so?

NV: One of them pulled me off of Wally and punched me in the face. Called me "a little skank" just like they did at school. Said they were "going to teach me a lesson that I'd never forget".

DC: What do you think they meant by that?

NV: You know what happened. My file is right next to you. There's color photos and everything. Do I really need to paint a picture for you?

DC: Yes, I've seen them, Nina. However, the reports are quite sanitized. It will help us much more to hear what happened in your own words.

NV: *[sighs]* They attacked me, Doctor. They hit me a couple times and knocked me to the floor. *[short pause as she took a deep breath]*… and they ripped off my skirt and panties and took turns with me. Two of them held my arms while the other one had his way. They ran a train on me! One after the other after the other! Is that what you wanted to hear? The gory details? It hurt more than any pain I had ever felt before, like I was being torn apart. I kept screaming but no one came to help me. No one stopped them. No one…

DC: I know this is painful each time you tell it, and I'm sorry, but it is necessary for your recovery. [He pauses as he consults the thick manila folder of files on the table.] In your previous statements, you state that you blacked out the last few minutes of the assault.

NV: The gang rape, you mean the gang rape.

DC: Yes.

NV: I can't be sure. It's all like a bad dream that I fade in and out of… All I saw were Wally's eyes staring at me as they took it from me. They took it…

DC: It? What is it? What did they take from you?

NV: [whispering] Why are you making me say it? [another lengthy pause] My virginity. They took it and I can never get that back. It was supposed to be Wally. It was supposed to be perfect… a night I would remember forever. [She laughs unconvincingly] I guess that part came true. I'll never forget what happened… no matter how long I live.

DC: Tell what happened next, Nina.

NV: I came out of my mental fog while Frankenstein was on top of me for the second time. They had me pinned, so I still couldn't move my arms. The other two guys… I knew I wasn't going to wrestle my way past them. They were way too big. Each of them had at least a hundred pounds on me and they were barely

The Specimen

breaking a sweat. I had to do something drastic or they might decide to shut me up for good.

DC: And what did you do?

NV: I bit him. *[A tone of pride enters her voice]* I pretended that I liked being used by them, so I put on a show for him, kissing his collarbone and neck and he kept pumping away between my legs. I tried to moan to make it convincing and it seemed to work, because they started saying shit like "Yeah, baby" and "You like that, huh?"
When I finally had the opportunity, I opened my mouth as wide as I could stretch it and clamped my teeth on both sides of his larynx… and then I bit him through his Adam's apple with all the anger I had saved inside of me.

DC: Describe what it felt like, Nina. You need to re-experience every emotion that happened in each moment. You need to face your trauma head on and defeat it. Reliving how you escaped is exactly what you need now.

NV: Have you ever tasted blood, Doc? I don't mean sucking your thumb after a paper cut. No, I mean… have you ever swallowed full mouthfuls of blood until it overflows your lips and leaks through your teeth?

DC: I can't say that I've ever had the opportunity, Nina.

NV: It is an experience you never forget. You always hear that it's salty… and it is, but more than the salt flavor, you taste the coppery metal and you feel how warm and sticky it is. It was almost gummy in texture… I chewed through Frankenstein's larynx like it was the cartilage on a drumstick from KFC. Blood just gushed out of the hole in his throat… all over my face and shirt, and he fell back trying to scream, but I must have perforated his windpipe because he could only make a high-pitched airy whistling.

The other two guys immediately freaked out and scrambled away from both of us. I stood up and spat the chunk of throat gristle back into Frankie's lap, and then I immediately high-tailed it down the hall to the kitchen where I knew I could get a knife.

DC: What did they do then? Did they chase you or not?

NV: I discovered later that the kid in the Dracula mask ran out the door and called the cops. He tried to say that I had invited them over… that the gang sex was my idea. Thankfully he was an idiot and contradicted himself a number of times… plus there was the issue of Wally.

DC: Yes, Wally. At least he was able to recover and counter their story…

NV: The black guy in the zombie mask didn't run. He chased me into the kitchen and managed to grab some of my hair, but I pulled away from him and left a clump of it in his hand. I ran right to the knife block and snatched the biggest one I could find. I

The Specimen

whirled around and saw he was immediately behind me, so I just started slashing and stabbing like a whirlwind. I got in a good 10 stabs before that fat bastard ran off, following one of his friends and leaving the other dying in the living room.

    DC: 37, actually.

    NV: 37 what?

    DC: You cut him 37 times. For a total of 358 stitches… Most of it through the mask on his face. It's all in the report, Nina.

    NV: [muttered under her breath] Should've killed him. All three of them.

    DC: Do you want to kill them? Do you still want vengeance?

    NV: What? No… of course not. That wouldn't get back what was taken from me. No… I wouldn't… That would be wrong.

    DC: Vengeance is a completely understandable desire, Nina. Vengeance. Not revenge. The two acts are entirely different from one another. Revenge is solely about passion. Rage. Fury. Vengeance, on the other hand, is about retribution for a crime done against oneself. Justice, in other words. Vengeance is about restoring the balance to the scales of justice. [He pauses, making a decision]. Nina, what if I told you I could provide you a chance to balance the scales against your two remaining assailants, Mr. Corker and Mr. Weeks?

NV: Wait… What? What are you saying? Is this a trick?

DC: Miss Valentine, do you want your vengeance?

NV: [burying face in her hands for a few seconds before yelling] Yes! Of course I do. I want to peel the skin from their screaming carcasses. I want them to suffer completely. How could I not want anything else? It will never happen, though. I'm going to be locked up here for an extremely long time.

DC: Perhaps not, Miss Valentine. Perhaps not. Perhaps we can help each other in the future. Our paths are not always predetermined. Sometimes what seems to be a dead end can reveal itself as a road to a better destination than your original one. *[He claps his hands, startling Nina and stands up from his chair].* In the meantime, our session is complete. I won't keep you any longer with my questions, but I will most definitely be in touch in the near future.

[Dr. Colfax walks to the door and presses a buzzer. Seconds later, an orderly unlocks the door and escorts Nina back to her room. Dr. Colfax once again closes the door. He returns to his seat, leans back and looks directly at a camera in the ceiling before speaking]

The Specimen

DC: So, we're done with the interview… Make the Council aware that I believe that, with the right conditioning and chemical assistance, Miss Valentine is a prime candidate for our team. In fact, I'll even wager that she will eventually turn out to be one of our most valuable assets…

[A deep voice breaks the sepulchral silence]

VOICE: The Council has already made its decision, Dr. Colfax. We agree with your determination. Proceed with the plan of action and have a team detain the two surviving boys who attacked Miss Valentine. Await further instructions.

DC: Understood [He points a remote control toward the bank of equipment and presses the OFF button.]

- END TAPE -

Pete Kahle

The Springfield Republican

Monday, November 14, 2005

AT LEAST EIGHT PERISH IN TRAGIC BELCHERTOWN INFERNO

By Michelle Colton, Republican Contributing Reporter

BELCHERTOWN – In what is being called "one of the worst fires in Hampshire County history", four hospital residents, one doctor and three kitchen workers lost their lives when a reported gas leak caused an explosion in the kitchen at the Belchertown State Women's Psychiatric & Addiction Center. By the time engines arrived, less than ten minutes after the fire was called in, the blaze was curling the leaves of the trees surrounding the institute and the outer wall of the cafeteria had already begun to collapse.

"It sounded like a bomb went off. For a second there, I thought we were being attacked," stated Robyn Willocks, a nurse at BSWPAC for the past five years. "Thankfully, it happened when the cafeteria was almost empty. Also, we have practiced our evacuation routes many times or there could have many more deaths today. We were really lucky."

The definition of "lucky" may vary, depending on one's perspective. For eight poor souls, it was the end of the line.

Assistant Director Sheldon Weingarten, 63, and four residents, Tammi Lynn Reese, 34, Valerie Salamone, 26, Wendy Alcorn, 35, and Nina Valentine, 18, were identified after their bodies were found buried under the wreckage of the cafeteria. Nearer to the center of the explosion were three kitchen workers whose remains have yet to be positively identified. Any information

The Specimen

regarding these individuals or the explosion should be submitted to the Hampshire County Sheriff's Department as soon as possible.

The fire started just after one in the afternoon as many residents were returning to their rooms for a regularly scheduled afternoon rest period after the day's lunch. "The gas appears to have been leaking for a few minutes before it was ignited. Long enough to fill the kitchen and seep in to the cafeteria," opined Hampshire County Fire Marshall Jim Kilkenny. "I doubt they even knew what hit them." Kilkenny went on to say that the blaze remains under investigation and the preliminary findings were based on conclusions developed from the evidence collected at the time of the fire.

Pete Kahle

The Springfield Republican

Thursday, November 17, 2005

FAMILY TRAGEDY ENDS IN MURDER-SUICIDE

By Michelle Colton, Republican Contributing Reporter

HOLYOKE – Most of us go our entire lives without being touched by the ice-cold hand of fate. Fortune may not always favor us, but neither do we fall prey to heart-rending tragedy. When this happens to someone in our towns, we gather at our churches and community centers to offer prayers and occasional financial aid to our friends in need, but on our return trips home we mutter mumbled gratitudes that we were not the ones afflicted.

"Poor bastard. Better him than me, though …"

"I don't care as long as it doesn't happen to me"

"I'm glad I'm not in her shoes."

We've all said this to ourselves one time or another and then we go about our everyday hum drum existences. We can barely imagine what such an incident would do to our families and friends. What would happen if misfortune lingers around an individual or group, striking them more than once? Could you and your loved ones even survive? It seems unimaginable. Lightning never strikes twice in the place, right? Except for one family…

On the morning of December 28, 2004, long-time Holyoke residents Donald and Crystal Valentine arrived home to find a group of squad cars parked outside their home. Crime scene tape blocked entry to their driveway and neighbors milled around across the street like paparazzi at a Hollywood red carpet event. Upon verifying their identities, they were escorted to Holyoke Medical

The Specimen

Center where their 17 year-old daughter, Nina, was recovering from an alleged home invasion and gang rape.

In the aftermath of the incident, one boy was dead, two more were on life support and in critical condition, and a fourth was accusing her of being a "blood-drinking witch". Despite the eventual corroboration of a witness, rumors of deviant behavior and Nina's past run-ins with the law soon cast doubt upon her version of the night's events. That, and the realization that she was suffering from a severe case of Post-Traumatic Stress Disorder, led to her parents admitting her to Belchertown State Women's Psychiatric & Addiction Center to undergo intense inpatient therapy. She was a resident there until another tragedy struck on Monday of this week.

Fast forward ten months to this past Monday when we reported that eight lives were lost in a gas fire at the same facility. For the second time in a year, Donald and Crystal met with officers from the Holyoke Police Department to learn some tragic news. This time, they discovered that one of the individuals who perished in the fire was their daughter Nina. According to friends, the news of her death devastated them and led them to their eventual downward spiral.

At approximately 2:30 this morning, Holyoke police were called to respond to complaints of a barking dog at 134 Ketchum Court. One of the respondents, Officer Theo Klotz, had also been there on that fateful night in December 2004.

"I'll be the first to admit that it felt weird as soon as I pulled up the driveway," commented Klotz. "What's that word? Déjà vu? Yeah, that's what I felt. It was exactly like it was when I rolled up to the same house last December. The dog was barking in the garage and all the lights were turned on throughout the house. The door was open so we announced ourselves and proceeded to enter cautiously. As soon as we walked in, we smelled the blood. Mr. and

Mrs. Valentine were in the family room and it was apparent that it was too late to save anyone".

Once all the evidence was gathered and the series of events were reconstructed, police determined that both parties had been drinking heavily last night. At some point before midnight, an argument broke out between the Valentines. Donald Valentine struck his wife in the face, fracturing her cheekbone. Crystal retreated to her room, returning with the pistol he had bought her for their 15th anniversary, and shot him three times in the face. After Donald's corpse slumped to the carpet, she dropped the gun and went to the master bath room to draw a hot bubble bath where she sliced open her wrists and drifted off into unconsciousness.

Some individuals may still believe that it isn't possible for lightning to strike twice in one place, much less three times. I challenge those people to read about these past few events, analyze them and still come to the same conclusion. If the Valentines were still around, they might have a bone to pick with you.

The Specimen

Springfield Morning Union

Wednesday, November 23, 2005

**PAIR OF MUTILATED BODIES
FISHED FROM WESTFIELD RIVER**

By Garrett Kearney, Union Contributing Reporter

WESTFIELD – As the sun set on a seemingly uneventful Tuesday in the peaceful suburb of Westfield, most families were preparing for the upcoming Thanksgiving feast on Thursday. Guest rooms were being prepared for visiting relatives. Cars were being packed for out of town road trips. Turkeys were being thawed out to be brined, stuffed and placed in the oven on Thursday morning. The officers of the Westfield Police Department, on the other hand, were pulling two waterlogged corpses from the shallows of the Westfield River.

The first body was discovered by Maureen Cullen, 15, and her younger brother Liam, 11, as they rode their bikes down the path at the edge of the river on their way home from school.

"Liam saw it first. He's always looking for frogs and bugs. At first we thought it was an old mannequin that someone had thrown into the water," Maureen stated. "But then, as we got closer, we could see the bones sticking out of its… um, neck hole. That's when we knew something was wrong."

Later, after the authorities responded to Maureen's phone call to 9-1-1, a second body was discovered while scouring the river bank for evidence barely fifty yards downstream from the initial find, lodged beneath a tree which had fallen into the river months earlier.

"Whoever dumped them here didn't try too hard to hide them," commented Westfield Deputy Ray Lister. "If it weren't for the freak snowstorm earlier this month, someone probably would've already stumbled upon them by now. There's always a lot of foot traffic and bikers on the path at this time of year, coming out to see the leaves changing. It can get astonishingly beautiful around here."

Neither body has been identified yet, but authorities are compiling a list of potential candidates from the Missing Persons reports from the surrounding counties. The Hampden County Medical Examiner's Office released the following information in order to aid in the identification of the bodies. Both individuals were extremely fit young men in their late teens to early twenties … probably athletes. The first body to be found was an African-American male, approximately 6'4" in height and weighing 275 pounds, while the second was a Caucasian male measuring 6"2, with a weight of 245 pounds. Both bodies had been severely mutilated and battered, both before and after submersion in the river. An anonymous source in the Office of the Hampden County Medical Examiner stated that most of the wounds appear to be bites or surgical excisions on the faces and genitals of the two men, further complicating their identification. The exposure to the elements and local wildlife further deteriorated any evidence.

"We will dedicate every resource available," said Sheriff Glenn Pearson when asked if he thought this could be the work of a serial killer. "I won't comment on the specific evidence because it's an ongoing investigation and we want to actually catch the perpetrators of this horrendous crime." Any information regarding the identities of these two individuals should be directed to the attention of Detective Rowland Crouch in the Hampden County Sheriff's Office at (413) 555-5353.

The Specimen

<<ACME EYES ONLY>>
What We Know: An ACME Group Primer on the Riders
J.P. Kilcannon/G. Suares/K. Morimoto, 11th Edition

Section E – Reproduction

Frequency – With the ability to move from host to host and their virtually immortal lifespan (barring injuries), the need for Riders to reproduce is minimal. When a host dies unexpectedly, however, Riders must find a new host within two to three days. Without one, the Rider will certainly die. When it becomes apparent that the Rider may die without a new host, the urge to release larvae - to continue the species - rears its head.

Rider reproduction seems to have two specific triggers, each of which results in the production of larvae. The primary trigger for reproduction seems to be whenever the Rider is in certain mortal danger. Less commonly, the release of larvae can come from a subconscious awareness of the need to replenish their numbers due to regional catastrophes, be they natural or man-made. Primary examples of such events are the Black Plague, the various Crusades, the Holocaust, the Armenian Genocide, the Stalinist pogroms, Hiroshima and Nagasaki, Hurricane Katrina, etc…

Implantation/Gestation - Appearing as pale yellow slugs, the larvae immediately scatter from the deceased host in search of new candidates to ensure that the genetic memory is passed on. Unlike the symbiotic nature of Rider and host, the relationship between larva and host is purely parasitic.

The larva is ingested by the host through any available orifice (either voluntarily or involuntarily), where it then implants somewhere in the chest or abdomen, burrowing into the flesh. Here it develops much like a pregnancy, regardless of the age or gender of the host. Within four to six months, depending on the health of the host, the larva will mature into a full grown Rider and emerge.

Eruption – A Rider can be removed surgically just before it is ready to exit the host. If done in time, the chances of survival for the host are better than 50/50. However, if the Rider is allowed to come to full term, the survival chances drop to zero.

The host's body undergoes rapid, dramatic physical changes in the hours before the Rider is ripe. Its skin grows translucent and blood vessels rise to the surface, outlining where the parasitic creature will exit. The muscles in the area begin to spasm and expand in an accelerated semblance of child labor as the new Rider presses outward at the eventual point of evacuation. If an orifice is available the creature will dilate it to its limits and tear its way out if needed. If not, the flesh will continue to distend and expand until it rips. In some cases, the aftermath appears as if a grenade has blown a hole in the host's flank.

Once the newly emerged Rider has regained its energy, evidence has shown that it will attack the first potential host it encounters in order to ensure its survival. It is currently unknown why the Rider doesn't simply bridle the host in which it has gestated, other than the fact that its birth often kills the individual.

If the first encountered host proves not to be compatible, the Rider will search for another at the expense of the health and mental state of the first, discarding it when a new host is found. The shock of the abrupt forced separation may have a negative effect on the first host, up to and including death.

Section F – Thralls

In addition to the parasitic relationship between Rider and Host, there are two other methods that Riders have been known to use to exert influence over other individuals/creatures.

The first one is the previously mentioned use of pheromones to project emotions upon another person. If the emotion is love or, less often, fear, the target can be induced to act in a specific manner while under the influence of the pheromones. The victim actually feels that she is in love with the Host. Any request from the host is considered reasonable, no matter the subject, and the victim does whatever she can to fulfill the request.

The Specimen

The older the Rider, the stronger the pheromones' effects will be. In the case of Elders, the Host can convince the victim to even commit murder, and then wipe the victim's memory of the incident. Eventually, however, it becomes impossible to maintain the pheromone output and the effect wears off. The strength of the pheromones directly corresponds to the age of the Rider and the time it takes to diminish.

The other more common method is through the creation of Thralls, or creatures bound into mental servitude to the Rider. In the vast majority of cases, thralls are animals that have been enslaved through the ingestion of a small bit of the Rider's tissue... a *bug*, if you will. These *bugs* are about fifty percent smaller and less complex than the larvae used to impregnate individuals with the seed of a new Rider.

The only recorded cases of humans being Enthralled happened centuries ago at the peak of the Rider population (see Section F. – Rider History). All other recorded cases have involved animals. Examples include rats, birds, dogs, horses, monkeys, and even larger wild animals, such as wolves, lions and hyenas. Some species seem to be more compatible than others to becoming Enthralled, but the fact that a species has not yet been recorded as a Thrall does not signify that it is not possible. It simply means that it has not yet been witnessed and recorded.

This is not to say that there are no longer Riders capable of creating human Thralls. Only that there are no records of such in recent centuries. Since we are constantly learning new information about the Riders, it is likely that we will discover more modern records of human Thralls.

Thralls, unlike Hosts and individuals under the effect of the pheromones, can only follow simple directions of two to three steps maximum. For example, a Thrall could be ordered to go to a specific location and attack an individual at a certain time, but it could not follow complex directions involving multiple tasks. On the other hand, Thralls are believed to maintain a constant psychic connection with the Rider, whereas individuals affected by pheromones only respond to verbal commands.

Historically, a Rider does not appear able to create Thralls until it is well over a century old. Once created, Thralls are believed to be mainly used for reconnaissance and, to a lesser extent, targeted violence - the equivalent of suicide bombers. When instructed to attack someone, Thralls focus all their energy on harming their opponent with no regard to protecting themselves. As a result, they tend to have a high mortality rate and are utilized less sparingly than in the past.

The Specimen

Chapter 21 - Sneakers

"Blood debts must be repaid in blood." – Chinese proverb

Modern Day – Chesterfield, MA

Grimaldi recalled his first kill as if it had happened yesterday. You never forget your first time. Truth be told, he remembered all of his kills, from the first to the most recent, his forty-third, not that he was keeping a tally. He was just wired that way. Nobody would ever accuse Grimaldi of being a member of Mensa, but his memory was uncanny. That and his talent for murder made him quite valuable in Quillian's eyes.

If anyone had witnessed Grimaldi's first murder, no one would have ever thought that he would someday make a profession out of killing people. It had been spontaneous, sloppy and amateur. Grimaldi was still astonished that no one had ever fingered him for it, but nearly twenty years later, the case remained unsolved. Most likely the main reason he had not been caught since that first event was the fact that he never once again made things personal. Murder was a profession for Grimaldi, not a hobby. He didn't enjoy the act, but he did appreciate when he completed a job efficiently.

The gas fumes were making him light-headed, not to mention the fact that he had been off on another trip down memory lane. He was not on his game tonight. Grimaldi shook his head to clear the cobwebs and continued dousing the rooms of the Monahan house with the contents of the gas cans.

The bodies of Chuck and Kate were laid out on their beds, while Hank's body had been dragged out of the kitchen and dumped in the middle of his bedroom between the king-sized water bed and the fish tank. A propane heater had been taken from the garage and placed in the master bedroom to serve as a decoy cause for the fire he was about to set. The house reeked of gasoline and propane fumes. *Gotta wrap things up before I pass out*, he thought. *Just one more circuit through the house and then it's barbeque time.*

Both of the girls were still alive, having been bound and gagged before being placed in the truck by Quillian. Murtaugh left with them an hour ago. By now, he should have arrived at Hartford compound where they would be held. Grimaldi and Quillian would be heading there later with the specimen removed from Monahan's flank. One this large hadn't been located in decades. Cultivated in labs, yes, but not naturally occurring like this one. Normally, the host would have been identified much earlier and any mass would have been removed well before it was much larger than a walnut.

In Monahan's case, he hadn't visited a doctor in nearly a decade, so the creature had been allowed to gestate nearly to maturity. Only when his wife had used a guilt trip on him into donating blood at a Red Cross blood drive sponsored by Sydney's high school tennis team was he flagged as a host by the Acme Group. What had been a generous donation that would possibly save someone's life had indirectly ended the lives of Monahan and his family. *Ain't that a kick in the kiwis?* thought Grimaldi.

Quillian was on his cell phone in the back yard, sending another crew to the hospital to check on that kid who was hit by the car. *He'll probably send Bohannon and Geist*, he thought. *If only Murtaugh hadn't messed things up with the kid. He's got a good eye, but no killer instinct at all.*

Grimaldi walked once more through each room in the house, drenching the shower curtains in each bathroom with gasoline and making certain the gas burners on the stove were turned on. He opened multiple windows on each floor to provide oxygen once the fire was lit. Finally, he checked the screened porch at the back of the house. Best to make sure there weren't any more witnesses besides that boy in the hospital. It never hurts to double-check. Apparently the original intent was for the porch to be used as an exercise room, with a treadmill and a weight bench next to a couple of bicycles hanging from pegs on the wall, but that seemed to not have lasted that long. All the exercise equipment was covered with a thick layer of dust, and much of the floor space was filled with stacks of cardboard boxes filled with the type of debris that families collect through the years, yet can't bear to throw out.

There was also a cat. Long-haired, mainly orange with black and gray patches on its legs and a black mask on its face, the animal was sprawled on top of a makeshift bed made from a cardboard box and an old

The Specimen

military blanket. It opened its eyes for a few seconds, flashed Grimaldi the feline equivalent of a sneer, then buried its head in its fur. The big man froze for a second, then crouched a few feet away, smiled broadly and called quietly to it, "C'mere, buddy... here, kitty, kitty."

* * *

Thirty-three years earlier, Grimaldi was orphaned as an infant when both of his parents were killed in a hit and run accident. The usual story... A drunk driver T-boned their car after running a red light. Baby Albert was the only survivor, safely protected in a new car seat that his parents had purchased that same day. He lived with his paternal grandparents for the next three years and, by all accounts, led a happy life, but when his grandfather died of a heart attack just after his 4th birthday and his grandmother suffered a serious stroke less than a month later, Grimaldi was placed in foster care. In his mind, this was the moment his life set him on his current path.

Labeled "an angry, sullen child", he bounced from family to family over the next seven years until finally he ended up with Martin and Gina Shawcross, a middle-aged couple who were obviously in the foster family game for the financial benefits. They weren't cruel, but it was soon apparent that they had no emotions invested in young Albert Grimaldi or his three foster brothers. He was the youngest at 12. The others were 14, 14 and 15. Normally he would have been a target for older children, but he had recently hit puberty and an early growth spurt had minimized the chances of any bullies focusing on him.

"Don't cost us any extra money. Don't bring the cops to our door. Don't expect anything from us but what we're required to do. Abide by those rules and you've got a place to stay until you're 18. Is that understood, Al?" Martin had said as he drank from a can of Keystone Light. The two of them sat on folding chairs in the dingy kitchen of the Shawcross house that afternoon in September, 1993. Gina was washing the dishes, but intentionally staying out of the discussion. Al would soon learn that she wasn't much of a conversationalist. Martin, on the other hand, seemed to love the sound of his own voice, and he was always willing to share his opinion with anyone who was within earshot. Despite this, Gina was able to shut him up with a single sideward glance.

Al nodded and mumbled, "Yessir." That was pretty much the end of the introductions. Martin showed him downstairs to the partially finished basement, which he learned he would share with his foster brothers. He opened the door, and ushered him into the room with a quick "This is Al. He's staying with us" before turning around and squeezing past Al on the way upstairs for another can of watery piss.

The basement was large, but with four boys in their teens (or in Al's case, close enough to it), it would soon feel cramped. On the far end of the room, opposite the door, were two metal bunk beds placed caddy corner on the right side. Two beat-up couches, both the same dingy green color, formed an entertainment area around a scarred coffee table and a monstrous console television. On top of the coffee table was a Nintendo system with multiple game cartridges scattered around it. A tall, skinny blonde kid with glasses was seated on one couch playing a game of Double Dragon on the NES with a stocky boy with buzzed brown hair and serious case of acne. The third occupant of the room was a short black kid on the right bottom bunk with his nose buried in a novel the size of a phone book (which Al later learned was The Stand by Stephen King, the only non-library book that he ever saw within the Shawcross household). All three glanced at Al, grunted in an approximation of a greeting and then went back to their activities. Al walked over to the bunk beds without speaking, climbed up to the unoccupied mattress on the top left bunk and went to sleep.

Later that afternoon, Al learned their names. The blond on the couch introduced himself as Kevin. The boy with the pizza face was Turkish with the awkward name of Osman Hamzaoğlu. Call me Ozzie," he said. Al gladly obliged. "That's Lewis," Ozzie said, pointing at the kid with his nose in a book. Lewis looked up, mumbled a greeting and went back to his novel.

The next couple of months living in the Shawcross house were quiet, but boring. Al tried to play Nintendo with Kevin and Ozzie, but he simply didn't have the knack for it. All Lewis did was read books that he borrowed from the local library. Once, Al went with him to see if there

The Specimen

were any books he might like, but came back empty-handed. Martin and Gina preferred their privacy, so the boys were discouraged from coming upstairs for anything but meals and laundry. There was a full bathroom in the basement, so, anytime they were not in school, they rarely went above ground.

As usual, school was an exercise in futility. Al stumbled through his classes with a D average and he probably didn't even deserve it. Most teachers considered him dull and colorless. When asked questions, his usual answer was a shrug. Occasionally they would toss him a softball question. His strategy was to mumble something he had heard repeated over and over again during class. He was correct enough times to maintain a semblance of attention. He made no friends, and his foster brothers were in high school while he was stuck in middle school, so he walked to and from classes alone.

The walk took well over twenty minutes each way. More if the weather was bad. It rarely bothered Al, though. Even though South Boston was not known for its neighborhood safety, nor was it the most picturesque locale, the walks to and from school were Al's escape. Those few minutes each day were when he felt most in control. He could choose which street to go down and what pace he would take. His favorite pastimes were to observe other people on his walks and to feed any stray animals he passed with scraps of food he collected from various dumpsters.

There were quite a few unconventional characters on his usual route home. He imagined their personal lives, their conversations, and their crimes. He created elaborate backstories in his mind if he saw them on a frequent basis. There was Scabby Abby, a woman he always saw standing on the same corner in a bright yellow dress. Maybe she had been pretty years ago, but now she looked old and used like a wadded up piece of toilet paper. Her makeup was always smeared and she had scores of scabs on her knees, elbows, and forearms. Every so often he would see her talking to friends in their cars pulled up to the curb. If the chats went on for a long time, she would always get into the car with them and drive off.

Another person he always regularly saw was Mr. Leung, an ancient Asian man who seemed to always be performing t'ai chi on a random street corner, ignoring everyone and everything around him. One day Al saw a car hit a large pothole filled with rainwater drenching Mr. Leung with the resulting torrent of mud and water. Astonishingly, Mr. Leung completely ignored what had happened. He progressed methodically through the ritual motions one by one until he had completed all 108 of the classic hand forms.

  Out of all the people he saw on his daily walks, only one rubbed him the wrong way; a burly, prematurely balding guy who Al privately referred to as T-Bird due to the 1974 Thunderbird he was always spotted driving up and down the city streets. With a metallic bottle green paint job and a cream-colored leather top, the car was always getting appreciative looks from pedestrians and fellow motorists. It was too bad that the car was the only thing nice about T-Bird. Al had taken an intense dislike to the man immediately. Al had seen him run red lights, cut off other cars, swerve around pedestrians in the crosswalk, and litter with abandon. He was, in Al's opinion, just a vile human being who deserved some come-uppance.

  Not only did Al see a variety of people as he went to and fro to school, but he also saw a wide variety of animals on the streets. Dogs, cats, pigeons, the occasional rat scurrying in an alley. Rather than throw it away, he began feeding scraps from his lunch every day to some of the cats as he walked home. One of the friendlier cats quickly became his favorite, a white tom with black markings on its ears and paws that he christened Sneakers.

  Sneakers became accustomed to his routine as well, often appearing at the same spot each time of day, yowling for his share of the food. Al made sure to spread the food around, but soon he was saving the better pieces for Sneakers. He knew Martin and Gina would never allow any of them to have a pet, but he still considered Sneakers his cat.

  Months went by and winter arrived. It snowed often, in dribs and drabs, but that year it never seemed cool enough for the snow to pack down hard. Most of the days, the street and sidewalks were covered with islands of dirty slush amid miniature streams of melted snow shimmering with the oil and effluvium it washed away from the pavement. Winter in the city was ugly. Snow rarely remained white, and sidewalks were rarely shoveled on many of the streets. If someone did clear off the snow a bit,

The Specimen

the narrow pathways on the sidewalks were barely more than furrows of mud and trodden dog shit lined with frozen Hefty bags of the week's trash.

In the alley, Al had set up a plastic milk crate with an old blanket in it as a bed for Sneakers. He occasionally checked on it and left a few extra treats hidden in it for Sneakers to find. He never saw Sneakers in the crate, but there was some evidence that the cat had been using it regularly. White cat hair had collected on the blanket and there were no other cats with his coloring in the neighborhood. When Al showed up with his daily bag of scraps, Sneakers would always slink up next to him within minutes, purring and showing his appreciation that Al had once again arrived as promised.

Right after school, he often sat on the crate in the alley, scratching Sneakers behind the ears and telling him what had happened in school that day. He talked more to Sneakers than he did to any person, revealing secrets and hopes and, occasionally, dark thoughts. Sneakers just sat in his lap contentedly and listened to the drone of his voice. Of course, he realized that the cat couldn't understand him, but Sneakers did seem to recognize and react to his moods. In later years, he would realize that Sneakers had been his best friend during that time, probably his only friend. His best friend ever was a cat. Pretty depressing when he thought about it, but in his mind it definitely justified his subsequent actions.

It was a Wednesday, at the end of January, and the streets were especially slick. Freezing rains the previous night, followed by a winter squall that covered the pavement with black ice, had turned the streets into a series of bobsled runs. Most drivers were smart enough to stay at home and off the streets, but there were a few reckless morons who didn't care.

School had been cancelled due to the dangerous roads, but Al still packed up a few leftovers for the cats and braved the weather in the early morning to walk to his usual spot just as the sun crested the horizon. As soon as he stepped outside, the below freezing temperatures caused ice crystals to form around his nose and mouth. The simple act of breathing hurt his lungs as he inhaled the morning air. He was slightly concerned about Sneakers and the other animals in this weather, but they had survived colder spots earlier in the winter and looked no worse for the wear. Most likely, there was a warm alcove or abandoned building where they all huddled together and rode the worst storms out.

The streets were empty and silent, except for the sound of a lone car engine growling blocks away. Someone was stuck in the snow and ice, revving their engine in futility and probably doing more damage than necessary. Al cut through the local playground and realized he was headed directly towards the vehicle that was the source of all the noise. Reemerging onto the street, he looked to his left and saw a green car mired in a snow drift and spinning its wheels. He walked closer and realized exactly whose car it was. Bottle-green paint. Beige leather roof. It could only be one person: T-Bird. Just who Al wanted to see on this lovely morning.

The Thunderbird's wheels stopped spinning and the engine shut off as the driver got out and cursed at the sky. As suspected, it was T-Bird who exited the vehicle in a fit of apoplexy. He slammed the door and began kicking at the mound of snow and dirty ice before moving on to stomp on a small pile of fur in the middle of the road while spewing a litany of obscenities.

Oh no. No...

Al froze in his tracks and squinted to focus. It wasn't a trick of his mind. He saw white and black and a few splashes of red. He took a few steps closer, eyes fixed upon the bloody mess flattened in the tread marks left in the snow. The body was barely identifiable, but Al knew exactly what it was. He continued toward the ranting man, steady and implacable.

The man he called T-Bird stopped stomping on the bloody patch of snow, turned toward him and snarled, "What the fuck are you lookin' at, kid?"

In that exact moment, milliseconds before a white-hot rage consumed his every thought, Al realized that T-Bird wasn't a man at all. He was still just a kid. Eighteen or nineteen years old at best, with acne-scarred cheeks and a wispy attempt at a mustache. Prematurely balding with a sunken chest and slumped shoulders. An angry little boy pretending to be something he wasn't.

He dropped the bag of food and closed in on T-Bird. The man cocked an eyebrow and looked down at the battered corpse in the snow by

The Specimen

his feet. The head was unrecognizable, a pulped soup of bloody white and black fur buried in ice and slush. The upper torso was completely flattened. The tire had disemboweled the animal by forcing the entrails through the anus to lie steaming in the frigid air between the two rear legs – legs which had the signature black boot markings of Al's friend Sneakers. Al stopped five feet from T-Bird, staring at the body of his friend and visibly shaking with rage.

T-Bird looked at him with a confused glare, and then laughed out loud, "Jesus, kid. You gonna cry? It's just a stupid fucking cat. Fucking thing ran right out in front of me. It's not like I killed your mom or something."

Al snapped.

He launched himself forward, swinging his fists wildly at the man and unleashing a barrage of obscenities intermixed with Sneakers' name. One blow glanced off T-Bird's left cheek, but the rest were deflected as the man backed away in shock.

"What the fuck? Kid! Kid! Cut it out…" screamed T-Bird as he retreated toward his car. He slipped in the pile of slush and fell to the icy pavement, flailing on his back and yelling for Al to stop. Al ran up and began kicking the fallen man in the side and the groin repeatedly. T-Bird rolled to his side wailing in pain and clutching his genitals for protection. Al leaped onto his back, plowing his knees into T-Bird's kidneys and pressing his face into the bloody snow. Al pressed down with all his strength until T-Bird's screams became muffled and his struggles weakened.

Sobbing, with rivers of snot running to his chin, Al crawled over to Sneakers' flattened corpse and dragged it back to where T-Bird lay moaning in the snow. He kneeled next to the battered man, grabbed him by the hair and lifted his head to scream in his face, "LOOK AT WHAT YOU DID!! LOOK AT WHAT YOU DID!!"

T-Bird tried to whimper an apology through his crushed lips, but Al refused to allow it. He brutally shoved the cat's entrails into T-Bird's mouth and nose, and then pressed him face first into Sneakers' matted bloody fur, leaning with his entire weight on the man's skull. T-Bird pounded the snow with his arms, kicked and flailed as Al bore down unrelentingly on his head and neck. Al heard something crack. The fight in T-Bird weakened and eventually stopped, but Al continued to press his face into Sneakers' ruined corpse for another few minutes until he was absolutely sure that his friend's murderer was dead.

Slowly, without a word, Al stood up and looked around. He was surprised, yet calm. Unbelievably no one had heard any noise from the fight. The morning was as silent as a graveyard. Not one house light came on. No figures stood in their windows clutching their phones as they reported the horrific murder they had just witnessed. A light breeze disturbed wind chimes at a neighboring building, breaking the peace with sounds of broken glass.

* * *

Much later, when a number of years had passed, Al would realize all the mistakes he had made. All the evidence he had left behind and how lucky he truly had been that the crime was never connected to him. Much later on, he would become more efficient and methodical with killing. Now, however, he was numb. Deadened to the blood in the snow. To the blood and gore on his hands and knees and the cooling corpse at his feet. Nothing mattered except for his need to return home and collapse into his bed.

He rubbed snow on his hands and knees to wash off Sneakers' blood, then turned and retraced his steps to the Shawcross' house. The sky slowly brightened as the sun rose over the roofs, but Al didn't feel any warmer. Along the way, Al threw the scraps into an alley to a crowd of yowling cats. They either recognized him or they smelled the food. Regardless, there was no sense in wasting it.

As he reached the street where he lived, he heard sirens in the distance from the direction of the Thunderbird. He looked over his shoulder and saw a faint red and blue light aurora illuminate the roofs of a few buildings blocks away. A tidal wave of exhaustion washed over Al and he realized that he would soon pass out if he didn't get home to bed. Minutes later, he was back inside the house with no one any wiser. The Shawcrosses were upstairs locked in their bedroom. Kevin, as usual, was

The Specimen

snoring like a saw mill, and Lewis and Ozzie had earplugs in to block him out. Al stripped out of his clothes and climbed into his bunk, falling asleep before his head hit the pillow.

* * *

Quillian was not very happy when Grimaldi opened the back doors of the van.

"What's holding you up?" he called from the driver's seat. "We're already cutting it close. The locals could be here any minute, and you know how I despise working with them when it isn't necessary." He continued, "I just spoke with Valentine. Something vitally important has come up, so they're leaving Greylock and meeting us in Hartford with their guest. They may have a lead on the location of the Greylock specimen as well, and I think Dr. Colfax will want to question him personally. We need to get over there immediately."

"Nearly done, Q," grunted Grimaldi as he placed a couple of crates in the van next to the stainless steel industrial cooler bolted to the floor, right next to the doors. Inside the cooler was the specimen removed from Monahan's flank. "Just being thorough. All that's left is to spark it and get the hell outta Dodge."

"Use one of the M14's. We need to be certain the whole house goes up."

"I was thinking the same thing," agreed Grimaldi as he opened a floor compartment and removed a large metal suitcase. "I felt some rain drops just now. Better safe than sorry." He unlatched the rectangular case and lifted open the top, revealing six cylindrical metal objects, all painted red with the letters **AN-M14 INCEN TH3** printed on the side in black bold lettering. Removing one carefully, he placed it next to him on the van bed and re-latched the case.

"I'll be right back," he stated, closing the van door. Grimaldi headed inside and quickly made his way to the master bedroom. Placing the white phosphorous grenade between the bodies of Chuck and Kate, he set the timer and hurriedly vacated the premises. Seconds later, a paralyzing bright flash streamed from the windows, followed by a muffled detonation and a chorus of shattered glass crashing to the ground, just as Grimaldi reached the van.

"Time to go," growled Quillian. "If they didna connect the kid to this house yet, they soon will. Let's get on the road. I'll be needing a glass or two of Kilbeggan when we arrive."

Grimaldi belted himself in and Quillian pulled the van down the Monahan's winding gravel driveway, heading for the back roads to I-95 South. In the rearview mirror, the house could be seen in full, white-hot conflagration, belching smoke from all windows and providing a beacon to the law enforcement and emergency services already in the area. A few trees looked as if they had also ignited in the explosion. Soon, sirens were blaring on the main roads as a convoy of vehicles raced to the site of the growing blaze. It was expanding quickly and would most likely occupy them for many hours.

Behind them, with a barely discernible mewl, a small figure leapt nimbly into Grimaldi's lap. Quillian yelped in shock and swerved to the side of the road, drawing and pointing his pistol at the creature in one fluid move.

"What. The. Fuck. Is. That?" barked the surly Irishman.

The orange and black cat in Grimaldi's lap stared at the gun in Quillian's hand, then calmly lifted his rear leg and began licking his ass.

"I didn't have time to tell you, Q." mumbled the burly man sheepishly. "He was in the garage and I couldn't let him burn… so I took him with us."

Quillian was utterly silent, visibly struggling to control his emotions as he re-holstered his pistol. "Dumbass," he snarled. "Control that thing. I almost shot you. And don't even get the idea to put any of this on me. Dr. Colfax will not be pleased."

He started the van again and pulled back onto the road. For the next few minutes, the only sound was the cat's contented purr, until Grimaldi said quietly, "I decided to name him Boots." Quillian chose not to respond.

The Specimen

*From the Personal Journal
of Dr. Saul Eckenrode
Clinical Director
Mount Greylock Institute*

October 8, 1965

    Young Harry is not the same, and he may never be again considering what those butchers did to him. I was able to visit him in his room and I could not believe this was the same, lively young man of whom I have become quite fond. He looked shrunken in his bed with large bandages around his head, neck and torso. He is also experiencing severe cognitive deficits since the operation. His speech is halted and he struggles remembering vocabulary and events from his past.

    I looked under his bandages yesterday afternoon when he was sleeping, and, as I suspected, the foreign tissue that I had seen attached to his flesh had been removed surgically. The discoloration on his skin seems to have advanced extensively, especially on his torso. I have no experience in dermatology, but I would assume that, similar to incidents when an individual's hair goes white from fear, the increased loss of melanin in his skin is due to severe stress.

    The only positive note I can take from this is the fact that Harry does seem at peace. He may have lost much of his memory - and in fact he struggles to remember my name or where he is staying - but he does not have the fear that was always present in his eyes. He does not cry anymore.

    If I were a better man, I would consider pursuing the option of adopting this young man, but the numerous bad choices I made in my youth prevent this avenue. Even if I were a proper candidate to become Harry's caretaker, his past with the ACME group - whatever it may be - would certainly impede any possibility of its conclusion.

    - S.

October 14, 1965

    Harry was returned to the general populace today and I made sure I was there to supervise how he reintegrated himself. Unfortunately, there wasn't much to watch. Harry wandered around in a daze for a few minutes before claiming an empty chair and settling in to watch the latest episode of *I Dream of Jeannie* with the rest of the residents who stared slack-jawed at the screen.

On the other side of the room was Angelo Scarpa. I still find it incomprehensible that he was returned to our facility. Stanley Wick was moved to another unit, so why couldn't they find a bed for this monster somewhere else, considering the history he has here?

Thankfully, he seems to be avoiding Harry. I may not have been consulted about where I feel Scarpa should be staying, but I was able to do something about his medication. He had been placed on a relatively moderate dosage of Thorazine, but I wasn't satisfied with the results, so I have adjusted his charts and tripled his dosage. I want this animal to be thoroughly subdued, responding to commands like a trained dog. Sit, Scarpa!

His nose, as expected, looks horrific. As a patient of the state, cosmetic surgery is not an option. He was simply cleaned, stitched up, and sent back the next day with that red gaping hole in the center of his face, leaking green snot down his lip like that one kid in 1st grade who hadn't yet figured out how to blow his damned nose. I could see deep inside his skull.

I've asked Jameson and Fenton to keep an eye on him. They didn't seem to mind. Unlike Drs. Coe and Colfax, I do not begrudge their company. Underneath their matching buzz cuts, they actually seem to have souls.

Wonders never cease.

-S.

October 21, 1965

I can't say how it might have happened, but we have lost a resident somewhere. Richard Hutchens, one of the most pliable patients we have ever had in this facility, has just vanished. He has been here since he was an adolescent. As such, he was determined to be a low escape risk, so he had not required restraints on his bed at night. In hindsight, we may need to revisit that policy.

The Specimen

    I asked Coe, Colfax and their lackeys Jameson and Fenton, but no one "had heard" of Patient Hutchens. Frankly, I'm not too certain I should trust them, considering our past history. Coe and Colfax haven't exactly been forthcoming with any information and the other two, though friendly with me, won't do anything to jeopardize their income.

    Thankfully, Hutchens does not have any relatives in the mix. He has been a ward of the state for years, and they aren't known for keeping track of their responsibilities all that well. Regardless, though, I need to come up with something to explain his absence.

    - S.

Chapter 22 – Government Men

"Hell is empty and all the devils are here."
– William Shakespeare

March 13, 1965 – Springfield, MA

Violetta Rooks was on a mission. *As she climbed into her 1959 Chevrolet Brookwood station wagon, she set the glass casserole dish on the passenger seat with her duffel bag-sized purse bracing it. She wasn't going to let it slide onto the floor and ruin her plans for the afternoon. The scent of Spam, mushroom soup, asparagus and noodles filled the car and set her mouth to salivating.*

"Hoo-wheeee! That Lucien Roumain is gonna get down on his knees and thank the Good Lord Jesus when he gets a taste of this," she giggled to herself. "You've outdone yourself this time, Violetta!"

She slid behind the wheel and checked herself in the mirror before starting the car and pulling away from the curb. Her rivals for the attention of Lucien Roumain had better get up pretty darn early to get the best of Violetta Rooks, especially those three harpies always sniffing around her man - Bella Pooley, May Witherspoon, and the worst of them all, that skinny slut, Ruthie Aubuchon. Violetta was about to jump to the top of the heap in the Seducing Lucien Roumain Competition with this masterpiece of a casserole.

Ever since the extra-large Casanova moved into the area a few years ago, he had always been surrounded with eligible women looking for a strong, reliable man with large appetites. Lucien Roumain definitely fit that bill.

Even so, there was something else about him that stirred her imagination. There was a depth to his personality. Something intangible. Women were always attracted to Lucien. Whenever Violetta was near him, the hairs on the nape of her neck stood on end and she felt a warm glow in her cheeks.

The Specimen

Her cousin Lucy would have said that he had an aura surrounding him. Violetta didn't know anything about that, but she did know that he smelled wonderful, like sunshine and spring, whenever she walked in the door to Bayou Lou's. It had to be some mixture of exotic oils and spices that he used as a cologne because there was no possible way he could smell like that naturally. She was sure the other women noticed as well, but she was determined to be at the front of the line, and since none of them could cook their way out of a paper bag, she was certain she had the inside track to his heart.

As she drove the seven blocks to the store, Violetta fantasized about how he would respond to her latest gift of food. Last week she had driven by with a mincemeat pie only to find a sign on the storefront stating that Bayou Lou's was closed for a couple days due an illness in the family. Along with the sign, she had found two notes slipped into crack between the door and the doorjamb, and of course she had to read them.

One was a message from the local beer distributor requesting him to call them at his earliest convenience. Violetta had replaced it back into the crack. The second one had been from Ruthie Aubuchon inviting Lucien over to her house for dinner next week for a "special meal". Violetta had shredded the note with pleasure, sprinkling the pieces in the gutter as she walked back to her car and already planning her next visit.

Bayou Lou's had remained closed until yesterday, when Violetta had seen the OPEN sign as she drove by on her way back from church. She immediately interpreted it as a sign from God and began planning her casserole offering for today's delivery. This time she was determined to see Lucien.

Turning onto the street where the store was located, she saw that both parking spaces outside the store were taken by vehicles – neither of which looked familiar. The first in line was shiny new turquoise Ford XL Falcon convertible. Behind it was a generic white panel truck - probably a delivery man. Violetta pulled up to the curb, parking across the street in front of a three story walkup, and crossed to the sidewalk, casserole dish clutched to her bosom.

"You watch out, Lucien Roumain," she murmured with a confident smile. "Violetta Rooks ain't playing games no more. One taste of this and Ruthie Aubuchon's bony ass will be in the rear view mirror."

* * *

"Some fat lady is heading over here, Jeffords," grunted the red-faced young man peering through the blinds. He wiped the ever-present sweat from his brow with a sodden handkerchief and glanced back at his older colleague. Tom Jeffords was guarding the door to the storage room where their other three team members were handling their recently ambushed target.

"What do you expect me to do about it?" answered Jeffords. "Get rid of her, Jimbo. Convince her that the store is closed. Do what you have to do to keep her outside the store."

"I'll try," Jimbo replied with a sigh.

"Don't just try, kid. You got what you wanted. You're on an Extraction Team now. No more desks. No more filing papers. Don't think about anything. Just do. Time enough to think later. We don't need anyone gumming up the works at this stage. Once the extraction is complete, we need to pack up our equipment and sanitize this place."

The young man nodded and stepped outside to confront the approaching woman. As the door closed, Tom knocked twice on the door behind him and opened it. Three other men, two white and one black, were standing around the unconscious Lucien Roumain on the concrete slab of the loading dock. The store owner's shirt had been removed, revealing the organism on his left flank, pulsating and deflating in time with his heart.

"It's a big one, Jeffords," said the black man at the center of the room. "Hell, it's probably the biggest I've ever seen alive."

"No surprise there, Mangual," he responded. "Considering the mess it left in New Orleans a few years ago, we pretty much knew it would be an Elder."

The Specimen

"It shouldn't have taken so much time to track it down," grumbled the grey-haired man on the right. "When I was brought into the Group, we tracked one down every couple of months ... and that was while we were fighting Adolf."

Jeffords and the other two men remained silent. No response would have served any purpose. Mike Pfeiffer, the man who had spoken, was the mission leader and he was universally considered to be a bit of a braggart and a dick. He was in his late sixties and most Acme agents who worked with him thought he should have retired years ago. Pfeiffer had over thirty years under his belt, more experience than the other four team members combined, especially that sweaty green desk jockey James P. "Jimbo" Kilcannon, who had only been with the team for the better part of a month. There was no denying that Pfeiffer, despite his loud complaints that most of the current crop of Acme Group agents were a bunch of incompetent bean counters, was a master at tactics. Even if his physical skills were fading, he was still better than most agents. If only he wasn't so arrogant.

Jeffords himself had the next most experience. He was in his fourteenth year on the Extraction Team and he had participated in over sixty Extractions. This was only his third Elder, though. Most of the specimens they had found were juveniles Riding their first or second Steed or still in the larval stage. Either the Rider population was dwindling or they had become better at hiding themselves in this modern age. Jeffords suspected it was a combination of the two.

The final two members of the team were Hector Mangual, the weapons expert of the group, and Gary Koonce, the medic. Mangual had his "baby", a .30 Kiraly-Cristóbal Carbine assault rifle, at his hip, ready to react in case anything unexpected occurred. Koonce was kneeling next to Lucien's body deciding how and where he should start the incision.

Jeffords glanced at the shirtless Lucien and the creature straddling his spine. The neural threads growing from the main mass pierced their prisoner's skin at hundreds of random points on his back and flank. He shuddered in revulsion. No matter how often he saw one of these things, he would never be able to reconcile the fact that some people welcomed these things with open arms. Without question, such people were traitors to the entire human race.

"Are you sure it's completely subdued?" he asked Koonce as the medic started the incision at the base of main body. "We don't want it waking up in the middle of the extraction, do we?"

"I gave him twice the normal dose for a man of his size. Any more might kill him which would immediately release the Rider," responded Koonce. "I've never dealt with one this large before. We can only guess about the specifics, but we do know that sedating the host also affects the Rider due to its direct connection through the circulatory, endocrine and nervous systems."

"Koonce, this isn't a training run. Cut the chatter," interrupted Pfeiffer before turning his attention to Jeffords. "We'll worry about our part back here. You just need to keep an eye out front with Kilcannon. Why are you here anyway?"

Jeffords explained that they had a visitor and that Kilcannon was attempting to turn her away. As soon as the words left his mouth, however, he realized his error and Pfeiffer confirmed it.

"What in hell were you thinking?" bellowed the team leader. "Get back out there and make sure he hasn't screwed things up beyond repair."

Jeffords clenched his jaw, holding back an angry retort. It wouldn't matter whether or not his words carried any truth or not. Pfeiffer was in one of his moods where logic and reasoning had little effect on him. Best to just bite his tongue and follow orders. He nodded curtly and closed the door before weaving his way to the store entrance. From the sound of it, Jimbo was not having any success exerting his authority.

Back in the storeroom, as Jeffords walked out, all eyes were on him and Pfeiffer. Their conflict had been brewing for a bit and the others were just waiting to see how it shook out in the end. Koonce and Mangual exchanged glances, rolling their eyes at the pissing match they had just witnessed.

The Specimen

On the floor, as their attention was distracted from the task at hand, a slight trembling ran up the left tendril as it detached itself from Lucien's flank. By the time the agents' focus returned to it, all motion had ceased and it lay in wait like a viper... biding its time for the perfect opportunity to strike.

Chapter 23 – Dirt Mall

"There is a time when even justice brings harm." – Sophocles

Modern Day – Hartford, CT

Every town has one. An eyesore on a secondary highway (state, not federal). A vast lot overgrown with weeds, cracked pavement and the faded lines denoting former parking spaces. Occasionally one or two stores may linger on in the location, dragging out their agonizingly slow deaths surrounded by the shells of Spencer's Gifts, Hot Topix, and Claire's Boutiques.

Whether locals called it the "dead mall", the "dirt mall" or "that place where there used to be a K-Mart", the most activity that they would expect to find in the abandoned buildings would be some vandalism or occasional drug use.

Not a secret international coalition dedicated to wiping out an alien threat that has been here for millennia, thought Murtaugh as he pulled into the former home of the Green Valley D-Luxe Mall. The place had been shut down in the mid-1990's when the economy was booming and all anyone wanted was bigger, shinier, and more modern places where they could ride the hamster wheel of capitalism until they died. Places like Green Valley were doomed once the internet boom happened.

As he pulled the van around to the entrance of the underground garage, Murtaugh thought, not for the first time, that he probably would have liked this place at its peak. He was a child of the late sixties and early seventies and the mall brought back happy memories. The décor of the mall's exterior was pure kitsch… old gold and avocado with the occasional dash of maroon. He could practically see the throngs of shoppers wearing plaid bell bottoms and all things suede. To Murtaugh, that decade was emblematic of innocence and all things good before the worst event in his life happened and he got sucked into this hidden world of monsters, assassins and mad scientists over three decades ago.

* * *

The Specimen

1984 – Newark, New Jersey

Despite many opportunities in his life, twenty-two year old Archie Murtaugh had never held a gun before. Now, as he hefted the pistol in his hand, it seemed as if the opposite were true... that he had been using them his entire life. Somehow, it felt right, as if it had been molded specifically for his grip. His fingers fit the weapon as they once had fit the hand of his dead girlfriend. For the first time in nearly two weeks, since Monica's body had been discovered in a dumpster, raped, decapitated, and disemboweled, Archie allowed himself to crack a ghost of a smile.

"You like? Good for you?" asked Vasily, a short, greasy-looking ferret of a man standing next to the open trunk of his rusty Chevy Impala. "I have more if you want. Bigger or smaller. You like chrome?" he continued in broken English, pointing at the dozens of pistols, rifles and shotguns spread out for display on a ragged wool blanket, including a metallic .45 that would have made Dirty Harry weep in envy.

Archie shook his head. "I'll take this one," he whispered, gripping the gun firmly and enjoying the sensation of the cold metal.

Vasily nodded in approval, "Good gun... Hardballer," he reiterated. "Good for what you need. You get the bastard, eh?"

"I'll get him. You can count on that... how much you want for it?"

"For you, special deal because it is for important business," the runty Russian stated solemnly. "$125, plus I give this for free."

Archie snuck a look inside it and saw a box of bullets with an extra six-round magazine. He grunted in acceptance at the price and handed the back alley arms dealer six crumpled twenties and a five.

"Listen to me, kiddo," Vasily instructed, looking seriously into the young man's eyes. "You get this fucker. You put extra bullet in his face for Vasily. What he did to your girlfriend. What he did to you. This fucker, he needs to die."

Archie nodded grimly, tucked the gun and the paper bag into a canvas knapsack, slung it over his shoulder and walked out of the alley with Monica's image burning in his thoughts. The only way he would feel that she would finally rest in peace would be when he put her murderer in the ground.

In Archie's opinion, the local police were completely useless. Even though it had been verified that he was working the door at McCoy's Pub the entire shift on the night that Monica had been raped and murdered, they still hounded him as suspect #1 for the first three to four days of the investigation. They were so certain that the simplest answer was the obvious one. They wanted the boyfriend to have committed the crime to make their job easier, so much so that they ignored any other possibility, regardless of the strength of the evidence to the contrary. Only the discovery of another victim with similar mutilations convinced them otherwise.

Archie had been in interrogation or under surveillance for three consecutive days when the second body was discovered in a dumpster. Yet even when he had finally been eliminated as a suspect, they refused to listen to him. He was certain he knew who the murderer was, but it seemed as if any information he gave them was completely ignored.

Archie had read somewhere that it was better to regret doing something after the fact and to live with the consequences than to regret never having done it at all and wonder about what might have been. Every day since her death, Monica's words rang in his ears throughout the day and caused him to wake up in a blind rage every night. She had known someone was following her, and she had told him of her suspicions of who it might be just the night before her murder.

Two years earlier, at the tail end of her senior year of high school before Archie ever met her, Monica had been set up with a young man named Wayne Duffy by a mutual friend. It had been a typical blind date. He was friendly, polite, clean cut, and exactly the type of boy her mother would have loved. Naturally, there were no sparks at all and thankfully each of them had seemed to realize it right away. They had parted ways amicably and she later heard from that same friend that he had eventually gone to college somewhere out west.

Monica had not thought of Wayne again until he suddenly showed up on her doorstep again a month ago. He was dirty, delirious and had a feverish gleam in his eyes. Frankly, he looked like he was sick. . Within seconds, the boy had professed his undying love for her and seemed to expect that she would return his affections unequivocally.

The Specimen

Things did not go as he had planned. As clearly as possible, Monica had told him that she was not at all interested in him, that he needed serious psychological counseling, and to never come to visit her again. She closed the door in his face and laughed it off later that day with Archie and their friends.

Monica didn't tell him until the last time he saw her that she thought someone had been following her for a number of days and that she was reasonably certain it was Wayne. Since then, the guilt had consumed Archie. He should have done something. Tracked the guy down and confronted him. Insisted that she report the confrontation to the police. Anything... but Monica wasn't worried, so why should he be? She claimed the guy was harmless.

For the thousandth time, Archie wondered how events would have unfolded if only he had been paying more attention. He would have seen that she actually was scared, but she didn't want to seem a burden. Instead, Archie had made her promise to always have a friend walk her home, but she must have felt safe because she went home alone one night... and Wayne Duffy abducted and slaughtered her.

Archie wiped away angry tears as he sat in his car a few hours after buying the gun. He had waited long enough and now it was time to make things right. This was about vengeance, not the law. Now that he had a weapon, Archie's plan was simple. He would wait in hiding here outside Wayne Duffy's apartment complex, force his way into the apartment that he shared with his parents, and convince the young man to confess to the atrocity. Using any means necessary until the scales of justice were balanced.

As night fell, a lackluster rain began to spatter on the pavement and intermittent gusts of wind blew through the streets. Within minutes, the exterior of grey industrial building was stained nearly black by the shower. He waited for a resident to enter the building a few parking spots away from the front door, engine turned off and gun already tucked in his waistband, ready to use if necessary.

An opportunity came sooner than expected when a hunched older woman with multiple shopping bags staggered to the main entrance under her load. Leaving his car, he paced his steps so he would reach the door just in time to hold it open for her. She glanced at him apprehensively, seemingly astonished that he wasn't trying to mug her, and then she smiled nervously and muttered a thank you as she ducked out of the wind and rain. When she was buzzed in by someone upstairs, he followed in her wake and entered the building.

He had already scouted out who lived where by scanning the names next to the buzzers earlier, so he knew that Duffy lived with his parents and three younger siblings in 10-G, the corner apartment on the top floor. The entryway was cluttered with layers of faded flyers stapled over one another. Stale cigarettes overflowed the ashtray that hadn't been emptied in months, a pile of crushed butts littering the peeling beige linoleum.

Just looking around the lobby, he felt dirty and unwashed. Places like this made Archie glad he had a poor sense of smell from having his nose severely broken twice in his youth, once when a wrestling match with his older brothers ended with his face hitting a coffee table, and the other time when he was jumped by a group of kids in high school. It was a wonder Monica had shown any interest in him with his crooked face.

He hurried to the dilapidated stairwell – he wasn't going to ride up in the elevator with the old woman - and began the long climb to the tenth floor. Something seemed off as he reached the landing between the ninth and tenth floors. A few of the lights had been broken long ago, cloaking the stairs in large patches of darkness. He made no attempt to be quiet after he realized that the stairs were coated with an adhesive substance that made each step he took sound like duct tape torn from a roll. Whether this was an intentional safety precaution by building management to improve traction or the result of years of accumulated filth was impossible to tell. Reaching for the door with a gloved hand, he opened it and stepped into the corridor.

The air in the hallway was stale with a hint of things old and putrid, as if it had been sealed for days without ventilation and the humidity had allowed mold to form in the dingy beige walls. The mottled maroon and green patterned carpet was worn down from decades of feet dragging home after the nine-to-five grind. Despite the obvious signs of years of wear and tear from the residents, there was an air of abandonment

The Specimen

lingering in the corridor. Archie stood motionless for a moment, listening for evidence of anyone living here. The only sound was a steady drip-drip-drip of water leaking through a spot on the ceiling halfway down the hall. He heard no voices, no television or music. Nothing that would serve as evidence that anyone actually lived on the other sides of any door on this floor.

There were three apartments on each side of the hallway. From Archie's snooping around, he knew that the first and third apartment on each side were two bedroom units while apartments C and D were single occupancy lofts sandwiched between them on each side. At the end of the hall on each floor were the larger family apartments: four bedrooms in a space the size of two of the two bedroom units put together. Duffy's family lived in the family unit at the far end.

Now that he had breached the walls of the castle, Archie experienced a momentary urge to flee back down the stairwell and abandon his plans of vengeance. He had already placed his hand on the handle of the door and was beginning to turn it when he abruptly felt the presence of another person watching him. Whirling back around, he squinted down the hall and looked for this individual. The lights were flickering and dim, but there was no way that anyone could be hiding from him. The hall was completely empty, and yet...

He felt as if, just out sight, someone was taunting him. Gloating that he had lost his nerve and was about to run off into the rainy night. The urge to leave was almost corporeal, as if spectral hands were pushing him away. Strangling him with fear. Stroking his lizard brain into its "fight or flight" mode.

Just at that moment, Monica's face came into vivid focus in his mind's eye, and all thoughts of flight vanished. He shook his head in fury at his hesitation and started down the hall to apartment 10-G, fighting the voices in his head with each step.

On a whim, he pushed the door, expecting it to be dead-bolted. Unexpectedly, it swung open with ease and he immediately went on alert. The entryway was a small alcove that led into a main room with hallways leading away on the left and the right. The living room was dark, with shadowy shapes strewn around the floor. Archie held his breath, listening for any sign of occupancy. On the far wall, dim light streamed in from an archway to another room – possibly the kitchen - allowing his eyes to slowly adjust. At first, the objects around the room appeared as random piles of clothes, perhaps laundry or pillows, but then he processed the information and they came into focus, revealing a scene of incomprehensible violence and carnage.

  The room was an abattoir. Archie had been correct in his assumption that many of the piles were clothes. What he had not seen were the contents inside the shirts and pants on the floor. Arms and legs bent in unnatural angles, torn from sockets with shards of broken bone piercing the skin. Piles of flesh peeled from bodies. Purplish entrails looped in precise coils from the lamps and drapery. Dried blood pooled on the hardwood floor and splashed all over the walls and furniture. A child's severed head cradled in a pair of woman's hands sat on top of an immense console television. The eyes were missing and blood streamed from the sockets like mascara in the rain.

  Any lingering doubts he had that Wayne Duffy was behind Monica's murder were dissolved immediately. In searching for a run of the mill thrill killer, he had stumbled into a den of evil so absolute he could feel it in the air.

  Archie stepped to the side of the doorway. In the light from the hallway, he would easily stand out as a target if anyone was still here. The illumination revealed more of the room now that he had moved to the side and he could see that the carnage was hours old at the very least. Perhaps even a day or two had passed since the slaughter had happened. Most of the blood had dried to a muddy reddish brown and someone or something had tracked it all throughout the apartment. Leaning closer, Archie could see a variety of prints –what appeared to be the bare footprints of an adult male interspersed with an animal's footprint, perhaps from a dog. They had crisscrossed the puddles of gore multiple times, marking their paths in chaotic patterns resembling paintings of abstract and morbid phantasms.

  From the kitchen came a muffled sound as if someone was dragging himself across the floor. Could there possibly be any survivors in this hellish place? Or was it simply a ruse to draw him into a trap? If anyone was still here, they had to know that he had entered the

The Specimen

apartment. With the door hanging open and the hallway light streaming inside, he hadn't exactly been that subtle.

The dragging sound continued and a small black shadow emerged in the archway to the kitchen. Archie let out a quiet sigh of relief as he realized that he had found the source of the dog prints from before. Backing into the hall with its jaws clenched around an unknown object was a miniature black and brown dachshund, clothed in a bloodstained pink dog sweater with the name "Noodle" stitched inside a bone outline on the back in bright green letters.

Archie crouched down and beckoned to the dog. Seeing him from the corner of its eye, the dachshund turned and dropped the object on which it had been gnawing to the floor. As it hit the ground, Archie could see that it was the bare foot of a young child... only the foot with a couple ragged ligaments dangling from the raw meat just above the ankle. The nails were painted neon pink and the smallest two toes seemed to already have been chewed off.

Noodle's eyes reflected a cancerous yellow in the light as she snarled deep in her throat and launched herself directly at Archie's face. Barely reacting in time, he blocked her attack with his left arm and scrambled backwards, spouting obscenities at the savage pooch. The dog latched firmly just below his elbow and bit deep through his sleeve into the flesh. Archie let out an incoherent shriek and fell backward on his ass. Noodle hung on with her teeth nearly meeting through the muscle in Archie's forearm as the young man punched the dog in the face again and again to no avail.

Blood streamed down his arm onto the floor. If he didn't get this beast to release soon, an artery would tear open and he would bleed out in minutes. Archie pried at Noodle's jaws, but only succeeded in lacerating his fingers, one down to the bone. The dog's grip was unrelenting. Abandoning that tactic, he gripped the dachshund by the skull and poked his thumb into its right eye. His thumb pierced the sclera and a bloody spew of vitreous humor washed over his hand. Noodle moaned in agony but she refused to release her jaws. Archie swung his arm at the doorframe. As he smashed the animal's body against the wood corner, the sound of bones breaking mixed in with the dog's whines and Archie's frantic sobs.

Still, Noodle refused to let go, scratching his chest with her hind legs. He was certain the dog was on the verge of dying, but he wouldn't be able to extricate himself from her grip until she was actually dead.

Finally, he was able to grab one of the dachshund's rear legs with his right hand and pin her down to the floor. Lowering his bleeding arm on the other side, Archie wedged his right knee onto her neck and dropped his full weight on it as he twisted her head. With a resounding CRUNCH, Noodle's neck snapped and her teeth released from his savaged arm. Archie hurled the little dog's corpse at the far wall and collapsed wheezing against the door.

"What. The. Fuck. Was. That?" he gasped when he was finally able to speak. He cradled his arm against his chest and was glad to see that, although the bite looked horrendous, the bleeding was actually slowing down somewhat. The dachshund's lifeless body had landed near the entrance the hallway on the left. It was hard to believe that this small lump of bloody fur had nearly torn out his throat a few seconds earlier. He looked at his arm again in concern. Could she have been rabid? That would explain her savagery. He needed medical attention, but before anything else could happen he had to see if Duffy had definitely caused this carnage that surrounded Archie… or if he would be found torn apart in one of these piles.

Archie stood slowly and pulled his previously forgotten gun from his waistband. He could have easily blown a crater into Noodle's skull and ended the fight right there, but he had wanted to avoid any unnecessary noise. That option had disappeared within the first few seconds he had entered the apartment, though. If someone was in one of the other rooms, there was no way in Hell they could have missed the noise. Frankly, no one could have missed it if they lived within two floors of the apartment.

Noodle twitched.

Archie froze, paralyzed at the sight and whispered, "No way. No fucking way."

It simply wasn't possible that the dog was alive with the injuries she had sustained. Her back rippled and undulated beneath the bloody sweater again.

The Specimen

No! No! He was not seeing this. It was impossible! Dead animals did not move. They remained dead and silent on the floor. Archie pointed his gun at the dead dog's body and slowly crept closer, muttering the words "Stay dead. Stay dead," as a mantra. Noodle's neck had been twisted around nearly 180 degrees when the corpse landed. Her eye was a gaping hole leaking a translucent blood-tinted discharge down her cheek.

She was definitely dead, but her torso continued to bloat and deflate intermittently, making it appear that something was artificially inflating her lungs well past normal capacity. Archie was frozen in fear. Each subsequent expansion of the chest cavity appeared to migrate up towards her head. Her neck stretched as the object moved up the esophagus and into the back of Noodle's throat. Seconds later, a mottled gelatinous finger poked out through the ravaged eye socket and lingered, tasting the open air.

Archie was overcome with horror and revulsion. Was that some kind of grub or worm? He reared back and stomped on the dog's skull with his right boot multiple times, reducing it into a messy blood and bone paste. Immediately before he crushed it, two fleshy worms darted out through the gaping eye socket. The first wriggled in Archie's direction and squirmed up his legs and chest at an astonishing speed. The slimy grub slid past Archie's lips just as he clamped his mouth shut, barely trapping the larva in time. He bit down and popped the invader with his incisors, releasing its bitter gelatinous innards onto his tongue. It burned his throat like an extreme case of acid reflux.

Archie gagged and spit out the wormy chunks onto the wall. The second grub crawled down the hall on the left. He watched it slither and weave like an albino leech until it reached the bare feet of a half-naked man standing there silently in the shadows.

Wayne Duffy stared at Archie with a facsimile of a smile. He stood at the edge of the light, shadows wreathing his face and torso. The worm-like creature climbed his leg like a snake slinking up the trunk of a tree, wriggled around his chest to his face where it pried open Duffy's lips and slid inside his mouth. He licked them as if he had just eaten the best meal of his life and commented, "I'm not sure if I should report you to PETA or the ASPCA, considering the condition of poor Noodle here. You certainly did a number on her."

"Fuck the dog and fuck you, you fucking psycho"

The man blinked as if offended, "Somebody's feeling a bit hostile today."

"I suppose you're Duffy," Archie stated when he found his voice, ignoring the man's words. "I was beginning to think you had left."

"Duffy? I prefer not to be called by that name. This is only his body. I'm so much more than that young boy. Duffy is only a microscopic piece of me now that he has stopped fighting. There are a myriad of lives spanning dozens of centuries inside me, many of which I Rode for decades."

"Sounds like a bunch of insane bullshit to me," Archie spat. "You're just a pathetic little punk with mommy issues who graduated from torturing kittens and pissing his bed to carving up the girls who ignored you in middle school."

"Nice speech. Did you come up with all by yourself? You must be Monica's boyfriend, Archie Murtaugh. Am I right? The mustache is a dead giveaway." He chuckled then continued, "You're earlier than I expected. I didn't think you would come here to settle business for a while. I was certain you would take at least a few more days to get the gumption to confront me."

"Did you do it?"

"Did I what? Oh, did I kill Monica? Of course I did, even though Wayne fought the urge for the longest time. He really didn't want to kill her… and in the end that was why I had to." He paused and looked around the apartment, waving his hand at the corpses on the floor. "You know … I really wish you had given me some notice. I would have cleaned up some of the mess for you." He took a couple of steps forward, emerging from the shadows and flipping a light switch on as he passed it. "But sit down, let's talk a while and see if we can work things out."

His initial instinct was to empty the gun into the lunatic bastard, but once Duffy revealed himself, all Archie could do was stare. At first impression, the young man appeared sickly and weak. The only clothing that he wore was a stained pair of jeans sagging around his bony hips. He

The Specimen

seemed to be near Archie's age, in his early twenties, but his wispy blonde hair was already receding in a widow's peak combed back into a greasy pseudo-mullet hanging past his neck. His skin was pasty white with freckles covering his entire torso.

Duffy had obviously not washed himself for days. Dried streaks of blood stained his pants and skin, and a stench emanated from him like rotting vegetation. None of that registered with Archie, though. He was fixated upon the three bile-colored tentacles that were wrapped around Duffy's torso. Each leprous arm measured two inches across, ending in a six inch bony spur that burrowed and clutched the tissue beneath his skin. As he moved closer, Archie could see veins, arteries, talons and hair sprouting down their lengths. The two lower ones constricted his chest parallel to one another. The third larger tentacle crawled over his left shoulder and pierced his pectoral muscle, melding seamlessly with the flesh.

Watching the alien flesh pulsate in time with Duffy's heartbeat, Archie was conflicted. He wanted to avert his eyes from the scabrous, veiny monstrosity, but he was compelled to stare, fascinated as if he had been passing a deadly car crash on the highway. After a couple seconds of silence, he managed to sputter, "What the hell is that… thing on your back?"

The bloody young man looked directly at Archie, his gaze penetrating to the recesses of his subconscious. In that moment, something TASTED him… a wraith-like tongue licked the interior of his skull, caressed the folds of his cortex and savored the hidden secrets inside him. He felt violated… as if his skin, muscles and subcutaneous layers had all been peeled back one at a time to reveal his true, inner self.

An entity within Duffy gazed into his skull and a choir of voices began to speak all at once. At first overlapping. Male voices. Female voices. A cacophony of tones, accents, languages and ages, all finally merging in unison into a genderless roar of a voice in his thoughts…

< WHAT AM I? YOUR INNOCENT QUESTION HAS MANY ANSWERS, BUT YOU LACK THE CAPABILITY TO SEE THEM ALL … MUCH LESS COMPREHEND THEM. IN A WORD, I AM A RIDER. THIS FEEBLE CREATURE CHAINED TO ME IS MY STEED. HE SERVES ME AND, IN TURN, HE IS REWARDED BY BECOMING PART OF ME. I AM

THE CONGLOMERATION OF THE CENTURIES OF EXPERIENCES OF ALL THE STEEDS WHO HAVE HAD THE HONOR OF BEING RIDDEN BY ME. BEFORE AND AFTER THEIR CHAINING.

ALL THEIR KNOWLEDGE IS MINE …

ALL THEIR DREAMS ARE MINE …

ALL THEIR LOVES AND HATES AND HOPES AND FEARS …

ALL THEIR RAGE AND JOY AND PAIN AND ECSTASY …

ALL THEIR LIVES AND DEATHS …

ALL ARE MINE.

I HAVE BEEN A TEUTONIC KNIGHT IN LITHUANIA AND A PEASANT GIRL ACCUSED OF BRUJERIA IN SPAIN.

I HAVE LIVED IN LUXURY IN THE PALACE AT VERSAILLES, IN A STONE MONASTERY IN ROMANIA AND IN A HUT OF MUD AND STRAW IN HISPANIOLA.

I HAVE TORTURED HUNDREDS OF MEN, WOMEN AND CHILDREN AND BEEN TORMENTED AND PERSECUTED TOO MANY TIMES TO COUNT.

I HAVE HAD MY TONGUE REMOVED, MY ENTRAILS DISEMBOWELED, MY EYES PUT OUT, AND MY MANHOOD SEVERED NOT ONCE, BUT TWICE.

I HAVE RAPED AND BEEN RAPED.

I HAVE FATHERED CHILDREN AND GIVEN BIRTH.

I HAVE RIPPED INFANTS FROM WOMBS AND THROWN THE CORPSES OF OLD MEN AND WOMEN INTO THE BURIAL PITS AT TREBLINKA

… AND MOST RECENTLY, I HAVE USED THIS CURRENT STEED – WAYNE DUFFY - TO ABDUCT, DEFILE AND SLAUGHTER NUMEROUS YOUNG WOMEN IN THIS FAIR CITY. I HAVE DONE ALL THIS SIMPLY BECAUSE I CAN. >

Archie lifted his fists to press his temples in a futile attempt to banish the voice. The man he had thought was Duffy turned away from him in order to reveal the passenger on his back – a grotesque alien monstrosity – in its horrid beauty.

< SEE MY TRUE FORM! AM I NOT MAGNIFICENT? >

The Specimen

The three muscular appendages wrapped around his torso and met in a softball-sized node embedded in the skin just beneath Duffy's right scapula. Migrating from side to side on the central mass was a cloudy yellow eyeball, a cancerous orb that extended toward Archie on a foot-long cartilaginous stalk. The pupil dilated to virtually cover the entire eye. A jagged scar – an ancient battle injury perhaps - almost bisected the eye, rendering it partially blinded by the opaque tissue. Two fleshy slits fluttered on either side of the lone eye in a mockery of respiration. An amber liquid started to seep from large pores on the main mass of the creature and an acrid musk tainted the air.

<PUT DOWN YOUR FEEBLE WEAPON AND SUBMIT TO ME. ACCEPT THIS HONOR AND BECOME MY NEXT STEED>

For once, Archie was glad for his scarred sinuses. He was becoming nauseated and unsteady from the powerful stench. If the smell of the creature bothered him this much, he could only imagine what it would be like for someone with a normal sense of smell. He snorted in disgust and retreated a step; gun aimed directly at the disfigured eyeball as it weaved sinuously in front of him.

Eying Duffy and his Rider for any sudden motion, he responded slowly and precisely, "No, you are most definitely not magnificent. You are the furthest thing from magnificent in my opinion. You are a fucking monster, inside and out… and whatever you may be, you and your kind should be wiped off the face of this planet. I would rather die here, completely in control, than ever consent to your offer."

The Rider and Steed turned back around until Archie was once again looking at Duffy's face, on which appeared signs of frustration and concern.

<SO BE IT. YOU HAVE MADE YOUR CHOICE.>

The attack was instantaneous.

One of the chest tentacles withdrew from Duffy's flesh and lashed out with the bony spur. The skin beneath Archie's left eye flayed open, sending a spray of scarlet weeping down his face. The pain was a shock, but it helped bring Archie out of the daze into which he had been slipping. He scrambled back out of reach of the whipping appendages and quickly sent two point blank shots at Duffy's head.

Somehow he missed. Even an amateur like him should have been able to blow out the back of this guy's cranium from that range. Shitty fucking gun. One bullet shattered a family picture that showed Duffy with his parents and sisters gathered around a snowman, each wearing the ugliest Christmas sweaters in creation. The other bullet lodged in the doorframe to the hall. Duffy - or not Duffy... like it actually mattered at this point – bum-rushed Archie and body-slammed him into the couch, flipping it over with the impact. He tried to soften his landing by rolling, but the arm Noodle had bitten gave way beneath him and he slammed face first into something rotting, warm and slippery.

Again, a tentacle whipped at Archie as Duffy grabbed him by the hair. Wrapping around his neck like a fleshy noose, the alien arm pulled him off the floor and he saw that he had just taken a header into the ravaged guts of one of the corpses in the room. A headless woman... probably Duffy's mother. She looked about two days dead and smelled like a bowl of wet dog food that had been rotting in the summer heat. From her condition, it appeared that Noodle may have thought so as well. Archie would have vomited but the chokehold on his throat sealed off his gorge and prevented him from adding to the mess on the floor.

Archie could do nothing as he was dragged brutally to his feet. Another tentacle wrapped around his left forearm – the injured one – and yanked it back well past its normal range of motion until his shoulder dislocated with a resounding POP. The joint felt as if someone was running a blowtorch along every nerve in his arm. Seconds later, the clammy tentacle clenched again, disarticulating his elbow, tearing out tendons and ligaments, and snapping his wrist in half. The hold on his throat loosened and he was allowed to scream.

<LISTEN TO THE MUSIC OF THAT AGONY! PERHAPS I WILL DO THIS TO ALL YOUR LIMBS BEFORE I REMOVE THEM ONE BY ONE. IT MAKES ME LONG FOR THE TIME WHEN ONE COULD HAVE SOMEONE DRAWN AND QUARTERED WHENEVER THE URGE STRUCK. HEARING THE FLESH TORN FROM BONE. THE ELASTIC TWANG OF TENDONS AND LIGAMENTS AS SHOULDERS AND HIPS ARE WRENCHED FROM TORSOS. THE COPPER SMELL OF BLOOD

The Specimen

MIXED WITH THE STENCH OF BOWELS. AAAAHHH, HOW I MISS ROMANIA!>

Bellowing in agony, Archie was amazed to see that he still clutched the gun in his right hand. Without a thought, he reached back and pressed the barrel into what seemed to be Duffy's ribs, pulling the trigger repeatedly until the gun clicked on an empty chamber. Immediately, the tentacles released him, dropping him onto the floor where he moaned and cradled his twisted, shattered arm.

The monster masquerading as Duffy retreated, clamping his hands over the multiple gaping holes in his sides. Streams of blood leaked past his fingers at a worrisome pace, trickling down his leg and pooling around his already bloodstained bare feet.

<SO... THE PUP HAS FANGS AND GETS IN A LUCKY BITE!> He lifts his arm and examines the extensive wounds. <THAT WAS DEFINITELY UNEXPECTED. I THINK THESE WOUNDS MAY BE ENOUGH TO RETIRE MR. DUFFY AS MY STEED. HMMM... NOW WHERE COULD I FIND ANOTHER STRAPPING YOUNG MAN TO PROVIDE ME A RIDE?>

Archie scuttled back on his remaining good hand and feet. He ran smack dab into the side of the overturned sofa and he was trapped – backed into the corner with no apparent escape. Not even one bullet remained in his gun, either to defend himself or to take the easy way out and permanently make himself ineligible to become a Steed. He looked around him for something... anything he could use as a weapon, but the only things within reach were the piles of rotting limbs and bloated torsos of Duffy's former parents and siblings.

The Duffy-monster kneeled a few feet away, no longer covering the bullet holes in his side. He smiled beatifically as the chorus of voices reverberated in Archie's head, <DON'T WORRY... AS THEY SAY, THIS WILL ONLY HURT FOR A BIT. YOU WON'T EVEN NOTICE IT>. The demented grin widened as he snorted and let out a series of child-like giggles. <THAT WAS A LIE. THIS IS GONNA HURT MORE THAN ANYTHING YOU'VE EVER EXPERIENCED BEFORE IN YOUR MISERABLE, POINTLESS LITTLE LIFE.> He bowed his head to the floor and the three-tentacled monstrosity began to forcibly remove itself from the fleshy confines of Duffy's body.

Weeping, Archie defiantly held the gun pointed at the center mass of his opponent as the sound of ripping flesh and bursting glutinous sacs filled the room.

So intent on the horrific scene before him, he didn't see the three masked figures in trench coats march into the room until they were right behind Duffy's kneeling figure. The men on the left and right of him each roughly grasped the closest tentacle in gloved hands. The middle man pointed a metal box at the central node on Duffy's back and pressed a large black button. Two metal darts shot from the box and lodged in the main mass of the Rider. Immediately afterwards, the man pressed a second button – this one was red – and the Rider and Duffy began convulsing as thousands of volts tore through them. Seconds later the two bonded beings collapsed to the gore-covered floor.

The stench of burnt hair hung in the air and the men removed their gas masks. The one in the middle was obviously in charge. He had salt-and-pepper hair buzzed to his scalp and a jagged ugly scar running from just below his right ear diagonally across his throat. He stepped towards Archie, stared him up and down for a second and growled in a voice that sounded like he was gargling shards of broken glass, "Give me one reason why I shouldn't just shoot you? Who the fuck are you and why are you even here? I'm this close to putting a bullet in you and blaming it on this sick fuck on the floor."

Archie said nothing. Placing his gun at his side, he slumped against the wall, covered his eyes and didn't speak to anyone for the next three days.

* * *

… And that was how Murtaugh met his future mentor James P. "Jimbo" Kilcannon.

A month later, after his release from the hospital, the scarred and battle-worn warrior showed up at his apartment one night with a bottle of

The Specimen

20 year old scotch and, ultimately, a job offer to continue the fight against these monsters for as long as he wanted.

    Murtaugh accepted on the spot.

Official Report on the Greylock Incident

February 15, 1966
To: Members of the Governing Council, ACME Group
From: James P. Kilcannon, Agent-in-Charge
RE: Greylock Incident (Hutchens Period)

Dear Council Members,

The next set of entries deal with Dr. Coe's continued side experiments with the Cluster, and the fortunately short period where the Rider was bonded with the patient Hutchens. This incident specifically led to the creation of a set of protocols, when attempting any Host Transfer in our labs.

- JPK

*   *   *

Day 51

I dreaded coming to the lab today. Even though I was able to get more sleep than I have had in weeks, it was restless and broken by dreams where I found the lab in various states of destruction. In the end, my concerns did not prove prophetic. The lab was as pristine as it had been when I left hours earlier.

When I opened the closet door, the organism was in the same exact position as it was when I locked it in last night. Part of me was disappointed. I half expected that it would have evolved in some unknown manner in the past ten hours. I knew this was unlikely, but the innocent child that has hidden inside me since my college years yearned for something marvelous.

The Specimen

Colfax was away for the day. I expect he was reporting to the Council again, listing my faults alphabetically or some other annotated list of petty crap. Do they take him seriously? I wonder. I'll keep him busy monitoring the original Rider for now. No need to bother him with this new side project.

Five more irradiated samples remain. Last night, I came to the decision that I would repeat the same procedure with all of them. I predicted they would all merge into the main mass, and that was exactly what happened. Though I observed the samples religiously, I somehow missed the actual process. One second the original was on the table with a new sample next to it, and the next second, I blinked and they had merged into one larger sample.

I experimented with samples from earlier tests, ones that had been exposed to heat, cold and other extremes, but no attempts to merge them were successful at all. The main mass ignored them.

Its mass is now 77.3 kg with a length of 1.15 m, width of .85 m, and height of .42 m. About the size of a large dog, such as a mastiff or a St. Bernard. I will monitor these numbers daily. One question to investigate will be how it gains any sustenance. As a living creature, it surely requires food.

- GC

Day 53

For lack of a better name, from now on I will refer to the creature as "a Cluster" considering its appearance and the method by which it was formed. Its growth seems to have finally stabilized and a solid core of neural tissue has formed in the center of its mass.

This morning, when I opened the closet, I found that the Cluster was no longer on the cart where it had been placed overnight. Instead it stood upright as if it were bipedal like a human. Even so, I am unconvinced that it is exhibiting intelligence just yet. This recent display could simply be mimicry as opposed an attempt to communicate.

Colfax returned the evening before last and he has been much less intrusive than before. Perhaps the Council set him straight on our respective roles.

Other things to note – the question about how the Cluster had been finding nourishment has been answered.

This morning as I first checked on its condition, I stepped on an object that crunched like a dry autumn leaf on the ground. Initially I thought that was exactly what I had found, until I picked it up.

It turned out to be a desiccated corpse of a rat. The skin was as thin and dry as decades-old parchment, with wisps of grey-brown hair and the features as flat as if it had every drop of moisture sucked out of its body, then pressed between the pages of a heavy book. It broke apart in my hands like a potato chip. When I dropped the dried rat dust to the floor, I saw a few more rat chips piled in the shadows.

The rest of the day ended uneventfully. I sent Mr. Willard to the store for some rat traps to be placed around the rooms, so we can see for ourselves how the Cluster handles its food. It should prove interesting. Perhaps we can move on to something larger later. Maybe a cat.

- GC

Day 56

The experiment with the rat traps has been delayed due to developments with Hutchens and the Rider that need to be addressed immediately.

Hutchens has been conscious for nearly a week now and, as expected, the Rider appears to be in complete control of him. Communication with the parasitic creature, however, has been extremely limited. We seem to have been correct with our prediction that Hutchens would be a blank slate, but we underestimated the effect that his autism would have upon the ability of the Rider to communicate.

The Specimen

Before the transplant, Hutchens often seemed to be lost inside his own thoughts. As long as he was not touched or moved, he could exist without any interactions with his fellow residents inside his own world. Even so, he seemed quite content.

Now, there exists a dark intelligence in his eyes that cannot communicate with us. I can see the frustration and the fury there. The powerful mind that was accustomed to dominating every individual it encountered feels impotent yet again. The mind that we thought would be easy for the Rider to control has become its prison cell.

We know only a few facts about the Rider's last couple Hosts, but the one thing of which we are certain is that they had extremely strong willpowers. Mr. Roumain seems to have been able to control the Rider all the time, except when his health was failing. Young Master Varney was strong as well, but it is unlikely he would have been able to hold back the monstrous ego of the Rider on a consistent basis. The only thing preventing the Rider from dominating him before was the combined effect of the numerous injuries that it received during the escape from our original abduction at Bayou Lou's.

Both Colfax and I have been taking turns speaking to Hutchens and the Rider, but we haven't even been able to get it to respond in any manner. Not even in the affirmative or negative answers to which Hutchens had been accustomed.

It has been an exhausting day filled with frustration, but I am certain our efforts will eventually succeed. I am returning to my quarters now. Colfax will take over with Jameson stationed outside the labs and I will continue tomorrow morning.

- GC

Chapter 24 - 'Round Back

"The only good human being is a dead one."
- George Orwell

March 13, 1965 – Springfield, MA

Something wasn't right, thought Harry as he pedaled his bike through the underpass to the other side of the tracks. He'd felt that way ever since he woke up a few hours earlier, and he instinctively knew that it had something to do with Lucien. Maybe he was finally leaving today! If that was the case, Harry had to catch him before he disappeared for good. He had to tell Lucien that he didn't blame him at all for the previous week's incident. He had to beg him not to leave.

It had taken three days before his mother and Nana would let him out of the house after he woke up from his head injury. Since then, Harry had ridden by Bayou Lou's three times to see if it was open, but each time he had been disappointed to find it closed. No sign stating when it would open again, nor were there any announcements of its imminent relocation. He was desperate to see Lucien again, but it was beginning to look like he might actually leave without a proper goodbye. Harry was distraught at the thought he might not get a chance to convince his friend to stay.

He saw the commotion outside Bayou Lou's as soon as he turned onto Alden Street. A strange chubby man in a rumpled gray suit - a white man, in fact - was blocking one of Lucien's most avid admirers, Miss Violetta Rooks, from entering the store.

From what Harry could see at this distance, it wasn't going very well for the man. Miss Rooks, who was not a small woman in any sense of the word, loomed over him with a casserole dish held over his head in one hand and her other forefinger poking him in the chest to punctuate each word that came out of her mouth.

Harry slowed down and approached the store in the shade of the flowering trees that lined the sidewalk, trying to catch some hint of what was happening while remaining out of sight. He hid behind one of the

The Specimen

larger trunks and peered down the block. The man's words were too quiet to be heard, but Miss Rooks' powerful voice easily carried across the intervening space.

"Like I care about your tin badge. Who do you think you are? Some sort of Secret Agent Man?" she ridiculed him before starting on another lengthy harangue. "I made this dee-licious casserole for Mr. Roumain and *I* will be the one who gives it to him. Not some two-bit government man."

The man briefly mumbled a reply, but Miss Rooks bulldozed over him with another tirade, "Don't try to butter me up now, Huckleberry. This ain't Alabama and I ain't about let some chubby cracker send me on my way before I see my man…"

The door opened and another man, colored and fit with a military demeanor, stepped out to confront Miss Rooks. Harry became even more concerned. These men did not fit in this neighborhood at all. They wanted something specific, and like Miss Rooks had said, they seemed like government men… the kind that only showed up when they wanted to take what they claimed was theirs, such as taxes, or property. Where was Lucien? What could they want from the owner of a corner store?

Suddenly, he realized exactly what they wanted. Lucien may have been careful to a fault to hide the existence of the Rider, but he failed to account for the weakness of others. Someone who knew about the creature he carried on his back must have let the secret slip, and before he knew it, there were secret government agents knocking on his door. This was straight out of the comics! If not for the revelation last week, Harry would never have believed such an extraordinary idea, but considering what he knew now, the evidence was clear. For Lucien's sake, Harry hoped his friend wasn't in danger. He had to investigate.

Harry took the opportunity to duck in the alley while the three were distracted to the point that he felt they would not see him when he dashed out from behind the tree. Head pounding, he hugged the brick wall, a bit shaky and disoriented from his sprint and lowered himself to his knees.

"Ugh… guess I'm still hurtin'," he admitted under his breath. "Still gotta take things easy."

He looked back across the street and muttered a few words that would have earned him a mouthful of soap if his mother had heard them. His bike was still lying on its side next to the tree where he had been hiding. If he ran back over there, he could easily grab it, but he would also surely be noticed. Best to move on and just hope that no one in this neighborhood took off with it.

Unabated, the argument could still be heard around the corner. Miss Rooks certainly was giving it to them, Harry smirked. He always had liked her, especially when she brought one of her legendary casseroles. Hopefully she would keep them busy while he peeked in through the loading dock in the rear of the store.

Having caught his breath, Harry rose to his feet and walked slowly around the back of the building. Alden Street ran along the entire length of Watershops Pond, a brackish lake in the center of Springfield. Many of the buildings on the street, with the exception of Bayou Lou's, sat almost flush against a tall wooden fence that had seen better days, with a narrow strip of pavement between the buildings and fence. Immediately beyond the fence was a steep twenty to thirty foot drop to the lake's rocky shore. Harry's grandfather had told him they had been built because a young girl had fallen to her death there a little over a decade earlier.

The back entrance to Bayou Lou's was three buildings down, about ten yards from the fence, leaving barely enough room for delivery trucks to pull in and unload their goods onto the loading dock. Harry scurried next to the fence in the shadows of overhanging trees before dashing up to the loading dock door. Voices leaked from within, but he didn't recognize any of the speakers as Lucien. From his vantage point, there were at least two men, possibly three, engaged in conversation.

He peered through the narrow seam between the dock doors. Three men in suits surrounded the motionless body of a fourth individual splayed on the concrete floor. Harry couldn't see very well through the crack. The man on the floor could have been dead or alive, but he lay in a

The Specimen

pool of shadows and all that could be seen were his legs. Two of the others were standing, one with a large assault rifle in his grip and the other with what appeared to be a dart gun aimed at the body on the floor. The third man was on his knees, hunched over the body, seemingly working at cutting something with a knife. Harry bit his lip to keep from crying out and squinted some more, hoping to dispel a creeping suspicion that he knew exactly who was lying there.

Seconds later, two things happened simultaneously that confirmed his fears. The man on his knees shifted position, giving Harry a line of sight directly to the body. It was his friend Lucien. The bloody flesh of his back gleamed red and wet as the man with knife sawed away. As he realized this dreadful fact, a wall was demolished in his mind and a familiar, sickening presence made itself known...

<CHILD, HAVE YOU COME FOR ME??>

The sibilant whisper licked him like a tongue along the interior of his skull, but impact of the creature's voice was anything but subtle. The Rider had been waiting for him, and it had struck at his conscience when he was off guard. The message was frantic and full of rage and fear.

<YOU MUST HELP US, CHILD! YOUR FRIEND IS IN DANGER! HE WILL DIE WITHOUT YOUR INTERVENTION! DO SOMETHING!>

Harry squeezed his eyes shut and held his fists white-knuckled against his temples. Not now. This could not be happening now, when Lucien was in peril. Harry knew that the creature spoke the truth, but, considering the last encounter and the hunger it had displayed for him, he knew that he absolutely could not trust it. How could he save Lucien without falling under the influence of this abomination? Even without that complication to the situation, how could he possibly think that he could even help? These men were armed and professional. Harry was just a kid interfering in the affairs of men much more powerful than him, and if he kept it up, he would probably be killed and dumped in the river.

<THEY ARE BUTCHERING US!!!>

And with that outcry, the Rider sent a mental scream that roared through Harry's psyche and, worst of all, shared the excruciating pain that it was currently experiencing. Harry was suddenly inside the mind of the Rider, its alien body scraped from Lucien's back like the skin of a deer being peeled from its carcass. He could feel that the razor-like blade cutting the Rider's flesh from Lucien's back was also severing the neural threads that connected their two minds, leaving each of them psychically incomplete.

Harry reeled back and flailed his arms at the psychic blast. All of his senses were eclipsed by the intensity of the pain. He felt as if he had been blinded by looking directly into the sun. All sound was drowned out by an explosion of white noise. His skin burned as if all his nerve endings had been exposed. Taste and smell were overwhelmed by a foul bitterness that flooded his mouth and gullet.

He fell backwards, insensate and barely clinging to consciousness. He tripped over a wooden pallet behind him and collapsed to the ground flat on his back. The silence was instantly demolished as the metal trash cans lined up against the wall were kicked over by his thrashing legs.

<THANK YOU, CHILD. YOU HAVE DONE WELL>, the Rider's voice said as it cut through the pain. Harry could not respond as he lay twitching on the pavement.

* * *

"Someone's at the dock doors," yelled Mangual at the sound of the crashing cans. He immediately aimed his rifle in that direction.

"Check it out, Mangual," Pfeiffer ordered, setting the dart gun aside and drawing his pistol. Both men approached the doors. Pfeiffer covered on the left while Mangual grasped the handle and slid the right door wide. Squealing on the metal rails, the door opened to reveal Harry lying on the pavement in the aftermath of his seizure.

"Just a kid having some sort of fit. What should I do?"

The Specimen

"Damn it to Hell. Can't leave him out there. He might have seen something. Bring him in here and tie him up. Make sure to blindfold him. I'll decide what to do with him later," grumbled Pfeiffer. "Koonce, let's wrap this up. We need to leave soon." He turned away as Mangual pulled the unconscious boy into the loading dock and bound him to the water pipes protruding from the wall.

Koonce refocused on the excision, gritting his teeth as he reached a particularly thick section of connective tissue. So involved was he in cutting the body of the Rider off of Lucien's torso that he missed the motion out of the corner of his eye until it was far too late to avoid the attack.

The long bony spur that had formed on the end of the Rider's tentacle darted forward and pierced his throat like a harpoon. Koonce collapsed backwards, grasping at the barbed appendage in a futile attempt to extract it before it did any more damage. The Rider retracted its tentacle like a whip, ripping out a golf ball-sized chunk of his trachea and sliding through his hands like a slimy strand of barbed wire. As he lay on the floor, Koonce tried desperately to plug the hole in his throat, but the torrential gush of blood spurted through his fingers down his chest and legs. He felt a wave of numbness wash over his body as the life bled out of him.

Mangual and Pfeiffer whirled at the sound of Koonce choking… just in time to see the Rider detach its remaining uncut cilia from Lucien's body and dart behind a pile of unused wooden pallets.

"CRAP!" swore Pfeiffer. "Go to the left. I'll take right. We need to corner it before it gets outside. We can't let it escape."

"Can I shoot it?" yelled Mangual with a grin. He clicked off the safety and circled around to the left side of the pile.

"If you have to … just don't let it get away!" Pfeiffer snarled as he went behind the pallets into the shadows, gun in hand.

* * *

James P. "Jimbo" Kilcannon wished to God he could just shoot this woman. She was still yelling and making a scene, waving her casserole dish around. Just about all of his patience had been exhausted with her, and Jeffords was only making things worse with his dismissive attitude. The only reason Jimbo hadn't invited her inside so he could plug her right between her piggy little eyes was the amount of paperwork he would have to fill out. He had requested this transfer to get away from the pencil-pushing and he didn't want to give them any reason to ship him back there. No… shooting her was out of the question. They would have to resort to something less messy. At the very least, he wanted to inject her with a sedative to shut her up, but for now it seemed better to just step back and let Jeffords take the lead. After a few more minutes of Miss Violetta Rooks' caterwauling, even Jeffords might admit he was beaten… at which point Jimbo would suggest the needle.

"Violetta Rooks' momma didn't raise no fool," she said again as she refused to go home. "Not until I can see my Lucien", she demanded. At one point, it looked like she might let the casserole dish slip and cover the three of them with Spam and noodles.

"Did your mama teach you to speak that way to a lady?" she asked Jeffords as he let a choice phrase slip. "If you were my son, you'd have so much soap in your mouth, you'd be spitting up bubbles for a week and you'd never think of mouthing off to me again."

Jimbo could see that his colleague was reaching his boiling point. He was on the verge of dropping a few subtle hints about the sedative when a large crash followed by a barrage of gunfire echoed from the back room … first single shots followed by the rat-tat-tat-tat of Mangual's assault rifle. Jimbo and Jeffords looked at each other in dismay, shouted at Violetta in unison, "Stay here!", and then bolted to the rear of the store. Seconds later, glass dish in her hands, Violetta ignored their command and followed them into Bayou Lou's, ready to slap aside anyone who got in her way. No one would be keeping her from her man. Not if they valued their lives.

The Specimen

Chapter 25 – Blue Light Special

"Never open the door to a lesser evil, for other and greater ones invariably slink in after it." - Baltasar Gracian

Modern Day – Hartford, CT

As the metal gate automatically lowered behind him, Murtaugh turned left off the ramp into the garage and backed the van up to the loading dock on the west wall. He shifted into Park and shut off the engine, taking a few seconds to savor the cool subterranean silence in the bowels of the mall. The engine ticked as it cooled, but other than that, no sounds echoed off the concrete walls.

Silence was a valuable commodity to him these days and Murtaugh took advantage of any spare second he was able to squirrel away. The girls were completely safe and secure where they were, anyway. They had at least three hours to go before the sedative would wear off and they would slowly wake up. Five or ten minutes reclining in the driver's seat was exactly what he needed. He leaned back, closed his eyes and let his mind wander as he relaxed.

Back when Kilcannon ran the show in this region, Murtaugh would never have considered such an action, but a lot of things had changed in the past decade. Quillian was now in charge after a series of inept successors who had quickly moved on to less important roles in the organization.

Not that Quillian was a poor team leader. He just had different priorities and methods than Kilcannon had. Before his "retirement", Kilcannon had been single-mindedly focused on the eradication of the Riders and related threats. Quillian, on the other hand, was too willing to assist with Dr. Colfax's side projects. If Kilcannon found a victim in the early stages of bridling, he would attempt to separate the individual from the parasitic Rider, but whenever he encountered a fully bridled Rider/Steed pair, he would riddle it with bullets without a second thought. Once the two beings were completely symbiotic, separation became a pointless endeavor. A separated Steed suffered from the worst case of Post-Traumatic Stress Disorder that Murtaugh had ever seen. Very little of the original personality remains after the bridling process. Most of it would have been assimilated into the hive personality of the Rider. The longer the Ride, the more that the Steed's personality comes to the forefront.

Quillian would take a more long-term approach in the same situation. If at all possible, he would order the team to capture the affected individual, or in some cases any related individual who may have been exposed. When a capture was successful, the new test subjects were brought here to Green Valley and passed off to the inscrutable Dr. Arnold Colfax, who would then conduct experiments on them and dissect them when they expired. They didn't die. They *expired*... like a gallon of milk going sour in a refrigerator. The doctor liked his euphemisms.

In Murtaugh's opinion, despite his subdued, almost shy demeanor, Colfax was just as insane as some of the subjects he treated. It often had crossed his mind that the doctor would have been an ideal colleague for Josef Mengele in Auschwitz. He was an unrepentant sadist and, some suspected, a pedophile, but he was undeniably a genius. A genius that had compiled much of the knowledge that was available on the strengths and weaknesses of the Riders and their kin. Without the data that he and his predecessor, Dr. Genevieve Coe, had collected, the battle against the Riders would have gone much more poorly.

Murtaugh realized early on in his life with the Acme Group that sometimes, no matter how much it disgusted him, it was necessary to work with a lesser evil in order to defeat a greater one. The Riders were undoubtedly the greatest evil. He hadn't been fighting them for the better part of thirty-five years just for shits and giggles. It was a lifelong vendetta on his part and he wouldn't stop fighting until the last one had been peeled off its victim and tossed into a wood chipper, Fargo-style.

Someone knocked on his passenger-side window and Murtaugh reluctantly opened his eyes and groaned. *Great. Just what I needed*, thought Murtaugh. *Tweedle Dipshit and Tweedle Dickwad.*

The sweaty, balding man at the window grinned maniacally, pressed his lips against the glass and inflated his cheeks like a chipmunk gorging itself on nuts. Behind him stood another man with mirrored sunglasses (despite the fact that they were underground nowhere near any sunlight) and curly black hair buzzed to the scalp. Both wore urban camouflage khakis and plain black tees straight out of the local Army/Navy store. Even with their cliché *Soldier of Fortune* outfits and their less-than-professional attitudes, Murtaugh knew they were not amateurs, but they *were* poster boys for gun control. The two of them had served as contractors with Blackwater during the first years of the Iraq War. Both had many kills notched on their gun belts. *Whoever gave these guys guns in the first place should have their asses kicked on a daily basis.*

"Taking a little nap there, Archie?" asked the fat one at the window. "The Doctor won't be happy about that."

"Thanks for the advice, Smolensky. You're always looking out for us in the field," Murtaugh replied. "I'm sure he won't mind the latest unsolicited dirt on your co-workers. LeDuke, what do you think?"

The other guard just grunted and shrugged his shoulders. Jerry Smolensky and Burt LeDuke were two of the rotating security contractors who guarded the way in or out of the facility. As far as they knew, they had been hired as corporate security for a pharmaceutical/medical supply company. Why that company would be based in the basement of an abandoned mall was never questioned by any of the guards. It was simply accepted and ignored. All that mattered to them was the exorbitant paycheck they got at the end of the week. If something hinky was going on, it didn't matter to them. The worst they had been told to expect was someone trying get in undetected for a little bit of corporate espionage, or maybe some eco-terrorism. *If they only knew,* thought Murtaugh. *They'd shit a whole palette of bricks.*

He opened the door and stepped out of the van, stretching his arms and legs before walking around the back of the vehicle.

"Who else is on the clock?" he asked them as he unlatched the rear door, swinging them open to reveal a large pile of metal crates.

"Huerta and Fowles," replied LeDuke. "They're on rounds upstairs today. Brawley's on the desk inside. Need some help there?"

Murtaugh nodded and the three of them awkwardly dragged out the largest crate and hefted it onto a flat metal handcart on the loading dock.

"God damn! What you got in there that's so heavy, man?" grumbled Smolensky. "A couple of dead bodies? These weigh a ton."

Murtaugh smirked, "Top secret, guys. If I told you…"

"…You'd have to kill us," finished the pudgy man. "You need new material, Archie. That was old even back when you had hair."

"Low blow, Smolensky. Low blow. Now I gotta break out the fat jokes. Hold the door for me, would ya?"

The two guards obliged as he maneuvered the wide cart into the dark hallway beyond. As soon as he crossed the threshold, the ceiling panels lit up, illuminating a white corridor. Much more modern than the outside area, it stretched ahead a few yards before ending at a T intersection. Murtaugh bid the two men goodbye, closed the door behind him and pushed the cart down the hall.

A right turn at the T and a left at the next intersection led him to a large metal door with a keypad lock. He typed in a 5 digit code and continued on in a similar hallway until he reached a large open room empty of everything except for two examination tables, an MRI machine and an array of medical tools. Underneath each examination table was a large circular drain where any blood could be washed away. Separated from the rest of the room by a wall of glass was a long desk with a row of flat screen monitors.

Murtaugh maneuvered the cart between the two tables and slid the crate gingerly to the floor, wincing as his back tightened up and he felt a slight spasm running just under his left shoulder blade. *Can't do this shit much if I keep falling apart like this every time I exert myself.*

He unlatched the crate and lowered the lid gently to the ground. Inside, lying in a bed of pink popcorn peanuts were two black nylon body bags. Murtaugh removed each bag and placed them on the floor between the two tables.

Unzipping the first bag revealed a sedated Sydney Monahan, still dressed in her pajamas. She was drenched in sweat and breathing shallowly. Her hair clung to her forehead in slick ropes. Her left cheek and lower jaw were colored dark purple and swollen to twice their normal size from Grimaldi's roundhouse blow. *Daaamn, that's definitely broken. Al went a bit overboard*, thought Murtaugh as he gathered the girl in his arms and laid her flat on the cold metal table. He then snapped cuffs built into the table around both her wrists and ankles.

The Specimen

Murtaugh turned to the second bag and quickly removed Dahlia, about twenty pounds lighter and six inches shorter than her buxom blonde friend. He placed her gently on the table and paused to look at her. Take away the Goth vibe and the heavily applied black eyeliner and she looked like she could be Monica's little sister. He gritted his teeth and shook his head, chasing away those stray thoughts. *You need to avoid distractions, Archie. The past is long gone and you chose your path.*

As he cuffed her onto the table, he winced when looking at her left hand. Apparently she had scratched a few bloody furrows into Grimaldi's forearm when he initially had tried to inject her with the sedative.

As a reminder of who was in charge, the thug decided to break all four fingers on her left hand. After some agonized shrieks, Dahlia had passed out, but she would be in the worst pain of her life when she woke up. Her hand looked like a crooked bundle of mottled red sausages, with a shard of a bone erupting through the skin at the base of her pinky finger. The subsequent injection off went without incident and she had not regained consciousness since then.

Murtaugh stared at her mangled fingers and made a quick decision since she was already sedated. Grasping each one individually, he gingerly pulled them straight – or at least straighter than they had been – and lined them up with each other. She moaned, but didn't wake up. If anything, he hoped he had stopped them from healing like a bird's claw.

After unloading the cargo, Murtaugh moved the crate to the far corner of the room, then walked over to the wall and pressed the button for the intercom.

"Yes?" crackled a soft accented voice from the speaker next to the button.

"Dr. Colfax?" asked the bald tough. Receiving no confirmation, he continued. "Murtaugh here. The two girls that Quillian sent from the Monahan hunt are in the examination room. Ready for intake whenever you want."

"That is good to hear, Archie. Any news on the target?"

Murtaugh winced at the sound of his first name and bit his tongue. He hadn't used it since his early twenties, but it still brought back memories from his youth that he would much rather forget. The doctor always spoke in an even calm tone that reminded him of Mr. Rogers if he had an Alabama twang, - simultaneously soothing and unnerving. He even wore cardigan sweaters on a regular basis due to the constant room temperature of a brisk 66 degrees. This, however, was no Land of Make Believe that he would ever have wanted to visit as a child

"Monahan had a ten or twelve pounder. Surprisingly advanced. Um… there was an incident, though. Involving a witness," Murtaugh replied.

"Yes, Quillian reported that earlier. I already have Geist and Bohannon taking care of the cleanup at the hospital."

Murtaugh let out his breath slowly and asked, "Is there anything else you need done, Doctor?"

"No. Carry on. I will be there within the hour. The subjects can wait."

Without another word, Dr. Colfax ended the communication, leaving Murtaugh to stew in the suddenly stifling silence. He stood there, head bowed for a good thirty seconds before turning around and approaching the examination tables. Unconscious, the girls seemed much younger to him than they had huddled against the wall of the Monahan's kitchen.

"Of two evils, the lesser must always be chosen," he whispered under his breath. He briefly brushed back the hair from each girl's face, then turned away and walked out the door, images of a long-dead girl named Monica in his thoughts.

The Specimen

Official Report on the Greylock Incident

February 19, 1966
To: Members of the Governing Council, ACME Group
From: James P. Kilcannon, Agent-in-Charge
RE: Greylock Incident (Hutchens Period)

Esteemed Members,

    Much of the records for the remaining months were destroyed in the disaster on the night of the Blackout, but we have been able to restore some of the key documents that should confirm what we suspect went wrong. From these records, we should be able to extrapolate what likely happened.

                            - JPK

                      *   *   *

Day 57

    I returned this morning to an abattoir. Something went terribly wrong in Lab 1 last night...

Day 58

    It is done.

    The last have taken up all my time, but now I am finally sitting down to document exactly what happened. In order to understand it all, I will try to write everything down so I may examine the facts and reconstruct the most likely sequence of events...

    After a restless night's sleep, I returned to the labs to relieve Colfax and Jameson. There was no answer to my knock, but I assumed that Colfax was simply distracted. No cause for concern in my mind. I disengaged the electromagnetic locks to the lab and knew instantly that something horrifying had happened. A distinct aroma like freshly minted pennies hit me in the face on the gust of warm air that escapes every time the lab door is opened. A lingering musk beneath the sharp tang dissipated as the warmer air rushed out to the corridor. Blood was everywhere. Bodies were crumpled on the floor.

Jameson was dead, Hutchens was dead, and Colfax was on the ground unconscious from an obvious blow to the head.

*   *   *

I stood in the doorway for close to a minute while my mind tried to make sense of what I saw. The lights were out and at first I could only see their silhouettes, but my eyes adjusted and the carnage revealed itself quickly in the light from the hallway.

Hutchens lay on the examination table, back arched as if he were screaming to the heavens. His head hung backwards over the edge of the metal table at an impossible angle. One hand still held the scalpel which he had used to gradually saw through his larynx and neck muscles all the way to the vertebrae.

In my shock, I'm embarrassed to admit that I giggled slightly. The resemblance of his neck to a Pez dispenser was uncanny. I imagined a large piece of candy – cherry, of course – sticking out of the ragged hole in his Adam's apple.

Jameson had been stabbed with something in the left eye, quite possibly the same scalpel which Hutchens had used to partially decapitate himself. A stream of blood and ocular fluid had leaked down his cheek from the savaged eyeball, but otherwise, there didn't seem to be any other damage to the rest of his body. Neither bruises nor abrasions from a struggle were apparent. I would have to examine him further, but I wagered that the weapon used to pierce his eye had also impaled his brain. He sat leaning against the wall opposite the table as if

The Specimen

he was simply resting, but the reek from his voided bowels and bladder betrayed his true state

I initially thought Colfax was dead, too. Blood was leaking out of his ears and his nose, matting his red hair and forming a small pool behind his head. He moaned when the light from the hallway hit him in the face, so I realized he was still alive. Pity.

Finally coming to my senses, I entered the lab, turned on the lights and closed the door. This must remain secret. Once I alerted Fenton and brought him in here, we could clean up the mess and continue the experiments.

Mention of the experiments brought to mind the Rider. Had the demon escaped? Was it the cause for the homicidal behavior of these men here? Where was it hiding? It had to be in the room, unless there was some other exit that we didn't know. Anything was possible, I thought. This building was built last century. There must be hidden alcoves or chambers throughout the walls. If I had designed the building, I wouldn't have been able to resist adding a few secrets.

Blood had dried in streams down the sides of the table where Hutchens was immobilized, or perhaps I should say "partially immobilized". The leather strap that should have bound his right wrist to a metal bar had been unfastened. Now his hand hung down the side of the table still grasping the scalpel he had used on his neck. He hadn't cut through the leather or pulled his way out of it. Someone had to have unfastened it for Hutchens and handed him the blade.

I pried the scalpel from his grip, almost certain that he and his flapping Pez head would lurch up, wrap his arms around me and beg me for a kiss. My morbid imagination was getting the best of me, it seemed. Hutchens remained dead and I placed the stained tool in the pocket of my lab coat before rolling him over on his side.

The Rider was gone.

I had expected it to be gone due to the carnage around the room, but it was still a shock to see the gory divots in Hutchens' back where the Riders' tentacles had penetrated his back muscles. Could it have escaped the lab? I wasn't certain, but I knew that it was long gone if it had found another egress. I couldn't be concerned about that yet, though. This mess was my number one priority now.

Next I turned to look at Jameson, leaning a few feet away against the wall. Colfax could wait. I checked his pulse, just in case, but he was definitely gone. Cold and clammy. The smell of his shit and piss nearly had me looking for a wastebasket in which to puke.

Up close, I could now see that whatever made the hole in his eye had penetrated much further back than the socket. Tiny bits of bone were stuck to his eyelids and cheek by the dried blood and ocular fluid. Whoever had stabbed Jameson had done quite a thorough job, stabbing through the eyeball multiple times until it was just a shredded hole of bloody skin. I searched his lab coat and found his electromagnetic key, his knife and a pack of Pall Malls. Nasty things. Never really saw the appeal.

He appeared to have been dead for at least 4 hours, since rigor mortis was starting to set in. Probably closer to six hours. His gun was still in his shoulder holster. I removed that as well and stashed it in my coat.

Colfax moaned again.

I cursed at him and walked over, tempted to kick him in the face. This was all his fault. I didn't have any proof, but I was certain of it. Besides the blood and fecal matter in the room, this entire mess just reeked of his interference. I will definitely be filing a report on his continued incompetence with the Council.

It looked like he had slipped back into unconsciousness. First I checked his pulse. It was weak but steady. I lifted his eyelids. No dilated pupils or hemorrhaging. The sclera were white and his gaze was focused. His nose and ears were still leaking blood. I rolled him over and nearly screamed.

The Rider was pinned beneath him in a pool of dried blood. I flinched before I realized it was motionless, quite possibly dead. Nudging

The Specimen

it with my foot, I confirmed its dormancy. What could have knocked it out? There were no electrodes attached to its skin. No method to administer the current either. Besides, as time had shown, the alien had required an increasing voltage each time it was applied, as if it was building up a tolerance. No, it had to be something else.

I rolled Colfax over and found the answer – a crushed syringe attached to a bottle of Halperidol. Blood stained the needle and an injection site could easily be seen on the creature's back. The bottle was empty. If it was full when injected into the monster's flesh, the Rider was given a dose of 25 milligrams, enough to subdue a psychotic outburst by the most violent of patients.

Surprising to say the least. Colfax hadn't completely screwed things up. However it had gotten loose, he had managed to immobilize it before it escaped the lab.

He moaned again when I rolled him off the sedated organism, revealing a gory wound on his left hand. Two of his fingers had been gnawed or torn off at the second knuckle. When I flipped over the Rider, I saw that it had formed a lamprey-like orifice on its abdomen. Red blood covered most of the creature's body, but, even though there was no definite proof, I was sure the severed parts were long gone, shredded to a pasty gruel in its gut.

No matter now, though. I looked around the lab again and saw an unused specimen jar half filled with water. I retrieved it and dumped the monstrosity inside, sealing it shut.

* * *

Colfax will live, regrettably, but he obviously needs a day or two of rest before he can get up and around again. Besides his two partially severed fingers, he has a cracked rib and the head trauma is ruining his equilibrium. He wants to get right back to work, but I won't allow it. I want him to be at full strength for the next phase of the experiment, and to be honest, I need some time alone to decide the next move.

Fenton arrived within fifteen minutes, and after his initial shock at Jameson and the rest of the victims, he quickly controlled his emotions and shifted into professional mode. I admire that in an individual.

Within an hour, he had completely sanitized the scene and wrapped Jameson and Hutchens in rolls of plastic, sealing them shut with tape. I get the suspicion that these aren't the first deaths that he has swept under the rug for the Acme Group. When he loaded the bodies onto a cart to transport them for removal, I told him to hold off for now. At my request, he delivered the two cadavers to Lab 2 because I decided to delay the disposal for a couple of days.

I might have another use for the bodies...

-GC

The Specimen

Chapter 26 - Unleashed

"All God does is watch us and kill us when we get boring."
- Chuck Palahniuk

March 13, 1965 – Springfield, MA

The air smelled of cordite and blood. *An entire shelf of jars had been shattered seconds earlier when Pfeiffer crashed into it in the firefight. Now he was huddled against the cinderblock wall, clutching his arm to his belly and trying to staunch the flow of blood from his right hand. Out of reach, his pistol lay abandoned in a pool of Koonce's blood and broken glass in the middle of the floor. Alongside the gun were three of Pfeiffer's fingers that had been severed when the Rider lashed him with its spurs.*

Mangual crouched next to him with his back against the wall, scanning the opposite side of the loading dock for signs of the Rider. He was sure he had hit the creature at least once, but in this mayhem there was no possible way to find any signs of its current location. That thing was lightning fast. It had fled into the shadows after he had sprayed it with bullets, and now it could be anywhere. Hopefully it was dead. He reloaded his weapon and slowly climbed to his feet, visibly wincing from the cuts and bruises along his back.

"Hang in there, chief," he whispered to Pfeiffer. "I'll take care of this."

Pfeiffer just groaned unintelligibly in response. His injuries and blood loss had taken the fight out of him. When he adjusted his arms, Mangual saw the reason for his stoic silence. His shirt was thoroughly drenched red and brown. Beneath his blood-soaked arms, Pfeiffer had hidden his main injury, a deep ten inch gash slashing across his abdomen. Purple ropes of intestine bulged through his fingers, leaking their contents into his bloody lap. All of his energy was focused on keeping his entrails inside his abdominal cavity.

Compared to him, Mangual was hardly scratched. The Rider had managed to whip him across the forehead with a tentacle as it leapt by, but the two inch laceration was superficial. A few shards of glass were embedded in his upper back as well. Nothing that he thought needed immediate attention, though. Time to focus on catching this thing and killing it if necessary, just as should have been done from the get go. If the scientists needed one of these monsters for experiments, they could capture one themselves. Otherwise, Mangual was all in favor of wiping these mutant sons of bitches off the face of the planet.

He sidled along the perimeter of the loading dock, eyes darting from shadow to shadow watching for any movement that would give a hint at its hiding place. Koonce's corpse lay on its back across the Roumain man's legs, and the boy from the alley was slumped in the corner with his arms tied above his head.

"This is getting messy," he muttered. "Glad I won't have to clean it up."

The door to the front of the store banged open, and the two remaining members of the team rushed in. For once, Mangual showed some restraint and didn't immediately spray the newcomers with a wave of bullets. Jeffords automatically assessed the situation and split off to Pfeiffer's side. A few steps behind, Jimbo froze, stupefied at the devastation and carnage in front of him. The overpowering metallic stink of blood filled the air, but it faded in comparison to the atmosphere of potential violence temporarily held at bay.

Something terrible is about to happen, thought Jimbo. Before he transferred to the extraction team, he had always imagined that it would involve more investigation and research than actual fights. Obviously, he had to reevaluate that idea, especially considering the foe that he was about to face.

"Get that woman out of here!" yelled Mangual.

Jeffords gestured to Jimbo to keep her back before turning his attention back to Pfeiffer. The fingers were lost for good on his wounded hand, but he might retain some of the function because he still had his

The Specimen

forefinger and thumb. The gut wound was another story entirely. Fecal matter had already leaked into his body cavity. This would almost certainly lead to a massive infection whether or not they made it out of here alive today.

The creature was much stronger than anyone had expected. The amount of sedative used should have been more than enough to keep it under for a few hours. Jeffords looked over at the two bodies in the middle of the floor. The only possibility that he could imagine was that Koonce had underestimated how much of a factor Roumain's size would be on the effect of the drug. Most of it must have been used to knock the man out, but not the Rider.

"Where do you think it is?" he called to Mangual

"I don't know," he replied. "I hit it at least once but it kept coming at us. I'll find it… I'll tear this fucking place apart if I have to."

"I think we should call in some backup," Jeffords suggested. "This operation's already blown."

"No way, man. I got this!" Mangual looked back at him scowling at the idea, and that's when it all turned to shit.

Later, when the time came to write an official report and list everything in the proper chronological order, Jeffords and Jimbo would each struggle to determine what happened first.

Looking over Jimbo's shoulders as he attempted to move her back into the main part of the store, Violetta Rooks finally noticed that one of the bloody bodies on the floor was Roumain's. She immediately ran towards him – sobbing "Lucien! Lucien!" Jimbo attempted to hold her back, but she easily shoved him aside, backhanding him across the face the second he tried to grab her by the shoulder.

In the same instance, the creature dropped from the ceiling directly onto Mangual's face and neck. The Rider covered his eyes and nose like a caul and, within seconds, he began shaking his head and screaming. Blood seeped out from beneath the alien flesh and streamed down his cheeks in dozens of red rivulets. Involuntarily, he squeezed the trigger on his Kiraly-Cristóbal and released a burst of bullets before dropping the gun to the floor and trying to pull the Rider off his face. The bullets barely missed Miss Rooks as she rushed toward her man, but two grazed Jimbo on the right temple and the cheek. Another one hit the casserole dish dead center, sending an explosion of noodles, Spam and shards of glass into Jimbo's face and chest. One piece of glass, the size of a poker chip, lodged itself in his larynx and clove his voice box in two. He immediately released Miss Rooks and collapsed to his knees, mewling in pain as he attempted to stem the bleeding from his throat. Miss Rooks, now on the floor, began to crawl towards Lucien's body.

Jeffords rushed forward and grabbed one of the flailing tentacles as it began to encircle Mangual's neck. Up close, it was apparent that the Rider had been severely injured earlier. One tentacle hung limp like a bloody shredded noodle, and two bullet wounds the size of golf balls perforated the main mass of its body. Blood and a yellowish ichor oozed from the wound. He gripped the slimy appendage, but it pulled free. The jagged spurs protruding from the tentacle slashed open the palm of his hand as it ripped through his grasp.

A quarter-sized blister formed on the dorsal surface of the Rider. The skin of the blister hardened into a scale which flaked away, revealing a mucus-covered orb with a slit iris. The eyeball met Jeffords' gaze as if the Rider were examining a new species of insect.

The tentacle whipped again, this time slapping Jeffords on the right temple. Instead of the bony spurs that had previously adorned the limb, it now was covered with hundreds of miniscule fanged suckers that latched onto the skin on the side of his head. In less than a second, neural threads had rapidly punctured his skin and drilled through to his cerebral cortex. Jeffords could do nothing to avoid the connection.

A pulse of white noise froze him in place, and then a voice echoed within his mind.

<SHOULD I KILL YOU ALL?>

The Specimen

Jeffords couldn't respond by speaking. He was paralyzed from head to toe. A small string of drool leaked from the corner of his mouth. All that he could muster was a mental yowl.

<OR SHOULD I RENDER YOU INCAPABLE OF COMMUNICATION?>

With a herculean effort, Jeffords croaked out the words "Please … don't"

<YOU WANT MERCY WHERE YOU WOULD GIVE NONE>

Mangual collapsed to his knees. His screams became a high-pitched keening as he continued in his efforts to peel the Rider from his face. Jeffords raged silently. He watched his friend suffer, but he could not move more than a twitch of a finger, a trembling eyelid or flared nostrils.

<AN EXAMPLE MUST BE MADE. YOUR KIND HAS FORGOTTEN WHAT HAPPENS WHEN YOU DEFY US. YOUR ONLY PURPOSE IS TO BE OUR STEEDS. WITHOUT RIDERS, YOU ARE ONLY CATTLE.>

Jeffords was forced to watch as the Rider slid down Mangual's face, revealing something dreadful. Where his eyes had been were only scarred hollow sockets. Dried blood rimmed the scabrous remains of his lids, but the rest of the wounds were completely clean of blood. After the removal of the eyeballs, the wounds had been cauterized somehow.

Acid, thought Jeffords in horror. Mangual's eyes hadn't been torn out. They had been dissolved. Digested.

Mangual tumbled bonelessly to the ground and the Rider swung on its two remaining tentacles to land on Jeffords' left flank. The yellow-irised orb migrated from its back to its upper perimeter to lock gazes with him and communicate once again.

<NOW I WILL TAKE … >

… but Jeffords couldn't recall what was said because there was a pause - a gap - and then something was inside his mind scouring through the events of his life like a person skimming through a book. Reading a

paragraph here, a sentence there. Tearing out pages at random. Crossing out passages. Looking for the action - and that part of his memory, those pages, had already been torn from the book, crumpled into tight little balls before being discarded like used food containers. A page here. An image there. A vivid memory of a deceased friend. The scent of a woman's perfumed skin. The flavor of his mother's meatloaf. Gone forever. He didn't know what he was losing or what he had already lost, but each page torn out was something. Important or not, each memory was a piece of him that could never be recovered. Bit by bit, his life became littered with holes. Spots of nothingness that would never be refilled.

All the while, as his mind was being plundered, that citrine orb stared at him, holding his gaze and scooping him out like the guts of a pumpkin. He could feel his self slipping away bit by bit. His identity was dissolving and circling the drain.

Suddenly, a black hand wielding a skinning knife jammed the blade through the Rider's eyeball into the central node of its neural core. Miss Rooks stabbed it again and again with Koonce's knife, retrieved from the wet red concrete next to his body. The knife pierced the creature through to Jefford's own flesh. He was released and, like an old rubber band stretched to it limits, he snapped back in control of his thoughts, but much weaker, and fell to his knees.

"Die, demon, die!" she screamed, slicing off another tentacle in a fury. "You killed my Lucien!"

Shrieking, the blinded and bloody Rider leapt off of Jeffords' chest and oozed away, leaving a trail of gore in its wake. Jeffords collapsed, shadows of his memories slipping through his fingers. He lay on his side, vision slowing going gray. The chorus of screams from Mangual and Miss Rooks and Jimbo's labored liquid wheezing were muffled as he sank into an impenetrable fog. The only sounds he could hear were the rasping slither of its pseudopods on the concrete as the Rider escaped, searching for a new Steed. The boy, he wanted to yell. Stop! The boy! Stop the boy…

The Specimen

Chapter 27 – The Burden of the Beast

"Though the man above might say hello, expect no love from the beast below" — Steven Moffat

March 13, 1965 – Springfield, MA

And so Harry ran. For the first few minutes of his escape, Harry was in something of a fugue state. He didn't know why he was running, nor did he have any idea where he was going, but he knew that he needed to run away as far as he could. He carried something on his back and his only coherent thoughts were to stay out of sight and avoid capture. Beyond that, he acted on a primal, instinctual level. He was compelled to flee much longer and with greater endurance than he ever would have thought was within his capabilities. Something pushed him past the normal limits of a young healthy boy. The clouds opened up and still he ran. Heedless of the freezing rain. Concerned only with avoiding capture.

Finally, after sprinting for nearly half an hour through the alleys and side streets of Springfield, Harry hid in a stone culvert to catch his breath and seek shelter from the sudden downpour. The rain fell in sheets at either at either end of the long tube, giving him the sensation that he was trapped behind a torrential waterfall. Crawling a few yards in, through matted leaves and a shallow stream of fetid runoff water, he sat and leaned, shivering, against the cold inside curve of the concrete tube only to find that something on his back prevented him from lying flat.

"Oh no," Harry groaned. "Please, no. It's not possible"

He pulled back the collar of his shirt and felt past his shoulder blade. He touched something foreign and recoiled, then explored the area again. Warm and wet gelatinous flesh melded with his own smooth skin, burrowing to connect with nerves and ganglia. No sign of cartilage or bone structure, either. The Rider was now fused to the muscle of his back and nothing short of a razor-sharp blade would remove it from his body.

Harry began to quietly sob. If the Rider was now attached to him, did that mean that Lucien was dead? He couldn't remember anything after he witnessed the men cutting his friend open on the loading dock and the creature invaded his mind. His next conscious memory was only from a few minutes ago when he realized he was running through the streets of Springfield. Fleeing something or someone. Now that he had some time to consider what had happened, Harry realized that he must have been fleeing the group of men who had been hell bent on removing the Rider from Lucien's body.

How had he even escaped? His wrists were sore and raw, so he must have been tied up at one point, but he wasn't strong enough to tear away any rope or twine that would have been used… was he? It must have been the Rider, using him in a burst of strength to rip free and run as far away from Bayou Lou's as possible.

It was strange, though, he thought. Harry felt nothing now besides the bulky lump on his back. No alien presence in his mind. He pulled his hand back out from under his shirt and instantly saw why the Rider's voice had gone silent. Stained red, his hand was covered from wrist to tip in blood and ichor. Somehow, the Rider had been severely wounded. Shot and stabbed. Judging by the amount of damage he felt, it had nearly been torn to shreds. Reaching back under his shirt, he could feel the many stab wounds and the clotted remains of its punctured eyeball. He poked it multiple times, but it only felt like a mass of dead fat. Most likely, Harry guessed, it was unconscious. The Rider needed to heal. It could be dead, thought Harry, but that didn't seem right. He could sense a shadow of a presence hiding in some dark corner of his mind. Waiting to heal, so it could once again take control. That was an option that Harry had to stifle immediately. He could not allow himself to even entertain any possibility that this might happen.

Somehow, he had to get this abomination removed from his back, but who could he trust? He couldn't do this alone, but he couldn't think of anyone who could hold on to such a secret without giving it away. The only one who would have understood his predicament was Lucien… and he was probably dead. Harry had only seen his bloodied body through the doors on the loading docks, but nothing led him to believe that Lucien had survived. He couldn't tell his family and he had no friends to share his

The Specimen

pain. There was nothing he could imagine that he could do to resolve this problem. If Lucien couldn't rid himself of this monstrosity, how could he? Lucien had lived by himself and he had been an adult, but Harry was still a child. He was still dependent on his family. He wept, huddled and shivering, as he mourned his friend.

A couple of hours passed before the storm finally slowed to a drizzle. Harry dozed on and off in exhaustion, but his sleep was fitful and filled with barely remembered images of blood and monsters. The water level in the tunnel had risen a few inches, forcing him to slide his back up the wall and soak his shoes. Debris and waste from the streets and gutter washed by him in an ugly brownish current that smelled of oil and rotting vegetation.

When the flattened corpse of a squirrel floated by, Harry realized it was time to head home. He needed to sneak into his house and change clothes before anyone noticed him in this condition. With the Rider on his back now, his choice would be limited to anything big and baggy to hide the bump on his back. Fine for now, but when the weather warmed up in the summer, he would be in big trouble. Walking around in a sweater and dungarees in the summer would not only arouse suspicion – especially from his mother and Nana – but it would also be physical torture from the heat. During the summer, Harry often went for weeks without ever wearing a shirt. That was not an option in his current condition.

He crawled out of the culvert and looked around to reorient himself. The day was still clinging to the remnants of the storm, clouds hanging gray and foreboding over the Springfield sky. After a few seconds turning in a circle, Harry recognized the steeple of the Church of Christ the Liberator over the roofs a couple of streets away. He headed in that direction and soon found that he was closer to home than expected. His mad dash had unconsciously taken him in a wide loop that centered on his neighborhood. One last glance at the stone culvert and Harry hurried home, wondering if he might soon need to make plans to protect his family from the menace riding his back… and to what extremes he might need to go.

Chapter 28 – Good Samaritan

"If you got something you don't want other people to know, keep it in your pocket." -Muddy Waters

June 4, 1965 – Springfield, MA

It may have been nearly half a century ago, but to Milton "Bud" Ritchie, it was just as clear in his memory as last week. Bud was sixteen years old and finishing his junior year at West Springfield High School in western Massachusetts. As editor of the school newspaper, Bud would regularly stay late into the afternoon to fine tune the articles and mock up the pages for the upcoming issue. On inordinately busy days, he would stay nearly to dinner time and then rush the two miles home before dusk. His mother encouraged his journalistic ambition, but family meals were sacrosanct. Showing up late earned him a wooden spoon upside his head, but worse than that was her cold shoulder for the next couple of days.

This time, Bud was extremely late. He would be receiving multiple whacks from the spoon, but for once he thought it was worth the temporary pain. Earlier in May, a dozen young men publicly burned their draft cards in New York City to protest the country's involvement in Vietnam. College students were marching against the war in cities across America, and Bud was hearing whispers of a similar sentiment in his own school.

It disturbed him. Personally, he didn't approve of the United States' presence in Southeast Asia, but he felt it was his duty to support the soldiers who were fighting under our flag. There was a price to pay for living in this country, and in his opinion, burning draft cards was the equivalent of throwing oneself to the floor and having a tantrum when your parents told you to do your chores.

Since the recent news of draft cards and protests, Bud had been consumed with writing an editorial that would voice his opinion succinctly and provide a contrast to the message of the protestors. It might not make him popular, but he was certain that many of his classmates shared the

The Specimen

same opinion. Perhaps his editorial would encourage others to speak out as well.

The sun had already sunk behind the buildings. The ambience had taken on an amber-like tinge, portending that soon the streetlights would flicker on. Bud was pedaling his bike strenuously, up streets and through alleys, attempting in vain to arrive home before sunset.

Without warning, as he cut through an alley, he was struck with an overwhelming wave of vertigo... nausea so intense and disorienting that he immediately careened into a large dumpster and crashed over the handlebars in a tangle of arms and legs. He ended up on his back, ensnared in an overgrown bush at the end of an alley. The wind was knocked out of him. He lay flat on his back in the shadows of the hanging branches, struggling to pull in some air for what seemed to be many minutes, but was more likely only thirty to forty seconds. After a couple of minutes, he was finally able to catch his breath. He moaned in pain as he realized that he had thoroughly abraded his palms and both elbows and knees. His bike seemed scratched, but unbroken, lying on its side in the middle of the damp alley a few feet away.

Bud attempted to sit up, but his wooziness forced him to fall back onto his side. Must have hit my head, he thought. I'll get up in a few minutes and try again. He rolled to his side and stared out into the street. Resting in the shade and waiting for his eyes to focus, Bud had a clear view for fifty or so feet up and down the empty pavement. He looked down at his knees and realized his khakis were ruined, torn through on both legs with mud and grease covering the length of them. Yet another reason for his mother to smack him with the spoon.

His head throbbed and he retched in the dirt until the bitter taste of bile filled his mouth. He didn't know why, but his nausea was getting worse. Concussion, he thought. Not good. Dusk was creeping up on him, but he couldn't force himself to stand. He closed his eyes for a moment to subdue the pain and possibly summon the strength to pull himself to his feet.

"You okay, Mister?" a voice broke through his fog. Bud opened his eyes to the sight of a skinny colored boy standing at the edge of the alley.

He was young, possibly ten or eleven, with short-cropped hair and a baggy green sweater about two or three sizes too large for him.

"I'll be okay in a minute," Bud grunted. "Just took a fall. That's all." *I've got to be careful in this part of town even though he's just a kid, he thought. He might try to rob me or something.*

The boy took two steps closer and peered at Bud in the waning light. He had a small white patch of skin at his hairline, and another blotch on his cheek. A weird sort of birthmark, Bud guessed. Then Bud noticed his eyes. They weren't shaped weirdly or colored strangely, but Bud sensed that he had nothing at all to fear from him. The innocence and pure goodness that this boy held inside him radiated outward through his eyes. Underneath the boy's aura, though, Bud could sense a sickness inside him that was being held back by the overwhelming positive energy he had.

The boy looked at Bud with concern, staying out of reach, but squinting worriedly at the blood on his elbows and knees. "Mister, you're all scratched up and bloody. Let me get someone to help you and take you home," *he stated.*

"It's not necessary. I just need a minute is all. I don't want to trouble anyone," *Bud said as he waved him off. He tried again to sit up, but the dizziness surged and once again he keeled over into the dirt.* "I guess I could use some help. My head is hurtin' somethin' fierce," *he admitted.*

The boy nodded and took off down the street. He had a mission to complete now, something to brag about to his friends later. Thank the Lord for Good Samaritans, thought Bud as he watched the young boy hurry down the sidewalk searching for any adult who might know what to do in an emergency.

The rumble of an engine approaching from the opposite direction startled Bud from his daze and sent a flash of panic through him. He hurriedly dragged himself further into the shadow of the hedge. Seconds later, a dark blue two-door sedan drove by slowly. 1958 Dodge Lancer, noted Bud automatically. As a result of his interest in journalism, he had trained himself to note details everywhere he went. A good reporter could break a story with one small aspect that your average Joe might miss.

Two large figures in the front seat of the Lancer seemed to be scanning the sidewalk for something or somebody. Other than the make

The Specimen

and model, Bud didn't recognize the vehicle or the passengers, but he felt that he could not let them see him. He flattened himself on the shadowed alley floor near the roots of the bush and willed himself invisible. The knowledge that he would be in a dire predicament if he was seen consumed every thought. Irrational though it may be, he somehow knew that the men in the car were not Good Samaritans. They would not help a stranger in need. Did not even have the capacity to do so, in fact. Bud held his breath and froze, motionless as a rabbit hiding from the gaze of a raptor soaring above its burrow.

The Lancer rolled down the road at a leisurely pace. The driver had the window open and Bud could see his hairy knuckles as he tapped a rhythm on the side of the door panel. Continuing on for another block or so, the sedan dwindled in the distance and Bud allowed himself to exhale as the ominous vehicle moved on.

Wait. Not so fast. Bud shrank back into the bushes as the car slowed and pulled to the curb abruptly. A small figure rushed toward the Lancer waving his arms and yelling.

It was the boy.

Bud wanted to scream out and warn the boy to stay away, but his throat was frozen. Paralyzed. He was incapable of uttering more than a squeak as he watched the events unfold. The boy, his Good Samaritan, walked up to the car window and frantically pointed in the direction of the alley where Bud lay. The man with the hairy knuckles listened to the boy as the passenger side door opened. Another man stepped out and circled around the front of the vehicle, approaching the boy from behind. As if suddenly realizing his situation, he looked back and forth between the two men and stepped backwards in dismay. He appeared to recognize them from somewhere and it was apparent he feared them, holding his hands up in a futile attempt to fend off their approach. He began to scream and cry, looking for a path of escape.

Bud was shaking with terror, frantic that he could not move as he watched the second man clap a cloth over the boy's mouth. In one fluid motion, the man caught the boy as he put up a minimal struggle, lost consciousness, and collapsed to the ground. The rear trunk popped open and the boy was lifted and placed inside within seconds.

They were abducting him! Bud had heard of such crimes, but never believed that it could happen here. Maybe in New York, Chicago, or possibly even Boston, but not here in Springfield. hings like this just didn't occur here.

The man closed the trunk and got back in the car. The driver turned the wheel and it became obvious that he was making a U-turn and heading back toward Bud's hidey-hole.

Adrenalin surged through Bud in a white-hot gush, galvanizing him and disintegrating the wall of terror that had held him in its sway. He lurched to his feet, gasping at the pain in his elbows and knees, but suddenly no longer suffering from vertigo. Hobbling to his bike, Bud climbed on and pushed it with his feet to the opposite end of the alley just as the Lancer came slowly to a halt at the bush where he had been hiding. The man in the passenger seat looked directly into his eyes as Bud looked over his shoulder and they met gazes. "I know what you saw," his eyes seemed to speak. He continued staring, "… and there's not one damn thing you can do about it." The man raised his left hand and pointed it at Bud, thumb raised and forefinger extended in the form of a pistol. "POW!" he mouthed, before smiling and lowering his hand. The Lancer moved on and Bud began pedaling maniacally toward home.

He was certain that the car would follow him and he would either be abducted, shot, or run down like a stray dog in the road, but he reached his house less than ten minutes later, safe from harm. His parents met him at the door, frantic with worry and a bit angry with him until they saw his condition and heard his tale.

Later that night he spoke with the police and reported everything that he had witnessed. Despite his eye for details, neither the car nor the boy were ever found.

The Specimen

Interlude: The Rider
The Festival of Red Smoking Mirror
Tenochtitlan, c. 1370 AD
The Flaying of Men - 1 Dog, Tlacaxipehualiztli

Cipac welcomed his imminent death. His village had been favored by the gods and now, as the sun set in its bloody brilliance on the western horizon, every male member of his extended family, from his infant cousins to his ailing grandfather, had been chosen to serve as blood sacrifices in the festival of Tlacaxipehualiztli this evening. Bound at the wrists with strands of fiber rope, he and dozens of healthy young men from his village were herded by ranks of cuāuhtli and ocēlōtl warriors down the main avenue of Tenochtitlan. Cipac was more successful at hiding his fear than most of his fellow captives, but he was still intimidated by the warriors' fearsome battle dress and weapons.

On his left, the cuāuhtli marched in full regalia, all with garish headdresses resembling the eagles for which they were named. Feather-lined cloaks, brightly colored breastplates and breeches added to the spectacle as they emulated the fierce raptors in the traditional battle dance. On the other side of the column, the jaguar warrior ocēlōtl, clad in spotted skins atop their armor with the partial skulls of their feline brethren incorporated into their helmets, brandished their macuahuitl in dizzying patterns. The flat wooden swords with embedded obsidian shards cut through the air near the captives, portending their approaching deaths.

They reached the main avenue and the column turned right, toward the field flanking the Great Pyramid of Xipe Totec, The Flayed God. This was one of the greatest festivals of the year, celebrating the planting of maize and praying for abundant crops. During the festival there was an endless parade of victims lined up along the field, leading to the apex of the pyramid, where the High Priest pierced their chests with an obsidian blade, removing their hearts before hurling their twitching corpses down the stairs. This had been happening for three days now and would conclude two days hence.

Cipac followed the rest of the prisoners, resigned to his fate, yet honored that his sacrifice would please Xipe Totec. He was determined to meet his death with his eyes open and his mouth empty of cries for mercy. He would enter the afterlife in peace.

Hours passed as the sun beat down on the field and the line inched toward the great edifice. Thousands of devotees writhed in ecstatic seizures while children danced among them in glee, cheering as each body tumbled from the top level.

At the foot of the pyramid, the line was suddenly stopped by a group of lower priests, painted with garish dyes, wearing giant headdresses and feather robes. They walked up and down the section of line containing Cipac and his cohorts, prodding each prisoner, raising their arms and examining their mouths for weaknesses and diseases.

"This one!" they shouted and signaled for Cipac to be removed from the line. The young warrior looked around in confusion. Had he been deemed unworthy? Was there a flaw of which he was unaware? Had he offended anyone? These thoughts and more swirled through his mind as he was led by a cadre of two cuāuhtli and two ocēlōtl to a small building at the rear edge of the pyramid. He looked back to his friends and family, but they had already begun the climb up the stairs to their fate.

Cipac entered the building flanked by the four warriors. Inside was a narrow stairwell, which led underground into a passageway beneath the pyramid. The thick stone walls lowered the ambient temperature from the sweltering heat outside to a cool, almost chilly dampness. Cipac felt the urge to ask why he had been taken from the line, but he resisted, knowing that none of the warriors would speak to him on pain of death.

The thundering drums and the cheers of the crowd were muffled but they could still be heard through the interconnected passages as they climbed the stairs deeper into the interior of the pyramid. The sounds of the festivities echoed throughout the narrow halls and chambers, merging into one voice clamoring for the blood of the sacrifices.

Finally, they reached a larger ceremonial chamber near the apex of the pyramid. Stone sconces of burning oil lined the walls, illuminating the room with an undulating, ruddy light. Scenes of Xipe Totec in various battle poses were represented in mosaic tiles throughout the room. Cipac's

The Specimen

escorts led him to stand on a red and black design in the center of the room where they stood and faced the curtained doorway that led to the platform at the top of the pyramid.

Minutes passed as the cheers grew louder and louder from outside. The drumbeats built to a crescendo, then ceased abruptly. Seconds later, a tall, painted figure entered through the doorway at a slow pace. He walked regally into the chamber, body stained yellow and tan. His limbs, mouth, eyes and ears were colored scarlet as if he were bleeding. Cipac watched the man in awe, realizing immediately that this was Tlatlaukitezkatl, the high priest of Xipe Totec. Garbed in a brightly plumed headdress with a feathered cowl and cape that hung down his back, the priest also wore the rotting skin of a vanquished warrior in honor of the Flayed God, as Xipe Totec was also known.

The skin was days old, shriveled like uncured leather and reeking like a rotten tapir carcass. It was tied to his arms and legs by thin strands of leather, dangling loosely off his elbows and knees. Tlatlaukitezkatl glanced briefly at Cipac and his entourage, then strode to a stone basin on the left wall. Two young attendants immediately appeared from a side room as he removed his ornamental headdress and doused himself with water. Underneath the layers of paint and jewelry, he appeared as shriveled as the flesh he wore. Tlatlaukitezkatl coughed wetly, spitting a mouthful of bloody phlegm on the floor. Another attendant rushed to clean it up as he turned to appraise Cipac.

Cipac was struck silent. This withered creature was the one known as Tlatlaukitezkatl? He was the high priest of Xipe Totec? How was that possible? Although the man was quite tall, he was bent over with a large hunch in his back. He stepped over to Cipac, looked him up and down and nodded in approval.

"He is worthy to wear the Skin," stated Tlatlaukitezkatl. "Prepare him for the ritual."

Cipac stood frozen in confusion. Wear the Skin? What did that mean? Only priests could wear the skins of the enemies. It was an honor that was not given lightly, certainly not to potential sacrifices. He did not resist as his escorts grabbed him by the arms and neck and led him to an adjoining chamber. Smaller than the previous room, every inch of the walls and ceiling were covered with mosaic patterns of precious stones depicting Xipe Totec in his successive stages of life.

In the first stage, the god was shown as an invincible warrior slaying his enemies on all sides as if they were stalks of maize in a field. Next, he was represented as peeling a thick layer of flesh from the back of a fallen foe. In the third panel, Xipe Totec was at the height of his powers, wearing multiple layers of flayed skin and towering over mountains of corpses. On the final wall, he shed the Skin and began the journey to Mictlan while another warrior took the shed Skin and donned it, becoming the next incarnation of Xipe Totec.

In the room were two slabs of obsidian the length of a man, stained with many layers of dried blood and gore. Cipac was pushed over to the slab on the right and forced to bend over until he was spread eagle lying on his chest. His head was turned sideways facing the opposite stone and fitted into a hollow in the slab. His arms and legs were tethered with leather straps to rings on the slab's sides. Another strap held his head down as well. Cipac attempted to look around, but could only angle his neck slightly before it became painful. He was confused. Why was he face down? If he was to be sacrificed, wouldn't he be placed on his back to allow the priest to carve into his chest cavity and cut out his beating heart?

One of the lower priests stepped into view holding a long obsidian blade with an ornamental jeweled handle. He stepped to the head of Cipac's slab and stood there waiting for a command. At the other stone table, Tlatlaukitezkatl began to disrobe, removing the feather cloak followed by the flayed skin, and finally his leather breechcloth. He stood there, stark naked, wrinkled and sagging, looking more like a beggar on the street than the voice of The Flayed Lord. He and Cipac stared into each other's eyes for what seemed an eternity before he whispered solemnly, "Go west with the Sun, child." With a final nod, Tlatlaukitezkatl took a corresponding position on the other stone, baring his back to Cipac and exposing an incomprehensible sight.

Nestled between his prominent shoulder blades was a multi-tentacled monstrosity throbbing and pulsating in time with the elder priest's heart. Two of the appendages snaked beneath the skin and gripped Tlatlaukitezkatl's ribs, while the larger tentacle pierced him just below the

The Specimen

nape of his neck. Other, smaller tendrils waved in the air like cilia, pointing in the direction of Cipac. They were tasting him. He was certain. The surface of the creature was pale and mottled, contrasting with the nut brown shade of the priest's skin.

Tlatlaukitezkatl turned his head to look at Cipac one more time, then closed his eyes and sighed, "Begin."

The priest next to Cipac began keening in an ululating warble as he slowly lowered the tip of his obsidian blade to the young man's upper back. Cipac shut his eyes and tensed up, preparing for the killing blow. The pain came quickly. Sharp, burning and unending. The blade did not penetrate his chest cavity as expected. Instead, he felt the priest carve a deep furrow from nape to tailbone, running directly down his spine, cutting through all layers of skin and meat down to the bone. The pain was so sudden and intense that he wasn't even able to scream, releasing only a high-pitched drawn-out gasp before the shock made him briefly lose consciousness.

The next couple swipes of the blade brought him back in time to feel the flesh on his back peeled slowly away from the underlying meat like the rind of a ripe melon. This time he screamed. The large flaps of skin were placed carefully next to him, hanging off his body like broken wings. Cipac's voice trailed off into a series of shuddering sobs as rivulets of blood trickled from his wounds and fell into gourd bowls placed to collect it.

On the adjacent block of stone, two other priests delicately severed the threadlike connections between the creature and Tlatlaukitezkatl's spine. When the last filament was cut, the high priest let out a deep sigh and his shallow breaths ceased. The chanting priests, instead of wailing at his death, continued as if nothing of importance had just occurred. In fact, the chant increased in tempo and tone. An earthy musk permeated the room masking the scent of blood and sweat.

Separated from Tlatlaukitezkatl's back, the creature opened a slit on its skin, revealing an eye near the base of the left tentacle. The entire eye was a bright golden iris, striated with scarlet capillaries and filled with an intellect many centuries old. Barely conscious, Cipac stared back and made eye contact. His pain faded as if washed away with a bowl of cool water. Fear subsided with the pain and he was overcome with a sense of wonder. Was this creature a messenger from Xipe Totec?

The priests gently placed the creature on the floor next to Cipac's stone. All the while, their eyes remained fixated on one another. It raised a tentacle and held it inches from the young man's face as the cilia brushed along his right temple. He sensed a warm energy run over his skin as a question was asked – a request for permission. Cipac nodded and closed his eyes.

The chanting increasing in intensity as the priests fell to their knees. Given consent from the young man, the creature pulled itself up Cipac's arm and settled in the center of the open wound along his spine. Immediately, thousands of miniscule venous tendrils penetrated his flesh, connecting the creature to his spinal cord and nervous system. The two closest priests each grabbed an arm as Cipac began to thrash and convulse from the sudden intrusion. Once the nerves were connected, more cilia extruded from the bottom of the tentacles transforming into capillaries as they burrowed subcutaneously into his torso. The small blood vessels bored into the walls of his aorta and vena cava, attached directly to the blood supply and instantly began to exchange blood and hormones. Cipac ceased his convulsions and settled into a deep healing slumber. Tlatlaukitezkatl's corpse was removed from the chamber and even more priests entered the room, joining the throng chanting around the altar.

Outside, the celebration continued as the crowds of worshipers anticipated something important and out of the ordinary was happening. Painted dancers circled the bodies piled in a large mound at the base of the Great Pyramid of Xipe Totec. Young women in feathers and beads handed out celebratory kernels of roasted maize, while mobs of children emulated the cuāuhtli and ocēlōtl warriors in mock battles throughout the crowded avenue.

The afternoon passed and the sun sank lower in the sky. Within the high priest's chamber, the young man stirred on his stone. His new passenger had completely melded with the wounded flesh on his back and the remaining exposed area was pink and new. he long flaps of skin hung in tassels from his torso. In the hours of his recovery, the priests had divided the hanging skin into long thin strips, dyed them garish colors to

The Specimen

match the feathers on the robes. His face had been painted and his nipples and the septum of his nose had been pierced to accommodate large jade plugs.

He stood slowly and held out his arms to be dressed by the attendants. They rushed to his side and draped the ceremonial feathered cloak over his broad shoulders and back. Another man handed him the priest's staff as he exited the pyramid to the sacrificial platform. The crowd roared its approval as he exited the dark chamber into the reddish evening sun.

"Behold!" announced yet another priest as he strode into sight. "Tlatlaukitezkatl is reborn!" The mass of devotees rose up as one, cheering at the sight of the young man in the ceremonial dress. Tlatlaukitezkatl smiled, still overwhelmed by the sensations from this new host body. Cipac, however, heard nothing as he began his long, final journey west into the sun.

PART 3
TURMOIL

The Specimen

Chapter 29 – A Glaring of Cats

"Those who'll play with cats must expect to be scratched."
- Miguel de Cervantes

Modern Day – Cambridge, MA

The cats were extremely agitated this afternoon. Tails swishing back and forth, they paced up and down the window sills, crouched on the furniture, and eyed the entryways with a palpable air of unease. Sprawled atop Elvira's antique cherry curio cabinet, Solomon surveyed his feline thralls like a general at the summit of a hill far from the front line. Elvira had tried to coax him down with his favorite liver treats, but her attempts were fruitless. Solomon would only come down when he was good and ready.

This phase of feline vigilance had begun as soon as Elvira had gotten off the phone with that pleasant young lady from the American Cancer Society who had called that morning and had asked for donations of clothes and books. It seemed as if the cats knew a stranger was coming to visit their lair and they did not particularly like the idea.

Elvira sighed and lowered herself into her recliner to work on some Word Jumbles until the girl arrived. Two grocery bags filled with the out-of-fashion detritus of seasons past sat at the door next to a box of old Ace Double science fiction paperbacks that had belonged to her late husband.

Even though she would never admit it out loud, she knew that her apartment had a constant underlying odor of stale cat food that, no matter how much cleaner she used or how many windows she kept open, eventually returned to permeate the rooms. It was hard to deny the facts. She was becoming a stereotypical cat lady.

* * *

Just over twenty-three years ago, on the day after she buried her husband Bernie at the age of forty-six, Elvira Dombrowsky drove to the

The Specimen

closest animal shelter and adopted a cat. Ostensibly, she had been planning on getting a pet for years and that day had been as good a time as any to do so, but a number of her friends and family felt she was simply filling the hole left by her dead husband. Naming the cat Bernie in his memory did nothing to help silence the whispers that she was going bat shit crazy, either.

Not that she cared one bit about what either side of the family said to her. The remaining family of her dearly departed Bernie Dombrowsky were all too eager to cut all ties with her, since they had always thought that any woman who was unable to conceive must have done something to deserve her barren state. As for her side of the marital fence, the majority of the Popeckys were some of the most insufferable fools she had ever known. She loved them all, but most of them couldn't have poured piss out of a boot even if the instructions had been written on the heel. So she named her cat after her dead husband and sometimes pretended he was still alive. If that was crazy, then she was fine with that.

The second Bernie was a bruiser of a tortoise-shell, a bit on the chunky side, with extra toes on his front two paws and, in Elvira's opinion, the most beautiful yellow-green eyes she had ever seen on a cat. He was her constant companion and she spoiled him as if he was the child she could never bear. Bernie lived for another sixteen years, more than twice as long as his predecessor had been married to Elvira. When her nephew Frank left his father and came to live with her after his mother's death in the fall of 2002, he immediately bonded with Bernie, who soon took to sleeping with the troubled young teen at night. Initially she was sad at Bernie's choice, but Frank needed companionship, and when she realized that there was no reason that she couldn't get another cat, Elvira felt the need to visit the shelter again.

This was how Solomon finally came into her life. The moment she walked into the Cambridge Animal Shelter, Elvira was drawn to the sleek ruddy-haired tom with penetrating copper eyes. Amid the yowling of the other cats and the plaintive whining of the dogs, the kitten soon-to-be-named Solomon sat at the door of his cage serenely, staring at her as if he knew she would take him home. And that's exactly what she did.

Nearly twelve years had passed since that day she brought Solomon home. The brash little kitten stalked directly up to Bernie, swatted him on the nose and quickly established the fact that he was now the alpha male in the apartment. Bernie, like his namesake, was not one to fight. He quickly backed down and let the little Abyssinian assume the throne. And this was the status quo for the next five years.

Frank left for college in the fall of 2007 and Bernie passed away less than a month later. One day, he just didn't wake up. Elvira knew exactly what had happened when she discovered Solomon curled around his old companion's body in the middle of Frank's bed. Sad to say, but Elvira grieved more for that cat than she ever had for her husband.

The next morning, she woke to a paw repeatedly batting her softly on her forehead. Solomon had a surprise for her. Mewling plaintively, he pounced off her bed and waited in the doorway to the hall for her to follow him. Bleary-eyed, she shrugged into her threadbare housecoat and trailed after him into the kitchen as he looked back at her and meowed impatiently.

"Hold on, Solomon! Mama's coming," she blustered as she hobbled down the hall. "You know I don't move well in the morning…" Her voice trailed off as she saw what Solomon had waiting for her.

Just outside the window to the fire escape were two young cats perched patiently, a beautiful Russian Blue female and a bony tomcat with black and white patches all over his torso, soon to be named Rusalka and Gemini.

Elvira stopped at the kitchen arch, dumbfounded for a few seconds, then she quickly made a decision and did what she felt was only right; she unlatched the window and let in the two newest members of her family. If she had any doubts that Solomon had known exactly what he was doing, they were all swept away when he repeated the same behavior seven more times over the next couple of years, recruiting Alexander, Domino, Cleopatra, Odin, Athena, Isis and Loki into the pride. Soon, they were one family unit… an elderly widow and her ten surrogate feline children. Cat lady or not, she was content with her lot in life.

* * *

The Specimen

Elvira woke to a staccato rapping at her door. In the cool afternoon breeze from the window, she had dozed off while waiting for the representatives from the American Cancer Society. Her Word Jumbles had not been effective enough of a distraction to hold her attention. Pulling her recliner into its upright position, she wiped a small strand of drool from her chin with her afghan, set the puzzles aside and called out, "Just a minute. I'm on my way."

She winced as she rose gingerly to her feet – damn arthritis – and carefully approached the door. A low, almost imperceptible keening rose up and permeated the living room as put her hand on the doorknob. She shushed the cats absentmindedly and looked around the room, surprised to note that every one of them were staring – no – glaring at the door. With their hackles raised and their entire bodies vibrating, all ten cats seemed ready to hurl themselves at whoever stepped in from the hallway. Something was making them homicidal, directing their hatred in one focused beam of energy, and she realized that it wouldn't be responsible of her to open the door right now and chance that one of her babies would attack anyone. The Cancer Society could get their clothes and books another time.

She unlatched the deadbolt, but kept the chain on the door as she peered through the crack at the two people in the hallway. A pretty young thing with reddish-blonde hair tied in a ponytail, stood there, holding a clipboard and pen. Normally, Elvira would have taken one look at her and thought former Girl Scout, but something seemed off. She glanced back into her apartment and realized that there was a musky scent in the air that seemed to emanate from her living room. That and the cats' reaction were having an influence on her, setting her on edge.

The young blonde was smiling, but it seemed plastic. Manufactured. Couldn't she hear the cats? She looked no older than twenty in her pink t-shirt and jeans, and that was being generous. Off to the young girl's left was a tall, balding black man in his fifties in a rumpled grey suit with a face like a basset hound's and teeth the size and color of lima beans. His smile was even more rigid and forced, as if he were enduring an especially painful bout of intestinal gas.

Even without the chaos occurring behind her, Elvira would have been hesitant to open the door to them. They gave off a sketchy vibe and she grew even more convinced that they were not in any way associated with the American Cancer Society.

"Mrs. Dombrowsky?" chirped the perky rep. "I'm Crystal Harris. We spoke on the phone this morning. This is my associate Ronald Mayhew. We're here for the donations. May we come in?"

Elvira didn't know why she felt uneasy or threatened, but she knew that she did not want to open her door to these two. The cats were becoming more restless by the second, a couple of them leaping down to the floor to entwine themselves around her ankles.

"I'm sorry," she replied through the gap in the door, "I meant to call you back and cancel the pickup, but I didn't have your phone number. I'm just not feeling too well at the moment. We'll have to arrange another time."

Crystal's smile wavered ever so slightly. She glanced at her partner and then looked back at Elvira and responded, "Well, now that we're here, let's just take your donations off your hands and then we'll get out of your hair... okay?"

Elvira hesitated, before a wave of fear, anger and aggression overtook her manners, making her snap, "I said some other time!" before slamming the door shut and engaging the deadbolt.

In the hallway, Nina Valentine shook her head in disgust and muttered, "Fuck it. Let's do it the hard way." She hadn't slept in over thirty hours and her temper was on a hair trigger.

Delano Stoopes was already pulling his pistol from his holster and aiming it at the door jamb. "That's what I wanted to do in the first place," he smirked.

"Just say 'I told you so' and get it over with, Stoopes," she responded. "You know you want to."

"Nah," he smiled a toothy grin. "That's not my style."

He turned to the door and squeezed the pistol's trigger twice in succession, blowing the deadbolt to pieces. Shards of metal and wood exploded as the door to the apartment swung open. Elvira cried out in panic and fled down the hall off the living room. Stoopes kicked the door

The Specimen

to the wall with his foot and stalked into the living room, sweeping left and right with his gun.

Nina followed immediately, making sure to stay behind Stoopes' considerable bulk.

"There!" she shouted, pointing at the stout figure of Elvira Dombrowsky hobbling through a doorway in a housecoat and slippers. Stoopes lunged in her direction and the room exploded on all sides with a chorus of hisses and yowls. A flash of orange, white and black streaked from the top of the television cabinet as something landed on the black man's back. The calico stabbed its claws through his jacket and bit his left ear. In a simultaneous attack, two others cats darted out from beneath the couch and the loveseat to latch onto both of his ankles with their fangs and claws.

"Aaugh! Muthah-Fuckah!!" howled the large man. He reached up with his left hand, grabbed the calico by the skull and squeezed as he ripped it off his bloody ear. The cat's skull collapsed like an eggshell in his grip as he flung it away. The animal's limp corpse slammed into the wall and knocked a large framed picture to the floor in a shower of blood and glass shards. Stoopes shook his left leg in the air, dislodging the fat tabby shredding his ankle, and slammed his foot down, just missing crushing its spine by inches as it darted away down the hall. The black cat on his right leg clawed its way up his inner thigh, coming within inches of his unprotected crotch before Stoopes jammed his pistol into its mouth and turned its head into a shower of gore with one pull of the trigger. The twitching carcass fell to the floor in a mound of brains, bones, and fur.

Nina rushed to the left as her partner was assaulted on all sides by another round of yowling beasts. She punted a fluffy white Persian into the ancient console television, knocking over a row of family photos like dominoes, and then dodged around a gray tabby that launched itself off of a bright yellow velvet ottoman. The air was filled with screeches and crashes as more and more cats entered the fray. The musky stench in the room burned Nina's nostrils, causing her eyes to water. She was overcome with a wave of rage and anxiety.

Pheromones? Where?... that means...

"Holy Crap, they're Thralls, Stoopes!" she called to her partner. "How is this possible?"

"I don't fucking know," he screamed as he held up a black and white cat by the tail and smashed it into the coffee table. Its bones broke like pretzel sticks and it flopped to the floor, twitching in spasms of agony as it bled out of all of its orifices.

"One of them must be leading the others. It must be in service to a Rider!"

"No shit, Sherlock," he bellowed over his shoulder as he kicked another cat into the wall. "I've been doing this for a bit longer than you. Seen dogs before. Falcons. Even a chimp once. Never cats, though… thought they were incompatible. SHIT! WATCH IT!"

Both windows exploded in a deluge of glass as another horde of cats swarmed into the apartment. Feral strays. A flood of alley cats of a leaner, deadlier breed. A gray one-eyed cat clambered up the side of the couch and sprang at Nina, landing on her back and immediately biting her neck. She shrieked a litany of curses as its front claws carved long parallel trenches down both of her cheeks. Covering her eyes with an arm, she slammed her back into the wall, crushing her attacker between herself and the wall. The one-eyed cat fell to the ground broken and twisted and tried to drag itself away, but Nina immediately stomped on its skull and ended it.

Stoopes shot two more cats as more than half a dozen others tried to climb his legs to get at his face. Nina leaned against the wall and scanned the room. A couple of the felines had run down the hall after Elvira, but the majority was focused on Stoopes. His sleeves were drenched in red from the wounds on his hands and the animals he had slaughtered. He used every weapon available to fend off the onslaught, even the bodies of other cats. He shot them, stomped on them, and hurled them out the window. Nina was doing significant damage on her own, but Stoopes was going through them like a buzz saw through wood.

There! On top of the curio cabinet!

A sleek reddish-brown tom surveyed the room calmly like the Sphinx, following each skirmish and seeming to direct which of the animals went where.

The Specimen

Nina cried out and pointed, "That one! The red one up there! Kill it, Stoopes!"

Both of them fired multiple shots at the animal, but it ran along the cabinet and darted into the hallway in the direction that the woman had gone. Immediately, the remaining cats surrounding the two of them rushed away down the dark corridor after their leader.

They both stood stunned surrounded by bodies of cats in various stages of carnage. Blood, brains and fur dripped off the walls and furniture onto the carpet. Two cats with their innards blown open writhed helplessly in pools of gore. Nina strode over to them and crushed their heads with her boot.

"Fucking cats," she snarled. "I was always a dog person."

"They fucked you up, girl," commented Stoopes, staring at her gouged cheeks while he pressed his hand to his ravaged ear. "Your face is a complete mess."

"Well, you always were a mess," she said wiping the blood from her eyes. "So I guess we make a matching set now."

"Let's end this," he said, starting towards the doorway where they last saw Elvira. Nina nodded and followed, gun out, a few steps behind him.

He crouched down at the door and burst into the bedroom, ready for another assault. Following him, Nina entered the bedroom a second later and found her partner standing with his gun pointed directly at the old woman. She was seated in a large, cushioned chair next to the open window, surrounded by a group of five remaining cats. A bright orange and green afghan covered her lap. Tears streamed down her face. The room smelled of rug deodorizer, cat urine and musk. Behind her, on the back of the chair, sat the reddish tom.

Abyssinian, recalled Nina. *That's what it's called. That's gotta be the leader.* She kept an eye on him while Stoopes confronted Frank's aunt.

"You're not from the American Cancer Society," stated Elvira. Her hands were bunched beneath the blanket. A black and white Maine Coon Cat of truly enormous girth planted its bulk in her lap and fixed its piggy glare at the two interlopers.

"I'm glad that's out in the open," said Stoopes. "I'm not a big fan of beating around the bush. This could have been a lot easier for all of us, but your damn cats had to fuck things up for everyone."

"I don't have anything of value," she insisted, sobbing. "You came here for nothing. You killed my poor babies for nothing!"

"Mrs. Dombrowsky..." Stoopes stated solemnly. "If you only knew the truth. We're fighting for the survival of the human race against the greatest threat it has ever faced and anyone who gets in the way gets taken out."

Confused, the old woman remained silent.

"All we want is some information," he continued. "The sooner we get it from you, the sooner we end this. Your choice. I don't care how long it takes."

"If you're going to kill me, get it over with," she said. "I'm just an old woman. I don't have any info you would want."

Nina interjected, "Frankie says otherwise."

Her nephew's name hit her like a gunshot. Elvira paled and lost her voice for a few seconds before responding, "What have you done with him? Have you hurt him at all?"

"Just a tiny bit," Nina smirked as she stepped even with Stoopes. "But I'm pretty certain he loved every minute of it."

Stoopes interrupted impatiently and wagged his gun, "We're not here to chat, lady. We only want to retrieve a very dangerous item that was stolen from us... From our property... By your nephew. Once we get it back in our possession, this will all be over for you."

"I wouldn't know of anything like that," protested Elvira. "You've made a huge mistake!"

Stoopes tapped his gun on his right thigh and sighed, "So that's the way you want to play it." He shrugged his shoulders and continued, "Okay then..." and pumped three bullets into the reddish cat seated behind Elvira. The cat's screech cut through the room as the impacts of the shots blew him through the air and out the window down to the alley below.

"SOLOMON!" screamed the old woman in anguish. The four remaining cats bolted behind the chair and under the bed. Elvira wept for

The Specimen

a second, then choked back her pain and turned around to face the two intruders, silent and ashen.

"If you didn't realize it before, are you ready to believe how serious we are now?" inquired Stoopes. "We will find the specimen and you will tell us wh…"

Suddenly there was a muffled pop and Stoopes coughed loudly as if he had inhaled a mote of dust or a small flying insect. He brought his left hand to his throat just as a gout of scarlet spouted from a small hole dead center in his Adam's apple.

Nina froze, blindsided by the turn of events. She stared at Elvira taking a few seconds to notice a small wisp of smoke curling up from a lump beneath the afghan blanket covering her lap. *Oh my God, did we fuck up*, she thought as she turned back to him and yelled, "STOOPES! DON'T!"

Streams of blood leaked through his hand, drenching his shirt as he emptied the rest of the gun's clip into Elvira Dombrowsky's chest. Job done, he slowly crumbled to the floor like a skyscraper imploding from a demolition.

Nina dropped to his side and attempted to place pressure on the hole in his throat, but the arcs of red spilled, spattered and sprayed with each pump of his heart, widening in a pool beneath him. Her pants became soaked in seconds as she knelt on the wet rug.

"No, No, No, No…. Don't you fucking die, Stoopes! You stupid black bastard. Goddamn you! You're not gonna fuck everything up and then leave me to clean up this shit!" she shrieked, realizing immediately that he was already gone. *What a sick joke*, she thought. *After everything he's done, this is how he dies. Bled out in seconds in this fucking cat lady's apartment.* "FUCK YOU!" she screamed, punching him in the chest a half dozen times.

She looked up at Elvira. The old bitch lay there, riddled with bullet holes, wheezing as her lips turned up in a smile and her eyes began to dim. Nina lurched to her feet and stumbled over to the chair, grabbing Elvira by her flabby shoulders and shaking her so her head wobbled to and fro on her turkey neck.

"Oh no, you don't! Not you too. You don't get to die before telling me where you put it!" She yelled in the dying woman's face. "Where is the specimen? Where did you hide it for Frank?"

Elvira's lips moved slightly, but her whisper was too low for Nina to hear. She lowered her head to the woman's mouth and was able to make out one word before a final gasp and Elvira Dombrowsky passed on.

"Bernie…"

"Bernie?" Nina yelled in disbelief. "Bernie? Who the fuck is Bernie?" She shook Elvira's body again, but the old woman had already moved on to a much better place. The cats ran out of the room, rendered harmless with their leader in a pool of blood in the alley below. Through the open window, Nina could hear sirens approaching and she realized immediately that the local police would be here soon. In order to avoid any unnecessary complications, she needed to take care of some arrangements before she dealt with the mess in here.

Removing her cell phone from her pocket, she held it to her ear and said, "Cleanup". Her voice activated a preset seventeen digit number. Three seconds later, there was one ring before the line was answered and a computerized voice said, "Report".

"This is Valentine," she stated calmly. "Mission has gone completely FUBAR. We require a diversion and sanitation ten minutes ago. Authorities are already en route." She rattled off the address of the apartment building and the authorization phrase before hanging up and standing at the window to see if she needed to vacate the premises.

She leaned out the window and heard the sirens approaching closer and closer from multiple directions when, nearly simultaneously, the cars reversed course and headed en masse in another direction where a sudden plume of black smoke was filling the graying twilight sky.

Nina gritted her teeth in a facsimile of a smile and started to pull her head inside when she saw motion on the alley floor five stories below. She recognized the wounded animal immediately from his sleek musculature and reddish coat. Though he must have cashed in all nine of his lives by surviving the gunshots and the fall, Solomon had managed to raise his body up from the puddle of blood and oil in which he lay and stagger away to the end of the alley, rear right leg dragging behind him

The Specimen

with a crooked trail of gore in its wake as if he was pulling a bloody mop. Nina cursed in frustration and, even though he should not have been able to hear her, Solomon paused and turned to look up at the window, meeting her eyes for a moment before disappearing around the corner of the building.

Official Report on the Greylock Incident

February 21, 1966
To: Members of the Governing Council, ACME Group
From: James P. Kilcannon, Agent-in-Charge
RE: Greylock Incident (Cluster/Scarpa)

Members of the Council,

    In the final week before the blackout, the absence of Dr. Colfax's watchful eyes appear to have led Dr. Coe to be careless again with the surgical protocols. Her ill-advised choice of the resident she used as the next Host, plus her reckless experiments in Lab 2 are evidence enough that she was slowly losing her grasp on reality. In hindsight, we should have seen what was coming...

- JPK

*　*　*

Day 61

    With the weather outside getting colder and windier, this building is now prone to icy drafts and strange whistling noises coming through various cracks in the walls and foundation. Not only is it not the most ideal working conditions, but it sets the residents on edge. I'm glad that I've been locked away in my labs lately, because everywhere else I go in this castle of the damned, I hear screaming and crying echoing through the corridors. It's quite distracting.

    The Rider is still somewhat sedated. I added another solution of Halperidol to the jar to keep it under for a while. As long as it remains subdued, we won't need to worry about any more incidents like what happened last week. In the next few days, I will designate a resident for

The Specimen

the Rider's next Host and we will begin the surgery. There are a number of fine candidates, but one stands out above the rest.

- GC

Day 62

In Lab 2, I have made great progress with the Cluster, especially with its diet. Fenton delivered the bodies to the lab after the cleanup of the evidence the other night. Since then, not one individual has asked about Hutchens or Jameson. It goes to show you how much our presence is noticed around here. It looks like we have been assimilated. I filed a report with the Council and asked for a replacement agent to be assigned in Jameson's place. I expect them to send one shortly.

The next morning, after Fenton was occupied with keeping an eye on Harry and, on my instructions, distracting Eckenrode in any way possible, I went to Lab 2 to examine the bodies and prepare them.

After dressing in surgical scrubs and a mask, I unwrapped each of them from their plastic shrouds, stripped their bloodstained clothes off and laid their cold, stiff corpses on the floor in front of the closet. Jameson had already started to bloat a bit. As I dumped him onto his belly, a wet fart sounded and I nearly got sick from the stench of rotting innards.

Keeping that in mind, I was a bit more careful with Hutchens. He was much lighter and easier to lift off the wheeled cart, but when I stretched him out, I saw that the flap of muscle and skin attaching his head to his neck was stretched and torn. It was obvious that it would be a pain the ass, so I grabbed it by the lower jaw and ripped his head free. Rather easily, I might add. Done with that, I set it on the ground next to his greasy grey cadaver. Time to see if my theory was correct.

I unlocked the closet and opened the door so the Cluster could see or smell or whatever it was it used for senses. I hadn't fed it in days and it might be more inclined to eat now. It had been a while since I had seen any rats. When I first came to Greylock two months ago, they were everywhere, just out of view, especially in the basement.

The light streaming from the lab illuminated the yellow gelatinous interior of the Cluster so that eddies and swirls inside the flesh cast shadows on the wall behind it. Floating in the center of the amorphous creature was a darker node, about the size and shape of a large potato. Threads resembling dendrites snaked off through the cytoplasmic interior like dozens of miniature bolts of lightning.

Each time I see it, I am filled with a sense of awe. I created life. I almost feel a maternal instinct, but I know I can't let myself become too attached to it. If it does turn out to be dangerous and untrainable, it will have to be put down. The Council will want to explore its potential as a weapon, but if it can't be controlled, I know that they will give the order to exterminate without hesitation.

I stepped back away from the bodies to give it some room and I waited. The Cluster just sat there for a few moments. Pulsating. Its outer membrane seemed to be dull and a bit foggy compared to how it had looked a couple of days earlier. Unlike the last time, I sensed more than animalistic instinct in its aura. I sensed an intellect. It was observing me. Watching my actions and filing them away to reexamine later. In the three days I had neglected to feed it, it had developed a mind, and for a second, I also sensed that it didn't like me very much. This was something that, in my arrogance, I had never considered would happen. I believed that, somehow, it would imprint upon me and regard me as someone who was in control.

In reality, this was an utterly unique being.

It slouched forward, slithering from the recess to stop a few inches from Jameson's bare left foot. For a moment, it appeared to act like a big puppy who was confused about what had been placed in its food bowl. A pseudopod about the size of a man's forearm extended from the central mass of the Cluster and, following the contours of Jameson's flank, examined the body less than half a centimeter from the skin surface.

The Specimen

Hundreds of pea-sized cavities appeared on the underside of its exterior, revealing bright yellow nodules that distended and leaked a transparent fluid that smelled like, of all things, half-sour pickles. A few seconds later, the amorphous mass flowed over and completely engulfed Jameson's naked bloated body. Once inside the cytoplasm, the body rose up to the center and curled into a ball.

The motion of Jameson's body startled me. Momentarily I had the paranoid thought that he could still be alive, suffocating inside its guts, but I soon realized that the Cluster was squeezing him, pulping him like an orange in a juicer. The various body fluids were flowing like faucets, leaking blood, bile, urine, and spinal fluid from all his orifices and even his pores.

The color of the Cluster gradually changed from a transparent light yellow, to a dark rusty brown with streams of scarlet peeking through the murk. Muffled sounds of bones splintering and cartilage popping filtered through the Cluster's mass. Though I was fascinated, my stomach did not agree. I turned away, but the thick liquid sounds were impossible to ignore. It seemed to last for hours, but in reality the feeding took fifteen minutes at most.

When the noises finally ended, I turned around and found the desiccated remnants of Jameson deposited at my feet. After the feeding, what was left of his skin, organs and pulverized bones resembled the largest twisted hunk of beef jerky I had ever seen. About a yard long, it thankfully retained no identifying characteristics. Jameson's hair and much of his outer skin had been dissolved by some type of digestive acid, while any moisture in the body had completely disappeared.

The Cluster had expanded up and out a few inches. The membrane was now taut, firm and flushed with health. It bobbed up and down as a lipless horizontal slit appeared in the side closest to me and a buzzing series of noxious belches sounded from the pseudo-mouth.

Only that wasn't exactly what happened. Not really.

In the hours since I left the lab, I've gone over the sounds in my head again and again, and I finally can admit that the sounds weren't just belches or an escape of gas from the interior of the Cluster. The more I replay the sounds in my memory, the more they sound like a voice... and I could swear that it said "Thank you".

Day 64

    Colfax is up and around, but he seems quite subdued compared to his normal arrogance. Perhaps the Hutchens incident has made him acknowledge his mortality. His attitude has entirely changed and he is finally acting with proper deference... as he should have from the beginning.

    His hand is healing well. Apparently the bite was not infectious, just ragged and ugly. There was enough remaining flesh for me to stitch a flap to cover the exposed bone on each of the two severed fingers. Since it wasn't his dominant hand, it should not present a problem in the future.

    Together we have reviewed a list of potential new Hosts for the Rider and, though we agreed on eliminating most of them, I had to make an executive decision once we got down to the final two candidates. Colfax wanted to bond the creature to the child Harry once again, to see if his memories would return. I find that theory unlikely at best.

    Instead, I decided to take a calculated risk on a resident who will present a challenge, but also has a high intellect that will prove useful in our attempts to communicate.

    His name is Angelo Scarpa.

                      - GC

The Specimen

The Poughkeepsie Journal

Friday, April 26, 1958

ACCUSED RAPIST LINKED TO SERIES OF BRUTAL MASSACHUSETTS MURDERS

By Charley Dexter, Journal Reporter

NEW PALTZ – In a lurid story that could have been pulled straight out of the pulp magazines, a man recently arrested for raping eight local children in the past two years has been linked to mounting evidence that he also may be responsible for the deaths of more than seven young women across the border in Massachusetts.

Angelo Scarpa, 31, a traveling flooring salesman from Amherst, MA, was brought in last week on charges that, over the last two years, he had lured eight children in the New Paltz/Poughkeepsie area into his car and brutally raped them for hours before dumping them in the parking lots of local hospitals.

The victims were of both genders, ranging in age from 8 to 15. The most recent victim, a 10 year-old boy from Wappingers Falls, was able to provide a detailed physical description and a partial license plate that led police in Scarpa's direction.

In the ensuing search of his apartment, a number of objects were found in a locked trunk that could be directly connected to each of the eight victims. Along with these objects were a large collection of souvenirs that did not match any of the children. Investigations now have revealed that these items were taken from the homes of at least seven different unsolved murders in Massachusetts that had occurred over the last decade. The investigation is ongoing…

Pete Kahle

The Daily Hampshire Gazette

Friday, August 22, 1958

DEFENSE ATTORNEY: KILLER BLOOD MAY RUN IN SCARPA'S FAMILY
By Dick Ransom, Gazette Contributing Reporter

AMHERST – Angelo Scarpa, the local man charged with brutally killing at least seven young women in the past ten years and raping eight children across the state border in New York, may have learned it from his grandfather when he was a child, argues Massachusetts public defender Gerald Pincebaugh.

Over two decades ago, Scarpa's maternal grandfather, Giacomo Rossi, allegedly left his eight year-old grandson waiting out in the car as he forced his way into the house of a man he suspected of having an affair with his wife.

Once inside, Rossi beat his victim, Johnny Benedetto, to death in front of Benedetto's wife and four children. Reportedly, the weapon used in the man's death was the victim's own shoe…

The Specimen

The Daily Hampshire Gazette

Friday, August 2, 1959

SCARPA COMMITTED TO GREYLOCK INSTITUTE
By Dick Ransom, Gazette Contributing Reporter

ADAMS – In what is hopefully the last chapter of this horrendous tale, confessed multiple murderer and rapist Angelo Scarpa was admitted yesterday to the Greylock Institute on a long term psychiatric commitment. For many who have been following this story since its beginning in May of last year, the verdict of Not Guilty by Reason of Insanity was a complete shock and, to some people, confirmation that our grand system of justice is irrevocably damaged.

Considering the number and severity of his crimes, Greylock may very well end up as his residence for life, but stranger things have happened with regards to the actual case.

Some believe that justice has been served, but other people were not as forgiving.

"They should just lobotomize the godless bastard and call it a day," commented Northampton resident Dick Rafferty. "I'm always in favor of rehabilitation, but some animals are just born evil down to the pit of their godforsaken souls. That's when you cut your losses, put one in the back of his head, and call it a day."

Ida-Louise Brundage, next door neighbor to one of the victims, was equally unsympathetic.

"In my opinion – and I'm not the only one who thinks this way, ya know – the first thing they should've done was to take that monster out to the barn and do to him what farmers do to horses that can't be tamed. Just cut off his man parts," she said with a steely glare. "That would've taught him something for sure."

Tempers certainly have run high in the community since the former salesman received the controversial verdict, but perhaps we can take some measure of consolation in the fact that a long term commitment with a history of crimes as odious as the ones he openly admitted committing is virtually equivalent to a life sentence…

Chapter 30 – Body Bags

*"I was walking in a government warehouse
where the daylight never goes.
I saw fifteen million plastic bags
hanging in a thousand rows ..."*
- Adrian Mitchell

Modern Day – Chesterfield, MA

"**Lockdown's been lifted,**" said C.C. Kennealy as the EMT climbed into the passenger seat of the ambulance. "We can finally head in."

"About time," grumbled her partner Billy Oestreicher. "It's been nearly 6 hours sitting here with these bodies in the back. What happened? Bomb threat?"

"Nah, we wouldn't have been waiting that long for them to clear a bomb threat," C.C. continued. "I heard it was something bigger. An actual incident, not a threat."

"Baby snatch, perhaps?"

"Possibly. I'm sure we'll hear shortly."

"Better be good. I wasn't planning on any overtime tonight," he grunted as he shifted out of Park and pulled the ambulance out of the Wendy's parking lot where they had been biding their time. "Any longer and our passengers would have started smelling ripe."

"They don't exactly smell like roses now, do they?" C.C. joked. "I don't think I'll be eating barbeque in the near future."

"That reminds me. I haven't eaten dinner yet"

"That's nasty, Billy."

"Doc Froehicke finds my jokes funny. Besides, you wouldn't want me any other way," he laughed.

"Yeah, well... Froehicke's a twisted old fuck. I guess you have to be one if you're the medical examiner."

Billy and C.C. had been working together as EMT's in the same ambulance for nearly four years and, in all that time, they had never fought once. Billy was creeping up on 50, but he was proud to still have a full head of blonde hair and only a small paunch that was easily clenched when necessary. In his opinion, his glasses and well-trimmed goatee made him look intellectual. Dress him in a corduroy jacket with elbow patches and he would easily pass for a community college professor. C.C. (short for Cicely Charleen, but anyone who called her that was risking his life) was the type of woman people referred to as "bubbly". Short and buxom with a liberally freckled face and curly auburn hair pulled back in a ponytail. C.C. was only 28, but she gave off a maternal vibe that could calm the most panicked accident victim.

They liked the same music (Country and Classic Rock), the same food (Thai and Mexican) and the same sports teams (Red Sox, Celtics and surprisingly, the Packers. Love those Cheeseheads). The two of them were a well-oiled machine compared to the other crews who serviced St. Frank's and other hospitals in the region, seemingly able to read each other's minds and anticipate exactly what was needed for each case. Many of their colleagues often remarked that, if not for their two decade difference in ages, they would have realized long ago that they were perfect for each other. What their friends and co-workers didn't know was that the two of them had each separately come to the same conclusion years earlier, but they were both too afraid to make the first move on the other and they secretly pined for one another as they sat alone in their respective apartments night after night.

Standard protocol stated that any ambulance transporting the deceased to the hospital morgue for autopsies had the option to use the lights and siren, but it was up to the discretion of the crew. Since it was his turn behind the wheel today, Billy opted for a quiet ride with only the lights running. Though they joked a bit, they soon became quiet, somber at the loss of life. Sadly, this was a regular part of the job. Deaths and traumatic injuries from motor vehicle accidents were quite a common sight to people in their line of work. The challenge was to not let these incidents affect their performance, but also not to become calloused and lose their empathy for the patients… dead or alive.

Life as an EMT was never monotonous with the variety of cases they saw each shift. Some days, their worst case was a sprained ankle in a pick-up game of hoops. Other days, they may have to utilize their

The Specimen

combined library of knowledge to maximize a patient's chance of survival. Other times, like today, even their expertise was not enough.

The three bodies currently in the transport were all from the same family and they were most definitely deceased - charbroiled and sealed in their body bags after having been extricated from the smoldering blackened remains of their family home. C.C. had overheard some of the officers talking about the details of the incident and, if what they said was true, this lurid tale of family horror would soon be the top story across the state. Not only did it appear that the son had bludgeoned both his parents to death, but he supposedly went to his room lay on his bed and immolated himself. Terrible what a confused mind would lead someone to do to their loved ones, thought C.C. as she leaned back in her seat and closed her eyes for a quick meditation session in the 10-15 minutes she had before they arrived at St. Frank's.

* * *

Behind the two EMT's, the three neon orange body bags containing the victims of the house fire were stacked in a pyramid at the back of the ambulance. In the top bag were Kate Monahan's remains. They had lost the most mass in the inferno, the fatty tissue having melted off and boiled away within minutes of igniting. Blackened and curled into a fetal position by the tightening of her shrunken tendons and ligaments, she resembled a bog mummy found in the wilds of Great Britain. What remained of her corpse barely weighed thirty pounds.

Beneath her body lay the bagged cadavers of the two Monahan men. Her husband's body was similarly shrunken and twisted by the conflagration, but much more meat remained under the shiny crackled skin. The gaping wound on his side had served as an open orifice into which the flames had licked and tasted his heart and guts until they had exploded from the boiling juices within. Even now, the body suppurated and leaked fats and other fluids into the body bag where they congealed on the inner plastic surface.

The third one - Hank's - was in much better condition compared to the other two... as dead bodies go. Rather than being charred down to the bones, his body had been subjected to a slightly lesser degree of heat due to his choice of bedroom furniture. The previous year, for his 15th birthday, young Hank Monahan had asked for only one present: a king-sized water bed. Against their better judgment, Chuck and Kate had bought it for their behemoth of a son.

As the house went up like a torch, the flames in Hank's room were doused when his water bed burst and flooded the room. Hank's 240 lb. body had fallen into the water-filled bedframe and stewed like a monstrous piece of pork fat in a giant crockpot. Soon after, any new fires that had sprung up were again put out when Hank's 110 gallon fish tank boiled over and drenched the floor.

Not that there was any chance that Hank had survived the blaze, but it did ensure that his body was cooked differently. The teen's head was scorched down to the bone, but the rest of the body had been cauterized and scalded. Rather than being turned into a charcoal statue, the torso had been roasted like a turkey with all the meat and juices sealed inside.

In the hours since the bodies had been removed from the burnt shell of the house and sealed inside the body bags, they had started the process of decomposition. Kate's and Chuck's remains had been leaking gases out various holes and orifices all along, but Hank's corpse had been building up gas inside the body cavity with no way for it to escape. Finally, the pressure became too great. Beginning at the blistered navel, a tear appeared in the flesh, unzipping all the way to the sternum in a great, oozing, purplish trench.

A plume of intestinal gas erupted from the rupture with a loud blare, eliciting groans about the stench from the EMT's at the front of the ambulance. The foul odor, a frequent event when transporting cadavers, distracted them from the motion beneath the plastic. As the internal fluids seeped out of the gash into the bag, two segmented tendrils snaked from within the body cavity, grasped the sides of the wound and pried it open. Attached to the tendrils, a bloody nodule of mottled tissue resembling a small hamburger patty emerged. Sprouting a number of thin spidery legs, it

The Specimen

skittered onto the exterior of the body's chest and spun in a circle, checking all visible corners for threats. A blister formed on its back, peeling open to reveal a luminescent orb resembling an eye.

For now, the organism remained still, waiting for a sign. The only motion was a small fringe of rippling cilia encircling the orb at regular intervals. Searching for another like it. There had been others before. Others who shared a common ancestry. Others who spoke to it soothingly as it grew to maturity within the boy's body, but they were gone now. It sat there on the crispy skin of Hank's chest and waited patiently as the ambulance approached the hospital. Waiting for a sign.

* * *

Barely five miles away, a large amorphous figure in the vague shape of a man slumped deep in the shadows of a large HVAC unit on the roof of St. Francis Children's Hospital. Cloaked in the darkness, with dusk quickly approaching, its features were indistinct until seen up close, at which point its preternatural form was quickly apparent. Though it had not been killed in the battle in the boy's room earlier that day, the Cluster had sustained a great amount of damage from its wounds and it required time to regenerate. Time which was quickly vanishing. Puddles of tissue which had sloughed off and necrotized lay in a ragged trail leading to its current location. Its "head" had reformed, but it lacked features, as if it had been born with a caul upon its face as a sign of its otherworldly origin.

As it recuperated from the damage, it remained vigilant in case a hospital employee decided to venture up to the roof for any reason. It sensed that, five floors below, the boy who now hosted its seedling was being moved to a waiting ambulance so he could be transported to a new hospital – one with significantly better security. Within days it would be able to communicate with the boy much more efficiently over long distances, but for now they were limited to basic empathic contact within an extremely small radius… at least until the seedling matured and became fully rooted in the boy's central nervous system.

Others were within its telepathic range, Riders of various sizes, powers and ages. Steeds and a lone, damaged Riderless that hurt to even touch its mind. So much trauma and pain in one being. It recognized this mind, felt that it had known this one before, but never had its pain been so palpable. Someday it would to search this damaged mind out, but not now when it had to heal and find the lair of the enemy, its creators, the zealots who sought to exterminate its kind.

Less than an hour ago, it had felt the deaths of dozens of its Thralls as they were slaughtered by agents of the enemy. A few had barely escaped, but it was now certain that their foes were on their trail. They were searching for the Elder that had been discovered in the asylum last month after decades of being entombed. The one that was so utterly damaged and scarred that it hurt to make contact. The one that had immediately cloaked its mind from fellow Riders and their kin. The one whose entire being radiated hatred and bloodlust before it vanished from the perception of the only beings who could possibly help end its suffering.

And now, for a fleeting second, there was contact with a new mind. Familiar somehow, yet fetal and completely inexperienced. Rather than a narrow, focused beam of thought, this mind flailed, whipping its thought strands in random, unpredictable patterns.

There it was again. A longer glimpse of the thought patterns revealed that the being flailing its newly discovered mental tentacles was barely out of the host. In fact, it was unformed, at least a couple months premature. The new being's thought patterns resembled the thoughts of the one that had been forcibly ripped from its Steed, Chuck Monahan, by the Acme agents. Similar, but they were unfocused. Layered. Almost as if there was more than one mind vying for control. Undeveloped.

Could another Seed have sprouted among the Monahans without anyone's knowledge? It sent out feelers once again and realized that it was much closer, approaching this very location within minutes. When it brushed against the amorphous bundle of mental energy, it lashed out quickly and enveloped the entity with a harness. Initially the other struggled, but it quickly realized the futility in its actions, recognizing its weakness in comparison to the overwhelming power of its captor. Once

The Specimen

the Cluster knew that it had complete control, it summoned the other being to the roof of the hospital… and it waited.

Chapter 31 – Rats in a Cage

"The beast in me is caged by frail and fragile bars"
– Johnny Cash

Modern Day – Hartford, CT

Dahlia was cursed. This current situation was undeniable proof. She had always suspected that there were unknown forces in the world manipulating events behind the scenes, but it wasn't until recently that she had realized that they were specifically aligned against her. Maybe she had pissed off someone in a former life and the constant river of shit in which she was always floating was simply karma's way of balancing the scales for the sins of her previous incarnations. Wrong place… wrong time. That was the story of Dahlia's life, epitomized by the current situation.

After she and Sydney had been thrown in the back of a van and injected with a sedative, Dahlia had woken in agony curled in a fetal position under a thin blanket. She turned her head and saw she was on a flat, stained mattress on a metal bedframe in a tiny cell. There were neither windows nor clocks and she had no way to tell how much time had passed since their abduction. Judging by the deep, ravenous ache of her hunger, she believed she had missed at least two whole days… perhaps more. Her lips were dry and cracked, her eyes were crusty, and a mule-kick of a headache was splitting her skull in two. She couldn't move her left hand at all. It was wrapped in a thick bandage and felt like all four her fingers had been broken. They were swollen and tight.

The better part of half an hour passed before she was able to pull herself to a seated position, where she moaned and retched, though nothing came out. Finally, she was able to lift her head and check out her surroundings.

Instead of being restrained by zip-ties, she was now on a chain leash. Her hands were now free, but a set of steel manacles connected her ankles by a thick chain, which in turn was chained to an iron ring set in the concrete wall next to the bed. A fresh bandage was taped a couple of inches beneath her left clavicle. Dahlia peeled back the tape and muttered an obscenity beneath her breath at what she saw. Someone had implanted

The Specimen

a device beneath her skin. One she had seen before when her Aunt Sophie had battled lung cancer a few years earlier. It was a common medical device called a *portacath*. It was used to easily inject drugs or draw blood from patients who were frequently subject to such procedures. Filled with dread, she couldn't breathe at the sight of the implant. What was it for? Were they injecting drugs into her? She certainly felt drugged. Or were they doing something with her blood? She examined it closely. The incision had slightly healed, meaning she could have been unconscious for much longer than she had originally thought. Perhaps a week or more.

She examined the structure of her cell. The three main walls were concrete cinder blocks painted the same shade of antiseptic sea green that was all the rage in elementary schools built in the 1980's. There was a metal toilet bolted to the floor, a metal sink bolted to the wall, and a mirror made of polished metal bolted above the sink. The front wall of the cell was made entirely of thick metal bars painted the same color as the walls. If she walked as far as possible with the chain and leaned forward a few inches to the bars, Dahlia was able to look into the cell opposite hers and the two adjacent cells on either side.

Sydney wasn't in any of those cells across the way, but the one diagonally to her right did have an occupant. Under a plain gray blanket lay what appeared to be a tall, lanky man curled tightly into a fetal position. For a few minutes, she thought he might be dead, but eventually she was able to see a barely perceptible rising and falling of the blanket. Breathing means alive, she thought. Are those blood stains on the blanket? She squinted but couldn't be sure.

Dahlia was taking a long time to move, and then it was only to sit up on the bed and lean with her back against the wall. Her thoughts still seemed as if they were in slow motion, but the drugs were wearing off and she was readily reverting to panic mode. Whatever it was that she had been injected with packed a fucking wallop. Her eyes felt like they were bleeding, her ears were ringing incessantly, and she had a headache that felt as if someone had whacked her a few times with the wrong end of a claw hammer, Oldboy-style.

The stillness was broken by a sob off to her right. *Sydney!*

"Syd, is that you?" she called through the bars. "You okay, girl? Babe, it's Dahlia. I'm right here in another cell."

At first, the only sounds she heard in response were a bout of retching and moaning, before a weak, muffled voice responded, "Yeah, Dahl… it's me. My head is spinning and I just puked my guts out." She held back another sob, "Oh God, my face. I think that big greaseball broke my cheekbone… I can't believe this is happening."

Dahlia agreed, but she knew that panicking would only exacerbate the situation. She had been in bad situations before. Nothing this bad, of course, but she had learned how to compartmentalize her emotions and look at situations logically. She had to do that here if she and Sydney were ever going to escape.

Sydney asked how she was doing and Dahlia verified that she was as good as could be expected under the circumstances. Sydney had a portacath implant as well, so Dahlia explained her thoughts about how long they had actually been there and why they would need a portacath. They both compared notes about their cells and soon realized that Sydney was two cells down to Dahlia's right. There was a fourth cell on their side, just to the right of Sydney's. On the opposite side, there were also four cells. The first, third and fourth were empty, with the second cell occupied by the man under the blanket. As far as they could tell, the other cells on their side were empty.

Across the corridor, the other captive began moaning. He threw the blanket to the floor and stumbled off the bed to fall to his knees. Hanging his head over the metal toilet, he began vomiting for all he was worth. Dahlia covered her mouth to prevent herself from crying out in sympathy at what she saw.

The tall man seemed to be in his late twenties, wearing only a pair of filthy jeans, and he had been brutalized extensively. Bloody wounds – bite marks and deep scratches – covered his back, neck and arms. They all appeared a couple days old, but the blood had completely dried in trails down his torso and no one had cleaned him up. He loudly emptied his guts in the basin and collapsed back against the bed. Dahlia could see that his face and chest were even worse than his back. Both eyes were nearly swollen closed. His nose was bent completely to one side and a large semi-

The Specimen

circular bite mark was apparent on his distended lower lip. On his torso were dozens of gouges and cuts, but the main injury that drew her eyes was a suppurating three-inch diameter hole where his left nipple should have been. The skin around the bite was inflamed and obviously infected.

Sydney must have seen him as well, because she could hear her whimpering in sympathy and terror in her cell. The blood-soaked man looked up and saw the two girls across the corridor huddled against the walls of their cells. He smiled in exhaustion, spit a bloody wad in the general direction of the toilet and said to them in a hoarse whisper, "I see the Sleeping Beauties have finally awoken." Getting no response, he nodded his head in acceptance and continued, "I was beginning to think you would sleep forever. Pardon my appearance. It's been a rough couple of days. Believe me, I look a lot better than I did the night before last."

Dahlia finally got up the courage to speak, "Who are you? What is this place?"

"Excuse my bad manners. I entirely forgot to introduce myself. I'm Frank Popecky, and this is Hell. If you're in here with me, you probably already know that we're in a shitload of trouble."

* * *

One floor above them, in what was formerly the sporting goods section of the department store that had once occupied this building, Dr. Arnold Colfax watched the three prisoners intently on an array of monitors. He was a tall angular man with more than a passing resemblance to a praying mantis. Fifty years earlier, in his early twenties, his hair had been a shocking orange, but now most of it was iron grey, slicked straight back from his forehead. His complexion was yellow and unhealthy. His freckles had evolved into dime-sized age spots and his once vibrant green eyes were now the color of diluted seawater.

Yet despite his obvious failing health, even more apparent to those who met him was the strength of his will. His intellect was intimidating, but it was his charisma that drew his acolytes to unquestionably follow him. In their minds, it was not possible that he could ever be wrong on any subject. Though he espoused no religious beliefs whatsoever, his underlings followed him as if he were the leader of a cult. A cult of science dedicated to the eradication of an invasive species, but no matter how well-intentioned the goal, it still resembled as a cult. People who met him said he gave off a vibe of complete control, and though he may intimidate them, he made them feel secure, too.

Perhaps, if they had known the true reasons for his current experiments, they would have been a bit less maniacal in their devotion... perhaps even a bit disillusioned in him. Add in the fact that the ACME Group had not sanctioned the majority of his recent explorations and side missions (in fact, they weren't even aware of the prisoners) and his disciples might start to question his judgment.

On the screen, the prisoners were finally discussing their predicament together. Colfax could have been listening since the cells were wired for sound, but he preferred to listen later in the evening after he had retired to his quarters. Right now, he was more concerned with his health than their panicked banter.

A sharp pain in his abdomen caused Colfax to suck in his breath and bend over at the waist. Pressure sometimes dulled the pain. Sometimes it made him vomit. This time was not as bad as it could have been, but he definitely needed to go to his quarters for more pain medication.

Only four more months, he thought. *Four months until I can roll back the clock a few decades with the fruit I have sown.* He looked at the prisoners again. *Don't worry, girls. No harm will come to you at all. I need to protect my investments.*

Another wave of pain hit, causing him to bite his lower lip until it bled. He stood up from his crouch and hit the intercom button on the wall panel.

"Mr. Quillian!" he barked into the microphone.

"Yes, doctor," answered the agent instantly. "How may I help?"

"I am headed to my quarters for a rest, but that does not mean that I am off duty. Understand?"

"Yes, sir. I'll call you when your attention is needed, but handle the minor shit myself," barked Quillian in his brogue.

"Have you found that cat?"

"Not yet, sir. We're pretty certain it ran away."

The Specimen

"I don't want you to be pretty certain. I want you to have the dead body in your hands. Find it and snap its neck as soon as you get your hands on it. After the fiasco with Stoopes and Valentine, we can't take any chances at all now. Do you need me to repeat this, or did you get it the first time?"

"Clear as crystal, doctor."

Good. Pass it on to Grimaldi, and Murtaugh if he's around. I'll alert you when I return."

Colfax signed off without waiting for a response and headed to the elevator.

* * *

"You heard all that? Especially the part about that damn cat?" asked Quillian, looking over at Grimaldi. The big man nodded, unable to take his eyes off the TV screen. The Mets were holding on to a 5-4 lead over the Braves in the bottom of the 8th and they had a runner on third with two outs. He wasn't just a fan. He was a fanatic in the original sense of the word. Anything related to the New York Mets would mesmerize Grimaldi, turning him into a drooling zombie, which was one reason Quillian didn't allow sports radio during stakeouts.

The other reason was the fact that Quillian believed that baseball sucked arse. Football was the only sport worth watching in his mind, and not that wanna-be rugby shite here in the States. Bohemians all the way, Boy-O!

"I'm not killing Boots," grumbled Grimaldi.

"I understand, but I told you so, Al. Don't say I didn't. I knew the doctor wouldn't go along, and the attack on Del and Nina directly led to Del getting himself shot.

We won't kill the cat, but we can't have him wandering the base. Understood? We'll take him to a shelter or something."

Grimaldi nodded, sulking like a child.

"Good," responded Quillian. "I'm an animal lover, too, Al, but you can't keep one around if it's a potential threat."

The Specimen

Chapter 32 – Ookla the Mok

"Cats don't like change without their consent"
– Roger Cara

Modern Day – Hartford, CT
Ookla the Mok was on the prowl.

In the hours since he had scampered away from the two goons who had taken him from his old house, he hadn't eaten much, but he had latched on to the scent of fairly large well-fed rodent in the past few minutes and he had chased it into the air vents. Not a place he wanted to go, but if that was where he must travel in order to fill his belly, then off he went.

The big ugly man was nice to him, but he called him by the wrong name and the food was terrible. The other man with the silver hair ignored him half the time and kicked him when the big man couldn't see it. One night of that had been all he could handle, so he left when the silver-haired man had conveniently left the doors to their rooms wide open.

Now, like the cartoon character after which Hank had named him when he was a kitten, Ookla was stalking his prey through the abandoned metal tunnels of a formerly thriving society. The moon had not been split in half and he did not travel with a barbarian named Thundarr, but this was certainly not the comfortable life to which the Monahans had him accustomed.

Up ahead, Ookla spied the rat he had cornered in a sealed off section of the air ducts. It was a big one, nearly a quarter the size of his own mass. The rodent screeched at him as he padded forward, stopping with a few feet. It clawed at the screen that it had found blocking its way to the passage beyond, but the mesh was razor sharp and caused its paws to bleed.

Ookla licked his chops. The bloated rat turned to face Ookla, spitting in its frustration and fury, and prepared to launch itself at its hunter. Suddenly, it froze as something that it had never seen before triggered an ancient memory of a deadly predator passed down through countless generations of rats.

Ookla yawned, widening his maw until his jaw popped and dislocated like a giant python. Flowing from his enlarged throat, a mass of viscous yellow larvae swarmed out and attacked the rat en masse, burrowing into its flesh through eyes, ears, mouth, nose and all other available orifices.

The rat thrashed for a second before it died, paws curled in agony. Minutes later, the larvae abandoned the desiccated corpse and returned to their Carrier, filing down his throat to their home in his abdominal cavity.

Ever since Ookla had discovered the corpse of Willie Brady months ago in the forest behind the Monahans' house, the larvae had been living symbiotically inside the cat's abdomen, waiting for true Steeds to become available. As each new one was discovered, one larva would leave and implant itself in that individual by slithering into an ear, nostril or throat and beginning the gestation period.

In return for hosting them, Ookla received all the benefits a Steed received from its Rider without any of the demands. He had never felt healthier than he did now.

Finished with the rat, Ookla popped his jaw back into place and turned around. He was content, but he had to keep searching for another scent he had briefly caught earlier… The scent of the girl from his family.

Sydney was here somewhere.

The Specimen

*From the Personal Journal
of Dr. Saul Eckenrode
Clinical Director
Mount Greylock Institute*

October 31, 1965

    Halloween. Not my favorite holiday. Understandable, considering the clientele at Greylock. Too many of them believe the legends and myths surrounding the holiday to the point of obsession, so we avoid mention of it altogether, temporarily raise the dosage of their medications, and focus on the seasonal aspect of this time of year.

    One of the benefits of our location on Mt. Greylock is the beauty of the trees during this time of year. The changing colors of the leaves and the sound of the wind in the branches work wonders on the residents' moods. On windy nights, the rustling branches serve as a natural lullaby. Everything is calmer.

    I'll admit it... the sounds of the leaves soothe me as well, even to the point where I can forget that we have not found Hutchens yet. We searched every corner of the building and the institute's grounds, hoping at first to find him hiding in the basement or wandering the woods.

    I have come to the conclusion that one of two possibilities happened. Somehow, however unlikely it may be, he escaped into the surrounding woods where he probably died of exposure. The other more likely prospect is the possibility that ACME has taken him for one of their tests, in which case he is as good as dead as well.

    If I were to begin asking questions, I would jeopardize my status here and it would be swept under the rug anyway.

    Sometimes you just have to close your eyes and let the sounds of the autumn leaves drown out your conscience. I've slowly learned that it's much safer that way.

    - S.

November 5, 1965

  Now Scarpa is missing. This is unbelievably **BAD**. I need a drink immediately.

      -S.

November 6, 1965

  It seems my concerns, though not unfounded, have been alleviated. If you recall, Resident Angelo Scarpa went missing yesterday and immediately I had visions of mass murder in the surrounding communities, followed by news organizations descending upon Greylock to cover the recent tragedy like the laughing hyenas they all are.

  Thankfully, although every instinct was telling me to prepare for the shit storm, staff has proven to have some restraint in this situation. The press has not been told, or they deemed the story unworthy for print. The latter is unlikely.

  Initially it seemed that Scarpa's disappearance was a result of being short-staffed. Jameson has still not returned from his sudden family emergency. In Jameson's absence, Fenton has stepped up and shouldered the load, throwing himself into the work with a frenzy. He seems more driven. Angry, even.

  Last night, though, Fenton revealed to me that Scarpa has not left the asylum, and that he is under the watch of Coe and Colfax in one of the labs. Heavily sedated.

  Although I find this distasteful, I am relieved that I don't have to explain his escape to anyone. Perhaps, once they're finished with whatever they're doing, they'll do me a favor and perform a lobotomy on him before he returns to the floor.

  If I could, I would have had him put down like a rabid dog a long time ago. Some people just need it.

      - S.

Chapter 33 – Elevator Music

"Somewhere, something incredible is waiting to be known"
- Carl Sagan

Modern Day – St. Francis Children's Hospital

C.C. tapped her foot to an inner beat as she waited for the elevator doors to open so she could deliver the bodies to the hospital morgue in the basement. All three body bags were piled together on a metal cart. Husband and wife on the bottom shelf. Junior on top. As soon as she got these three crispy critters to the morgue, she would finally be able to head home, wash off the day's accumulated filth in a long hot shower and have a large glass of merlot before getting some well-deserved slumber. Billy had invited her out for a late dinner, but she simply had no energy and the last thing she wanted to do was appear sweaty and disheveled, smelling like burnt cadaver, in a possibly romantic encounter. Someday she might get enough courage to tell Billy how she really felt and then jump his bones, but today was not that day.

Out of the corner of her eye, she caught a quick glimpse of something moving on the cart. She flinched and then laughed at herself. It was most likely a bug or spider that had crawled into one of the bags while it was open and on the ground. They were supposed to ensure that no contaminating substance or insect made it into the body bags with the remains, but it happened occasionally no matter what precautions were taken. It was just part of the job.

The elevator dinged and the doors opened. A group of sleep-deprived young residents exited, followed by a family of four: Mom, Dad, teenaged daughter (wrinkling her nose at the lingering porky stink of the corpses) and hyperactive little brother (who stopped his constant chatter as he stared at the body bags in pure awe). C.C. smiled at the family in greeting and pushed the cart into the elevator car. All to herself and the Monahans. A truly hideous Muzak version of Nirvana's "Come as You Are" provided a soundtrack as she set the cart flat against the back wall. She pushed the button for the basement level and leaned back against the wall. *Slowest elevator in the world*, thought C.C.

Something definitely moved in the bag this time. A significant bulge in the orange plastic tented up for a few seconds before settling back down. C.C. was pretty sure it was the bag containing the body of the boy, Hank. *There! Again! Holy Crap*, she thought. *Is there any chance he could still be alive?* As the elevator finally began its descent, she stepped up to the cart and unzipped the bag a bit to look inside.

A small shadow instantly skittered forward and launched itself from the bag at her face. *Facehugger!* At the sight of the fleshy tendrils and leech-like mouth, she instantly thought of the creature from the movie *Alien*. Her best friend in 4th grade, Laney Briscoe, snuck a video-taped copy of the original movie to a sleepover at her house and she had been utterly terrified at anything resembling the monster that burst from that alien egg since then. She ducked and swatted the thing with her right arm, screaming like a terrified child.

It ricocheted off the wall, landing on its back near the elevator doors. The pale grey-pink organism was about the size of a mouse with a dozen or so wriggling yellow feelers waving in the air and a gelatinous nerve cord for a rat-like tail. C.C. stared at it in dismay and shrieked again, maneuvering herself behind the cart with the body bags.

"Help!!! No! No! Ohmigodohmigodohmigod!!!" she hyperventilated and wailed while the elevator continued down to the basement at its usual leisurely pace.

Rather than flip itself over, the creature's feelers retracted into its thorax and sprouted through the bottom, immediately skittering beneath the metal cart. C.C. continued her howling as the elevator finally reached the basement and the doors slid open.

C.C. gasped in relief and launched herself out of the car, abandoning the three cadavers on the cart. The wheeled table rolled forward, preventing the elevator doors from closing. As she ran down the empty hall, calling for help, she heard the repetitive clunking of the doors rebounding again and again. No one seemed to be around, but most likely

The Specimen

Dr. Froehicke, the medical examiner, was working on a body with his headphones blasting Metallica at ear-bleeding levels as was his standard routine every day.

Too late. It darted toward her as she stumbled down the corridor. A light touch on her left ankle and suddenly the nimble critter was spiraling up C.C.'s pants leg. She yelped again and fell to the floor, writhing in a last-ditch attempt to crush it beneath her weight. It slithered past her hips, honing in on the center of her spine and puncturing her flesh on either side of the vertebrae. Within a split second, its two barbs drilled into her spinal cord and started to co-opt control of her motor functions. Her shrieks were cut short as a numbing sensation washed over her entire body and she was wracked with violent convulsions that bashed her head repeatedly on the floor.

Seconds later, she went limp. Eyes rolled back in her skull. Motionless, except for an occasional spasm in her fingers or fluttering of her eyelids. The corridor was all but silent. A whisper of music leaked through the doors to the morgue around the corner, and the elevator doors hit the hospital cart and rebounded every few seconds. The sole witness to the incident was an unmonitored camera at the end of the hallway that recorded everything and saved it on a server in case anyone wanted to review it. The current tape would never be seen, eventually filed and forgotten among thousands of other videos.

Exactly two minutes and thirty-nine seconds after C.C. collapsed, she opened her eyes and stood up slowly. She retrieved the cart and delivered it to the morgue, leaving the decedent forms on the top body bag. Shawna, the morgue attendant and Dr. Froehicke were hunched over a body, in the process of removing the organs and weighing them. They didn't even see her as she left the morgue. Walking to the elevator, she waited silently, entered when the doors opened and pressed the button for the top floor. She had an urgent appointment on the hospital roof.

Pete Kahle

<<ACME EYES ONLY>>
What We Know: An ACME Group Primer on the Riders
J.P. Kilcannon/G. Suares/K. Morimoto, 11th Edition

Section G – Rider History

The following is an overview of a few significant moments in recorded history where Rider influence has either been confirmed or overwhelming evidence exists that they had a hand in the outcome. This is not meant to be a complete catalog of such events. Many other events involving the Riders in one way or another have been documented since the founding of ACME, but, of the ones we have discovered, the following examples are believed to have had the most significant impact on the course of history. It is also quite likely that there are many other instances where the influence of the Riders was far greater, but we have yet to understand the evidence.

1298 CE (Germany) - The Rindfleisch Massacres
In the town of Röttingen, a local knight identified as Lord Rindfleisch, called together a mob that slaughtered and burned all Jews in the local area for the alleged crime of desecrating a consecrated host. Continuing through the summer, the throng eventually eradicated 146 more Jewish communities, killing more than 5,000 members of that faith. King Albert I subsequently had Rindfleisch captured and hanged publicly, before being cut down, slashed open and left for the scavengers to eat. When his body was finally removed days later, a mass of rotting alien tissue attached to Lord Rindfleisch's carcass had been completely ignored by the crows as if were poisonous. This was considered to be "demonflesh" and was taken as proof that he had been controlled by an evil, otherworldly entity.

14th – 17th Centuries CE (Europe) – The Black Death
For three centuries, the bubonic plague ravaged Europe, killing over 200 million people in the 14th century alone. During this period, knowledge of the Riders' existence appears to have been much more commonplace. What seemed apocryphal in other eras and parts of the

The Specimen

world was accepted as fact here and now. No one was immune from suspicion. Anyone could be taken on any day. They were seen as Devils. Harbingers of Doom. Bringers of the Plague. Some of the more notorious Rider/Host pairs were referred to as The Horsemen, insinuating that they were heralds of the approaching Apocalypse.

Especially damning was the fact that their Hosts glowed with unearthly health at a time when half of the population was dying horribly in most regions, and some lost as much as 80% to the pestilence. People truly believed that agents of Hell walked among them, so much so that the Riders became complacent, expecting that nothing would even consider challenging them.

In some areas, the Hosts and Riders were quickly hunted down and burned at the stake or tortured to satisfy the bloodlust that had grown with each death of a family member. In rarer instances, Riders were able to hide their forms, using the chaos to direct suspicion and anger at their tormentors. Even so, the Rider population plummeted during this period, especially among the younger specimens. With the number of worthy Hosts dropping, the younger Riders were much less cautious when choosing their new potential Hosts. Less cautious and ultimately more vulnerable.

The Black Plague has been estimated by historians to have killed more than 1 out of every 3 people in Europe, but it decimated the Riders even further. Ultimately, we now believe that the population of Riders had dropped by 80 to 90% by the time the plague moved on from Europe.

This drastic reduction in the number of Riders had two traceable results. First of all, what had been considered commonplace then was now inconceivable to most people. Monsters riding the backs of their fellow man was the stuff of nightmares and cracked minds.

Additionally, in order to replenish their numbers and stave off impending extinction, the Riders began to produce and release many more larvae to seed the population. Choosing Hosts became much more indiscriminate. The vast majority of the Riders that had survived the Black Plague were already quite old – all Elders, many over one thousand years. The wave of new Riders were juvenile and undisciplined, prone to arrogance and always placing themselves and their Hosts in severe peril. Very few of them would reach Elder-level maturity by present day.

Lastly, the Riders began to migrate much further abroad. This is not to say that there were never any of them who had ventured outside of the original European radius. Prior to the Plague, some had moved to other countries and continents, but the majority had stayed on in the Old Country, cultivating flocks of their thralls and waging wars against their tormentors as well as fellow Riders. Now, however, the prospect of new lands to explore, new cultures to exploit, and new Hosts to Ride was too tempting to pass up. In the end, the Black Plague may very well have saved the Riders from stagnation and eventual extinction by providing a drive to expand beyond Europe into new lands and cultures.

1518 CE (Holy Roman Empire) - The Dancing Plague
In July, a number of individuals in Strasbourg, Alsace were overcome with the compulsion to dance frenetically in the streets. Over the next few weeks, the number of dancers swelled to over 400 participants, dancing continuously day and night. Eventually, some of the dancers perished from exhaustion, heart attack and stroke. Survivors of the month-long craze claimed that they felt they were possessed by evil spirits and found it physically impossible to stop.

1701 CE (Japan) - The 47 Ronin
The daimyo Asano Naganori is ordered to commit seppuku by Shogun Tsunayoshi after attempting to kill the corrupt kōke Kira Yoshinaka. As an act of vengeance, 47 of Naganori's former samurai planned for nearly two years before killing Yoshinaka. Witnesses to the battle later claimed that Yoshinaka had an oni (demon) riding on his back.

1841 CE (USA)
President William Henry Harrison dies from a blood infection contracted after a juvenile Rider is surgically removed from his back

The Specimen

days after his inauguration. Following his death, the news was circulated that he had passed away due to pneumonia contracted during his lengthy Inaugural Address.

1888-1891 CE (England) - The Whitechapel Murders

Eleven women are murdered over a span of thirty-four months by a vigilante identifying himself in letters to the London papers as "Jack". Over the next few weeks, he is given the sobriquet "The Ripper" for the increasing brutality of each murder. In the post-mortem exams, Coroner Wynne Edwin Baxter, an agent of ACME, determines that three of the victims showed signs of having been implanted with Rider larvae, nearly all of which had been excised from the victims' bodies while still alive. The remaining eight fatalities showed no signs of alien infection, despite the increasingly savage vivisections perpetrated by the killer.

The identity of the Ripper was never discovered, but it is now apparent that he was aware of the existence of Riders. Additionally, he somehow was initially able to identify victims who had Rider larvae implanted in them. What remains uncertain is why he lost the ability and whether or not others were involved in the hunt. As one of the greatest mysteries in ACME history, many theories have been put forward. From rogue ACME agents to an insane Host that remained dominant, ideas have been explored, but none have been verified.

1898 CE (Italy)

In Milan, General Fiorenzo Bava-Beccaris orders his troops to fire upon an unarmed crowd of protesters with muskets and cannons. Over 200 people died in the massacre. Decades later, Bava-Beccaris became an avid supporter of Benito Mussolini. He was long suspected by the ACME Group to be carrying a Rider. Multiple attempts were made to kill him, but none were successful.

1900 CE (Italy)

King Umberto I of Italy is assassinated by Gaetano Bresci in retaliation for honoring General Bava-Beccaris' order to shoot at the protestors in Milan. Bresci was actually the lone ACME agent in the region acting upon reports that Umberto had been compromised by the Riders years earlier. Whether the King was a Host or simply influenced by someone else with a Rider was never discovered.

1912 CE (USA)

John Flammang Schrank attempts to assassinate former president Teddy Roosevelt, but fate intervenes and the bullet is slowed by a steel eyeglass case and the fifty-page copy of a speech that he would end up giving later that evening. Schrank was later captured and taken into custody by agents of ACME, who had been unrelatedly following him for months on suspicion of hosting a Rider. Forced into action, they secretly transported Schrank to an ACME facility and performed a removal of the juvenile Rider he had on him. The procedure was a success and the Rider was incinerated per the policy at that time. Schrank's mental state was permanently affected and he spent the remainder of his life at the Central State Mental Hospital.

1932 CE (USA) - Lindbergh Baby Kidnapping

On March 1st, the 20 month-old son of famous aviator Charles Lindbergh was reportedly kidnapped and killed by a German criminal named Bruno Hauptmann. This man was tried both in the criminal courts and the court of public opinion, and found overwhelmingly guilty. Hauptmann was executed for the crime, but he was only a convenient scapegoat. The truth was much stranger...

In the 1920's, a faction of ACME had splintered off for ideological reasons - not the first time this had happened. Generally, these splinter groups were motivated by a goal of complete eradication of the Riders, whereas our original charter preferred to capture, examine and experiment before executing the entwined creatures.

The faction in this case was the leadership council of the Free International Society of Teutonia, a pro-Nazi Party German-American organization. One of the primary objectives of FIST was the continued purity of the human race, which understandably required the total extermination of the Riders, regardless of the human cost.

The Specimen

Unbeknownst his family and friends, Charles Lindbergh was secretly a member of FIST. He learned of anomalies in Charles, Jr.'s anatomy through the family physician, a fellow member of FIST, and communicated his concerns to colleagues, a number of whom had experience with Riders through their prior time with ACME. They immediately realized that a Rider larva was growing inside the boy and approached Lindbergh, revealing what they knew and detailing what they believed should be done

After a few days of deliberation, Lindbergh agreed to allow them to perform whatever procedure was necessary to free his son from the grasp of the Rider. The kidnapping was staged by FIST, and that era's equivalent of a media blitz began.

Regrettably, the plan was not successful.

Two months later, the child's corpse was found decayed and in pieces in a lot near to the Lindbergh house. An officer involved in securing the scene reported, unofficially, that it "was a couple of weeks old and it appeared as if a small bomb had gone off in the kid's gut."

The surgery had obviously not gone well. The procedure triggered a premature exit for the developing Rider, and any chance of saving the child's life was destroyed. Lindbergh and his colleagues deflected the investigation away from the family an evidence was eventually found that pointed authorities towards the aforementioned Hauptmann.

Lindbergh remained involved in FIST for the next couple of decades, publicly becoming a prominent face in the growing anti-communism movement. As the years passed, he also became a huge proponent of eugenics, stating that "Racial strength is vital." His experiences with the Riders and the death of his son affected him for the rest of his life.

1933-1945 (Europe) - The Holocaust

If historians knew the extent to which Riders were involved in the formation of the Nazi Party and, later on, the Final Solution and the concentration camps, they would be astonished that Rider/Host pairs were just as likely to be among the victims of the industrialized mass murder as they were the perpetrators – the SS officers, the gas chamber attendants, and the horrid doctors who performed grotesque medical procedures on children, twins and whoever else struck their fancy.

If not for an internal struggle within the Reich between opposing factions of Riders, the war's outcome could have been much different. Over six million people were slaughtered in the concentration camps, and countless others were killed in many conflicts across the globe. The lives lost during the war were the most seen since the Black Plague ravaged populations from Asia across Europe, and as should be expected, the percentage of Riders that died were also at its highest since that time.

Again the world was presented with an opportunity to rid itself of this alien plague. After the war, we estimated the number of remaining Riders worldwide to be between 15,000 and 20,000, less than 5 percent of whom were presumed to be Elders. Yet our organization still needed to remain in the shadows.

Despite this potential chance to deal a final blow to these parasites, public exposure could have ended up being fatal for ACME as well. Many top agents had perished in the war, and just as the majority of Riders were now extremely young, the core of the ACME agents were young and inexperienced.

As a result, we are at somewhat of a standstill at this point in the history of our organization. Our agents are gaining valuable experience. However, in the past few decades, the only Riders that seem to be easily found are the juveniles. The Elders have all but disappeared into hiding. The few that have been caught only gives us clues of an imminent disaster. No other information was gleaned from the interrogations. All that can be done is to bide our time and keep our collective eyes open.

The Specimen

Chapter 34 – What is Left of Me

"Fear of a name increases fear of the thing itself."
- J. K. Rowling

Modern Day – St. Francis Children's Hospital

The creature known as the Cluster waited, slumbered, and regenerated on the roof of St. Frank's. It did not think of itself by that name, but it was self-aware. It had heard that name screamed at him by the agents of Acme in their many encounters. The creature knew that name was chosen by its creator, but it did not accept it. A name was an assignment of an identity. A name was permanent and sacred. A name was earned.

In the half century since its genesis in a cement-walled laboratory in Greylock, the creature had learned much. It had learned to survive in the wild and among humanity. It had learned camouflage and stealth and deception. It had learned to identify danger and to protect itself against attackers. Through its feline and rodent thralls, the creature had even learned empathy and a sense of belonging. However, it had never found a name that it considered worthy.

Now, the creature rested as it waited for the other being to arrive. Each second, damaged cells by the thousands were sloughed off and replaced with newly created copies. The wounds it was healing were some of the most grievous injuries it had ever received. Multiple shots to the head and torso. Though none of the bullets had damaged its neural core, healing was taking quite a long time. If the creature had been able to spend a few hours in the boy's room with the female agent's corpse, it could have digested her body and used her cells as building blocks for regeneration. Without such sustenance, it needed to cannibalize its own flesh to recover fully. Such a process was slower and less efficient. By the time it was complete, its mass would be reduced by nearly forty percent. Now, more than halfway restored, the creature had shrunk to approximately the size of an average man. The head was almost recognizable and the bullet holes had filled in to the point where they were only shallow divots in its flesh.

A few yards away, the metal hatch flew open and hit the gravel surface as the woman it had summoned climbed up the ladder onto the roof. Smoothly and precisely, C.C. Kennealy pulled herself to her feet and walked slowly into the shadows where the creature lay. She stood facing it for a second before lowering herself to a kneeling position on the gravel. Her serene expression masked the fact that she was completely unconscious. Unaware of where she was or what she had done since her collapse in the hallway outside the morgue.

With a mental touch like a feather, the wounded creature reached out to the mind of the small passenger inside the woman, whispered to it soothingly and coaxed it out. C.C.'s mouth opened and hung slackly as the smaller creature it had contacted, recently born from Hank Monahan's cauterized cadaver, and ventured past her uvula. Slick, moistened with mucus, her throat expanded like a snake's to allow for its slug-like body to pass. It undulated down her EMT uniform, leaving a wet trail on the rough surface of the roof leading to the edge of its more massive relative.

The larger creature examined the smaller one with great interest, recognizing it as the larval form of a Rider. Rare, since due to their potential to live many millennia, Riders rarely reproduced. The birth of a Rider was a notoriously messy affair as well. Unless removed surgically, the larva would seek out the closest orifice of its host. If none were immediately available, the larva would create an exit out of necessity and burst through it in a violent and sloppy display. It had seen Riders within days of birth, but never had it seen a premature larva outside the host body like this. Strangely, it looked similar to the collections of cells it used to harness the thralls to him.

It beckoned to the larva. When the smaller organism did not immediately advance and meld into the mass of its body, it recoiled, confused. With a gentle psychic probe, it sent visuals of serenity and protection to the larval Rider, cajoling it to join together. It even expended some precious energy to release some pheromones to compel it forward. Finally the larva slithered up and touched the surface of the larger being, whereupon it was immediately engulfed and absorbed into the mass. For a moment, the shape and details of the larva could be seen within the

The Specimen

amorphous form, but this quickly faded as the larva was dissolved into its base components.

The creature was surprised. Something had been... different about this larva. Alien. Normally, when one of the Thralls' bugs returned, it gradually dispersed the information it had collected. The knowledge gained was examined and then filed away in the creature's internal library. The bugs were then dissolved and recycled.

This time, however, there was a stowaway on board. Instead of being mindless and wholly instinctual, this larva was filled to the brim with memories and a psychic imprint of another intelligence. Genetic memory. A ghost made tangible.

Before it realized what was happening, all the ghostly memories flooded throughout its neural core. A life cut short was replayed and experienced instantaneously by the creature. The thoughts and patterns of this individual filled the gaps in the creature's mind and redirected them as if it were a program being updated from an outside server. The psychic maps of the creature were suddenly given multiple new routes on which to travel. Back roads, side streets and dark cul-de-sacs. And among all of these new thoughts, emotions, and passions that were infinitely foreign to this creature as alien as the one known to its enemies as the Cluster... *was an identity... a NAME.*

This name sounded strange to the creature, but it felt right. It was a name that had belonged to the ghost whose memories now were shared by this creature. A name of a young man who had witnessed his father being slaughtered on the kitchen floor of his house. A young man who had died only hours earlier of smoke inhalation as his bedroom went up in flames. A young man whose corpse had been covered with water from an imploded water bed, protecting the Rider larva that had been growing inside him for months without his knowledge.

The larva had the essence of this young man deep inside. The memories of the teen were its memories. Some individuals of a spiritual nature might even believe that the spark of life that was carried inside this larva was the young man's soul.

The name of this young man had been *Hank Monahan*... and now it was the creature's name as well. His name and memories saturated the former Cluster. Over the past decades since its flight from Greylock with the young boy, it had practiced its abilities so it could camouflage itself enough, with pheromones and physical modifications, that it could go unnoticed among humanity, avoiding any but the most perceptive of humans – usually the very young or those in their dying years.

Even so, it had only experienced one emotion in all that time. It was quite familiar with the sense of loneliness that came with avoiding contact with others of its kind, even though it was not a member of the human race, and now the wall around its inner self finally gave way. Sinking to the gravel, it released all the pain it had been accumulating since its accidental birth. It wept long and savagely while C.C. looked on in a semiconscious daze waiting for new instructions.

The Specimen

Chapter 35 – The Dudes Abide

*"I hear the secrets that you keep...
When you're talking in your sleep."
The Romantics - "Talking in Your Sleep"*

Modern Day – UMass Medical Center

Deputy Simone Booker sat outside Scott Ritchie's new room at UMass Medical Center on the most uncomfortable chair of her life. She had been standing guard for the better part of four hours now, and she was counting the minutes until Sloan arrived to fill in. Her ass was numb and her left knee was throbbing relentlessly because her arthritis had flared up again. Who got arthritis at the age of 42? Though it wouldn't do her much good, she swallowed three more ibuprofen with a cup of tepid cafeteria coffee and prayed for a little respite from the pain.

Standing up to stretch the kinks from her body, she peeked into the room. Scott was buried under a pile of blankets, snoring away as if he hadn't nearly died a couple of days earlier. He still had casts over most of his body, but his mobility had improved immeasurably and the doctors here at UMass had determined that he no longer needed to be in traction. Quite surprising, since the initial diagnosis had projected a recovery of well over six months.

She wished that she could do something more than babysit Scott, but Sheriff Smucker had made it clear that he was not going to leave the boy unguarded after the incident at St. Frank's. He was only a year or two younger than her son. *That could be my Simeon in there*, she thought. *What kind of person shoots a kid his age?*

According to statistics, Chesterfield was supposedly one of the safest towns in Massachusetts. Simone had moved her family out of Boston to the suburbs to be safer and get a better education. If something like this could happen in Chesterfield, no place was truly safe. She clucked her tongue in sympathy. She didn't think that Scott had anything to do with the Monahan home invasion. On the other hand, she also didn't think that he was telling the whole truth, either. Some of the story had been left out. What it was and whether it was important remained to be seen.

Scott writhed on his bed and called intermittently for his parents, family and friends. He had been in a deep slumber for well over an hour, occasionally mumbling and babbling, but now he had calmed down. Simone shook her head and sat back down. Her shift would be over soon, and she could head home and wash the day's filth off of her. Leaning back against the wall, she heard Scott speaking someone's name clearly and repeatedly …

* * *

"Scott? Dude?"

Scott knew he was dreaming, but it seemed as if his eyes were open and he was looking at another ethereal plane layered on top of the main reality. Objects from this plane were wispy and transparent, flickering like the varied exposures of the film in a silent movie.

In the center of the room stood his dead friend, scintillating silver grey and wavering in and out of focus. Hank was wearing his usual outfit from their video gaming sessions: ratty grey flannel robe, his favorite baggy Joe Namath replica jersey (he was a Jets fan just to piss off his dad) and a pair of beige cargo shorts. With his long blonde hair, he was a virtual teenage version of The Dude from one of their favorite flicks, The Big Lebowski.

"Hey, Scotty the Body. How's it hanging?" Hank's specter grinned like a buffoon as he looked Scott up and down. "You look like a warm, steaming pile of shit."

"Hank …"

"You said that already, you tool. Twice, in fact. Did you land head first when that minivan smoked your ass?"

"Hank... Dude, this isn't real. You're dead. I'm dreaming all this."

The Specimen

"Well, you're right in some ways, and you're wrong in others. I am dead... but I'm not."

For a moment, Scott was at a loss for words. He looked around the room and considered whether he should call for Deputy Booker before turning back to the apparition.

"I saw that guy taser you in your kitchen until you shit yourself, Hank. They cut apart your dad, beat your mom to a pulp and just a while back I found out they burned down your house with the three of you inside! Who knows what's happening to Sydney and her friend?! They're probably dead too. This whole situation is fucked up beyond belief... and now I'm hallucinating things!"

"Dude ..."

"And here I am in the hospital with bullet wounds, broken bones, and the cops are acting like I have something to do with your family getting killed!"

"Scott ..."

"What, Hank? What can you possibly say that will make things better? Why did this have to happen? Haven't I lost enough people in my life? Why did you leave me too?" Scott's rage gave way to tears as he slumped onto the hospital bed.

The image of his best friend grew hazy and formless. A babbling chorus of voices battled with each other for dominance before coalescing once again into Hank's familiar rasp.

"Scott," he said, sounding more serious than he ever had in life. "That's what I'm trying to say to you. I'm... not... dead. I don't know how and I don't know why, but something has kept me from moving on. I don't even know what kept me from dying. There is so much more that I need to tell you, man, but I can't right now. I've changed in ways I can't explain. The only way you'll believe is if you see me. See what I've become. When I finally can come to you and show you what I am, you'll probably fear me in my new form, but if you let me show you that it really is me, you will recognize and accept me as I am."

Scott stared at Hank's wavering shape. Could this possibly be true? Was Hank some sort of revenant? Or was this a sign that Scott was going insane? He glanced around the room, then back at the apparition. Even though the voice and the intonation were exact, something vital was missing from this Hank.

No, that wasn't right. The opposite was true. It wasn't that something was missing. On the contrary, it felt as if something or someone was speaking through a Hank Monahan filter. The dust of another mind was leaking through and fleshing out the parts of the young man's identity that had been destroyed... burnt away in the inferno that took the lives of Hank and his parents.

It was all so confusing. Scott rubbed his eyes and spoke again in a much softer tone, "I don't know what to believe now. When will I see you?"

"Soon," answered Hank. "I need to recover from my injuries, but I'll check in. I know how to find you. Wherever you happen to be, I will be there when I can."

Scott closed his eyes and nodded. "I'm holding you to it, dude."

* * *

When he opened them again, Hank's shadowy form was absent, and Deputy Booker – until now he had just thought of her as Simeon's mom - was seated next to him with a glass of water. She offered it to him and smiled, "Good morning, Scotty. I figured you might need this. You scared me a bit. You were screaming yourself hoarse a few minutes ago."

Scott thanked her and drained the glass in one giant swallow. No ghostly images of former friends. He realized the whole dream must have just been a nightmare. That was all.

A vivid, detailed, utterly convincing nightmare …

The Specimen

* * *

Hank severed the tenuous mental tether between him and his long-time friend, Scott. It had only been a couple of hours since his rebirth, so he still struggled with the idea that he had died and reawakened as the main consciousness in this "body". Even so, he had adapted to the abilities of his new form almost instantly. He sensed that the previous consciousness had been subsumed by his own invading mind… or had it willingly stepped aside? When, after reviewing this body's memories, he had realized that Scott was already connected to him by a thrall seed, he nearly cried out in joy.

The former mind of this being lingered in his subconscious, rearing its head whenever Hank drew on one of its memories or attempted an ability, but it was more instinctual. He didn't need to make an effort to access it. He just did what felt right to him, just as he referred to himself as a he, even though he was well aware that, technically he was genderless or asexual. He identified as a male. That might change in the future, but for now, Hank Monahan was still a young male.

Later on, he might utterly lose his shit and have a complete mental nuclear meltdown, but for now he was throbbing with life. He hadn't even had time to register the information he had culled during his short stay inside C.C.'s mind. The fact that his parents were now dead and that Sydney and Dahlia were missing were lost in the myriad of thoughts swirling inside. Every sense of this body before his annexation was there for him to re-experience as if it were the first time, but for now he had to find a way to meet up with Scott, and as soon as possible.

He looked at C.C and reached out with a feather-like mental touch to the thrall seed he had implanted an hour or so earlier. Unlike the Hank larva, this organic node in her brain was not there to grow a new Rider. The way Hank understood it, the seed enabled telepathy between himself and the thrall, and it served as an organic GPS, allowing him to hone in on the location of the thrall as long as it was within a specific radius.

It wasn't his intent to keep C.C. enthralled for long, but until he was able to sort out his new existence and make contact with Scott and others, he would keep her this way. After all, how else was he going to find transportation? *For that matter*, he thought as he examined the bloodstained shreds of the scrubs he had on earlier, *where am I going to find clothes to wear?*

The Specimen

Interlude: The Riders
Lucifer's Concubine
Cartagena, Spain - December 19th, 1602

Just before the dawn sun washed away the dark stain of night, His Excellency, Bishop Juan de Zúñiga Flores of Cartagena, the Grand Inquisitor of the Spanish Inquisition, descended warily down the stone stairs of the ancient cathedral into the depths of Hell. The steps were slick from condensation and the bishop's usual attendants were not with him, nor were they aware that he had ventured out of his room without an escort to meet with the latest guest of the Inquisition.

This was not a visit he wanted to publicize. His robes, though made of fine cloth, were a simple gray without adornment. At times like these, it was best to fade into the shadows without sycophants fawning over every movement he made.

The walls of the stairwell were lined with tarnished brass sconces in which oil lamps flickered every twenty steps, descending into the bowels of the old structure. The amber light from the lamps was weak and the dancing shadows filled the area with blackened ghosts of previous passersby. Soot stained the rock walls in abstract patterns from centuries of burning oil. Underlying the odor of the oil was a subtle reek of rot and corruption that grew stronger as he descended into the earth. The great Italian poet Dante Alighieri would recognize this hellish stench, for it truly seemed as if the bishop was beginning a long journey to the Inferno made vivid by Alighieri's words.

At the bottom of the long stairwell was an intersection of three passageways that appeared to have been formed naturally as opposed to the manmade construction of the edifice above. The ceilings were low, cramped and filled with smoke from the sputtering lamps. Above ground, the wind had whistled through crevices in the crumbling foundation, but here a deathly silence ruled, stifling any stray whimper or muffling the cries of agony that often permeated the halls of these catacombs.

Taking the extreme right passage, the bishop stooped to avoid hitting his head and continued down a slight decline for a few dozen yards to a small chamber where he could once again stand erect. A solitary guard standing at attention before a barred cast iron door genuflected to the bishop, and then turned to raise the iron bar, allowing access to the dimly lit corridor beyond.

Ducking through the entryway, the bishop turned back to the sentry and said in a calm, firm tone, "Bar it behind me. I will return within the hour. Let no one pass until I return and speak no word of my presence within."

The guard nodded assent and closed the door. The sound of the bar clanging into place echoed down the narrow hall. The bishop looked down the passage and took a deep breath. This would be a great test of his faith, indeed. In the six short months since he had been named Grand Inquisitor, he had witnessed many affronts to the Word of God, but none as immediate and tangible as what was present in the prisoner he visited at this hour.

Along the right wall of the carved stone tunnel were five doors, all constructed of solid oak and secured with padlocks the size of a man's fist. The bishop passed the first four doors, stopping finally at the fifth chamber, the only room with an occupant.

On each door was a shutter covering a barred opening the size of a window. If anyone wished to speak with a prisoner without entering the room, the shutter could be slid to one side, revealing the opening.

The bishop paused, listening for movement within. A rustle of cloth or a muffled whimper - anything to betray that there was a tenant in the dank and fetid cell - but there was no sound at all, only the stench of unwashed flesh and human waste emanating from the dank chamber and overpowering the odor of burning oil from the lamps on the wall.

Reciting the Pater Noster, he performed the sign of the Cross and took a lamp from the sconce to his right before opening the cell with a large key on a ring at his belt. The glow from the lamp hardly pierced the shadows, but he stepped forward without hesitation and raised his hand to aim the light higher on the back wall of the chamber.

There she was. The foul whore. Lucifer's concubine. Leaning against the far wall with her head in the crook of her arms, the woman lay unmoving, chained by a shackle around her neck to an iron ring set in the

The Specimen

floor. Was she asleep or feigning it? He stood there in silence for a few seconds, examining the chamber for any changes. Nothing stood out. Waste was piled against the far left wall. A wooden bowl with a greasy lump of congealed gruel sat untouched near the central ring, apparently ignored for hours. A matching cup half-filled with tepid water next to the bowl gathered dust. The only evidence that the woman was alive was the barely perceptible rise and fall of her chest and a slight occasional twitch of her feet.

The lamp guttered and sparked, briefly brightening the cell. The bishop held his breath against the vile reek and took one step closer to the huddled captive to look at her more closely in the lamplight.

She was an old woman, a crone, clothed in a ragged gray robe, stained with vomit, blood and fecal matter. Her hair was matted and hung to her waist, dingy dark brown with heavy streaks of gray permeating the entire length. Her hands and feet were scabbed, covered in sores and blemishes that were obviously infected, and twisted into painful contortions due to years of arthritis. Her name was Inez Jimena de Lima y Contreras, and, if her claims were true, she was eighty-seven years old, an age that few ever reached.

"Open your eyes, harlot," pronounced the bishop. "You cannot hide from God's judgment any longer. The evidence of your sin is plain to all servants of the Church."

The woman raised her head and turned toward him with a concerted effort. She moaned in pain and moved gradually into the amber glow of the lamp. When her eyes made contact with his, he again crossed himself and suppressed a shudder. A dark intelligence seemed to lurk within the depths of those yellowed orbs. He could almost smell the sinful musk of her thoughts as she slowly examined him from foot to crown, crawling over his skin like the tentacles of a subterranean wyrm.

"You must confess to Him," he continued. "Would you die to protect the abomination that defiled your body? Or the spawn you harbor within your diseased womb? Will you condemn yourself to the fires of Hell?"

The woman attempted to speak, but her response was lost in a paroxysm of coughing as he persisted with his inquiry, "Even now you choke on the fumes of the Abyss. Speak, woman! Redeem yourself! Confess and save your cursed soul! Your body may be lost, but you can still atone and enter the Gates of Heaven!"

"I have not sinned," whispered the woman in a hoarse croak. "I have a disease, a sickness... of the body, not of the soul" She coughed loudly and a copious spray of mucus and blood landed at the bishop's feet, causing him to step quickly back in disgust. Her body shook violently as she choked and retched in undeniable agony.

"Your sin is what sickens you, woman! Why can you not see this?" The bishop swung the lamp low, illuminating the swollen lower half of her torso. "Your memories may have been scoured, but your body knows your evil actions! It has become a reflection of your sins. Can you deny it, puta? Can you not see that an abomination has taken root in your womb?"

"No!" she cried, amid continued bloody retching. "I have done nothing that you say I did. You see demons where none exist! I worship God! I am not the devil's bride or a whore of Babylon… I am dying!" She held her belly as a jolt of pain visibly washed over her.

As Inez continued to heave and quake, he reached down and tore open the tattered robe, exposing her bare body to the lamp's glow. Making no attempt to cover herself, the tortured woman fell to the cell floor, clutched at her abdomen and howled in pain, "Aauughh! It hurts. It hurts! It's tearing me inside!"

In the light, her arms, torso, and legs appeared normal. Withered and sagging with age as one would expect on a frail woman in her late years, with a few bruises and sores from her time in the cell, but otherwise unremarkable. None of these features were noticeable, however, when her abdomen was revealed.

She was grotesquely swollen. Engorged with blood like a monstrous tick, her belly was blotchy purple and shiny like an eggplant. The skin of her abdomen and hips were taut with pressure from the interior, pressure so great that her navel had inverted. Sweat slicked her skin and a sweet odor of decay emanated from her pores as she thrashed in agony.

The bishop was struck silent with shock. She had grown to more than twice her previous girth and now appeared even more unnatural.

The Specimen

Only weeks before when she was brought to his attention, despite all evidence to the contrary and the impossibility that a woman her age could conceive, Inez had appeared to be pregnant, with a rounded abdomen and a flushed complexion. The impossibility that she had become impregnated by a man at her advanced age was all the evidence needed to prove that the father was unnatural... a spawn of the eternal fires of damnation.

Now, however, the hellborne source of her offspring was becoming more apparent. Her flesh was mottled – the color of an aging bruise- with shadows of burst blood vessels in concentric circles growing darker as they came closer to the core of her gut. What had been perfectly round only a few days earlier was now distended and ovoid, marked with irregular outgrowths and fluid-filled sacs covering the bottom half of her abdomen.

With a drawn out shriek, the old woman arched her back at an excruciating angle, hurled herself into the air, and then slammed her whole torso to the ground. The bishop jumped back in fear at the sound of her bones breaking from the impact, followed soon by disgust as her bladder and bowels voided noisily. She continued to thrash on the chamber floor. The sounds of cartilage tearing and joints disarticulating were drowned out by her agonized screams.

Finally... silence. Her body lay at awkward angle, sprawled in a puddle of blood, mucus, pus, urine and shit. The smell was even more repulsive than it had been earlier. The bishop covered his mouth with his robe and breathed through the sleeve like a filter. Careful to avoid the body fluids, he stepped around the puddle and leaned to examine her more closely.

"Madre de Dios," he whispered in dismay. "Is she dead?" He nudged her body with his foot, but there was no response. Her robe splayed open, exposing her naked bulk, which seemed frail despite the bulging mass in her abdomen. Could it have been that easy to expel the demon inside her? Or did the stress of her condition combined with his endless indictments contribute to her demise?

It seemed too unlikely, though. She had survived nearly two weeks of alternating isolation and interrogation. From what he could see in the flickering torchlight, she had given up on using the clay bowl provided as a chamber pot and decided to just defecate in the far corner. She had wept, cursed, begged, bargained and railed against his persistent accusations and demands that she repent.

At times the bishop had even felt some pity for the old woman. Despite her dreadful sins, she was truly a victim. Few could withstand such a constant onslaught by Hell's minions and lust was one of their most powerful weapons. Even his Excellency had sometimes felt the pull of sinful desires while conducting an especially feverish interrogation with a ripe young subject. A couple hours of self-flagellation with a barbed lash usually were enough to tamp down those fires, though.

The bishop rose to his feet and gathered his thoughts as he strode toward the cell door. The remains must be cleaned up and burned and the cell must be exorcised of her foul taint, but he would want to examine the contents of her womb first. Over the years he had had firsthand contact with many slaves of darkness, in forms both natural and unnatural, but he had never had the corpse of a demon to inspect closely for an extended period of time. He intended to take full advantage of this opportunity. The knowledge gained from this specimen would be incomparable.

The noise of something dragging across the cell floor broke the silence. The bishop whirled away from the doorway to an incomprehensible sight… Inez's corpse heaving up and down like the bellows of a blacksmith's furnace. The flesh of her abdomen stretched and pulsated as something inside seemed to be probing for a weak section of the muscle wall through which to exit. Multiple areas of the necrotic skin bulged outward as the life inside her carcass strained for egress from its fleshy sepulcher.

The bishop stared frozen in terror as the woman's skin ruptured with a loud rip and the first glimpse of the organism that had formed within her body burst through the remnants of her navel. Leaping backwards in an attempt to escape, he collided with the closed door, hitting his head and spilling scalding lamp oil onto his left hand and forearm. He dropped the lamp, screeching in agony as his hand blistered and bubbled. Flaming oil splattered down his robe and onto his legs beneath. His robe ignited and he collapsed against the door as flames quickly enveloped him, first his clothes, then his hair and face.

The Specimen

With a feeble lunge, he instinctively attempted to roll on the floor to smother the inferno, but it was much too late. Skin blistered, then charred. His lungs and throat were scorched as he tried vainly to breathe. The aqueous humor in his eyes boiled, then burst. Streams of bloody gore ran from his eye sockets down his cheeks. His efforts soon diminished and he burned until finally his body lay in a charred fetal position next to the corpse of Inez Contreras, clinging to consciousness as his life seeped out of him. Unable to speak through his seared throat, he stared blindly at the cavity in Inez's torso with empty cavities where his eyes had been. He heard the plaintive cry of an infant in distress, reached out to comfort it, and died.

*   *   *

The bishop's blackened remains were discovered midmorning next to the savaged body of Inez. The cell and corridor doors were left open and since the guard had inexplicably disappeared from his post, he was used as a convenient scapegoat. The Church moved quickly to erase all signs of the cause of the bishop's demise and he was buried in the graveyard behind the cathedral in which he died. A new Grand Inquisitor was quickly chosen and all mention of the mysterious circumstances of the bishop's death was erased from the public record.

Soon, any rumors of the true circumstances of his death were stifled and removed from Church archives. The subterranean prison was cleansed, both physically and spiritually, and the entrance was sealed as if it had never existed. Weeks later and miles away, the bloated remnants of the guard's body washed ashore near the city of Toledo. He was never identified and Inez's offspring was never found.

PART 4
ENTROPY

The Specimen

Chapter 36 – A Piece of Me

"I am an unfortunate and deserted creature …
I am an outcast in the world forever"
– The Monster, <u>Frankenstein</u> by Mary Shelley

Modern Day – Cambridge, MA

Thousands of insects were crawling under her skin. Sioux just wanted to tear the stitches out and gnaw at the palm of her hand. Chew it down to ligaments and bloody bone. Suck the marrow out and make sure nothing remained. Anything to alleviate the incessant itching that had begun a day after she had sliced her hand open on the lid of the specimen jar. One frantic trip to the emergency room and twenty-two stitches later, it wasn't until Wyatt discovered the grooves in the side of the lid and the razor edges that Sioux had admitted to herself that she hadn't been bit by the thing inside the jar. Chet and Wyatt had some fun with her the following day with their usual juvenile pranks, but finally they toned it down a bit and now, three days later, she only had to endure the occasional jibe.

Goddamn, this itches.

The doctors said she should wait a few days more before removing the stitches, but this was getting to be unfathomable torture.

"Don't scratch it!" warned Chet as he emerged from the storeroom at the back of the store. "I'm not paying for another hospital visit if you tear open the stitches. This one's all you." He was lugging a battered cardboard box filled with an assortment of animal skulls and pseudo-Halloween decorations to the front of the store. Even though more than a month remained until the holiday, Chet was determined to maximize the advertising impact of the season. *Schrödinger's* and Halloween were a natural fit. Customers came in droves looking for the perfect creepy accessory to their costume or decoration for their front stoop. In past years, the store had averaged three times as much profit during the month of October as it earned in any other month of the year. Chet needed this month to be one of the best Octobers ever to even have a chance to break even and hold off the creditors at the end of the year. So far things were

The Specimen

looking pretty good. It wasn't even noon yet on a Tuesday and there were already a half dozen or so customers milling around the front of the store

"It might be worth it," groaned Sioux, rubbing her hand right below the bandage. "This is more painful than when it happened, Chet. I don't think I can wait a couple more days to have these stitches taken out."

"Once they do take them out, I expect you to carry your weight again, Sioux," Chet grumbled. "We can't stop for a moment this month."

"Yessuh, Massuh," she replied, bowing her head in and returning to her paperwork. Since she was not able to lift anything for a few more days, Chet had her working the registers and balancing the books most of the time, occasionally helping customers on the floor when it was busy. Not her idea of fun, but at least she didn't have to sit near that jar anymore. It creeped her out. Of course she knew it hadn't bitten her, but she still felt a weird vibe around it – as if it was watching her with its slimy thoughts, waiting and planning.

Chet rolled his eyes at her comment, and said, "You don't need your hands to talk to the customers. Get off your butt and help someone out now. There's a young blonde woman up by Lumpy. See if you can steer her towards a purchase. Chop, chop!"

He turned around and called up to the front of the store, "Wyatt, make sure you move the Wiccan Literature display closer to the front. We need the customers to take notice and make the connection as soon as they push through the doors"

"Sounds good, boss man," Wyatt answered. He wiped the sweat from his brow and once again pushed his glasses up his nose. His hair was tied back in a scraggly ponytail and he was wearing a sleeveless black tank top from which dangled a pair of red ear buds attached to his IPod, but he was still drenched in perspiration. It figured. Up front, as Chet had noted, there was an extremely hot blonde customer whom he'd been stealing glances at for the past fifteen minutes, and he looked like a sweaty orangutan.

The late September heat wave had unfortunately coincided with Chet's decision to cut down on the electricity bill and shut off the air conditioners. The ancient contraptions rarely worked, but, combined with the lone ceiling fan way above their heads, they normally cooled things down to bearable levels. Now, with only the fan running, everyone was suffering. Even Sioux, who was pushing the legal limits of decency with her black denim Daisy Dukes and hot pink bikini top, was looking a bit bedraggled from the humidity.

Wyatt slipped his ear buds back in and continued with his current project. He had been given free rein by Chet to get creative and design a window display to go along with the month's theme. After a bit of brainstorming, he came up with a plan to gather together a collection of items that could be found in the laboratory of a stereotypical mad scientist such as Dr. Frankenstein from James Whale's film of the same name, or Dr. Pretorius of the sequel, *Bride of Frankenstein*.

He had been working on it since yesterday. So far, there was a large wooden table devoted to medical equipment from the 19th and early 20th centuries: calipers, forceps, lancets, probes, and bone saws. He had gathered a potpourri of chamber pots, and a trephine that appeared not to have been cleaned since it was last used to drill a hole in someone's skull. They had surgical kits that had been used from the Civil War to Vietnam. Straitjackets and manacles from a wide range of asylums. There was a large collection of laudanum and ether bottles, test tubes, decanters, flasks, tubes and funnels of all shapes, colors and sizes. He had even found an intricately detailed medical model of a cadaver's head made of wax, untouched on the left half and completely dissected on the right.

On the shelves to the left of the table, Wyatt had lined up dozens of old anatomical texts from the late 19th century, each bound in leather with hand drawn illustrations on sheets of vellum. Bookending the volumes were a variety of skulls, both human and animal, each with some abnormality that had earned it a place of honor in *Schrödinger's*. The piece de résistance of the entire display was the large specimen jar containing the unfairly accused nemesis of Sioux… Lumpy the Teratoma.

Wyatt had placed the jar in the center of the top shelf where the afternoon sun permeated the citrine liquid, setting it aglow. Initially, Chet hadn't been certain he wanted to display the jar so prominently, but the way it gleamed and cast a glow, it was already having an amazingly positive influence on sales. Passersby responded to the shining like a beacon, a lighthouse luring them to enter the store and browse the items

The Specimen

for sale. They often seemed as in awe of the jar as he had been when he first encountered it. Only a few recoiled in disgust at the sight of the chaotic biology under glass. Some even appeared offended that such an abomination could exist. Most of the customers, however, reveled in the sheer grotesquery of its form. In a certain slant of light, the specimen even appeared to breathe, as if it were in hibernation waiting to emerge from its long winter slumber. Of course, that was simply an optical illusion caused by the occasional jostling of the shelves, swirling the liquid and stirring up the sediment at the bottom of the jar.

Since yesterday morning, when he first brought the jar to the front of the store, pedestrians had been lingering on the sidewalk or meandering inside, just to get a closer look at the specimen. Some were even compelled to place their hands on the glass surface. Wyatt completely understood the urge to do so, but because he had to prevent any possible damage, he moved the jar to a higher shelf out the reach of less careful admirers.

No one had shown enough interest to submit a monetary offer, but Chet still seemed to think that it could fetch somewhere in the neighborhood of $10,000. Perhaps that was wishful thinking, but Wyatt didn't think he was too far off the mark. Supply and demand set the price, and this appeared to be a wholly unique item. Somebody would buy it. For now, though, it was certainly helping sales.

Wyatt put the finishing touches on the Mad Scientist display, after which he told Chet he was taking a short cigarette break outside. He stepped onto the sidewalk and pulled out a yellow crumpled pack of his favorite brand: American Spirit Mellow. He flicked open his Zippo, lit the cig and took a long, deep drag on it, exulting in the sensation with his eyes closed and his face angled toward the sun. He was down to half a pack per day, but didn't think he could go much lower than that. Someday he would have to quit cold turkey, but not today.

It was good to get outside and feel the sun on his face after nearly a full day of grunt work. Even though it was still quite warm and the humidity was stifling, the cool breeze took the edge off Wyatt's discomfort. That, plus the bevy of eye candy strolling by in this unseasonably hot weather, had him in quite a content place. He shut his eyes again and leaned against the brick exterior of the shop, just appreciating the fact that he was twenty-six years old with no debt and a job he enjoyed that gave him enough money to carouse about Cambridge a couple of nights per week and still save a good amount for the future.

Listening to the sounds of the streets around him, the hustle and bustle of activity near and far, was somewhat of a ritual for Wyatt. He noticed sounds with his eyes shut that he would normally overlook. It was easier to single out individual voices and sounds when the white noise from the other senses that were buried for the moment. Wyatt had tried it the other way around (wearing soundproof headphones while watching the passersby), but the results hadn't been as successful.

He could hear a street musician playing the drums a couple blocks away in Harvard Square. In one of the apartments above the store, a young couple was arguing heatedly in Laotian or Cambodian (Wyatt couldn't remember exactly what their nationality was). An angry driver leaned on his horn as traffic backed up at the end of the block. Dogs yowled. Birds sang in the trees lining the streets providing a melodic counterpart to the hum of passing vehicles and the drone of dozens of conversations fading in and out as the participants walked by store. A few feet away someone was moaning and sobbing…

Wyatt opened his eyes. A familiar figure stood ten feet away, collapsed against the glass storefront and weeping.

"Old Harry? Is that you?" Wyatt put out his cigarette and approached the man cautiously, initially unsure whether the individual actually was the well-known Harvard Square character. The distraught man looked over and Wyatt's suspicion was confirmed. "Old Harry? It's Wyatt. What's wrong, bud? Did someone jump you again?"

A little over a year ago, some drunken frat boys visiting from UMass-Amherst had decided that the best way to spend a Saturday night would be to torment a number of the homeless who were constant fixtures around Harvard Square. Old Harry had been a frequent victim, and though he was never seriously injured, his trust in strangers was severely shaken. Since then, Wyatt, Sioux and Chet had helped him out with some food or a couple of bucks here and there. He generally visited the shop nearly every day.

The Specimen

Come to think of it, though, this was the first time Wyatt had seen him in nearly a week. Had something happened to him? He looked exhausted and bedraggled and his clothes hung on him as if he had lost a great deal of weight. Normally, Old Harry was clean-shaven. Wyatt knew that it was a point of pride with Old Harry to be well-groomed, but today his face was covered in patches of salt-and-pepper whiskers. His shirt was stained and rumpled. As he turned to face Wyatt, his eyes were glassy, bloodshot and unfocused and he smelled of alcohol, urine and perspiration. With a long, drawn-out moan, he repeated the word, "Nooooo!" as he sank down to his knees on the sidewalk and crawled away from the storefront.

Wyatt looked him up and down, aghast at his appearance. Old Harry's sudden weight loss and lack of hygiene were certainly causes for concern, but what was most shocking was the condition of his face and hands. What had been an extremely localized case of vitiligo had become severe in a matter of days. When Wyatt last saw Old Harry, the loss of pigment had covered most of his fingers with random splotches on his hands trailing up to his wrists. Other affected areas had included the top of his left ear and a quarter-sized blemish at the corner of his right eyebrow. Since then, it appeared that the vitiligo had increased tenfold. Both hands were completely bleached of color, except for the tip of his right thumb. The bleaching continued up from his wrists and forearms past his elbows. His face was even more drastically affected. The blemish above his eyebrow had expanded to encompass the upper right quadrant of his features. His right eye, originally brown, was now a pale washed-out yellow. The skin around the eye was now bleached up well past his hairline and down to his upper lip. On the left side, his ear was now ninety percent blanched and his cheek was spattered with numerous pale spots.

Wyatt approached Old Harry slowly and squatted next to him. The elderly man continued to shake and sob on the sidewalk. He flinched as Wyatt laid a hand gently on his shoulder and suggested, "Why don't you come into the store, Harry? I'm sure Chet will let you clean up."

Old Harry recoiled in terror, shouting "No!! Noooo! It's evil! It can't be here! It died in the fire!"

Wyatt was confused. Old Harry was staring over Wyatt's head at the store with such abject fear that he felt compelled to look behind him just to be certain that a chainsaw-wielding maniac wasn't sneaking up behind him… broad daylight be damned. Harry began to wail incoherently, occasionally shouting "No!" and "Not again!" Some pedestrians studiously ignored his hysteria, walking on past with feigned indifference, while others hurried across the street to ensure that they would not become involved in an incident that might derail any of their plans. Through the doorway, Wyatt could see Chet striding in their direction bearing a concerned and slightly annoyed look.

Inside *Schrödinger's*, a couple of customers had wandered closer to the storefront to gawk and see who was causing the commotion. One in particular, a pretty young blonde in her early twenties named Crystal, had been asking Sioux incessantly about the specimen jar in the display case. Requesting information about the ugly thing that Sioux had no possibility of knowing. Now, however, she seemed distracted by the scene out front, especially the fact that Old Harry was fixated on the same object in which she had been intrigued. She pulled out her cell phone and pressed "5" to speed dial her boss.

Abruptly, Old Harry tore away from Wyatt's grasp and crawled backwards into the gutter to press his back against a parked car. His wails turned into screams of anguish and his eyes rolled back in his head. He began clawing at his face, carving bloody furrows into his cheeks with ragged fingernails.

The old black man began to rock back and forth, moaning "I saw it die. I saw it die at Greylock. It can't be here. It died in the fire."

Wyatt froze. *Did Old Harry just say "Greylock"? Like the Institute listed on the specimen jar? Could he actually have recognized that thing from his past?* Wyatt was still unsure if Old Harry was going to curl up in a ball or attack him and try to eat his face next like that bath salts guy down in Florida. Chet stood in the doorway paralyzed at the sight, while Sioux rushed forward and knelt next to him, imploring Old Harry to calm down and let her help.

Throughout the entire incident, not one person thought to look and see what it was that had caused Old Harry's meltdown. No one had

The Specimen

their eyes on what was happening in the specimen jar on the top shelf. Not a soul watched the liquid churn and froth as the organism mushroomed open, unfurling tentacles and segmented feelers from within its grisly husk. Nobody saw a long leprous tongue with wriggling feelers at its end unfurl from an orifice at the bottom of the specimen. No one saw the central nodule on its flank swell and bloat until it split down the middle. A small vertical fissure appeared and peeled open, revealing its eye: a mottled, fulvous orb with a striated amber and crimson iris. An eye that stared directly at Old Harry's cowering figure.

If they had continued watching the specimen, they would have seen it lock gazes with Old Harry, soon after which the elderly man began convulsing and foaming at the mouth. They would have seen it press against the glass wall of the jar and turn its attention to the young blonde woman standing in the doorway of the store. They might have seen it lick the inside of the jar and ferociously bump against the glass. Seconds later the tentacles and feelers retracted into its body as the woman snapped her phone shut and looked at the jar one more time before walking swiftly away down the sidewalk.

Chet performed CPR on Old Harry for ten minutes, preserving his life until the ambulance arrived and the EMT's took over. Soon after, standing on the crowded sidewalk off to the side of a crowd of looky-loos, Sioux sobbed in Wyatt's willing arms and Chet spoke solemnly with a pair of police officers while Old Harry was lifted into the ambulance and rushed to the nearest hospital.

Of course, no one was watching the specimen. No one saw the squamous bruise-colored tongues slide hungrily again on the interior of the specimen jar, but, as always, it watched them and planned.

Chapter 37 – Stalking the Bandersnatch

"A cat's rage is beautiful, burning with pure cat flame, all its hair standing up and crackling blue sparks, eyes blazing and sputtering." - William S. Burroughs

Modern Day – Cambridge, MA

Solomon had been hunting, following the rapidly dispersing scent of the bad woman for two days now. He did not have a concept of names. Unlike the fictional Jellicoe Cats, felines were identified to another as a mélange of smells – each one completely unique to the particular animal. The same was true for most humans, though they often masked their natural scents with pungent chemicals that were redolent of machines and disease. The bad woman who attacked his family was an exception, though. She smelled of decaying oranges and old blood. Normally easy to follow in the city's miasma, if not for his injuries.

If anyone had noticed the reddish Abyssinian lurking in the alleys and cross streets of the neighborhoods in the past two days, they would have instantly seen the horrific injuries that he had suffered. Bullet wounds and broken bones that should have left him bleeding out behind a dumpster in one of many filthy alleys in this neighborhood. None had seen him, though. Just as the homeless are ignored by pedestrians most of the time, stray animals rarely earn a glance as they huddled in corners or dodged the relentless parade of feet.

After he was shot, he slept most of the first night lying under a pile of broken-down cardboard boxes while the alien tissue inside him caused his body to more efficiently seal his wounds and regenerate the lost flesh. He woke the next morning ravenous and weak, but no longer in danger of bleeding to death.

Even so, Solomon remained too feeble to hunt when he woke. He sent out a clarion call to any other changed feline brethren within the range of his mind. Within minutes, cats of all varieties were flocking to his alley with offerings of food to help him replenish his energy. A twitching

The Specimen

rat corpse. The remnants of a cheeseburger. A day-old fish head snagged from a dumpster. All gobbled down in minutes.

Now, Solomon barely seemed like the same cat. The only evidence that he had been shot and broken some bones were a couple of shiny hairless puckers the size of dimes on his right flank, a perforated right ear, and an extremely crooked tail. His right eye was also cloudy beneath a small hairless furrow by his ear. One centimeter to the left and he would have been killed by the bullet, but now none of these scars appeared recent. In fact, they appeared at least a year old.

Yesterday, Solomon had returned and scouted out the apartment he had shared with Elvira to find any survivors and to catch a scent from the battle. So many of his herd had been slaughtered defending the old woman who cared for them. The few who were not killed had fled to parts unknown. Solomon sensed them, but they were far off and faint. He smelled her blood as well and, though he could not feel sorrow, he felt an absence. The large black man's stink had ended here in a pool of blood, but the bad young woman's scent had been overladen by people whose sole reason for existence was only to muddy up the olfactory map he wanted to follow.

Her trace had eventually led from the apartment building to a parking spot two blocks away, which was now occupied by an entirely different car at the unpaid meter. The trail petered out, so Solomon continued his quest by methodically searching the surrounding blocks and following an unseen grid up and down through the back corners of Cambridge. When night came without any more discoveries, Solomon retraced his steps to the alley where he ate another sumptuous feast of scraps and alley rats that had been left for him by the other cats.

He set out again soon after dawn the next day, weaving around the street debris and avoiding the feet of single-minded morning pedestrians. After a couple of fruitless hours retracing the same path, a breeze carrying the bad woman's tell-tale scent crossed his path and Solomon stumbled onto a trail so fresh that the woman must have passed this location only moments earlier.

It wafted out from a stairway from an underground T station and swirled down the side streets away from the Charles River. Solomon took off after the scent, darting in and out between people's legs. He turned left at the next block and raced across the street amid a crowd of tourists and local Harvard students. A number of blocks later, the russet cat pulled up short at the foot of a clump of trees sprouting from the sidewalk. Across the street was a large shop with an imposing cast iron store front, through which the bad woman's spoor lingered.

He stayed hidden, though. Now was not the best time to sneak into the store. A throng of people were gathered around an emaciated old black man sprawled on the sidewalk. Another black man, this one younger and chubby, was pressing on the older man's chest until an Emergency Unit arrived. Directly next to them was a young, weeping girl and a tall, gangly fellow trying to keep back the onlookers.

Off to the side, standing in the doorway of the shop, were three customers in complete rubbernecking mode, watching the spectacle on the sidewalk. The couple in front were taking pictures to immediately post on their joint Facebook photo albums. Behind them was the woman from the other day. The bad one who try to kill him. The bad one who killed his friends. Solomon stared at her from his hiding spot, ready to follow her if she suddenly left in a hurry.

But then everything changed in an instant. Something horribly astonishing caught his eye and he forgot about her for the moment. Many other cats were here as well, milling about all within fifty yards of the doorway. All were thralls like Solomon, and all were focused on one thing – the object floating in the murky, liquid-filled specimen jar on the top shelf of the display in the shop's window.

Hackles raised, Solomon froze in place, overwhelmed by the sheer force of his emotions – foreign emotions for which he had no frame of reference.

Awe. Hostility. Sympathy. Disgust. Reverence. Fear.

These feelings all came from within Solomon, but not from him. They radiated from the flesh buried inside his body that made him a thrall

The Specimen

to the Cluster. He recognized what was inside the jar… and he realized that the specimen recognized him and his fellow felines, identifying them as tools to be utilized if needed and nothing more.

Solomon understood this just as he realized that this creature could easily wrest control of all of the thralls within range. Considering the distance between them and the Cluster, as well as the weakened condition of their sire, the question was not if this would happen, but when. Solomon could already sense the mental tentacles of the creature probing his mind, just as it did the same thing to his fellow cats.

The ambulance and police arrived within moments and, after attending to the man on the ground, the EMTs loaded him into the vehicle and took off for the hospital. Within seconds, the crowd of looky-loos broke up and dispersed to search for more tragedies that would give credence to their delusionary beliefs that they were more "blessed" than the victims because they had been spared.

The bad woman was nowhere to be found. A fresh scent trail led away from the store at a hurried pace, but Solomon ignored it for now. The specimen had other uses for him and she would have to wait.

Chapter 38 – Ghosts and Shadows

"I became insane, with long intervals of horrible sanity."
- Edgar Allen Poe

Modern Day – En route to UMass Medical Center

Harry was bleeding out. Arterial spray painted the walls of the ambulance. Scarlet arcs in rhythmic ebbs and flows. Every scar had been torn off simultaneously. A pool rapidly covered the entire floor of the vehicle with sticky coppery tenacity, and steadily rose with every passing minute. Blood leaked from his pores. Seeped from his nose, ears and eyes. Gushed from his throat with gobbets of freshly torn flesh floating in the puddles of gore. The tide of blood washed over his face in waves each time the ambulance careened around a turn. He screamed so long and loud, his larynx ruptured and emitted a long high-pitched whistle. Just as the whistle seemed it couldn't screech any higher …

It stopped.

Instantaneously, as if a new scene had been spliced onto the film of his life, all the blood was completely gone - vanished - and he was finally awake in the ambulance on the way to the hospital. The hallucination that he was bleeding to death was over. He was strapped down to a stretcher but all the memories he had suppressed for the past half century were coming to the surface. With a vengeance. The sight of the Rider, the monster that had once been a part of him, had blindsided him.

Like a leviathan eel lying in the centuries-old muck at the bottom of a stagnant lake, the horrors from his past stirred up the muddy debris of his mind with its convulsions, sending once hidden fossils to the surface. Just as the imaginary tsunami of blood had once flooded the ambulance, his restored memories rushed past his former mental barriers and he felt as if he was reliving them simultaneously…

Jarvis Harold Varney, Jr. was three years old and he couldn't get to sleep because his big brother Earl had told him that he would grow a

The Specimen

watermelon inside his belly if he swallowed some seeds. He was scared something awful. It was too late to do anything about it since he had already swallowed a couple seeds by the time Earl had shared this nugget of knowledge with him. Harry (Mama only called him Jarvis Harold, Jr. when she was mad at him) didn't want to die from a watermelon busting open his tummy before he grew up and got to be a daddy himself...

And then Harry was five years old, waiting at the door for Daddy to come home from work. They had a brand new television in the family room and Daddy said he could stay up tonight and watch all the cowboys shoot things up on Rawhide because he had done so well in school...

He was seven and crying in the middle of the street next to the shattered, bloody body of his cat, Fred, after he had been flattened by a speeding taxi...

He was eight and Willie Faraday was on top of him on the playground, punching the snot out him because he had told Eddie Sowders and Calvin Pinckney that he thought Willie was kinda dumb. He should've known better than to say something to Eddie because he was worse at keeping secrets than his big sister Maisie and that was pretty darn bad...

He was ten and he and his little sister Flo were hiding in their room under the bedcovers covering their ears. Momma was yelling at Daddy again about his constant "drinking and carousing with them cheap whores."...

He was eleven, just moved from New Jersey to Massachusetts to help take care of his sick grandparents. "It looks like we'll be here for the long haul. At least until they kick the bucket," he overheard Momma say to Daddy one night when he was supposed to be in bed...

He was twelve, watching three men mutilating a fat black man on a concrete floor – a man he somehow knew - and he was too scared to help him...

He was thirteen, pinned against the wall in the common room at Greylock, watching one man bite another patient's nose completely off, then crunch on it like a piece of celery on a crudité platter...

He was strapped face-down and spread eagle on an operating table as unseen surgeons carved the Rider off his back and fragments of his mind were excised along with the creature ...

He was curled under his bed at Greylock when the lights went out for hours as howling groups of the most violent inmates ran pell mell through the corridors ...

He was being carried through the trees by a massive person. The bright orange glow of a burning building raged through the trees behind them...

He was lost in the mountains, huddled in the hollow of a tree as a freezing autumn squall soaked him to the bone ...

He ate a raw fish that he found floating in a stream, then spent the next day sobbing for his family as he hid in a small cave, puking and shitting himself ...

He saw a skeletal homeless man roasting a dog over a fire under a bridge in Worcester ...

He was searching from some shelter in an alley when he found a boy who had died of an overdose in the middle of the night, needle still hanging from his arm. Harry took his shoes ...

He was vomiting behind a restaurant after eating the scraps of a chicken parmesan dinner from the dumpster. There were maggots in his puke ...

He was panhandling in Davis Square when a young Mexican girl brought him a warm bowl of menudo that was quite possibly the best meal of his life ...

He was jumped by a couple of drunk frat boys who found it necessary to compensate for their insecurities and inadequacies by beating on a defenseless old black man ...

And on and on and on ...

The specters from his past whipped by faster and faster until they appeared like an endless deck of cards, flipping past each individual image

The Specimen

in a blur until they exploded in a shower of spades, diamonds, clubs and hearts...

Fifty-Two Pick-up.

Official Report on the Greylock Incident

February 24, 1966
To: Members of the Governing Council, ACME Group
From: James P. Kilcannon, Agent-in-Charge
RE: Greylock Incident (Scarpa Implantation)

Council Members,

The remaining entries complete the lot of Dr. Coe's notes we were able to retrieve and restore to legibility. We believe that, even with the missing pages, a clear narrative is obvious. The causes of the disaster here at Greylock were a combination of hubris, poor judgment, and finally, simple bad luck.

- JPK

* * *

Day 67
    As expected, last night's surgery was a complete success. The Rider, still sedated by the Halperidol in its solution, seemed to flow directly onto Scarpa's spinal cord once it was placed on the exposed nerves.
    Colfax was even able to assist me in the surgery. His fingers have healed quite nicely. I feel like he finally has realized how lucky he is to have the chance to work with me. And to do it on a project of such importance. To study these creatures and understand their abilities is the path to their eventual extinction. We must find a way to eliminate every last one of them. If it takes generations to find a weapon against them, so be it.

The Specimen

They have lived among humans for thousands of years. Exactly how long may never be known, but every fact we learn about the Riders is another weapon to add to our armory.

Scarpa is now recovering in his room. I also performed some minor surgery on his nasal cavity to slightly camouflage a wound he received in August when another patient supposedly bit his nose off in a fight. The pretense to take him into surgery was a minor cosmetic fix, one of many to come that would eventually rebuild him an entirely new nose. Of course, this is a lie. We will only need him as long as we can use the Rider for experimentation. I don't expect that he will be the last Host we require.

- GC

Day 68

The Cluster has continued to surprise me. It has begun to mirror my actions and when it attempts to speak, it is obviously attempting to mimic my vocal intonations as well. Although it hasn't advanced to the point that I can hold a conversation with it, it does seem to understand me more and more each day.

It seems that Jameson's body will sustain the creature for quite some time. In the days that followed its last meal, it has shown no interest in any meal whatsoever. Hutchens' corpse had to be removed because it was quickly rotting and stinking up the lab. I had Fenton collect the corpse and dispose of it, but there is still a stain on the floor in the vague shape of his body, caused by the fluids that leaked out over four days.

Yesterday, the mimicking was taken to a new level. Since the first day, the Cluster has followed me around like an overgrown, gelatinous puppy. The pseudopods and tentacles that it formed were always in motion. Feeling surfaces, tracing letters, and occasionally attempting to grasp items off the table or from my hand.

This time was different. I wasn't around as much these past few days as I had been the previous week, and I am amused to say that the Cluster seems to have missed me. Or possibly it simply missed interaction with a living being. When I entered the lab and opened the door to the creature's room (I can no longer think of it as the storage closet), it slid forward and sat there, bouncing up and down waiting for my full attention.

I made it wait a few seconds to assert my dominance, before turning my attention to the creature. It sat there, quivering in what seemed to be excitement, about the size of one of those prize-winning pumpkins seen at your average county fair. It went still, then suddenly *morphed* its mass in an instant to an immediately recognizable form.

I stepped back, startled at its transformation. Looming over me now was a featureless manlike figure, well over six feet in height, and easily more than three hundred pounds. Two arms, two legs, and a gourd-sized lump for a head. The Cluster stood there in its new form for a few strained seconds before collapsing down into its original blobby form.

I was shocked for a few seconds before whispering, "Do something else."

Shuddering again, its flesh flowed sinuously in a spiral, thinning out and stretching to a length of nearly 20 feet. Like a serpent, it raised what would be its head and swayed, level with my face. I held my clasped hands up and pulled them apart. The Cluster mirrored them by opening like the bloom of a flower

For the next few hours, as I gave it instructions through detailed gestures and short commands, it went through a variety of forms as I tested its capabilities. Eventually it was able to form rudimentary scales, horns, claws and teeth. At one point, it even started to mimic my facial expressions. All this in one afternoon.

I feel like I've found a new pet.

- GC

The Specimen

Chapter 39 – A Meeting of Minds

"Most people are other people. Their thoughts are someone else's opinions, their lives a mimicry, their passions a quotation." - Oscar Wilde

Modern Day – UMass Medical Center

The old black man was dying. *He looks dead already*, thought Scott as he looked over at his new roommate. *If he didn't snore like a gorilla with a deviated septum, they would have already taken him to the morgue.* The man was gray and deflated, tucked behind a partially closed curtain partition. A single monitor occasionally beeped, tracking his heartbeat. The only other sound Scott had heard was a hacking phlegmy wheezing every few minutes. The man's two friends, a chubby black guy with glasses and a smoking hot Latina girl in her early 20's, had stayed for an hour before leaving a few minutes earlier. If Scott hadn't been in a partial body cast, he would have tried to talk to the girl. *Pffft! Who am I kidding?* he thought. *I don't have the balls to say one word to a girl like that. I would've been too scared.*

Scott had the television tuned to the SyFy Channel and muted, but the only show on was that ridiculous Sasquatch Brigade reality show and there's only so much close captioned idiocy one can take in a single sitting.

Since he had been transferred from St. Frank's two days ago, Scott had the room all to himself, until this afternoon when the old man had been wheeled in on a stretcher. Despite the fact that the man hadn't yet woken up, Scott was glad for the company. Even when his grandparents had come to visit, he had felt as if they looked at him differently now… as if they thought he would kill himself like his father had. The sheriff and his two deputies were also keeping him at arm's length. *Could they actually consider him a suspect in the Monahan family's deaths?*

Deputies Booker and Sloan were nice to him, especially Booker because Scott knew her son Simeon from the school play last year, but Sheriff Smucker… Well, let's just say he was a piece of work. He looked like a bloated rooster, puffing out his chest every time he entered the room, and he always had a different colored toothpick in his mouth that he rolled back and forth from one corner to another, stopping every so often to suck on it as he pretended to ruminate over what had just been said to him.

Scott could see right through the little man's bluster. It helped that his grandparents apparently thought that the Sheriff was a buffoon as well. His grandfather rolled his eyes nearly every time that Smucker opened his mouth, but he didn't say anything. Scott's grandmother, on the other hand, wasn't shy about showing her feelings. She had known Smucker when he was a teenager and he was "a puny piss-ant back then, too." Unable to hold back, she had burst out laughing yesterday afternoon when Smucker had barged into his hospital room and stated that they were making "good progress" on tracking the monster who had slaughtered Hank and his parents and kidnapped the two girls. The Sheriff obviously hadn't appreciated her lack of faith in his abilities by the way he had stalked out of the room, purple-faced and fuming.

Thankfully, there hadn't been any voices in Scott's head since that first day he had switched hospitals. He wanted to chalk that incident up to a concussion he probably had suffered when he was hit by the car. *And shot twice. Don't forget that,* he thought. It was either that or just a case of shock. Most people would have gone completely off the deep end after having witnessed his friend's family get murdered, getting chased through the forest by a gun-toting goon, and finally shot twice by said goon before tumbling into the path of a mini-van that ran him over. All this before waking up to a hospital room with three corpses in it. Two of them riddled with bullets and one ground into meat pulp. It was beyond surreal.

Even weirder were the stories he had heard about the man who had stopped the two fake cops who had tried to kill him. The only characteristic that anyone could agree on was that he was huge – over seven feet tall and about 350-400 pounds. Sheriff Smucker had questioned the lone security guard who had survived and he quickly dismissed his report, calling it the ramblings of a senile old coot.

"Stupid-ass gomer thinks it was a monster", sputtered the Sheriff when he heard the report. "That's all I need now. A buncha Hollywood

The Specimen

monster hunters walking all over town ridiculing our way of life. I won't put up with it," he had growled.

One of his current doctors had said that he might be suffering from PTSD. He looked up the definition on his tablet - Post-Traumatic Stress Disorder – and he didn't think that was the cause. Wasn't that the disorder that caused kids in school to go all Columbine?

The strangest part about the whole incident was that his injuries seemed to be healing much faster than anyone could explain. Oh, he still looked like hell. His face and torso were painted with blackish-purple bruises and his arms and legs were still in casts, but the swelling had receded quite a bit, and he could raise his arms and bend at the hips. His pain was nearly nonexistent, and his doctors seemed confused the last time they had examined him, as if they wanted to say something about his condition, but feared they might jinx him. *You don't talk about a no-hitter while the pitcher is still tossing the ball,* his grandfather was often fond of saying.

Scott didn't care about what a medical miracle he supposedly was. He only wanted to leave the hospital as soon as they would allow him, and try to see what information he could dig up to help the police catch Hank's killers. He had overheard the Sheriff speaking with his grandparents the previous evening when he was pretending to be asleep. Hank and his parents, Chuck and Kate, were all confirmed dead, but Sydney and Dahlia had not yet been found, which meant, however unlikely it may be, they could still be alive.

The old man snorted again in his sleep, and then woke up with a plaintive cry. Scott heard some confused muttering and rustling of sheets before a weak voice trembled from behind the curtain, "Hello? Is there anyone in the room with me?"

Loathe to answer, but feeling as if he had no choice, Scott answered him, "You're in the hospital, sir. I'm your roommate, Scott, but I'm stuck in my bed so I can't help you out."

The curtain was slowly pulled aside, revealing the old man seated on the side of his bed. He was wearing a baggy threadbare hospital gown that barely made it to his knees. His hair was unwashed and frizzy, his eyes were rheumy and bloodshot, and his exposed skin was covered in a motley pattern of white blotches from his forehead to his ankles. He was skinny and looked like he hadn't eaten (or washed) in days.

Looking around nervously as if something would jump out of the shadows at him, the old man stood slowly, wincing as he straightened and hobbled a few steps closer to look Scott up and down. He smelled sour.

"You… ain't kiddin'," he agreed, looking at Scott's multiple casts. "I bet… that hurt." He spoke slowly, carefully as if he was out of practice with the act of speech.

"I don't remember much of the accident, but it's not as bad as it looks. The doctors say I'm doing really well"

"Could've … fooled me… You look like … you … got hit by a truck"

"A mini-van, actually. At least that's what they told me."

The old man looked up with a restrained grin, "No… Shit? Didn't nobody … tell you not to play … in traffic? You look smarter… that that … son."

He looked around the room and saw the lavatory door. He groaned, "Don't go nowhere… Gotta piss… be right back."

With a belabored turn, he hobbled to the restroom with his gown open in the rear for all to see. On his back, past the gap in the gown, the flesh was a giant keloid scar roughly shaped like an inverted triangle, shiny and smelted like the molten wax on the side of a candle. The flesh beneath the scar was sunken and concave, appearing as if a giant ice cream scoop had carved out a few pounds of muscle.

Scott tried to look away but couldn't stop staring. He wondered what hellish injury could have caused such a mark. Oblivious to his scrutiny, the old man entered the white and chrome bathroom, closing the door behind him.

* * *

The Specimen

Before all this happened, Scott had wished for his life to change. He had stumbled through school, asleep half the time, ditching it altogether with Hank a couple days a month so they could hide out by the local quarry and get high. His main goal in life was only to smoke enough or drink enough to muffle the harsh, bright reality of everyday monotony. Boredom was his main complaint. Of course, his grandfather had an answer for his problems when he let it slip out one day after an especially mind-numbing day in school.

"Boredom is underrated. Be careful what you wish for, Scotty," he had said with a serious look at his grandson. "I heard somewhere that the Chinese have a curse for their worst enemies that means 'may you live in interesting times.' Now I don't know if it's bullshit or not, but to me, it's just another way of saying, 'It could be worse'. "

Scott didn't have a response for that

"And, believe me," Bud Ritchie had continued. "You don't want to know how much worse it could possibly get."

* * *

Scott heard the toilet flush and water running in the sink before the old man came out, looking a bit more refreshed. He had wet his hair and slicked it back. Hobbling over, he sat on the chair next to Scott's bed with a deep sigh before introducing himself, "You said you were Scott… right? Call me… Harry."

Scott nodded and they shook hands.

"Why are you in the hospital?" Scott asked. "I don't mean to be rude. If I am, I'm sorry. Your friends came in with you but I didn't get a chance to speak with them before they left."

Harry grimaced, took a deep breath and said, "I saw something… that I thought was… dead, and I became very frightened.

Scott, commiserating with Harry, replied, "I can understand that. I was so scared, just before my accident, that I thought I was going to be killed. Almost did, too."

He continued speaking and eventually told Harry about what he had seen through the windows of the Monahan kitchen, the ensuing chase through the forest, and even what he had been told about the incident at St. Frank's with the giant man-monster saving him from the counterfeit police. Harry remained silent throughout the entire telling of the story. Scott spilled everything. What he saw. What the men in the Monahans' house had looked like and their horrible actions. Hank's death and Sydney's abduction. He didn't know this strange old man from the streets, but he felt an inexplicable kinship with him. When Scott finished, he fell silent.

Harry was still. His eyes were wide open, but he was frozen, blind to his surroundings as if he was looking directly into the headlights of a Mack truck about to splatter him all over the pavement. Tears trickled in the wrinkled crevasses of his cheeks. He whispered plaintively, "No... not again."

"Harry? Is something wrong?" Scott asked. "Should I call for a nurse? You look horrible."

Harry shook his head, released a long, deep sigh and replied, "No... Scott. I just realized... something dreadful and... from the de...scription of your experiences... I'm afraid you are part of it, too."

Scott was confused, but over the next half hour, as Harry told his fifty-year-old tale from the start to the finish, he became silent and, soon, as his own tears ran down his face – no matter how astonishing the story seemed - he believed it all.

The Specimen

Chapter 40 – No Pleasure without Pain

"God is a concept by which we measure our pain"
- John Lennon

Modern Day – Cambridge, MA

If Wyatt Ferris had ever stopped to ponder what it would be like to have a taser applied to his genitalia, he wouldn't have even come close to imagining the sheer agony that he would feel right at that moment. He screeched at the top of his lungs, trying to cup his groin and fend off another attack, but the young woman wielding the taser easily kicked his hands aside and jammed the prongs into his groin again. She pulled the trigger, sending another blast of electricity directly into his man parts. Collapsing to the floor, he curled up into a fetal position and whimpered quietly.

"Stay down, Shaggy," she ordered him. "Or next time I'll give you a prostate exam with this little toy of mine. And I won't use any lube."

Jerking and convulsing, Wyatt was unable to respond in any way except nod his head. Mortified, he realized that he had lost control of his bladder and pissed his pants. Not completely, but enough to leave a noticeably wet stain on his crotch. Strange as it may have seemed, he didn't want this young woman to find out about the wet pants. Even after this unexplained taser attack, Wyatt didn't want to be emasculated any more.

That ship has long since sailed, he thought to himself. *Who is this chick anyway? And why is she acting like we have something she wants? What could she want in this place?* She didn't look like their usual customers at all… and Wyatt was beginning to realize that he should have been suspicious of her from the start.

* * *

Less than four minutes before ...

Chet had decided to close the store for the rest of the day after Old Harry's sidewalk meltdown. He asked Wyatt to clean and close up shop for the day while he and Sioux headed over to the hospital to check on the old man. Wyatt was only glad to oblige. He hated hospitals. Every time he had ever been in one of these death factories had been to visit someone who was dying. He even hated going to the veterinarian. The last time he had visited one was when his beagle Gus had to be put to sleep five years earlier.

Wyatt had counted all the receipts and cashed out the drawer by 7pm. It would have been a pretty good day if they had closed on time, but now, nearly three hours early, they were hundreds of dollars below the target sales. Chet would not be happy. If only the caller who had inquired about the jar had come to the store as she had promised. Perhaps she would have purchased it and Chet could have been able to hold off the creditors for a couple more months.

Wyatt sighed and shook his head. Chet had no idea that his financial problems were common knowledge, but it wasn't all that hard to figure out since Wyatt worked there full time and saw the gradual decrease in customers and sales. He finished wiping down the counter and grabbed the rolling ladder. The upper windows at the front of the store needed to be cranked shut. Chet had opened them in the morning to create some circulation and dilute the stagnant air, but the forecast of rain tonight made it necessary to seal them. Moisture and old artifacts didn't usually go well together.

RAP! RAP! Wyatt cursed under his breath and looked toward the front window display. Some idiot was knocking on the door to *Schrödinger's* and he or she was obviously ignoring the CLOSED sign in the window. Wyatt slowly sauntered toward the front of the store with the intent to gesture at the sign and then return to his work after dismissively inserting his ear buds and turning away. At least that was his plan until he realized that the *idiot* was the hot young blond woman from before. *Off the charts hot*, thought Wyatt. He stopped in his tracks for a few seconds before realizing that he was staring. She smirked at his dumbstruck

The Specimen

expression and, giving a shy little smile, tapped on the window again with a long red fingernail and gestured to the doorknob. He shook his head free of cobwebs and opened the door.

"I'm sorry, miss, but we're closed for the night," he stated with what he hoped was a truly regretful look. "The owner had a family emergency that needed immediate attention."

"Aww, that's too bad," pouted the woman. "I was interested in a specific item that I saw the other day."

She was extremely fit, dressed like a soccer mom going out for a run – tight black yoga pants, track jacket with a low cut pink Lycra top and cross trainers. A bit too light for the current weather, in his opinion. The sun had just set and a chilly breeze was already swirling through the streets.

The young woman's eyes were so large and such a deep sea green that Wyatt nearly missed the only flaw she seemed to have. Two vertical scratches ran the length of each of her cheeks as if some animal had tried to use her face as a scratching post. She had attempted to camouflage the wounds with cover-up, but it was as plain as day that they must have hurt like hell. He was caught staring again and she stepped closer, challenging him with her eyes.

"Um… anyway," he stammered after an awkward silence. "We'll be open again tomorrow at ten. Maybe you could come back then?" He could smell her perfume. Something citrusy and clean-smelling that probably came in a bottle shaped like a ballerina.

She furrowed her brow and answered, "Hmm, maybe…" Pursing her lips, she looked behind her to the left and right. "I don't think tomorrow works for me. It has to be today."

As she spoke, she pulled a small metal tube similar to a halogen mini-flashlight from her pocket. With the push of a button, two metal prongs extended just as she pressed it into his armpit and pulled the trigger. Wyatt was immediately paralyzed as thousands of volts coursed through his body and disrupted his nervous system. Every centimeter of his skin felt as if it were engulfed in flame. Every muscle, ligament and tendon became taut as razor wire on the verge of slicing through the layers of his flesh.

She pulled the taser away from his side and kicked the door shut behind her before jamming the prongs between his legs and pulling the trigger again.

"That one's for staring at my tits," she snarled.

Wyatt rolled to the side and vomited on the floor. The combination of pain and nausea had rendered him speechless. As he writhed in a fetal position, the woman closed the door behind her and strode into the store, heading directly for the display with the specimen jar on the top shelf.

"Well, well," she said. "Look what we have here. This is what all the fuss is about? Well, damn, this ugly thing had better be worth all the trouble it's caused."

Smirking, she turned around and asked Wyatt, "Where's the ladder, Carrot Top?"

Chapter 41 – That Special Feeling

"The future starts today, not tomorrow."
– Pope John Paul II

"That turkey panini was actually pretty good, honey. How was your soup?" asked Rosemary Ritchie as she and her husband Bud left the hospital cafeteria. Not expecting a response, she rummaged in the purple saddlebag she called a purse, pulled out a squeeze bottle of hand sanitizer, pumped it liberally in one palm and thoroughly rubbed it over her hands before offering it to Bud.

Lost in thought, Bud shook his head and grunted noncommittally. Rosemary glanced at him with a concerned frown. She knew these past couple of days had been nerve-wracking for the two of them, but Bud normally wasn't this taciturn. He was certainly getting crotchety as he got older, but he had never been the type to just clam up and keep his thoughts to himself. Since Scott had been sleeping earlier, they had left his room to do some shopping and take their minds off the situation for a few hours, but it hadn't had any effect on Bud.

Rosemary was worried. She hadn't seen Bud this down for so long since they had heard about Vic's suicide a few years ago. Back then, he had seemed to be holding in a white-hot rage at his only son for being so selfish and abandoning Scott when he had needed his father the most. This time around, however, he was cold and preoccupied, ignorant of how his mood affected those around him.

"Milton Schuyler Ritchie," Rosemary said, stopping in her tracks and switching into her legendary schoolmarm voice. "Cut the crap. If you want to mope around, you have every right to do so. It's not like I haven't been irrational and moody at times over the years, but don't think you're shutting me out. One thing we've always done is communicate and we're not stopping now."

Bud turned to her and rubbed both hands down his face before reaching out and grasping her hand.

"Damn it, you're right, dear," he muttered. "I should know better than to try and hide anything from you."

"Someday you'll figure it out," she smirked.

"I hope so," he replied as they entered the elevator. He pushed the button and waited for the doors to shut before he continued, "I'm getting that feeling again, Rosie. Just like with Vic. It won't go away."

"We've talked about that, Bud," she chided gently.

"I know, I know. It doesn't change things, though. I feel like something is crawling slowly up my spine, and as it climbs higher, my body gets weaker."

"Maybe we should have a doctor check you out, honey. It could be something else."

"It's not."

"I know you feel that way, but I also know that you avoid doctors more than anyone I've ever met. You just hope things go away and when they don't, you suffer even more."

The elevator opened on the 4th floor and they stepped out, turning right toward Scott's room. They could see Nate Sloan seated on a rickety folding chair at the end of the hall. The young deputy had his hat over his eyes and appeared to be asleep, but when they approached, he flipped up his brim and nodded.

"You look like shit, Nate," greeted Bud.

"Why, thank you, Mr. Ritchie," grinned Sloan. "I always have appreciated your blunt perspective on life."

"Anything happen while we were gone?" asked Rosemary, sidestepping the witty male banter.

"His new roommate finally woke up," replied Sloan. "They've been talking for over half an hour. Seem to have really hit it off."

The Specimen

"Really?" she replied. "Huh. I'm surprised. What do you think, Bud?" She turned to her husband and saw that he was holding his chest and looking green.

"I think I need to sit down," said Bud. He pulled open the door to Scott's room and stopped abruptly at the sight of the mottled old man sitting next to Scott's bed, deep in conversation with his grandson. The old man looked up, their eyes locked and suddenly Bud knew.

It couldn't be him. Could it? He had to be dead. It's been more than fifty years. The patchwork patterns on his skin, though they were much more widespread than when he first saw him, were in the same spots on his face and arms. And his eyes... There was an innocence there that Bud recognized, a strong willful kindness that Bud had never seen in anyone else since that fateful day when he saw the boy abducted.

It must be him.

Rosemary stepped forward and introduced herself warmly before stepping aside and subtly hinting to Bud that he should follow suit, when a familiar hideous sensation drowned Bud in nausea and vertigo. *Something truly dangerous was coming*, and his ability to sense it was again working to take him out of the picture.

He vomited on his shoes and collapsed to his knees, but before everything disappeared in a curtain of blackness, he looked directly at Harry, pointed and said "Samaritan."

Bud fell to the floor unconscious.

Chapter 42 – Opie and Little Miss Psycho

"I say violence is necessary. It is as American as cherry pie." - H. Rap Brown

Modern Day – Cambridge, MA

Valentine was feeling extra grumpy tonight. She had wanted to take her time with the hipster store clerk and release some of the tension that had been building since that fiasco at the old bitch's apartment the other day, but Dr. Colfax was adamant that she collect the specimen and return with it right away. No time for extracurricular fun. If anyone else had tried to keep her from practicing her hobbies, she would have just ignored them, but Dr. Colfax was special. He always knew what was best for her, and he never lied. He was the only person who really understood her needs, but he also knew that there was a time for business and a time for play. Fun time could wait until after the objective had been met.

Instead of a lengthy cutting session with Alfred E. Neumann here, she would have to make it quick and neat. That didn't mean that she wasn't allowed to take a couple souvenirs with her for later, did it? Perhaps an eyeball, or maybe a testicle. Something she could roll between her fingers on the ride back to Hartford. That should keep her from fidgeting and biting her nails to bloody nubs again.

Some of her colleagues were freaked out by her strange habits, which was why she hadn't been assigned a new partner since Stoopes had gotten himself killed. Normally, a new one would show up, scientifically chosen by compatibility, within a day, but it seemed that Valentine would be going solo for the next week or so. At least until they could coerce another person to make the ultimate sacrifice and partner up with Psycho Bitch, as she was known in Acme circles.

"Hey, Ron Weasley, hurry up with that stepladder," she barked at the tall clerk as he hobbled out of the storeroom. "Or I'll give those little nuts of yours another zap!"

The Specimen

* * *

"I'm coming," muttered Wyatt. He was sweating heavily, more from fear and nervousness, than the actual heat. The stepladder had been hanging on the wall from a hook. Next to the ladder were a couple of similar hooks from which hung Wyatt's battered ten-speed bike that he rode into work every day. Behind the bike, on another smaller hook, was an old Rastafarian tam that had belonged to Chet's father, Marvin, and had been there since the day the old man had passed away over a decade earlier. Beneath the tam was a small black button set into the wall that had never been pressed since it was first installed fifteen years ago. When activated, a silent alarm alerting the Cambridge police was triggered and officers would be sent out as soon as possible. At least, that's what was supposed to happen, but to be truthful Wyatt had no idea if the alarm even still worked.

When Wyatt reached into the storeroom and took down the metal stepladder, the edge of the door partially obscured him and he took his chance. Whether he had suddenly been afflicted with a wave of reckless insanity or a moment of pure clarity, he pressed the button beneath the tam and prayed more than he had prayed in decades.

Nothing happened,

Of course, that was to be expected. It was supposedly a silent alarm after all. He turned back through the door, handling the stepladder awkwardly with both hands and nearly stumbling into the beautiful blonde sadist who was holding him captive.

"Careful there, Opie," she admonished him. "You wouldn't want to bump into anything now, would ya?"

Wyatt just grunted. *Opie? Ron Weasley? What happens when she runs out of nicknames for me? Better for me to keep my mouth shut, do what she wants and hopefully stay out of trouble with Little Miss Psycho here*, he thought.

Thirty seconds later, he leaned the ladder up against the stack of bookshelves at the front of the store. He stepped back and received a quick kick in the shin when he didn't start climbing.

"Get a move on," she said pointing up the ladder. "Climb up and bring that puppy down here."

"I'm not sure I can," he said, as he clenched his teeth against the pain. "Carry that down from there, I mean. It's heavy. We needed two people to put it up there in the first place."

"Do I look like I give a good goddamn?" she snarled. "Do it or I'll be eating your nuts with my scrambled eggs tomorrow for breakfast. Understand?"

Wyatt shut his mouth and nodded in submission. He took the first two steps of the ladder warily, then looked up at his target, the glass jar four shelves above him. Squinting, he noticed that something changed since he last looked at the jar. From this angle, the yellow liquid seemed cloudy. Almost as if the sediment had been churned or shaken. Lumpy was an indistinct, shadowy form drifting in the muddy liquid.

A rapid flash of motion whipped by in the jar, almost leaving an afterimage on his retinas. He flinched slightly, and came within centimeters of falling backwards. Ten or twelve feet to the floor and the woman with the taser.

What the... What in Hell was that?

"If you drop and shatter the jar, you'll be picking up the shards of glass with your mouth. Understand me?" she hissed at him when he recovered his balance.

He nodded, mumbled "Okay", and started up again, gripping the ladder tightly. Something was causing the turbulence in the jar, but what could it be? The obvious answer just was not possible. Lumpy was a dead piece of meat. The turmoil inside the specimen jar had to be coming from outside. A subsonic earthquake? Vibrations from traffic? Whatever it was, it didn't matter now.

The Specimen

Wyatt drew level with the jar and braced himself as he attempted to figure how he could possibly carry it down the ladder by himself. The residue of blood and dead tissue swirling in the container obscured any sight of the jar's resident. The mixture was so cloudy and muddied, it reminded Wyatt of oily broth from a foul stew. Leftover shreds of dead flesh churned in a constant whirlpool allowing only infrequent glimpses of Lumpy.

He squinted and leaned forward, his nose mere inches from the glass. Condensation fogged the inside glass. How was that possible? That would indicate a cycle of moisture, wouldn't it? Damn it. What was causing the motion in the jar?

Lumpy drifted closer to the glass, spinning in time with the current. As it bumped against the interior of the jar, Wyatt noticed that the large nodule on its side now had a vertical slit down its center that was slightly parted. *It looks like it wants to kiss someone*, he thought. *Or eat them...*

"Are you admiring the view up there?" called his captor. "Pick up the pace, cowboy... or do you require some more motivation?"

"Just trying to figure this out so I don't drop it," he answered, looking down at her. She did not look like she was inclined to be patient.

He turned back to the jar and recoiled in terror. The specimen in the jar had unfurled to nearly twice its original size. Multiple tendrils flailed against the glass, surrounding a mottled yellow eye and a tooth-lined orifice that was sucking the glass insistently.

The thing was alive!

Wyatt squawked out loud and instinctively put his hands in front of his face. He stumbled back and suddenly he was falling, plummeting with barely enough time to think *Oh Shi-!*

The woman jumped out of the way and swore as Wyatt slammed the back of his head off the corner of a table. He hit the ground in a tangle of limbs and tumbled into a display. Bones and books and various bric-a-brac collapsed on top of his unconscious form.

"Idiot!" Nina Valentine shrieked. She kicked him in the side, but he was out cold. Above, on the shelf, there was a clatter as the upper window flew open and an army of feral beasts entered the building yowling and hissing.

The Specimen

Interlude: The Rider
The Night the Lights Went Out in Greylock
The Greylock Institute
November 9, 1965

Dusk had just fallen when the power went out across the Canadian province of Ontario along with seven states in the Northeast United States: New York, New Jersey, Vermont, New Hampshire, Massachusetts, Connecticut and Rhode Island. Most of the affected area remained powerless until 7:00am the next morning. In the weeks following the blackout, many stories of tragic incidents that had happened during the widespread power outage were told and retold across the country. Each telling elaborated and overemphasized certain salacious parts until most of what people heard were pure falsehoods.

UFO sightings increased and a reported mini Baby Boom was later found to have no basis in fact. One story, however, about a series of murders at an insane asylum in Massachusetts during the blackout turned out to be completely true, and in some ways, it was much worse than anyone could ever have imagined.

* * *

Dr. Saul Eckenrode had a secret that he had never told anyone. Nevertheless, it was a secret that he had prepared for long ago, when he had first walked into this very office and accepted the position of Clinical Director of Greylock Institute seven years earlier.

He was deathly afraid of the dark.

When he had seen the horrible wiring in the building, he had predicted that an outage such as this would happen one day, and as a result, his preparation for such an incident was thorough and detailed.

In his office, he had over four dozen candles, four industrial sized flashlights and a horrendously expensive kerosene lantern that was meant to be used on camping trips. He was prepared for hurricanes, Nor'easters, and whatever the weather would throw at them, but it was still surprising that the lights had gone out on such a dry, wind-free night.

Since it was still quite early, Dr. Eckenrode figured that the vast majority of the residents would be out in the recreation room, having just finished dinner. Each of the staff would have access to emergency flashlights on each floor, but it wouldn't hurt to circulate and pass out the extra flashlights to the staff members he could trust while keeping the immense lantern for himself. Eckenrode lit the lantern, gathered the flashlights and set out.

*   *   *

Angelo Scarpa was almost happy. After weeks of walking around in a complete mental fog, he had slowly come to his senses within the past hour and discovered that his nose was growing back. He couldn't see it in a mirror, but he could feel that skin was starting to cover the holes to his sinuses and cartilage had begun to reform.

Despite his good mood, he was tied to a table face down with leather straps and something that weighed about 10 pounds was on his back, and now, the light had been extinguished and the entire room was black as midnight.

<Hello, Angelo> said a voice in his head.

"What? Who the fuck is that," he exclaimed. "Where are you?"

<I am your answer to the question. I am your ticket to freedom. Just help me and I will help you with every wish you make>

"What kind of horseshit are you spouting? And just how do you propose to do that?"

<A friend of mine is coming to free you. Once he does, I will show you how to do things you never thought were possible. Trust me Angelo. You and I are going to be great friends. We're like two kernels of corn grown on the same ear.>

The Specimen

"Wait? What? Don't you mean two peas in a pod?"

<That metaphor works as well>

"Why can I only hear your voice in my head? Where are you standing? Tell me who you are and what you really want from me."

<Okay, if that's the way you want to do it, but don't blame me if you don't like what you see.>

A dim yellow glow slightly illuminated the room just above Scarpa's head, then another yellow light brightened the room even more. Scarpa felt a weird motion on his naked back, as if something was pulling slowly, steadily on the muscles deep within his back. Two glowing rubbery ropes dangled from behind his head into view. They began weaving sinuously in front of him, as the ends began to expand like small balloons to the size of tennis balls.

"What fresh hell is this?" Scarpa muttered.

In that exact second, the two balls on the ends of the ropes popped open, revealing bright slit yellow irises in the center of two bulging alien eyes… and then one winked at him.

Scarpa stopped screaming after about five minutes, then the door opened and someone else came in. The straps came off, and the fun began. Scarpa was screaming again, but this time he was screaming with laughter.

*   *   *

It had taken nearly an hour, but finally Eckenrode had passed out enough flashlights and candles so that every staff member and nurse had at least one. The residents had been calmed down and were currently being escorted back to their rooms in an orderly fashion.

Content that no real problems had occurred, he was heading back to his office when he realized that he should check in on Harry. As the youngest resident in the building, he might share the same phobia of the dark and probably would appreciate some company.

Eckenrode recalled how he had felt when the lights went out in his youth. Even though electric lights hadn't been as common as they were now, they were widespread enough to miss them when the power went out, especially when the radio stopped working. Here, with all the lights on and familiar faces, his panic was held safely at bay.

Wait a minute… The power went out… No electricity. That's it! Eckenrode realized that the electromagnetic locks on the ACME lab doors may have stopped working, which meant one of two things. Either they were locked and couldn't be opened until the power went back on, or they were open and couldn't be locked!

He immediately changed his destination and headed toward the South Wing where the labs were located. He was sure Harry would be fine until later.

* * *

Harry was not fine. No, he wasn't fine at all.

At that exact moment, he was fleeing down a random hallway in a part of the asylum he had never seen before.

He had been ushered back to his room by one of the guards. Stan was his name, Harry remembered. When they arrived in Harry's hallway, it was obvious something was going terribly wrong.

At least half a dozen patients were milling around every which way, panic-stricken and crying. One old man was seated against the wall, slamming his head backwards with enough force to leave a wet, red stain. At least two, maybe three bodies were in a pile at the end of the hallway, and a few feet from the door to Harry's room lay a familiar figure. The creepy doctor that looked like a one of those giant green bugs who bit the head off the males after they were "done with them". (Harry had heard his daddy say that once a couple years back, but when he asked him what they were "done with", his daddy never told him) was lying on the floor with a large cut on his head and it was bleeding pretty badly.

The Specimen

Crashes and screams could be heard from Harry's room. He wanted to run away from the noise. He didn't care where he went. Anywhere else, because he had a hunch about what was trashing his room, and he didn't want to see it ever again.

Stan told him to stay where he was before hustling down to where the commotion was. Nearly slipping in a pool of blood, he caught himself on the wall and rushed into the room, baton held high.

Five seconds later, Stan's broken body flew out the door and made a very unnatural crunching sound as it hit the wall head first, leaving a smear of brains and skull fragments as it slid to the floor.

Following Stan's impression of a rotten pumpkin, a man walked out and looked up the hall directly at Harry. The boy's stomach dropped in terror. Ten yards away, covered in blood and other fluids, stood Angelo Scarpa, but that wasn't the worst of it. Scarpa was shirtless and, on his back, rode the Rider that had been removed from his back only weeks ago.

"YOU!!" Scarpa roared, pointing in his direction.

Harry fled, disappearing around the corner, and Scarpa chased him, gnashing his teeth as he went.

* * *

The door to Lab 1 was already wide open. Shining his lantern inside, Eckenrode saw it was a mess, with specimen jars, empty and full, littering the ground. Notes covered the desks and tables surrounded by a variety of very expensive medical equipment. Seeing nothing of immediate importance, he decided to try out Lab 2, at the opposite end of the hall.

Eckenrode smiled to himself as he pulled open the door to Lab 2. Unlocked again. He looked inside, shining the lantern ahead of him. This time, there was a strong smell, redolent of spoiled meat and vinegar. What had they been doing in here? It almost reminded him of corpses. Had they stored dead bodies here?

This laboratory was much more organized than Lab 1. Still cluttered, the equipment was lined neatly along the walls and there was no large table in the center of the room. Instead, much of the lab was open space, as if it was intentional.

Wait... What was that noise? There was a noise coming from a closet in the corner of the room. Its door was closed, but motion could be seen behind it. Eckenrode suddenly became aware of the encroaching darkness. He was tempted to leave well enough alone, but then he remembered Hutchens and Scarpa (not that he cared much about the latter) and that they had disappeared. What if they were imprisoned and needed help?

Emboldened by the prospect of exposing Coe for the evil bitch that she was, Eckenrode walked up to the door and swung it open.

Immediately, he regretted his decision.

Slithering forward, like an immense translucent slug, came this massive THING. A few years earlier, Eckenrode had seen the Steve McQueen movie, The Blob, and thoroughly enjoyed it. This thing reminded Eckenrode of the title creature in that movie, and, since the movie version had consumed anyone or anything that got in its way, he was absolutely terrified.

Scuttling backwards like a crab, he reached the doorway, jumped to his feet and raced down the hall in the direction of Harry's room. The lantern lay abandoned on its side, leaking kerosene all over the floor. Dragging its undulating bulk, the giant creature rolled right over it, shattering the glass as it followed him out the door and down the hallway.

* * *

If Dr. Eckenrode had lingered long enough to shine the lantern on the other corner of the room, he would have found the body of a woman intentionally hidden beneath another desk. Blonde, with her features completely unrecognizable. Her face had been pushed in from the

The Specimen

battering until all that remained was a concave hollow of bone, blood and brains. Next to her was the heavy metal microscope that had been used as a hammer on her once-beautiful visage. Even with a complete absence of features, her identity was pretty obvious – Dr. Coe. Scarpa had killed her and stowed away her body soon after he had escaped.

    Around her were left years of research, priceless knowledge that she had never published and would now be lost forever. In the remnants of the shattered lantern, the kerosene ignited from the smoldering wick. The flaming puddle trickled over to one of their desks, and soon, all of the papers were on fire and the room was burning from floor to ceiling.

*   *   *

    Harry raced around the corner and ran headlong into Dr. Eckenrode. Both tumbled to the floor in a tangle of legs and arms as guards and residents ran past them shouting and crying.

    The frantic boy screamed at him, "Run! Run!"

    The doctor helped Harry up and tried to drag him back the way Harry had come. Harry screamed again incoherently and pointed. Lumbering down the hallway towards them was Scarpa, and Eckenrode could see why Harry had been running. From fingers to elbows, both of the murderer's arms were painted in blood and gore past his elbows.

    Behind them, though it wasn't visible yet, he heard the monster pursuing him as it dragged its bulk through the hallway, sometimes rolling over bodies in its way and grinding them to a paste.

    Looking back and forth between the two options, Eckenrode decided that, if he was going to be caught between a gelatinous alien monster and a murderous psychopath, he would take a chance with the known evil and run towards the human. Hopefully he would be able to bull his way past the man and turn down another hallway.

    The massive monster wobbled into view and Harry's eyes goggled.

"What is… that thing?" he screeched.

"I think it's the Blob… Don't go near it!" shouted Eckenrode, pulling him in the other direction. He ran toward Scarpa, manhandling Harry and dragging him behind him. "Get out of the way, Mr. Scarpa! You need to run. There's something horrible behind us!"

Scarpa smiled and stepped aside. Eckenrode, completely shocked that it had worked, started to run by the blood-covered resident when he felt something warm and slick coil itself around his right arm. He looked back at a yellow tentacle rippling over Scarpa's shoulder. It squeezed him tighter until his arm became entirely numb and his hand swollen and purple.

Slowly, with the sound like a millstone grinding corn, the bones in his arm were pulverized to a slurry. The skin on his fingers split down the middle and meat mushroomed out from under his fingernails like sausages that had been boiled too long. Eckenrode shrieked and told Harry, "Run! Run! It's got me!"

Harry screamed, "NO!" and launched himself at Scarpa in defense of the only friend he had in the asylum. He wrapped one arm around the man's neck and the bulk of the Rider and clawed at Scarpa's face with his other hand. He scratched furrows down the psychopath's right eye and cheek before rearing back for another blow. Scarpa spun away from Eckenrode, releasing the doctor as he slammed Harry between the wall and his shoulder.

Harry's second attack was either perfectly aimed or tremendously lucky. Either way, it had a deadly effect. His curved fingers punched right through the new skin covering Scarpa's nose-holes, burying them three knuckles deep into the folds of the sinuses before scooping out a slimy chunk of flesh as if he were helping himself to a generous portion of peanut butter from a jar. As he pulled them out, the skin tore downward in a long strip, exposing the glistening wet meat of his mouth.

Scarpa keened in pure agony. He threw Harry to the floor and covered his mangled face with both of his hands. The Rider bucked on his back and flailed its ropy tentacles in fury at the damage done to its Steed.

The Specimen

Harry lay stunned and dizzy on the floor. He tried to stand and run, but his left knee gave out on him. When Scarpa had slammed him down, his entire left leg had gone numb and he couldn't put any weight on it. He began pulling himself along the floor, but Scarpa followed him every step, yelling incoherently.

The Rider's voice broke through the mental panic Harry was feeling, <YOU MAY HAVE HURT MY NEW STEED, BUT I WILL KILL YOU, LITTLE BOY. I HAVE NO NEED FOR CHILDREN WHO WEEP IN THEIR SLUMBER. I WOULD RATHER HAVE THEM SLEEP IN THEIR GRAVES! >

Harry rolled over to see Scarpa's foot raised above his head, ready to stomp down and break his skull like an egg. He felt helpless as Eckenrode yelled behind him, "Harry, get out of there! It's coming!"

* * *

The Cluster was very confused. Dr. Coe was dead. It had smelled her blood and heard her end just minutes ago, and it was experiencing emotions that were foreign to it.

Anguish.

Loss.

Rage.

More people than it had ever seen in one place were running through the hallways. Some were running in his direction, only to turn tail and flee back down the hallway.

The man who had freed it was lying against the wall, obviously injured, and his attacker, bleeding and screaming, was about to assault a child. On the back of this man was a creature that felt like kin, but smelled of danger and acted like an enemy. At first, it couldn't decide, but then it smelled something on the skin of the second man and lost control.

It smelled blood.

Familiar blood.

Dr. Coe's blood.

This was no kin. This must be the one who had killed her. It was definitely an enemy. And enemies had to be killed.

Approaching the pair from behind, it reshaped into one of the forms that it had practiced, long and serpentine with a mass of individual tentacles where a mouth would be. It reared up over Scarpa and slammed straight down just as he was about to drive his foot through Harry's head.

The Rider caught a glimpse of the tentacle covered maw in the corner of its eye and twitched aside at the last millisecond. The muscular wyrm missed him by a hair's breadth and plowed its head into the plaster wall. Scarpa fell off balance, allowing Harry to crawl back a couple more feet to Eckenrode's side. Both of them stared at the two combatants in shock. Somehow this Blob creature was on their side.

Once again, Scarpa dove at Harry. Eckenrode blocked the attack with his remaining functional arm, but his strength was waning and Scarpa was larger, younger, and had a symbiotic alien attached to him. The odds were overwhelming and he realized that he wouldn't make it out alive. Decision made, he jumped at Scarpa yelling for Harry to flee. The wounded boy pulled himself up the wall and leaned on it as he hobbled away, dragging his bad leg and sobbing for yet another friend who was going to die.

Right arm dangling at his side, Dr. Eckenrode lunged at his opponent, only to be backhanded to the floor. The Rider's tentacles snaked over Scarpa's shoulders and wound around the doctor's waist and chest, squeezing him like a vise as it lifted his limp body in the air near the ceiling where smoke was beginning to accumulate. Scarpa cackled in insane glee and the Rider spoke…

<NOW YOU WILL SEE WHAT HAPPENS TO ARROGANT LITTLE MEN WHO DARE TO CHALLENGE ME!! I HAVE BEEN A KING! I HAVE BEEN A GOD!! I HAVE HAD ENTIRE CITIES SLAUGHTERED IN MY NAME! I HAVE RULED EMPIRES ON BOTH SIDES OF THIS WORLD. ALL OF THESE I WILL DO AGAIN!>

Eckenrode felt his ribs splintering into dozens of shards inside him, piercing vital organs and shredding his guts. Weak and tired from losing so much blood, he was resigned to his fate. He knew his time was

The Specimen

coming to an end, but he suddenly grinned as blood leaked through his teeth and whispered, "Do it."

From the ceiling, something resembling a gigantic lamprey snaked down and engulfed Scarpa's skull to just past the upper lip. The muscles along its length flexed, and Scarpa's head imploded in a shower of white bone, grey matter and red blood.

Eckenrode was dropped to the floor as the Rider's tentacles released him immediately. The voice had instantly been cut off, but Eckenrode was certain the creature was screaming in pain and fury at the sudden demise of its Steed. Scarpa's headless body teetered for a second, then collapsed in a boneless pile next to the doctor.

Before it hit the floor, the Rider had already torn itself from the man's back and skittered down the hall along the wall in fear for its sudden mortality. The Cluster moved to chase it down the hall, but Eckenrode's voice made it stop.

"Save the boy," he rasped. "Please, save the boy!"

The smoke was getting thicker as the fire in the labs grew too large to be confined. Any patients left in the corridors began streaming for the front of the building where some of the remaining staff corralled them outside into organized groups.

The Cluster hesitated, then went in search of Harry.

* * *

Minutes later, Dr. Colfax raced from his quarters at the command of the Rider, his only goal to collect the creature and hide it somewhere safe and impenetrable. The voice of the Rider screaming had roused him from his evening meditation when the creature summoned him for the second time that night.

Earlier, he had been in the recreation room when the power went out. The next thing he knew he was cutting away the straps that were pinning Scarpa to the table in Lab 1. Something was compelling him to do as the madman said. He had blacked out again and discovered himself back in his quarters. For all the thoughts of stress, he still had that fear inside him that he would lose control of his own mind, and now it appeared that he had done just that. The Rider was without a Steed. Something must have happened to Scarpa, he realized. Something deadly.

<BIND WITH ME, CHILD. BE MY NEW STEED.>

Dr. Colfax was overcome with an immediate urge to find the Rider and allow it to take control, but this time he was ready for the mental onslaught and he resisted with every fiber of his being. One of his abilities was to separate his emotions from his logic in order to make the most rational decision.

He now realized that, somehow, the Rider had found a way to influence his mind directly. It couldn't be pheromones. The distance between them was too far. Could he have larvae inside him? That was the only logical explanation… and it was a terrifying one. Beyond life-threatening brain surgery, he knew there was no known way to remove it. The immediate concern, though, was how to suppress the influence of the Rider now and find a way to keep it out of his head for good.

He sat there on his bed for a few seconds thinking over his options when another mental blast blew away his resolve and, after grabbing a couple of essential items, he raced out the door.

* * *

Ron Fenton was seriously thinking of changing careers. Yeah, the money was great and the opportunity to shoot actual monsters and fight for the freedom of the human race was nearly as cool as it sounded. He worked above the law as a preternatural hit man for a shadow corporation, taking out the creatures that used to inhabit his nightmares, and now were only notches on his belt. Hell, a couple of years ago, he and Jameson had even captured and tortured a Soviet spy for vital information on the location of a lab where the KGB was trying to breed Rider/Steed combat drones. They made a difference.

Lately, however, Fenton had been feeling worn out. First, they had to clean up the mess that Pfeiffer's team had made in Springfield,

The Specimen

squirreling away the survivors and hunting down Harry. Then, they were assigned as his babysitters here in the middle of nowhere, as if watching a little boy was in their job description.

When Dr. Coe had informed him that Jameson had been reassigned without any notice was when this job had really turned sour. Fenton realized that Coe and Colfax weren't all there, and he had intended to file a report detailing his various suspicions this week.

Now, none of that mattered.

The entire south wing of Greylock was on fire. Patients and staff were fleeing from multiple exits. Drs. Coe and Colfax were nowhere to be found, and even the director, Dr. Eckenrode, was missing in action.

The only person of any authority who was currently present was the head janitor, Charlie Willard, a friendly old coot who seemed to do nothing but constantly mop the floor, smoke Pall Malls and talk about his beloved Red Sox.

Willard was shuffling around the front of the Institute, shouting orders to an impromptu bucket brigade, and attempting to bring some sort of order to the chaos. Fenton stood off to the side, ostensibly keeping an eye out for Harry, who was still his responsibility. The brigade seemed to have slowed the blaze down, containing it to the South wing, but it was not enough to do more than hold it at bay.

Above the blaze, Fenton heard the sound of glass shattering over on the west end of the building near the edge of the forest. Looking in that direction through the smoke, he saw what appeared to be a large four-legged golden animal – like a bear or a mountain lion with an inner glow – leap from the second floor balcony to the grassy hill below. The beast was too far away and moving much too fast to catch, but as it disappeared into the dark forest, Fenton saw a sight that would stick with him the rest of his days.

Clinging to the back of the creature for all he was worth was the boy. The last Fenton ever saw of him was as Harry looked back in his direction. He raised his hand in a perfunctory wave, wishing him luck, and then Harry was gone.

* * *

Colfax clutched the jar in both hands as he unlocked the door to the basement of the Greylock Institute. It was a bit larger than needed, but it was the only jar that he could find on such a short notice. The label was still on it from the early days of the dissections.

The Rider shifted sluggishly in the jar, nearly sedated from another triple dose of Halperidol that Colfax had ambushed it with a few minutes earlier. Even now, he struggled to control himself. He realized that, if the Rider had not been weakened by the battle and the shock from the death of Scarpa, he might very well be under its control right now...

There was no way in Hell he would allow that to happen.

A mind as magnificent as his should never be shackled to the whims of another creature. In some ways, he admired these Riders. The strong should rule the weak, and, in most cases, the Riders were made to be the dominant half of a Rider/Steed combination. The strength of a human, enhanced by the mental powers of the alien half, was an example where the sum was definitely greater than the parts.

The basement was pitch black, but Colfax had a small flashlight and the only items down here were the boxes for the equipment from their initial move back in August. Colfax had supervised their storage after he had arrived, and, in his curiosity, he had discovered the hidden alcove inside the chimney. Right now, he couldn't think of a better place to hide the jar in the limited time he had. He doubted anyone else even knew of it.

When the time was right, he would send a team back to retrieve the jar, but he didn't want to risk being around it any more, especially with the thing's larva in his brain.

He ducked into the large brick chimney, climbed the rungs gingerly up to the hidden shelf, and placed the heavy specimen jar as far back as he could put it.

Climbing down again, he ducked back out into the main basement and was knocked sprawling by a last ditch mental blast from the Rider.

The Specimen

<BETRAYER! YOU SHALL PAY WHEN I ESCAPE! I WILL COME FOR YOU AND CRAWL THROUGH THE SHREDDED MEAT OF YOUR CORPSE AS I WEAR THE SKIN I FLAY FROM YOUR SCREAMING FACE! YOU WILL SUFFER!>

Colfax stood painfully and glared back at the chimney before continuing on. Perhaps he would never send a team to retrieve this foul creature after all…

PART 5
MAELSTROM

The Specimen

Chapter 43 – Exodus

"Flesh perishes. I live on." – Thomas Hardy

Modern Day – Cambridge, MA

Officer Marisa Vega flipped on the lights and siren, checked for oncoming traffic and roared onto Putnam Avenue as her partner confirmed to dispatch that they were en route to the location. A silent alarm had sounded in a freaky little antique shop and they were the closest unit available.

"I know exactly where it is," said Barry Strickland as he set down the mike. "Right near the intersection of Brattle and Church. Take Mass Ave. through the Square."

"And how would you know this?" she asked. "Do you have some sort of secret life that you hid from those of us at the main office? Do tell, Barry. Are you into that latex Goth scene?"

"No, no. Of course not," he protested. "And don't go making anything up now, Vega, okay? I already get enough crap from the guys about my weight. Watch out. Old lady. Two o'clock."

"I see her."

Vega careened into the left lane around the oblivious tourist in the crosswalk before turning right onto Massachusetts Avenue. She had been reprimanded for her reckless driving before, but most of her fellow officers would secretly admit they were envious of her skills behind the wheel. Strickland hadn't taken the driver's seat in the four years they had been partners and he was totally fine with that arrangement.

"Laura likes to go there for costumes for the community theater. That's all it is. I swear."

"Suuuure," Vega replied. "Blame it on your wife. I won't forget this next time we have dinner together with our families."

The Specimen

They laughed, then rode the rest of the way in silence, mentally prepping themselves for any situation that may arise at the store. Most likely it would end up being a routine snatch-and-grab, which meant they would be filling out reports all day long tomorrow.

Less than two minutes later, they pulled up to the curb and stared in disbelief at the chaos unfolding in front of them.

"What the heck?" Strickland muttered, breaking the silence. "Vega, is it just me or does it look like that store getting overrun by a shitload of cats?"

* * *

Solomon was the first inside. The Abyssinian immediately leapt from the windowsill to top of the nearest bookshelf. He saw the bad woman and directed the others to intercept and attack her. Behind him swarmed at least three dozen other cats, climbing down the drapes and launching themselves to various shelves and tables around the room. Skinny. Fat. Long-haired. Short-haired. It was almost as large an attack as the one a few days earlier at Elvira Dombrowsky's apartment, the only difference being that many of them were still recovering from wounds suffered the other night.

A scrawny tabby dove directly at Valentine, while three others jumped to the ladder before flinging themselves, claws extended, at her back and face. She met them head on. Catching the tabby in midair, she snapped its neck and flung to the floor. She broke the back of another assailant with a brutal stomp, but the other two snuck past her defenses and sank their teeth into her flesh.

As the bad woman kicked at her attackers and flung them aside, Solomon focused on the only thing that mattered … the commands in his head. The commands did not come from the voice it usually heard, but they were very similar, and much, much more powerful. Solomon had no free will remaining at all. He must do what the intruder told him to without question, even though his instincts raged against them.

An odd-eyed white cat clung to Valentine's back as it savagely bit through the cartilage in her ear. Blood streamed down her neck. Its front paws were tangled in her hair as it raked down her flank with its back claws.

Valentine slammed her body violently backwards into a supporting column, crushing her passenger between them. It fell to the floor twitching and flopping like a fish out of water. She continued cursing incoherently and slammed her boot on the cat's head, pulverizing it to a paste of brains and gore.

Backed against the column, she drew her gun and blew away four cats in four shots, one in midair as it dropped from a cabinet filled with giant insects encased in Lucite, and the other three as they charged at her from around the columns.. A deep scratch on her forehead trickled blood directly into her left eye. As she wiped it away, she looked up and recognized Solomon climbing across to the bookshelf holding the specimen jar.

"Get the Hell away from that!" Valentine yelled, jumping towards the ladder. Even as she began to run through the fray of spitting, screeching felines, she knew she was too late. The damned cat was only a couple feet from the jar and its trajectory was unmistakable. It barely squeezed its body between the jar and the wall, and it began to push. The jar moved ever so slightly, centimeter by centimeter to the precipice.

"NOOOOO!!" Valentine screamed in futility as she reached the foot of the ladder. Solomon looked directly at her with his dead eye, hissed defiantly and pushed even harder. Finally, bracing against the wall for leverage, he managed to get the jar past the edge to its tipping point and it fell.

The distance from the top of the immense bookcase in the storefront display window to the sunken main floor of the store was close to fifteen feet. The jar tumbled end over end, seeming to descend in agonizing slow motion. Valentine reached in a fruitless attempt to catch it,

The Specimen

but the slick surface barely allowed her to feel the glass before it slipped through her grasp and exploded in a shower of liquid and glass on the stone floor.

Right at her feet.

* * *

Bright, sudden, flashes from within the store were followed immediately by the sharp retorts of gunfire. The two officers dove behind their car doors just as they were exiting the vehicle.

Vega triggered her mike and shouted, "Shots fired! We have gunfire inside the store, dispatch! Requesting backup immediately."

Strickland squinted at the storefront, attempting to see inside, but all that was visible was a lone woman's silhouette battling against the horde of cats. About five feet away was another figure, this one of a man on the floor, covered with debris.

"What in God's name is going on in there?" Vega asked, gun at the ready. "There are dozens of animals in there."

"I don't have a clue at all. Rabies?"

"Maybe," she responded, "We need to call for backup and an ambulance."

"How about Animal Control? We need someone who has more experience with these situations."

"Already on it."

She sent the request in to the confused dispatcher, then crouched behind the car door again to decide upon their next action. At just that moment, a loud scream pierced their ears. Looking at the store again, they saw a large jar, nearly the size of a cask of ale, tumble off the top shelf of the display to shatter at the foot of the figure in the store.

* * *

The explosion of glass drenched Valentine in a massive splash of yellowish-brown soup. The foul, warm liquid was viscous and slick. What hadn't covered Valentine's clothes seeped around her feet in a slowly expanding pool in all directions. Wyatt woke, blindly retching, as the edge of the sludge reached his cheek and lips. This was not formaldehyde or any other chemical used to preserve organic tissue. No. That would have certainly been disgusting, but this was gross beyond anyone's imagination.

This vile, viscid soup, in fact, was five decades of collected filth sealed in a glass tomb. Clotted blood. The debris of shed flesh fermenting in the bilious silt of the jar. Concentrated foul waste marinating the leprous chunk of meat that now lay on the floor amid razor shards of glass, fresh blood and cat hair.

Valentine collapsed to her knees and vomited in a violent spew. Her palms and knees were sliced open by the broken glass and the blood swirled in the puddle around her, forming scarlet streams.

That wasn't the worst of it, though.

It was the astounding, unbelievably horrid stench filling the air that laid everyone low. Imagine a broth of rotting meat, blood, fecal matter, urine, and body odor soaking together for decades. Every person and creature in the room was overcome. It seeped into their pores, permeated their sinuses and dropped them choking for air to the floor. A half dozen cats perched on shelves and tables slumped bonelessly and dropped in piles of skin and bones to the cement floor.

Yet underneath it all was a pungent musk. Years of Rider pheromones trapped inside the jar had intensified and concentrated into a chaotic mixture. Fear, rage, lust, joy and despair swept across the room and out the door.

The cats were affected the most. Many were knocked senseless by the sheer strength of the emotions that were stirred up. Those lucky

The Specimen

enough to remain conscious near the door staggered outside and fled with no thoughts except for a clean getaway.

Inside, the remaining cats were caught up in the frenzy. Here a formerly white Persian was painted red after tearing the throat from an orange tabby kitten. In the display window, a pair of tortoiseshells were playing tug-of-war with the entrails of a gutted calico. Solomon lay on the top shelf of the display case playing with his tail and looking around dreamily as if he had hit the mother lode of catnip. All around the store, cats were mating and killing, screeching and yowling.

… And in the center of the chaos, lying on its side like a discarded chew toy in the pool of cooling sludge was the former occupant of the specimen jar. The Rider. It shuddered slightly. The eye peeled open and extended on a ropy stalk, scanning the room in a circle. Despite the chaos and carnage surrounding it, not one individual noticed its presence. Any cat that came within a few feet suddenly changed direction as if they had encountered a barrier. All eyes looked past its location, unconsciously avoiding any confirmation of its presence.

Pausing at the prone body of Wyatt, the Rider scuttled closer, and examined the young man from one end to the other. It bobbed up and down on unseen pads for a while, then turned away and headed straight for the other person in the store.

Valentine had no chance.

On her hands and knees, she dry-heaved, covered with a mixture of her own sick and the contents of the jar. In addition to the nausea, the pheromones were overwhelming as well. Where the cats had lost their inhibitions toward homicide and rabid lust, Valentine had exhumed all her insecurities and fears. All her buried rage and sorrow and feelings of isolation poured out, first in muffled whimpers, then in wailing cries.

The Rider approached from behind her and stopped just out of sight as she sobbed, unable to do anything besides kneel there in the filth. Beneath its piss-yellow eye, another two pores irised open and a pair of segmented limbs emerged. It sprang onto her back and nailed its forelimbs into the muscle, anchoring well beneath her skin.

Valentine reared back in agony. A whip-like tail unfurled from the Rider's back and encircled her waist as the main body slid beneath her blouse and straddled her spine. Seconds later, the neural fibers of the Rider were connected to Valentine's spinal cord and their nervous systems were acclimating to each other. She slumped against the table and began to convulse.

* * *

"Strickland! Wait!" shouted Vega as her partner raced ahead, dodging around the bloodied cats streaming from the store. She swore under her breath and followed him into the shop after radioing in their situation.

Gun braced in his hand, Strickland barreled through the open door and veered to his left behind a display of Civil War medical equipment. Immediately the cloud of pheromones enveloped him. He grimaced at the carnage and destruction. At least a dozen cats lay broken and bleeding on the cement floor, A few still mewling as their lives leaked out into the ever-widening pool of excrement. A scarred reddish-brown tom hissed at him from atop an immense set of shelves before leaping out of a second floor window.

"Gross! What in God's name is that smell?" complained Vega as she came in behind him. "Strickland! What are you doing just standing there? Wake the fuck up! We've got two bodies here."

Strickland turned to face his partner, tears streaming down his cheeks. Unable to speak, his eyes were bleary and bloodshot, betraying the pain he felt. Since he had entered the shop, he had been drowned by a deluge of emotions swirling out of the sea of his subconscious. He hadn't cried in over ten years. The last time had been at his mother's funeral, but now he couldn't stop crying. He couldn't remember ever being this distraught. All his effort was focused on preventing himself from collapsing in a sobbing heap at Vega's feet.

The Specimen

Vega looked at her partner in disgust.

"Pull it together, Strickland!" she snarled contemptuously. "Did you leave your balls in the cruiser? Stop crying like a little bitch!"

If she hadn't been so furious at her partner, Vega might have stepped back and examined the scene. She might have wondered why she was suddenly overcome with rage at everything. She might have realized that something was influencing her and Strickland's mental states, but at that point, she was too far gone to care. If he didn't stop his bawling, Vega was seriously considering putting her pistol flat against his temple and spraying his brains all over the floor. In fact, that was sounding more and more like an excellent idea. Before she realized what she was doing, she had unsnapped her holster and was raising her gun slowly toward his face. She was one second away from adding bits of Strickland's skull and gray matter to the soupy mess on the floor when the red-headed dork at her feet began giggling.

"Don't do it," the skinny white guy said from beneath the closest table, covering his mouth to hold back the snickers that were threatening to burst forth. "Something's messing with our heads. I can't stop laughing."

He snorted, "Now you'll probably shoot me instead. I think I'll shut up now"

The clerk curled in a fetal position, laughing so hard he could barely breathe. Gasping, he rolled onto his stomach and began wriggling towards the door, every so often stopping to take big, gulping breaths as he inched along the floor.

Behind her, Strickland whispered, "Vega! Look!"

Vega turned around quickly, ready to pistol whip him until he could tell his fortune with his shattered teeth on the floor if need be. Luckily for him, though, Vega wouldn't follow through with that plan. She turned her gun away from Strickland and pointed it at the woman who was slowly pulling herself upright. Ten feet away, dripping with vomit and other vile fluids, she looked at Vega briefly before, arching her back to the breaking point, she stretched her mouth until her lips seemed about to rip and began to howl.

Chapter 44 – Demons

*"It's almost as if a demon might have
passed from one host to another."*
- *John Forbes Nash, Jr.*

Modern Day – Cambridge, MA

Seconds earlier, Nina had been in the throes of a grand mal seizure. Blood trailed from her chin onto her neck and blouse from the large hole she had bitten through her lower lip. Her head and feet beat a staccato tempo on the bare wooden floor as she and the Rider waged an internal battle for control of her muscles, and an even more vicious brawl to determine which mind would become the dominant personality …

She was back in the house where she grew up. Where she had been happy for the first few years of her life before reality hit her in the face when she was gang-raped by three of her classmates who had broken into her home. Where she was reliving the horror right now …

Nina was pinned to the avocado green linoleum floor in her kitchen. The three boys surrounded her, sporting Halloween masks that seemed much more realistic than the ones they had actually worn. Rather than cheap rubber, these false faces appeared to have been peeled from actual cadavers, then decorated with Halloween makeup.

A dog howled in the garage, clawing at the door so he could save her… Fenris. She missed that dog more than anyone from her former life. No one had ever been as loyal to her at that beautiful beast had been.

Frankenstein and a zombie had her arms spread out and held in place while Dracula thrust into her frantically, wheezing like a bulldog behind the rubber mask he wore. He stunk of stale beer and armpits. Every few strokes, Drac would stop and clench his entire body spasmodically as if he was holding back a painful sneeze, before starting up again for a few seconds.

Finally, after a few cycles of resisting the sneeze, the Prince of Darkness shuddered and collapsed on top of her, before rolling off to the

The Specimen

side and switching places with the zombie. Frankenstein had already taken his turn in the driver's seat. He had been fast, rough and machine-like, starting her off bloody and bruised for his friends.

Now, Nina focused on the ceiling rather than looking at her next assailant in line. Her left cheek throbbed where she had been punched a few times by Dracula. It was swollen to the point where the purple and black bruised flesh nearly completely obscured her eyesight on that side.

The zombie climbed aboard the Nina-Mobile and took it slow, clutching her tight and moaning sweet nothings to her as if it was the night of the Prom and she had eagerly lay on a blanket in the back of his dad's Range Rover to make beautiful memories together. He was a small kid in all aspects... height, weight, and, thankfully, between his legs. After Frankenstein's brutal turn, this kid's swizzle stick was barely noticeable.

Again, Nina tried to fight back, but she was paralyzed and her attacker was much stronger than he looked. The only movement that this hallucination... dream... vision... nightmare ... allowed was the ability to squeeze her eyes shut.

"Yeah, you like that, baby? Is that what you wanted? Best you ever had, I'll bet. There's more where that came from." he cooed into her ear.

NO! NO! NO! OHMYGOD! OHMYGOD! NO!

Nina wanted to scream in his face and bite his throat. She wanted to fight and scratch and gouge out his eyes. Sever his tongue. Tear off his ear with her teeth.

She couldn't do anything of the sort. This memory was not following the script. Though she had attacked her rapists and fought her way out, she lacked the will or the way to send this ship back on its original course. She was at the mercy of her subconscious mind... just a passenger wherever it took her.

As the zombie's whispered seduction continued, the voice gradually changed. The young man's voice became deeper, taking on a guttural, raspy smoker's quality. The weight on her body increased and the individual on top of her grew heavier and taller.

"Open your eyes, l'il buddy," the new voice said in her ear. Nina flinched. She knew immediately who spoke. She snapped her eyes and confirmed her fear. Her dead partner Stoopes lay astride her and smiled his big toothy grin. His skin was ashy gray, having begun to sink into his flesh. A small hole in his throat continuously seeped blood. He coughed and Nina could hear the bullet rattling inside his throat like a peanut in a tin can.

"Miss me, girlfriend?" he asked as a partially clotted lump of mucus and blood fell from the hole in his neck to land on her cheek. "I thought I'd come back for a bit to see how you were handling everything. Maybe get myself a piece o' that ass you were always strutting around in front of me."

Nina tried to scream again but her vocal cords were still frozen. She relaxed her arms in the grips of Frankenstein and Dracula, hoping to lull them into a false confidence so she could wriggle free and fight back with every weapon she had. Literally tooth and nail.

"You don't look happy to see your old partner," said Stoopes after another bout of coughing sprayed a mist of scarlet in her face. "Didn't you miss your old Stoopsie-Poopsie? I would have thought you'd still be mourning me because of my untimely departure. Maybe the next person on this train will get your juices flowing?" Stoopes signaled to the other two monsters on either side. He then let go of Nina and held both thumbs up to his throat.

The nails on his thumbs were black and thick, ridged with edges as keen as a scalpel. With almost nonchalance, he pierced the skin at the center of his jawline with his nails and followed it back on each side, slicing through the skin, to just above each ear. Stoopes grasped each side of his face and peeled it back, in one piece, past his mouth, nose and eyes. The sound it made reminded Nina of a long piece of duct tape tearing away from a roll.

The Specimen

The meat beneath the skin was red and wet, raw and weeping blood, but the new features were recognizable. She knew who it was even before the whole face was revealed.

Her dead father stared at her silently. The three bullet holes in his face leaked bloody tears down his cheeks in a guise of sorrow. His eyes were deflated and sunken, but a spark of life flickered behind the clouded corneas, accusing her for her numerous crimes. He said nothing as more blood and brain matter slid from the holes in his face like toothpaste from a tube.

Unable to answer his glare, Nina was flooded with guilt. She wanted to ask why he and her mother had forgotten about her when she was locked away... why they blamed her instead of the monsters who had raped her. Did they think she had invited them in? That she had encouraged them and teased them with her torn stockings and black lipstick until they could no longer control their animal lusts? Did they actually believe that everything that had happened was her fault?

Donald Valentine raised his left hand to his cheek. He extended his forefinger and inserted it slowly, deeply, past the second knuckle into the largest bullet hole, directly beneath his left eye. He pulled at the layers of skin, tearing them away in grisly strips down past his neck and over his scalp. Soon, another familiar face was revealed.

It was Wally.

Her old boyfriend smiled ear to ear, a sight that normally would have warmed her heart made horrific by the fact that he had no lips. Obviously dead, patches of ivory bone were visible through the rotting flesh on his skull. His throat bore the blackened imprint of ligature in the swollen flesh and his jaws clicked as he began to speak.

"You look surprised, babe. Didn't your parents tell you what happened to me a few weeks after you went away to that hospital in Belchertown?" he asked, leaning closer over her.

Nina tried to close her eyes and avoid his gaze, but found that she couldn't even do that. Whatever had brought her to this nightmare was controlling every muscle in her body now. She was helpless. Frozen in terror.

"No, I guess they didn't want to stress you anymore," Wally continued. "After all, you were in a delicate state, right? The knowledge that your boyfriend had hanged himself might have sent you over the edge. Better to let you think I just couldn't stand to see you anymore because you were defiled by those three beasts. Is that what you thought, baby doll? That you were used goods and I wouldn't want that sweet ass anymore?"

His breath smelled like a meat locker that had thawed out and sat in the sun for days. Sweet, cloying and rotten. He ran his cold oozing hands up under her blouse and whispered in her ear, nibbling at her earlobe, "That's okay, Nina baby. Water under the bridge and all. I forgive you. Now that we're finally back together, we can finally do what you were planning that night we were so rudely interrupted. I have so many ideas."

He opened his lipless mouth and slid his slick wormy tongue up her neck like a monstrous slug. A couple of maggots wriggled out of his left nostril and fell onto her cheek as he stared directly into her eyes and said in his best Barry White impression, "Give me some sugar, baby. I've been waiting such a looong time for this."

Nina Valentine's mind dissolved into thousands of razor shards. What was left of her sank wailing into the abyss of her subconscious.

The Specimen

Chapter 45 – Howl

*"Nature is one great big wood-chipper.
Sooner or later, everything shoots out the other end
in a spray of blood, bones and hair." - Doug Coupland*

Modern Day – Cambridge, MA

Isolation is a gradual form of torture. Whether the isolation is physical, mental or social, the effects may not be readily apparent, but they exist. And they grow. Like an insidious infection, they begin as a swollen tenderness in the flesh and then they fester and decay. Sometimes the infection is in the mind and sometimes it rots the soul. This was the case with the Rider in the specimen jar.

For over fifty years, it had been secreted on a hidden shelf in a chimney in the basement of the Greylock Lunatic Asylum. The grievous injuries it had suffered at the hands of Drs. Coe and Colfax in their laboratory, as well as the horrific burns from the night of the blackout, were never given time to heal.

Without sustenance, left in the dark, the Rider was forced to cannibalize parts of itself and feed on its own waste to survive. All of its mental powers were focused on repelling any associate of the ACME Group from its hiding place in the months that followed.

Eventually it was forced to enter a form of hibernation, only reviving occasionally to psychically probe for potential Steeds that it might lure to where it was hidden. Its location was so remote that few opportunities existed once the asylum was abandoned.

In its previous incarnations, it had often held unbelievable power, exerting complete control over its Steed. From conquering 9th century England as the Viking warlord Ivar the Boneless, to being worshipped as the god-king Tlatlaukitezkatl for over three centuries in pre-Columbian Aztec Mexico, it had lived multiple lives ruling entire cultures. Among the many Steeds that it had complete dominance over were a Roman centurion, a Spanish Crusader, a Hungarian countess, and most recently, before coming to New Orleans in 1947, an SS Obergruppenführer in Nazi Germany and later, Argentina.

Many other times, the control it exerted on its Steed was met with greater resistance than would allow it to have full dominion. Only in times of great stress or when the Steed was incapacitated, was it able to wrest control of its Steed's body without resistance. When it encountered a Steed with the strength of personality to hold it at bay, it only had two goals. One was to search for any weakness in the Steed's mental armor so it could possibly become the dominant personality. Simultaneously, the Rider was always searching for a new, more compliant Steed.

If another Steed was found and the Rider was able to convince the current one to release him, the transfer was a simple process. All that was necessary was for the Steed to allow the Rider to detach itself, preferably near a potential new candidate, and Rider and Steed could part ways. One beneficial side effect of the detachment process was the loss of nearly every memory that happened during the period they had been connected. She would suffer from amnesia

Every so often, though - as was the case with Lucien Roumain – the Steed held the belief that releasing the Rider to enslave another human being was evil, a mortal sin. Roumain, in particular, was a devout Catholic who considered himself a modern Job being tested by God Almighty. The Rider was his burden alone. God would not give him any task that he was not strong enough to handle. Roumain would never willfully pass that task onto anyone else. He believed that doing so would condemn him to an eternity in the fires of Hell, and he was determined to take the Rider to the grave with him.

If not for the ironic untimely intervention by the ACME Group – the very organization attempting to wipe the Riders from the face of the Earth – Roumain might have succeeded in taking his unwanted passenger with him to the grave. If the Rider had not been shot multiple times ... if it had not been perilously close to death for the next few months ... if it had not been well below its normal level of abilities, it may not have ended up imprisoned in a specimen jar for the better part of 50 years.

The Specimen

Now, when the perfect opportunity presented itself, it had drawn upon the remaining energy it had gleaned from the meager offering of blood from the girl a week earlier. It sensed a number of Thralls in the local area and it had compelled them to arrive en masse and release it from its glass prison.

It was finally free, and its new Steed was one of the strongest it had ever Ridden, yet it had found it surprisingly simple to subdue and Bridle her by bringing past trauma to the surface of her conscious mind. Even better was the fact that she was affiliated with the ACME Group, the organization most responsible for its torture and imprisonment. Once it had her under its control, it felt its abilities returning to their full strength immediately

Finally, for the first time since it had been Bridled to Lucien Roumain, it felt free. Free to satisfy its darkest cravings. Free to seek out its enemies and take vengeance upon them. Free to howl its fury and elation to the world and announce its triumphant return.

... AND SO IT DID.

* * *

Half a century is a long time to hold a grudge. Most individuals would feel the anger slowly fade away into a dull ache that was barely worth the effort to revive, but this grudge had been the only thought on its mind during its imprisonment in the hidden alcove where Frank Popecky had finally discovered it. Instead on burying the pain, the hate it felt toward the individual who had ultimately betrayed and abandoned it had been cultivated like a rare plant, fed on the same diet of vitriol and agony and pure focused rage for the duration of its confinement and now it was released into the ether like a landscape-cleansing nuclear bomb.

The psychic howl radiated outward for hundreds of miles in all directions, felt by dozens of other Riders and Thralls within that widening circle, none of whom were even within millennia of this one's age. In addition, any person inside that area who had ever had contact with a Rider also heard the cry. Each individual was affected differently, depending on the nature of their prior relationship. Some passed out immediately. Others began vomiting as their equilibrium was thrown into chaos. A few lucky ones only experienced a mild headache and decided to turn in early that night.

Some were not so lucky...

* * *

Martha Pepsick, a three-term state senator, who just happened to be a thrall and hadn't even known she had been under the thumb of an otherworldly being for decades, suddenly stopped in the middle of a ribbon-cutting ceremony for a children's museum in Billerica and repeatedly stabbed herself in the eye with the giant set of scissors in her hands.

* * *

In the third quarter of a 44-17 drubbing of his school's rivals, the Bedford Buccaneers, Treyjohn Colpepper, star running back for the Concord-Carlisle Patriots, collapsed on the 10-yard line without even being hit, after a 57 yard dash that would have surely finished in the end zone. Colpepper was transported to the hospital by ambulance where he was diagnosed as having a slight concussion. He would miss the next two games, but eventually he would return to lead the Patriots to a state championship.

* * *

Arlene Dowling, 57, of South Boston, was cooking herself a late dinner of fried chicken and potatoes when she slumped to the floor

The Specimen

unconscious, pulling the pan of hot bubbling oil over her face, neck and chest. She was found seventeen days later after her beloved but starving Shih-Tzu, Little Miss Fancy Pants, had already eaten most of her fried chicken-flavored face and chest.

* * *

Shawn Hudley, 22, a bicycle messenger with a larva growing inside his chest wall had a massive aneurysm while crossing Massachusetts Avenue and crashed into a taxi stopped at a red light. His package, containing signed copies of a contract between two multi-national corporations, flew into the street and was promptly soaked and destroyed by the parade of cars running it over. The merger fell through and millions of potential dollars in profits were lost as a result. Shawn died immediately from the aneurysm and subsequent head injuries.

* * *

Diego Escalera, 27, was waiting at the Copley T station on his way to propose to his girlfriend, Elena. He had finally gotten the promotion to manager that he had wanted, and now it was time to man up and ask her to marry him. This was going to be the happiest night of his life. He stepped to the edge of the platform as he saw the train approaching, when suddenly he felt dizzier than he had ever felt before. Falling forward, his last sight was the front of the train just before it hit him and turned him into a splash of entrails, meat and brains all over the platform and his fellow commuters. The bouquet of roses he had purchased for Elena lay untouched on the edge where they had fallen.

* * *

And then there were the ones directly connected to this Rider…

Let's begin with the cats. Although they were not its direct thralls, it did sense a bloodline between them, carried over from the Cluster when that being had originally enthralled the horde, and so its ability to hijack them as its thralls was definitely due to the common ancestry between them. Unfortunately for them, they were also closest to the mental blast and they were hit the hardest.

As soon as Nina/Rider screamed out loud and unleashed her mental blast, a dozen of the cats fell to the ground yowling in agony as blood streamed from their ears, eyes and noses. They were dead within seconds.

Solomon was the exception. Perhaps he was armored by the time he had spent bridled by the thrall larva, or perhaps his instinct to escape was the right one all along. He had been the first to be enthralled, and he had been personally responsible for recruiting over a hundred more cats to the cause. Of course, almost all were dead now, but Solomon always survived. Perhaps he was just lucky.

Solomon, realizing something dangerous was about to change the dynamic in the store, darted from his perch out through the window and clambered down the wall to hide under the rusty recycling bin in the alley behind the store just as the psychic wave rippled outward from the bad woman. It slammed into him and knocked him unconscious, but the metal barrier provided just enough protection for him to again survive, battered and bruised, but alive.

Moving outward at the speed of thought, the wave not only announced the Rider's proclamation of its liberty to those who could sense it, but it also acted as a psychic Emergency Broadcasting System. Every being who tapped into it was momentarily connected to every other receiver on the same psychic channel. Most were overwhelmed by the sheer number of minds all linked at once, but a few significant individuals recognized each other and instantly knew the location, status and mental state of anyone with whom they were familiar…

The Specimen

* * *

Scott and Harry were hit first. After Bud had been rushed off to a room of his own to recover from his intense bout of vertigo, both had dozed off to a repeat of *Seinfeld*. Harry hadn't watched much television since the 60's and Scott had agreed to anything but the news. Now, nearly simultaneously, both jolted awake shouting names.

"Hank! Sydney!" cried Scott while his roommate called out for someone named Lucien. For a moment, they saw everything the other was thinking. The two looked at each other, frantic with their new knowledge, and immediately knew what had to be done.

"He'll be here... soon," said Harry, sliding to the edge of the bed.

"I'll need a wheelchair," nodded Scott. "We'll have to meet them downstairs."

The old man agreed. He put on his robe and headed for the door.

"There's a deputy still here. We need to get by him," said Scott. "How are we gonna do that?"

Harry just smiled and said, "We'll... find a... way."

* * *

Luckily for C.C. and Hank, Billy was driving the ambulance to Mass General. C.C.'s partner had proved to be especially susceptible to Rider pheromones (perhaps due to many years of marijuana use), and he did whatever Hank instructed him happily, without questions. When the psychic wave hit them, it passed Billy harmlessly since he had no larva inside him, nor was he enthralled like C.C, who was knocked senseless in the passenger seat for a few minutes.

Hank was hit the hardest, but it affected him differently. Instead of simply feeling a wave of rage, the psychic energy was precise, like a scalpel. Rather than cutting anything, the wave targeted his emotions with the pain and suffering the Rider had felt during the half century of confinement in the jar.

Hank understood the Rider and he hated him even more.

*   *   *

The next person to be hit with the wave was a man who had just celebrated his 103rd birthday at Sweet Valley Resting Home in Amherst, Massachusetts. He was sipping a glass of lemonade, freshly squeezed of course, and he was smiling as he reminisced about the 46 wonderful years of marriage he had spent with his beloved wife, Violetta, after she had saved his life twice back in '65. Once, on the loading dock in the fight with the Rider, and next by helping him lose over 150 pounds by changing his diet. Without either one, he wouldn't have lived past sixty.

She had passed on peacefully in her sleep two years earlier, and Lucien, or Bayou Lou as everyone called him here, had been biding his time, every day since, waiting for the Good Lord to call him home to be with his Lettie.

To his friends rocking on the porch with him, that time must have come. He dropped his glass of lemonade on the ground, exclaimed, "Oh, Harry… No," with deep regret, and then passed on to be with his love.

The stress of the wave was just too much for Lucien Roumain's old heart.

*   *   *

The wave had weakened quite a bit by the time it got to Hartford, but it still had its effect on those susceptible to its energy.

The Specimen

Frank Popecky, Sydney and Dahlia all fell back on their beds, clutching their temples as a painful flash hit them with the knowledge that they had made contact, however brief, with Hank, Scott and others who they didn't recognize. Dahlia puked in the corner, while Frank bit his tongue, drawing blood.

Seconds later, high on the wall in Sydney's cell, a plaintive meow emanated from the small air conditioning grate where Ookla the Mok had just arrived. The cat batted the grate with its paw and knocked it to the floor, before leaping down to Sydney's bed.

"Ookie!" shrieked Sydney in amazement. "What? Oh my God!! How the heck did you get here?"

The cat just snuggled up next to her and purred.

* * *

Grimaldi was approximately three hundred yards away and two floors up, searching for his cat Boots on the main floor of the mall above the laboratories and the prisoners' cells. Streams of rain were spraying in through a partially broken pane of glass in the skylight three stories above the floor. Graffiti and tags marked the walls of the mall, remnants of the period after it closed and before the ACME Group had purchased it through multiple shell corporations.

When the wave smashed into him, it felt like a knitting needle had jammed into his left eye and impaled it on the back of his skull. He sank to one knee and tried to alleviate it with pressure, but it was too intense. He fell, unconscious, to the linoleum. His left eye was still open and the sclera had become awash with blood.

* * *

Three floors below, in his private quarters, Dr. Arnold Colfax was twenty-two minutes into a one hour cycle of his personal sensory deprivation unit. At the exact moment the wave struck him, he was practicing labyrinth meditation. With all his senses muted by the chamber, Colfax was working his way through an immense maze he had unconsciously designed in his mind. He was almost at the point where he would reach the center, the most serene location of which he could conceive. Once there, he would completely surrender himself to his inner thoughts. In a successful meditation, after navigating to the center, he would contemplate for a spell, and then work his way out of the labyrinth just as the time in the sensory deprivation unit ended.

Tonight, it was a complete failure.

As he stepped onto the center of his inner labyrinth, the wave crashed into him, devastating his mental creation from end to end. The pristine black marble walls he had imagined shattered into dust. The silent black sky became lit with a boiling red sun searing the flesh from his bones. Each way he turned, the blazing sun would follow him, always staying at the exact point on the horizon which made it impossible to block with his hands. The floor became a mirror of scalding liquid glass, reflecting the hellfire from the rogue sun onto his sooty flesh.

He held his hand up to block his eyes and the meat and skin began to bubble and blister, boiling away until his bones turned into ash. The red sun bored a hole directly into his eyes and he knew the sun's face. Once before he had seen the face in his mind. Fifty years ago when he had nearly become the Steed of this creature.

Tlatlaukitezkatl, the Living Incarnation of Xipe Totec. The Wearer of Skins. He who Flays Men. This was the face he saw hovering over the blasted plains of his imagination, burning every plant and animal within his view to ash. This was the Rider who lived as a God-King in ancient Mexico for over three centuries, slaughtering hundreds of thousands of men, women and children to satisfy its unquenchable lust for blood. This was the Specimen he and Dr. Coe had tortured and cut to pieces hundreds of times only to watch it grow back again and again. The one he had defied and hidden from sight in the basement of the asylum.

The Specimen

Now, as the face hung directly above him in the sky of his mind, it looked directly at him with its demonic, glowing, yellow eyes and screamed, <I AM COMING FOR YOU, COLFAX!! BETRAYER!! DEFILER!! DENIER!! YOU WILL SUFFER FOR YOUR PRIDE. ARE YOU TOO GOOD TO BE MY STEED? ARE YOU TOO PROUD? WHEN I FIND YOU, YOU WILL WISH YOU HAD ACCEPTED ME!!

NO MATTER WHERE YOU HIDE I AM COMING FOR YOU!!!>

Colfax exploded out of his sensory deprivation chamber, dripping wet, covering his eyes from the bright light and gasping for air. He crawled out naked, sobbing and certain he would be dead by the end of the night.

There was a good chance he was right.

Chapter 46 – Road Trip

"Things are as bad as you fear they are. People are as bad as you think they are. The Universe does not care."
— Charlie Huston, <u>Sleepless</u>

Modern Day – Cambridge, MA

In another life, it was called Tlatlaukitezkatl. Now it Rode Nina Valentine. No longer screaming, she stood observing them as clinically as an entomologist would regard a new species of insect. The glistening yellow body wrapped around her torso, piercing her flanks with its talons.

"Give me a second here to figure this out," it said with a piranha smile as it. "Which one of you is the good cop? And which one of you is bad?"

"Stop! Keep your hands where I can see them," shouted Vega at the blonde gore-covered woman slowly walking towards them. A sideways glance at Strickland told her that her partner was still pretty useless. He had fallen to his knees wailing for help, and his gun was nowhere to be seen.

Perhaps that kid who crawled out the door was right … maybe something was twisting their emotions, but first she had to deal with this psycho who was definitely up to no good. It looked like she was carrying an object on her back – a knapsack or something – could that have been the source of whatever was causing all these cats to go berserk? Maybe a chemical weapon or a drug?

Vega pointed her gun at the woman and instructed her again, "Do not come any closer, ma'am. I want you to stop and take off your backpack, and then I want you to lie face down on the floor."

The woman stopped mid-stride, then stared at Vega with a ghost of a smile.

The Specimen

"I don't see what's so funny," fumed Vega. It was all she could do to hold back from pumping this woman full of bullets. "I repeat. Take off your backpack and lie down now."

The woman shook her head and looked Vega directly in the eyes as she held out her arms. What had appeared to be the straps of the strange-looking backpack were nothing of the sort. They were organic. Part of some animal. Pale yellow sinewy muscle rippling with each thought.

"As you can see, officer," she responded with a smile. "That's not an option. Why don't you put down that little gun and we can talk about it."

For a second, Vega was astonished at the enormous cojones on this chick. A surge of boiling rage blinded her. She spat, "Are you kidding me? My gun? Fuck that —"

She pulled the trigger. From a distance of less than ten feet, the bullet should have hit the woman square in the middle of her face, leaving a hole the size of a saucer on the back of her head. Instead, the blonde *twitched* just as Vega fired and the bullet missed. Barely nicking her right ear, it shattered a large mirror on the wall next to the register.

"Well then," said the woman seriously. "If you want to play that way, I'll gladly oblige." Lashing her arms like a pair of bullwhips, the woman cast the two tentacles at Vega. Bone spurs on the tip of each one punched through the officer's eyes, into her brain, and out the back of her skull. She was dead before she hit the ground.

The new Nina smiled in satisfaction. The tentacles retracted from Vega's skull, slipping out of the jagged punctures with a pulpy suction. Off to the right, curled in a ball, Strickland whimpered as she approached him.

"So, Officer… Strickland," she said, reading the name off his name tag. "Is that your squad car out there?"

Strickland, still crying, nodded in confirmation.

"Excellent! How convenient," she said, grinning widely. "Get up now. We're going on a trip. I have an old friend in Hartford that I want to surprise with a visit."

* * *

Wyatt watched the police officer and the blonde woman leave the store and get into the cruiser. He held his breath tightly until the engine started and the cruiser began backing up. He was huddled behind a pile of broken-down cardboard boxes next to the store's recycling bin, having crawled there only minutes before when the shit went down. As the police cruiser raced off and turned the corner, Wyatt exhaled gratefully and began to giggle again.

He stood up and hobbled back to the store, clutching his swollen testicles as if he was afraid that any moment someone would attack and give his balls another zap. This was something he had already experienced, and frankly, once was more than enough.

The door was wide open and light from behind the counter streamed out into the night. Wyatt stared at the destruction and the dead bodies, both feline and human, through the entryway. Shattered glass littered to floor and tables. Considering the aftermath, it was hard to believe that no one had heard or seen the commotion. True, they were located on a side street, but there should have been enough pedestrians on streets. The sun had barely set when that taser-wielding harpy had knocked on the door. Usually there were students, shoppers and diners wandering the streets until ten or eleven at night.

The destruction would close the shop for weeks and it might even shut it down for good if the insurance company was unwilling to cover everything. Everyone, from employees to customers, knew Chet had been having financial problems, and this might bankrupt him. One thing was certain, though. Wyatt wanted to be miles away when Chet learned what had happened.

The Specimen

There was no doubt in Wyatt's mind that Chet would completely lose his shit when he saw the destruction in his shop. He slumped to the sidewalk under the awning, and leaned against the doorframe in exhaustion. A chorus of sirens wailed in the distance. Soon the police and emergency would be here with endless questions, and there were very few answers he would be able to provide.

A shadow moved away from the wall and came at him. Wyatt flinched and covered his face, then lowered his hands as he realized that it was just a big red tomcat who wanted some company. The cat was scarred and obviously recovering from a number of injuries, but he was still majestic in his bearing as he climbed into Wyatt's lap without hesitation and settled down for a nap, purring in contentment.

The skinny young man stroked its reddish-brown fur and sighed as the rain intensified its melody on the canvas awning and thunder rolled in the distance.

He murmured to the cat, "You need a home, buddy? I could use some companionship after that fiasco in there. Huh? Yeah, I think I'll call you …"

Solomon.

"Yeah, Solomon!" Wyatt exclaimed. He didn't know where the thought had originated, but it fit his new friend well. He continued to pet the animal, noting the scars and lumps from old injuries.

"You've had a rough life, buddy. Haven't you?" he whispered as he closed his eyes. Minutes later, when the authorities finally arrived, both of them were asleep under the awning.

Chapter 47 – Haulin' Ass

"Know when to walk away, and know when to run ..."
– Kenny Rogers, "The Gambler"

Modern Day – Along I-95 South, MA

Larry Hazewood cursed under his breath and flicked on his right blinker on as he pulled over to the side of the road. He didn't need this crap right now. Red and blue lights flashed in his mirror as the police cruiser pulled in behind his rig and parked.

I hope you get drenched, he thought as he watched the officer step out of her vehicle. Due to the darkness and the downpour, he couldn't see much about the officer except for the fact that it was a woman. The rain was coming down in sheets and it wasn't likely to let up for a few hours. As a result, driving was painfully slow on I-95. Too slow to be stopped for speeding, so Hazewood was confused. *Why did she stop me? She's not even a state trooper.*

He looked in the mirror again, noting that the officer seemed to be reading the hazmat sign on the rear of the tanker. It looked like he would be late with this shipment, something that had been happening all too often lately. This run he was hauling 11,000 gallons of liquid propane to a number of distributors in the New York/New Jersey area. Normally, at this hour, Hazewood would have already stopped for the evening, but the weather and the idiots on the road made it necessary to keep moving for another hour or two. It was either that or he would have to wake up at the ass-crack of dawn to beat the early morning rush hour, and he did not want to do that.

The officer finished reading the warnings and started walking toward the front of the tanker. Hazewood checked himself in the mirror. Nothing wrong with using a bit of good old fashioned Southern charm to talk his way out of a citation. Besides, he knew he was easy on the eyes. With his silver hair and beard, he may have looked a bit older than his actual age of 52, but he was in better shape than most guys ten years

The Specimen

younger, much less his own age, and most girls who met him had a daddy complex that always seemed to work in his favor.

Just last summer, a truck stop Trixie down in Memphis told him he looked like a cross between Kenny Rogers – the Gambler, not the pitcher - and Tom Selleck in his Magnum P.I. days. Five minutes later, she was gobbling his knob while he leaned back in his cab seat while listening to the Man in Black sing about a ring of fire on the radio.

That hadn't been the first time he had sweet-talked a little lady into the sack, but he wasn't about to try that approach here. Anything like that would result in a quick trip to jail. The further north you were, the more careful you had to be with your comments. Harmless flirting back home was considered sexual harassment by the damn liberals up here. All he planned to do here was crank up the homey down-south charm and he'd have her blushing and sending him on his way with just a warning. Unless she was a lesbian. This was Massachusetts after all. Goddamn Puritans or perverts – every one of them.

Hazewood rolled down his window and peered down at the officer just as she strolled up. The wind swirled and spit rain in his face as he leaned out. He couldn't see much at all, squinting as she aimed her flashlight right at his eyes.

"What can I do ya for, officer?" he asked, attempting to smile as another gust of wind blew rain in the window. Wiping his face dry with his sleeve, he tried to look past the glare of the flashlight, but all he saw was a very shapely silhouette in clothes that did not look like a police officer's uniform in the least.

She held the flashlight pointed directly at his eyes for a few more seconds, and then lowered it to point at a spot just beneath his window. Hazewood could see that her blond hair was pulled back into a wet ponytail. She was soaked through to the skin – just as he had hoped – and that she wasn't even wearing a police uniform. Except for an oversized navy blue windbreaker with the Cambridge Police Department shield on it, none of the rest of her clothes looked like something a policeman would wear. *Heck, were those yoga pants?*

"I'll ask the questions, sir," she said as she blinded him once again with the flashlight. "What's your cargo?"

Hazewood bit his tongue and smiled. *So it's gonna be like that, huh? Might as well get this over with as fast as possible.* "Liquid propane, ma'am," he replied.

"How much propane are you carrying in this truck?" she gestured at the tanker behind them.

"What?" he asked, thrown a bit off guard by the tangent. "Eleven thousand gallons. Just like it says on the manifest here." He held up the clipboard with the necessary paperwork on it.

The officer ignored it and continued with her line of questioning, "Eleven thousand... that would make a pretty big fire, wouldn't it?"

"I'd imagine so... Wait, what?" answered Hazewood. He looked her up and down again, before coming to a decision. "You're not a cop, are you? What do you want?" Something was definitely wrong with this woman. Even through the rain, he could see she had what he referred to as *dead eyes*. Nobody was home behind that thousand-mile stare.

Belatedly, he realized she could be some sort of terrorist. Since 9/11, he had been required to take emergency response training every two years as part of renewing his Hazmat license, and he knew now that he should have been much more prepared, but he had become complacent in the intervening years. And who would have expected a short blonde woman to be a terrorist, anyway? Every example in the training course had been a bearded man who looked like Osama bin Laden or some other Arab, not Little Miss Yoga Pants here.

No weapons of any kind were within reach. He had a pistol, but it was packed away in the sleeping area at the back of the cab somewhere under a pile of dirty clothes. He doubted that he would be able to reach it in time. He quickly looked around the cab before lighting upon his CB radio. Perhaps he could press the mike and get some sort of message out.

The Specimen

"Not bad," she said before he could act. "You figured it out faster than I would have expected. No matter, though. I've made up my mind. I'm taking the truck."

An instant later, a sinuous whip-like tendril lashed out from somewhere behind the officer's back and entwined itself around his left forearm. Yellow-tinged with purplish-grey blotches, it resembled an old, bruised and boneless tail as it tightened on his arm like a tourniquet.

"Jesus Christ! What the hell is that?" shrieked Hazewood. "Get it off! Get it off!"

The tentacle was covered with a slick mucus-like substance oozing from its pores, but it did not slide off. Along the underside, a line of tiny barbed hooks dug into his skin like a strip of Velcro covered in snot. Hazewood tried to pull it off his arm, but the slime made it impossible to grip. The rain blowing in the window diluted the blood leaking from beneath the tentacle into rivulets of pinkish water.

"Just let it happen. Soon it won't matter at all," said the woman, standing calmly in the downpour. "You won't even remember why you were fighting it. You know I'm right. Just submit."

The silver-haired trucker shook his head, whimpering in fear. Cars roared by on the highway every few seconds, oblivious to the battle happening on the side of the road.

The tip of the fleshworm curled up, swaying to and fro inches from his face like a cobra mesmerized by a handler. Hazewood leaned back into his seat while grasping at the thing. It slipped through his fingers multiple times, slicing through calloused pads and knuckles with its needle-like burrs.

"Stop fighting. Just give in," she repeated soothingly as the torrential rain cleansed the earth around her.

Hazewood opened his mouth to protest and it struck.

A small segment of the tendril, perhaps two inches in length, pinched off from the main body and wriggled along his arm and up his neck. Hazewood clamped his lips tight, moaning in horror as it probed for access to his mouth. He fell backwards, kicked the steering wheel and shrieked in agony as the larva slid up past his lips and forced itself up his nostril. Within a second, blood streamed from his nose as the alien grub bored through his sinuses into his cerebral cortex. Almost immediately, a lattice work of neural threads permeated his brain and connected him to the Rider, stopping his frantic convulsions instantly.

He was enthralled.

The Specimen

Chapter 48 – Comes a Reckonin'

"Fate loves the fearless" – *James Russell Lowell*

Modern Day – Hartford, CT

There is a saying that when someone is struck down without warning that he "didn't know what hit him." It's a bit of a copout, providing the excuse that what had happened wasn't the individual's fault at all. That it couldn't have been avoided and no one is to blame.

Frankly, that's just a bunch of hokey horseshit.

* * *

11:48 pm - Burt LeDuke and Rob Fowles knew exactly what hit them. They were simply too damned stupid to get out of the way. They both were raised on a diet of *Delta Force*, *Dukes of Hazzard* and NASCAR in their misguided youth, before spending most of the last two decades as security contractors in various countries across the Middle East and Central America.

This gig for ACME was supposed to be a side job that had become semi-permanent when the U.S. pulled out of Afghanistan. Now they felt like overpaid mall cops with very large guns and nothing to keep them occupied. They had been itching for action for months. So when their current employer, Dr. Colfax, told them to prepare for an incursion of an "unknown variety", they broke out the big toys.

As Larry Hazewood's tanker truck entered the parking lot of the abandoned Green Valley D-Luxe Mall and bore down on the ramp to the parking garage, they simply strolled out onto the empty pavement, aimed their M-60's and began spraying the cab with a rain of bullets. That part worked quite well. The windshield imploded and Larry was perforated a few dozen times in the span of five seconds. The interior of the cab looked like it had lost a paintball fight to the red team in epic fashion.

Luckily for Larry, he was already dead when the truck crested the hill into the parking lot, because that was when the tanker hit the spike strips that had been laid across the entrances. In succession, every tire on the tanker blew, but as anyone who has taken a class in high school physics knows, there is something called momentum, which makes it extremely difficult for objects moving at a high rate of speed to stop in a short amount of time. Simply stated, larger objects require much more force to stop them, and a tanker truck with 11,000 gallons of propane is an extremely large object.

After slicing open all of its tires on the spike strips, the tanker didn't stop as they had expected. Rather the opposite. It jack-knifed and flipped, causing a flood of propane spurting from the many holes shot in the tank. Sparks cascaded as the tank scraped along the ground and the propane ignited all at once.

This was about the time that Burt and Rob, in unison, screamed "Oh Shit!" as the flaming cylindrical tank rolled right over them at more than thirty miles per hour, completely flattening their bodies like roadkill. Three seconds later, the tank crashed into the entrance to the underground garage and the entire container detonated in a cloud-shaped inferno that rained burning metal over the entire mall compound.

* * *

11:49 pm – The detonation shook the mall to its foundation. The lights in the girls' and Frank's cells flickered off and on before shutting off for good. The only illumination in the hallway came from a dim source out beyond the open doorway at the end of the hall.

"Well, *that's* not good," exclaimed Frank.

Dahlia screamed and began to cry, while Sydney just held Ookie tight and repeated her brother Hank's name over and over again. Since their simultaneous headaches, just before Ookie showed up, Sydney and Dahlia were both under the impression that Hank and Scott were,

The Specimen

somehow, coming to rescue them. How they would manage to find them... for that matter, how they had even survived the home invasion a couple days earlier, was not explained. All that was certain was the belief they felt that this would happen.

Frank was a bit more pessimistic. The only lasting image he had retained from that mental flash was his aunt's favorite cat, Solomon, knocking a large jar off a shelf so it shattered on the floor.

Not exactly an awe-inspiring, heroic premonition if you asked him. Then again, he wasn't Nostradamus. Just a one-nippled twenty-something slacker who enjoyed exploring old buildings.

"I should never have taken that damned specimen jar," he muttered under his breath.

* * *

11:50 pm - In one massive blow, the electricity and cameras had been severed, leaving the entire compound virtually blind and incapable of coordinating countermeasures for an incursion. Within the main staging area, the emergency lights came on and provided just enough emanation to avoid bumping into the furniture or walls.

"Fowles... LeDuke... Report!" Quillian barked into the microphone looped over his ear. "Shit! No response, Doc. We were hit with something big."

"You have a keen grasp on the obvious, Mr. Quillian. We need to evacuate soon. This place has been compromised. Surprising strategy. I expected a focused attack, avoiding any involvement of local law enforcement. Where are the rest of your people?"

"Besides Swanson and Brawley here, there's Grimaldi, Huerta, Murtaugh, Titus and Smolensky. Murtaugh's guarding the prisoners. The other are at their assigned posts... uh, except for Grimaldi"

"And where is he?"

"...Chasing the cat."

"This is not the time for humor, Mr. Quillian."

"Understood, sir. But I'm not trying to make light of our situation. He started looking for it hours ago when you asked about it, I sent him off to find it. He hasn't checked in since."

"We need to find him immediately. Swanson and Brawley can stay here. You gather the others, scout out the situation, and find that stupid cat-lover. If he wants to play with animals, send him to a petting zoo."

"Yes sir."

"And if you see that fucking feline, destroy it. Make it road kill."

"It's dead meat."

"And I want you to listen closely on this, Quillian," the doctor hissed. "Obviously, anyone you don't know could be the Rider. Shoot first. Ask the questions later. You can't trust anyone."

"Clear as crystal, Doc. Heading out now."

Quillian turned and headed out the door. As he passed Swanson and Brawley in the hallway to Colfax's office, he knew that they had heard the whole embarrassing exchange. He knew by their sour expressions and raised eyebrows that they were each thinking the same thing: *What a complete dickhead.*

*   *   *

11:50 pm - A hundred yards away from the initial explosion, on the north side of mall, an entire axle from the tanker cab crashed through the skylight and landed in an empty concrete fountain. Less than twenty feet away lay Grimaldi, still knocked out from the psychic assault earlier that night.

The crash had woken him, but it was the stench of burning rubber and propane in the black smoke washing over him that finally spurred him

The Specimen

to crawl to his feet. The courtyard would have been pitch black if not for the burning debris littered around him acting as torches in a dank, underground cavern. His head throbbed mightily, especially behind his blood-filled eye, as he stumbled back toward the access stairs to the basement level where the prisoners were being held. Only one thing was on his mind as evidenced by his mumbled mantra, "Must. Find. Boots."

* * *

11:53 pm - At the far entrance to the Green Valley D-Luxe Mall, a lone figure watched the flames and explosions light up the moonless night. She sat on the hood of a Cambridge Police cruiser, a couple hours out of its jurisdiction here on the outskirts of Insurance City.

The Rider, wearing Nina Valentine's body, was waiting to see if anyone else had been stationed at the front exit. If someone ran out, he would simply put that person down like a dog.

Next to her on the hood of the cruiser was lined up an impressive display of weaponry. In addition to her own favorite handgun, a Kimber Custom Royal II, with its blue finish and rosewood grips, she had both officers' pistols and a Mossberg 930 shotgun.

Not that she needed them at all. Her plan was simple.

1. Break in.
2. Find Colfax.
3. Peel his skin off and wear it like a poncho.
4. Kill everyone else.

If she needed guns to accomplish her goal, then so be it, but she'd be damned if she was going to kill the doctor quickly. He needed to suffer for the five decades of torture she had lived through.

She lit a cigar and inhaled deeply. It wasn't nearly as good as the rolled tobacco leaves she had smoked in ancient Mexico, but it would do well enough. She had liberated the box from Hazewood before sending him on his one-way mission. There was no reason for them to go to waste.

Speaking of going to waste...

She jumped off the hood, walked around to the back of the cruiser and popped open the trunk. Lying there, jammed in among the various confiscated items and equipment, was Officer Strickland, or at least what remained of him. He gargled in terror when the trunk opened. Cuffed and bound, he was a sorry sight. Nina had been practicing her craft on him every so often, in order to brush up on her skills with a blade. So far, he was missing his lips, ears, eyelids and fingers. *Oh, look. It appears he has chewed off his own tongue. How cute.*

She looked down the hill at the fire, and decided that she had about 15-20 more minutes to let off some steam while she waited to see if anyone would try to flee the scene. If no one had shown up by then, she would venture inside and finish it all, but for now she only wanted to cut and peel to expose the secrets beneath the flesh.

"Sorry, officer. I don't think I'll be killing you just yet. I still have tricks up my sleeve that I want to show you."

She went to work.

* * *

11:59 pm - "I think we've found them," said Scott, pointing off to the right side of the highway over the barrier fence and a long stand of pine trees. A distant orange glow of fire backlit the trees and sent their shadows clawing at the passing cars as if they could tear the drivers from their seats. C.C. rolled down the window and the smell of smoke was obvious. Whatever was burning had to be less than a mile away.

"Take the next exit, Billy," she said to her partner. Billy smiled contentedly and followed her directions to the off ramp. He hadn't said more than one syllable in a row since Hank had hit him full force with a

The Specimen

monster-sized dose of pheromones as soon as they saw him. Billy had never had a chance to resist. As far as he was concerned, he was on the best high of his last ten years, and possibly, of his entire life. Nothing bothered him at all. He was just going to roll with whichever way the wind blew them.

The five of them, Harry, Scott, Hank, Billy and C.C., had been chasing the ghost of the Rider's psychic blast since just after 9 pm.

Scott looked around the ambulance and couldn't imagine a motlier crew. C.C. and Billy, the two EMT's up front, were both firmly under Hank's influence. Harry lay dozing on the lone stretcher, the mad dash to the ambulance bay having taken a lot out of him. To Scott, sprawled on the opposite bench, he looked feeble. looking out the window and occasionally stealing glances at the creature that now housed the memories of his best friend, Hank, who now sat at the rear of the vehicle concentrating on the psychic trail that they had been following like a GPS unit for nearly three hours.

* * *

It had been surprisingly simple to leave the hospital. At 9:00 pm, just as Harry and Scott were concocting an elaborate plan to escape, Deputy Sloan was relieved by the third Bristol County deputy, J.P. Smucker, the Sheriff's namesake and only son. If the Sheriff was considered a rooster, then J.P. was an emu. At 30, he towered over his father by nearly a foot and had more than a passing resemblance to Baby Huey. Although folks liked him a whole lot more than they liked his father, he was widely considered the laziest individual to ever put on the badge of the Bristol County Police Department… which probably meant he would be the next sheriff if the elder Smucker ever decided to retire.

J.P. was also notorious for being an unrepentant pussyhound. His sole purpose in life seemed to be to bed as many of the fairer sex as he could fit into his schedule. Even though he was not an attractive man, J.P. had some of that "Aw, shucks" country charm that made a certain type of woman feel like they were in their own Hallmark Channel Movie of the Week. In other words, J.P. was always on the prowl. Morning, noon and the dark of night. Which was why he was chatting up the nurses around the corner from their room as Harry wheeled Scott down the hall to the elevator. Over two hours later, there was a good chance that their absence hadn't even been noticed yet.

C.C., Billy and Hank had been waiting for them in the ambulance bay. When Scott first saw the form that now housed Hank's mind, he was instinctually petrified. Its form was alien in the truest sense of the word, and, even with five thousand years of human civilization, humanity has always been preprogrammed in their ancient lizard brains to fear the unknown. To flee from it. To run screaming and gibbering into the safety of the light. Luckily, sealed inside a body cast, that was the one thing Scott could not do.

Harry was the first to approach Hank.

"I know you," the old man whispered. With his memories restored after being locked away for nearly fifty years in his mind, Harry felt a camaraderie with this creature. Judging it by appearance only, there was an obvious kinship between it and the Riders. It, too, was yellow and amorphous. The neural core could be seen floating inside its body, just as one could be seen in a newly formed Rider. Beyond that, the physical differences were quite significant. Hank had at least twenty times more mass than your average Rider, and his outer membrane was not scarred from thousands of years of horrific injuries piled one on top of the other as had been on the specimen in the jar.

Harry and Hank each reached out, hand to pseudopod, made the lightest of contacts and their past encounter surfaced from the deepest regions of their memories.

* * *

The Specimen

The Cluster fled through the trees, shifting forms as needed: Amorphous... Quadruped... Serpentine... Humanoid... whichever worked best on the terrain ahead. The young boy, nearly catatonic from shock, cradled in its grasp as it dodged trees, swung through branches, and leapt over brooks and streams. Smoke from the burning asylum carried on the wind, chasing the ghosts that had escaped.

Running. Hiding in the crooks of trees. Wind. Storm clouds. A deluge of rain. The boy woke up. Screamed for a while. Slept again. When the night grew cold, it warmed the boy. Hungry. It ate some squirrels and a raccoon that grew a bit too curious one night. It put some meat in the boy's mouth, but he threw up. It fed the boy some of its flesh and he accepted.

Two, three days and the boy became feverish. Delirious. Instinct led it to a small town where it left the boy in the parking lot of a bowling alley late at night. Watching from the forest on the other side of the road, it saw that he was discovered and taken somewhere by ambulance, then it left to learn the world and its place in it.

* * *

Seconds after they made contact, Harry turned and addressed Scott, smiling, "I was r... right. I once knew this creature, but your fff... riend. He is in...side. It's not just... memories. He liiives in there."

Hesitantly, Scott reached out and touched its flank. Within seconds, he knew it was true and he wept for his friend. Hank roped a tentacle around his wrist, then carefully slid it under Scott's cast. It slithered and examined Scott's injuries beneath the plaster, then, coming to a decision, flexed. All the casts dissolved in a cascading of plaster dust.

Scott couldn't believe it. Though he was quite sore, everything else was healed to the level he had been before the car impact. Some people would call it miraculous. Scott knew it must had have something to do with his earlier contact. It was impossible that he could have healed so quickly, but he had, and now wasn't the time to freak out about it.

In the following hours, as they raced down I-95 to save their friends, Scott and Hank didn't speak once out loud, but they held a lifetime of conversations in their minds. It felt like old times.

* * *

12:05am – Murtaugh's pocket was buzzing. Not the usual *your phone is ringing again* buzz, but the *super-secret clandestine buzz* that meant someone very important from the Council wanted to speak with him immediately.

He answered, "Murtaugh."

A man with a raspy voice spoke with him this time, "Murtaugh, this is Central."

"Yes, sir. Ready when you are."

"Abort mission. The location is compromised and the local police and firemen are en route. Leave immediately, taking only your data and your weapon. Report via standard code to the designated board."

Murtaugh was silent for a heartbeat.

"Are there any questions, Agent?" asked the voice.

"None, sir," he replied. "Orders acknowledged. Contact will be reinitiated when I am certain there is no trail."

"Excellent. We await your report."

The call ended abruptly. Murtaugh stared at the blank screen for a second, then dropped it on the floor and crushed the phone with his foot. He leaned over, fished out the sim card and snapped it in half. Done with that, he began transferring all his data to an encrypted USB drive capable of holding up to 1 terabyte. While it transferred the files from his laptop, he pulled a jacket from his closet, tore open the lining and removed a dozen stacks of hundred-dollar bills. Five minutes later, the data transfer

The Specimen

was complete. His money was secured in a money belt and his weapons were loaded. It was time to blow this popsicle stand.

He just had one more item on his "to do" list.

* * *

12:07 am - "It looks like the fire is coming from that abandoned mall off to the left," Scott noticed. "Let's see if there's still an access road."

They made a couple turns after exiting I-95 and were now driving south on Green Valley Rd, a minor highway that had seen better days. Local strip malls, cheap motels and gas stations lined the road. All, excluding some of the motels, were closed for the night.

"There it is!" Scott pointed out to Billy as they approached a left turn leading into a copse of pine trees.

They turned in. Halfway down the road they passed a faded retro sign that welcomed them to Green Valley D-Luxe Mall, complete with a mascot that was a blatant rip off of the Green Giant and Paul Bunyan. Potholes were abundant and the encroaching branches of the trees looked like they hadn't been trimmed since the mall had closed decades earlier.

Even though it looked like the last place they would find Hank's sister and her friend, they knew they had reached the right place before they crested the ridge. The reddish-orange glow confirmed that the fire was ongoing, but the squad car located a few yards off to the right proved that the Rider and its Steed had already arrived. The psychic afterimages in their memories had led them all here. For Scott, it was like experiencing a litany of déjà vu moments each time he recognized something the Rider had passed only moments before. It was unsettling, yet encouraging because they knew they were getting closer as the images grew stronger.

They parked off to the side, realizing at once that the Rider had already left to infiltrate the laboratory.

"We only have the one flashlight," Scott said. "Harry, can you take that?"

Harry nodded, "What about… weapons?"

"All we have is this flare and a couple of rescue knives."

"Better than nothing… I guess."

"I don't plan on using mine. Besides, we have Hank to watch out for us. Here, take a knife. I'll keep the flare and the other knife."

The three of them, Hank, Harry and Scott, left the safety of the ambulance to explore while C.C. and Billy stayed behind where they would hopefully stay out of trouble.

The trunk to the cruiser was cracked open and some suspicious maroon rivulets had dried to the bumper. Harry walked up and pulled open the trunk, staggered back and immediately vomited. It was something he would regret for the rest of his life. Scott and Hank joined him. When they saw the remnants of Barry Strickland, they didn't get physically sick, but they realized that they were going up against a true monster.

Distant sirens wailed from multiple directions. Company was about to arrive. It was time to head inside before it was no longer possible.

* * *

12:13 am - Smoke had filled the interior of the mall quickly, drawn inside by the draft caused by the broken skylight in the central atrium. Four men walked in a phalanx down the center aisle of the mall. Quillian, left of center in line, swung a Surefire P27X Fury flashlight back and forth as they walked slowly, looking for any sign of intrusion.

"I don't think that thing has the cojones to come into our place and confront us," grumbled Jerry Smolensky. "It wants to pull us outside - in the open - where it can pick us off, one by one. This is fucking pointless, Q."

The Specimen

"Keep your pessimism to yerself, Smolensky," spat Quillian. "I don't want to hear that whiny shit now. Just do your fuckin' job."

The chubby man turned to snarl some childish witticism at his team leader when a razor-edged whip lashed out of the smoke and opened his abdomen up. Smolensky gaped down at the foot-long gash in his gut as his entrails looped out onto the floor. He fell to his knees and collapsed into a pool of his own blood and fecal matter pouring from his ravaged intestines.

"What the fuck, man?!" swore the man next to him. He spun around and sprayed the darkness with bullets.

"Huerta! Save your bullets until you see a target," shouted Quillian. The Irishman yelled to the agent on his right, "We can't lose our focus, Titus. D'ya hear me?"

The burly African-American nodded calmly. He smiled and opened his mouth to say something when a bony spur burst through his throat and a woman walked out of the smoke behind him, pointing a shotgun directly at Quillian's midsection.

"How's it hanging, Q?" asked the girl he knew as Nina Valentine. The Rider gripped her shoulders with one tentacle looped around her waist and two others writhing above her head. She continued, "I'm borrowing Nina's body for a while. I hope you don't mind, because Nina doesn't. She has opened up her mind to me and now I know all her secrets."

She withdrew the segmented tentacle from Willie Titus' neck and he crumbled to the floor.

"Nina..." Quillian moaned sadly. "No, not you."

"Oh, that's right!" grinned the girl. "You two were each other's fall back when either of you wanted to relieve a little stress! You'll be happy to know that she actually liked you, Q. It was totally a daddy fetish on her part, but it worked."

"Let her go."

"Now, Q, you know that's not gonna happen. I need a Steed, you know and Nina here is truly one of the best I've ever Ridden. She's a natural."

"Fuck this!" Alberto Huerta shouted, running forward and releasing a burst of bullets at her. She fell back into the smoke and was silent.

"Why did you do that?" shouted Quillian.

"What the hell, Q? Just shoot the crazy bitch!" answered Huerta. "Valentine's already dead with that monster on her. You know that!"

"You're right, but I had to distract her. We had her out in the open, but now she's hidden by the smoke. She could be anywhere."

"No, man. I got her. I'm sure of it."

The smoke was getting thicker and the effort to breathe was making them both lightheaded. The rotten egg scent of propane was dissipating and a new sweet smell melded with the smoke. Quillian was starting to feel a bit dizzy.

"We need to head back. The smoke's getting too thick. She could be anywhere or you could have killed her, but we can't stay here."

"Yeah," agreed Huerta. "It's starting to affect me too." He turned to go and nearly ran into the false Valentine.

She smiled at him, but her eyes were filled with fire, "That's not just the smoke, Alberto. I added a little something special to it. I like to think of it as a mood stabilizer."

She circled the man languidly, without a concern at all, as if he hadn't just tried to cut her in half with a barrage of bullets. Quillian and Huerta were unable… no, more like unwilling to move.

She completed the 360° circuit of Huerta and whispered in his ear. Quillian couldn't hear what she said, but it became quite apparent when Huerta, grinning like a school kid, turned his gun on himself and shot a full burst of bullets directly into his groin.

The Specimen

He screeched, dropped the gun and fell, clutching the shredded meat of his man parts in both hands. The blood pumped from the severed femoral arteries in his thighs like water from a garden hose. He bled out within seconds, whimpering as he sank to the floor.

Done with him, she turned to Quillian and grinned like a mischievous school girl, "So, where were we? Oh yes. You were just about to agree to take me to my dear Dr. Colfax."

* * *

12:15 am – Outside the burning end of the mall, half a dozen fire trucks, two ambulances and a handful of police cars formed a line surrounding the blaze. While the firemen worked at containing the fire, the police pulled back to the mall entrances and cordoned off the entrances in preparation for the inevitable swarm of reporters, rubberneckers and firebugs. The ambulance and the squad car on the far ridge looked like they fit right in.

* * *

12:17 am – The man with the shaved head unlocked the door and entered the hallway. Frank and the two girls stared at him quietly. He had been here before, and although he hadn't been anything other than polite to them, they were still quite apprehensive around him. He wasn't the one who had broken Sydney's jaw or crushed Dahlia's fingers... and he most definitely did not bite off Frank's nipple, but he had a quiet menace about him, like he was always angry at someone or something, perhaps even at himself.

Holding his Maglite at his side and his handgun in his other hand, he scanned the cells as he walked past them, stopping at Sydney's when he saw Ookie curled under the blanket on her bed.

"So that's where he went," he said with a wry grin, "We thought he had run away."

He produced a key when he received no response from them. "I have a surprise for you three." He unlocked the cells one by one and addressed all three together, "I'm releasing you. You're free to go."

The three looked at him incredulously, but made no move toward their cell doors. *This had to be some sort of test. Or perhaps a sadistic trick?*

He continued, "Not that I'm suddenly feeling any remorse over my team taking you hostage, but the building above you is about to go up in flames, everything has gone FUBAR and I'm not cruel enough to allow you to burn to death."

Dahlia squinted her eyes, stared at him and whispered, "Thank you," before rushing into Sydney's cell and hugging her friend. Ookie jumped to the floor and circled them, winding in and out of their crossed ankles

Murtaugh said nothing as his eyes lingered on Dahlia.

Frank limped out of his cell and said, "I don't know why you're doing this, man, but thanks."

"Sometimes, in my line of work, we forget that there are some lines you should never cross," replied Murtaugh. "No matter how important your goal is… The end does not justify the means if you end up just as bad as or even worse than the monster you're chasing." He cleared his throat and continued, "When you head out, don't just run in any direction. Stay right until you hit the main concourse. By then you should be able to see the fire. Just head in the opposite direction and you should find a way out of here. Good luck."

He turned abruptly and walked out the open door before he changed his mind and further disobeyed his orders.

* * *

The Specimen

12:22 am – Dr. Colfax was furious. Everything he had planned had completely turned to shit. All because one unforeseen factor had been introduced into the mix, years of planning had gone down the tubes. The amount of research and live specimens that would burn up in this blaze was enough to make him weep. Colfax had his database downloaded onto a portable hard drive, but compared to touching and seeing the actual flesh of the subjects involved, there was no comparison.

He had waited for the others as long as he felt was safe before ordering Swanson and Brawley to pack up and bug out. For a second he thought about taking the prisoners with him, but decided they couldn't afford the time to travel to the labs and retrieve them. He hated to waste such valuable resources, but he could always start over again. Cultivating the larva and implanting it would be the easy part. More difficult would be the acquisition of more subjects.

It definitely wasn't as easy now as it had been back in Greylock. There, he and Dr. Coe had the pick of the litter. Human subjects of all ages and sizes. They had all been male, but later on, the gender line had been crossed when he had accepted his position as the Psychiatric Director of Belchertown State Women's Psychiatric & Addiction Center. Even so, over the years, he had found it necessary to supplement his herd (for lack of a better word) by abducting the occasional runaway.

Now he was running like a scared little child, just like he had once before in Greylock Institute fifty years ago. Pitiful. Soon, however, they would be outside and he would be able to contact ACME to be picked up.

Ahead of him, Brawley signaled with his hand that they should stop and retrace their steps.

"What is the problem?" he hissed at the bearded grunt. As usual, Brawley said nothing.

Swanson answered for him, "Look down that hall! It's a wall of flames. We can't continue that way! The only way out is to go down to the first floor and search for a window to bust out. If all else fails we can just go to the opposite end of the structure and exit via the loading docks."

"Damn it! You're right, let's do it."

* * *

12:25 am - Scott, Harry and Hank entered the mall through the open loading dock at the back of the old Sears store. It was far away from the blaze at the other end, but they could already smell the smoke.

"This could be the stupidest thing I've done in quite a while," muttered Scott. "Your sister had better appreciate this, Hank."

A pseudopod smacked him on the back of his neck.

"Dude!" he continued. "That was NOT what I meant."

Harry whispered, "Ain't we… supposed to be quiet? Let's… go."

They walked through the empty open space inside Sears, keeping the flashlight pointed toward the floor to keep from drawing attention. Hank was in his nearly human form and, in the darkness, Scott could almost imagine his friend's trademark saunter and shit-eating grin plastered across his face. He only hoped they made it out of here alive, so he could get more accustomed to the new dynamics of their friendship. Right now, Hank reminded Scott of Gleep and Gloop from The Herculoids cartoon, but perhaps he should keep that to himself for now.

The shattered glass entrance from Sears to the mall and some questionably-spelled graffiti was evidence that they weren't the first to enter this way. There was a good chance that they would run into the Rider and its Steed if it too was escaping the fire. More than likely, though, it was the one who had caused it.

A few minutes earlier, as they entered the loading docks, they heard a quick exchange of bullets. Since then, nothing but their footsteps echoed back at them. They kept walking, following the psychic map that was gradually fading with each step.

* * *

The Specimen

12:33 am – Grimaldi had been wandering for over half an hour in circles. Each time he thought he was going in the right direction, he got turned around and passed another fountain he had passed earlier. Or had he seen this one? Having gone up and down a number of inoperative escalators, he couldn't even remember what floor he was on now. He had been in the basement, but the prisoners were gone. Colfax and the others had left and their former chambers were scorched. The smoke and flames had taken over the walls and ceiling. Pieces of plastic molding had melted and fallen to the lower levels. Toxic fumes filled the air, burning his lungs and causing his head to swim. He couldn't see out of his bloody eye anymore and his right ear felt like it was filled with fluid.

Something was seriously wrong.

He ran, seeking escape, any way out of the inferno.

The smoke and the heat were unbearable, turning his stomach. Everything was spinning and he felt ill. Grimaldi ran to the closest railing and leaned out to throw up onto the floor below, when he heard the girls' screams and, soon after, the gunfire.

* * *

12:37:22 am – By his last count, in his twenty-two years with ACME, Quillian had participated in the execution of eleven Riders (four of which had been Elders). He had exterminated nearly sixty Thralls, both animal and human, including a chimpanzee and three falcons, not to mention the numerous larvae that had been extracted from unknowing victims, a majority of whom had survived. It had been an extremely successful career, one that he hoped would eventually lead to a position on the Council.

Now, though, it appeared that it might be ending prematurely. The Rider, in Nina's body, was leading him at gunpoint to an ultimate showdown with Colfax. A tentacle looped around his neck twice, ready to pop off his head like the bloom of a dandelion, and a handgun was pressed into his spine. Quillian had one more hidden card to play, but it was worthless without a perfectly timed distraction.

Her directions were unerring, focused on the psychic signature that was coming in their direction fleeing the flames. Colfax was escaping the burning building and the Rider was determined to end things here and now. Other minds were near them, but they were insignificant to her. If they got in the way, they would be killed before she met up with Colfax. If not, they would be killed later as she resumed her rightful place in this world.

A few doors up from them, the ceiling collapsed in on a former Orange Julius and flames licked along the adjoining beams crossing the canopy above them. The temperature in the open area of the mall was already over 100 degrees Fahrenheit and steadily climbing. Ahead of them, it was even higher. Soon, it would be too late for anyone to escape. They would all be broiled like roasts in the oven.

Just beyond their sight, shadows reared up in the smoke and screams filled the air. The figures grappled in the shadows, finally revealing themselves to the Rider as it forced Nina and Quillian to approach.

"Well, well. Look who's here," she called. "I did not expect you at all, but I guess I'm just lucky. Some days, everything just falls your way."

She tightened the loops around his neck, then removed the gun from his spine and aimed it over Quillian's shoulder at the tallest member of the new group, pulling the trigger three times. Simultaneously, Quillian took the only chance he might ever have and made his move.

* * *

12:37:26 am – Sydney and Dahlia were getting desperate, running back and forth through the smoke, hoping to find a store with an obvious back entrance. Frank limped behind them, carrying Ookla the

The Specimen

Mok. In much worse condition than them, he was feverish, and dressed only in a pair of bloodied jeans with numerous infections on the bite marks covering his body. The smoke and heat were causing him to wheeze and he had cut his feet a few times from walking barefoot through an abandoned mall that was currently wreathed in flames.

A kiosk that had once sold personally engraved jewelry had been melted into a pile of ash and plastic just beyond an elevator that yawned open, permanently frozen awaiting passengers that would never come. A staircase wound in a spiral around the elevator shaft, descending from the second floor. Smoke swirled like a living shadow on the other side of the staircase and a sudden light illuminated three silhouettes, two small, and one extremely large, approaching from around the stairs.

Sydney and Dahlia froze, peering at the trio, before shrieking and running full tilt directly in their direction.

* * *

12:37:28 am – Without any warning, Scott was attacked from both sides. He never stood a chance. A screeching multi-armed beast tackled him to the floor and pinned his arms to his sides, wailing and lunging at his face.

He almost pissed his pants in fear before realizing that he was in the embrace of Sydney and Dahlia, both hugging and kissing him on the forehead and cheeks with tears streaming down their faces in relief. Asking how he found them and where Hank was. Scott was amazed that he actually had found them. Sitting up, he tried to calm them down when Harry jumped in front of them shouting, "WATCH OUT!!" as he pushed them to the side just as the sound of gunshots shattered the air.

* * *

12:37:29 am – Hank immediately recognized the auras of his older sister and Dahlia as they rushed out of the swirling smoke and took Scott to the ground.

The seven-foot tall bipedal protoplasm stood back and waited for it to end. His reasons for doing so were twofold.

First, he knew Scott was in virtual heaven in the arms of two extremely cute girls, even if one of them was his big sister, and in his previous life, if the tables had ever been turned, Hank would have wanted to stretch out the experience for as long as possible.

Secondly, he had no idea how the girls would react to his new form. Until he could convince them to make physical contact, as Scott had a couple hours earlier, they would almost definitely see him as an otherworldly abomination. He wanted to avoid that pain as much as possible.

Ultimately, it didn't matter. That decision was taken out of his hands when Harry shouted, "Watch out!" and pushed the three of them in Hank's direction. Acting on pure instinct, Hank stretched his body like a protective blanket and bundled his friends entirely inside him just as three gunshots cracked through the air. Like a ball, he rolled away into the smoke.

* * *

12:37:32 am – Quillian stabbed the taser into the tentacle wrapped around his neck and held the trigger down. In the Rider's arrogance, it had only relieved him of his guns, completely missing the device secreted on the inside of his belt.

Set to maximum, the weapon discharged an eight megavolt charge throughout the body of the Rider. Unfortunately, since they were in direct contact with the creature, both Nina and Quillian received a full discharge as well. All three collapsed insensate to the ground as the mall continued to burn around them.

The Specimen

* * *

12:38 am – Hearing gunshots behind them, Colfax, Swanson and Brawley raced back to find complete chaos. Quillian and Nina, with the Rider attached, lay convulsing from the taser jolt on the floor. Twenty feet away, holding his hands to his bloody abdomen as he leaned against the stairwell, was an older black man with white patches all over his skin. Beyond him, crying and cradling a soot-covered cat, was the male prisoner he had left behind in the cells. Obviously he had escaped somehow.

Colfax nearly giggled in glee as he looked around at everyone. "If I had wished for this to happen, I don't think it could have been more perfect. Serendipity, this certainly qualifies!"

He stalked forward and kicked Nina in the back. No response, as expected. Turning to Swanson, the de facto leader of the regiment, Colfax ordered, "Shoot them all, even the cat."

"Even Quillian?" asked Brawley.

Colfax turned to him and replied dryly, "Now you speak, huh? No, not Quillian. That wouldn't be very nice of me, would it?"

The agent shook his head negatively and walked over to Frank Popecky, ready to execute the order, when a gunshot broke the silence and Brawley's head exploded in a plume of blood, bone and grey matter.

* * *

12:39:11 am – Grimaldi staggered down the stairs and shot Swanson in the face until the hammer clicked on an empty chamber. Blood ran from Grimaldi's right ear and nostril, while his ruined right eye was completely rolled back into his skull.

Finished, he turned, ignoring Frank and spoke directly to Ookla the Mok, slurring, "I took care of him for you, Sneakers. Nobody's gonna hurt you no more."

Now it was Colfax's turn. Grimaldi dropped his gun and pulled a very large knife from his belt. He wanted to make this up close and personal. The evil bastard deserved it.

Grabbing Valentine's gun from her limp grasp, Colfax yelled at Grimaldi, "You stay the fuck away from me, you stupid, greasy mook."

He aimed the gun at Grimaldi and pulled the trigger until the gun was empty. Nobody could miss at that range… unless he was an amazingly bad shot like Colfax. Only one even came close to hurting him as it cut small furrow in his left shoulder. Seconds later, Grimaldi grabbed the doctor by the throat and buried his knife to the hilt in Colfax's right temple.

* * *

12:39:37 am – In the sixty or so seconds that the girls and Scott were wrapped in Hank's amorphous flesh, an eternity of images were exchanged between the four of them. They saw all that had happened to each of them since the home invasion at the Monahans only three days earlier.

Sydney and Dahlia learned the fate of Sydney's and Hank's parents. They knew immediately that Hank had been transformed on the outside, but his entire identity – what some would call his soul – had been relocated into this physical form. Hank learned of the physical torture the girls had received at the hands of Grimaldi, and the medical procedures each had performed on them.

Sydney learned about Scott's crush on her, and Scott discovered that Dahlia actually thought he was cute. They learned that and much more before Hank released them away from the combat, then rushed back to end it all.

The Specimen

* * *

12:40:49 am – Nina Valentine woke from a long dream of white noise and opened her eyes.

* * *

12:40:58 am – Hank lumbered through the smoke prepared to fight for his friends' lives only to find Grimaldi kneeling on the ground next to the corpse of Dr. Colfax. The entire right side of the big man's face was covered in blood weeping from his right eye, nose and ear. Sprawled purring in Grimaldi's lap was the legendary feline beast that Hank had christened Ookla the Mok when he adopted him over eight years ago.

"I'm too tired to fight," slurred Grimaldi. "Mind if I take a rest first? I need to talk to Sneakers a bit."

Hank nodded the part of his body that represented his head, and Grimaldi continued, "Besides, I think your friend needs you more."

Hank turned and followed the man's finger to where he saw Harry lying on the ground in a pool of blood. Sliding to his side, it was obvious that Harry was not doing well at all. Shot twice in the gut, the old man was dying. This was not the type of injury from which anyone could recover.

Hank placed a pseudopod on Harry's forehead and sent him a short message, asking him a very important question. Eventually, without saying one word out loud, Harry smiled and nodded.

Hank pulled the old man in for a deep embrace. His flesh flowed over Harry's face into his ears, nose, eyes and mouth. After a few moments, as the conflagration increased around them, Hank disengaged and a new tenant lived with him inside his conscious mind. Harry was with him forever now.

Returning to his friends, he saw that Grimaldi had passed on quietly. Whatever you believe… wherever he went… he went there with a smile on his face and peace in his heart.

* * *

12:57 am – Scott, Hank, Sydney, Dahlia and their new friend Frank exited the mall through the loading docks where they had entered with Harry nearly an hour earlier.

They were painted in blood, sweat and ashes, but they felt cleansed. There was still much to do. Their lives had changed in endless ways and there were many changes to come, but they would face them together.

They reached the crest of the hill behind the mall just past 1:00 am in the morning. By 1:15, the fire had spread to every corner of the mall and it was, in some way, hauntingly beautiful.

* * *

1:11 am – Nina lay still on the floor while flames erupted around her. Inside her mind, the Rider raged and wailed in an attempt to reclaim her body, but this time Nina was ready and she was not giving in. Never again would she submit to anyone else.

<OBEY ME, STEED! I WILL NOT BE DENIED MY TRUE DESTINY. YOU MUST… YOU WILL SUBMIT TO ME!>

Nina smiled and replied defiantly with only one thought over and over again as the walls and ceiling fell in flames and cinders around her.

This is my body.

This is my body.

The Specimen

This is my body.

This is my body.

THIS IS MY BODY.

Epilogue - Brunni

Modern Day – Las Máculas, AZ

The wailing had been heard throughout the compound since the early dawn hours. Cries of anguish, fury and loss sounding from the chamber of The Anointed One. Mixed in with his howls for retribution were sounds of objects thrown against the wall and smashed on the floor.

Below, at the foot of the stairs leading to His chamber, the penitent devotees tore their flesh open with whips they had personally made from the tanned, braided skins of Those Who Failed and shattered glass shards. Each piece of glass had been individually glued to the lash by the devotee as one of the many tasks they must complete to advance along the Path to the Divine Bond. By now, the skin of their backs, flanks and shoulders was sliced and slashed so that bone and sinew were visible beneath the weeping blood that pooled at their knees. This was their Duty, to punish themselves for His Sins.

Finally... silence. The devotees ended their self-flagellation and waited, panting, wheezing, and bleeding to hear His Voice.

Sister Amelia, First Consort to The Anointed One, climbed the cast iron spiral staircase and entered His chamber to receive His Message. The room was lit with a dim amber light. All of the windows were covered with tapestries. Along the walls were immense bookshelves filled with religious texts in dozens of languages, writings of history's greatest philosophers, and volumes of The Anointed One's own journals.

The only other furniture in the room was a custom bedframe large enough to fit two California King mattresses side by side. A large mirror was now in hundreds of pieces on the floor. In the middle of it all sat a large, pale, blonde man in a simple black robe on the edge of the bed with his face buried in his hands. At his feet lay the twisted body of a teen girl, obviously dead. From her injuries, it appeared she had been thrown into the walls and furniture many times. Her head lolled back and to the side.

The Specimen

"May I speak freely, Brother August?" asked Sister Amelia. Stepping around the debris and stopping at the foot of the dead girl on the floor, she looked around the room and waited patiently for his response. This wasn't the first time he had fallen prey to his most primal urges, and most likely it wouldn't be his last.

"Speak, Amelia," grumbled Brother August. "Eventually I will relent to your perpetual nagging, so I might as well do so now and save my energy. What is it that you want?"

"Two things. One, if you keep this up, soon you'll run out of devotees. Heather here was the fourth one since last month."

"This time it was unintentional, Sister. I had a Shift in control without any warning. When I regained the wheel and saw what had happened, she was already this way. Despite her unfortunate death, I have an astonishing reason for this. Something that I believe you will deem of utmost importance."

"It must truly be unprecedented, Brother…"

"How about letting HIM tell you? You may then judge its importance for yourself!" said Brother August, his voice lowering in pitch as he stared directly into her eyes. The room filled with a scent somewhere between freshly cooked bread and hot chocolate. The irises in his eyes lightened from dark brown to a golden amber glow. Brother August stood and the robe fell to the floor. She was, as always, awestruck. He wore no clothes, but all she could see were the appendages rise from the creature melded into his back. Like the golden wings of an angel - or in some eyes, a demon - they writhed and danced as He spoke in another's voice.

"Sister Amelia, I sense that you doubt my actions. Do you care to voice them? Speak freely, Sister, for I am most merciful."

Amelia sank to her knees and genuflected before her living god and begged, "I meant no offense, O Great One. I only seek to understand. Your divine reason is sometimes difficult for your followers to comprehend. We only seek enlightenment."

Brother August paused, then smiled. "Listen then," he said. "Long ago, when I first came into the world of Man, I was not alone."

Sister Amelia slowly sat up and gazed at him, rapt in his words.

"I traveled across many kingdoms in numerous lands with another like me for numerous centuries. Millennia, even.

He was my brother.

We lived many lives and ruled together over many nations, but eventually we felt the mutual need to separate. To make our own paths and find our own destiny. We went our separate ways. He traveled to the New World while I went south to Africa, then eventually east to Asia.

We were able to sense each other and even communicate in a fashion, so we knew the other was healthy and doing well. Occasionally, every few centuries, we would meet and renew our friendship for a year or two, and then we would part ways once again. This went on, until, in the past few centuries we both noticed that humans were becoming stronger. Some could resist our influence, while others could even control us when we took them as Steeds. We each came near death a number of times."

The odor in the air began to change, as if the bread and chocolate from before was burning and becoming more acrid or bitter.

"There came a time when neither of us could sense the other's presence, except in times of extreme emotion… or extreme stress. The last time I heard my brother was over fifty years ago when he was in agonizing pain, and then he just disappeared. Just like that. After a decade of hearing nothing, I had resigned myself to the fact that he was most likely dead…

But then, last month, I heard his voice again. It was weak, but it was there, I began to plan to meet with him again. Perhaps to bring him here to join us in the Holy Bond for some time."

Last night, however, something struck him down, and this time I truly felt my brother Kalev die. I felt him burn to ashes. And then… I felt nothing. This time he was gone forever.

The Specimen

Yes I raged, Sister Amelia. And I wept. And I vowed upon my very life that I would hunt down every last individual who had anything to do with his death. This I swore..."

- TO BE CONTINUED -

ABOUT THE AUTHOR

Pete Kahle has been dreaming about writing novels since his teens, but after flirting with the idea in college, he spent 25 years working in a variety of careers before he finally stopped talking about it and started writing.

He has lived in New York, Arizona and Spain, but now he resides in Massachusetts with his beautiful wife Noemi, his two amazing children Zoe and Eli, one dog, two hamsters, two guinea pigs and two frogs.

Pete is a voracious reader of horror, thrillers and science fiction novels and he writes in the same vein. He is also an insane fan of the New York Jets, despite living deep in the heart of enemy territory near Gillette Stadium.

The Specimen is his first novel, but it certainly will not be his last. There are many other twisted tales percolating inside his head, among which is a sequel to *The Specimen*, and now that the dark closet in his subconscious has been opened, the monsters are clamoring to come out for a visit.

Follow Pete:
Website - http://www.horriblepete.com/
Twitter: @HorriblePete
Facebook: https://www.facebook.com/metsgeek

Printed in Great Britain
by Amazon